WOLF'S BANE

BOOK THREE OF THE DEMIMONDE

ASH KRAFTON

Red
Fist
Fiction

Cover art: Red Fist Fiction

Interior design/formatting: Red Fist Fiction

First edition published 2014
Second edition published 2016

Contact Information can be found at www.ashkrafton.com

ISBN-13: 978-1-946120-02-1

WOLF'S BANE
BOOK THREE OF THE DEMIMONDE

BY
ASH KRAFTON

ASH KRAFTON

DEDICATION

To my Beloveds—
My husband, my children, my family

Dear Sophia,

Salutations and blessings from the Pacific Northwest Conclave of American Demivampire.

We are writing to thank you once again for your guidance and your immeasurable consideration during last month's DV retreat. Although our envoy was nearly two hundred souls strong, you had ministered to each of us as if we were your own children. May God bless you with long life and all His protection for the countless Saves you have performed.

Words cannot adequately express our unfathomable gratitude. Your untiring efforts during the week-long healing sessions have earned our deepest devotion and sincerest respect.

Each of us enjoyed our stay in your city and look forward to enjoying your presence at the upcoming summer retreat.

Yours in redemption,
Leah Stephenson
PNCAD
Chair, Committee of Sophia Affairs

The man sitting across from me absolutely hated himself.

I didn't need to unzip my barriers to make that assessment. The way his shoulders crept up his neck, the curve of his back that left his face parallel to his thighs, the way he avoided looking at me or anyone else—body language said it all. And when he did finally raise his too-heavy head to look at me, his eyes were stony and hollow, too dead to even care what anyone saw in them.

He wore his self-loathing the way I wished I wore Jimmy Choos—right out there for the whole world to see. Difference was, he didn't care who looked.

I glanced at the Demivamp who hovered behind him like a first-year teacher. She toyed with the end of her braid and looked ready to throw herself onto him if need be. Maybe he was a flight risk. Maybe he was a danger to himself.

Maybe he was a danger to me. In that case, the other DV wasn't necessary. I didn't worry so much about myself anymore. I'd learned a thing or two about staying alive.

Not to mention, I had an entire courtroom full of DV that perched on the semi-circles of benches, elbow to elbow, each waiting their turn with the Sophia. I knew full well every single one of them would fling themselves between me and whatever peril might arise here.

I was well-guarded. Perks of being a national treasure.

I flicked my gaze up to the DV who stood behind my client, dismissing her. Once she took her place in the audience, I sank into my Sophia sight. Finding my center, I called up my barriers, peeling away the outermost layer and expanding it until it encompassed us both in an invisible but completely soundproof bubble.

A nifty little trick I'd learned since Dorcas removed the last remaining obstacles between me and my power. She hadn't been much of a dresser and had a weird thing for vampires, not to mention acting like the scariest damned thing I'd ever seen, but I had to hand it to her. She'd done me a solid.

When the barrier went up around us, there was a little ear-pop of sensation. He seemed to notice me then. His eyes took up a pale light, gleaming like the teeth he hid behind the disdainful curl of his lips. His power seethed out like the odor of a hot dumpster—the feel of it decayed and ugly and absolutely desperate.

I smiled, grim and hard. This guy might be the farthest gone DV I'd ever meet. He was going to be a challenge.

Good.

I decided to start the same way I always did, knowing this one might not end the same way. "What's your name?"

He stared me down for several moments. "You want my current name or the one that's waiting for me?"

Obviously, he was referring to the name change that happened when a DV Fell. Vampires never kept their DV names. All part of the whole born-again (dead-again?) persona of a newly-minted vamp.

"You have one name," I said, my voice like tungsten. "And you're going to keep it."

"Like you can stop me."

I smiled again, glad I had chosen to wear lip gloss because my mouth was so dry, my lips would have split without it. "I can. And I will."

"Look, lady." He leaned forward, elbows on his knees. The pale light in his dark eyes looked like an early hard frost on a green lawn. Untimely end of a sweet season. "I know who you are, and I know what you do. Sometimes, you just gotta let nature take its course."

"This isn't nature. This is self-punishment."

He smiled, open-mouthed to show all his teeth. Sharp, elongated, a mouth full of knives. A vamp's mouth. "And I earned every single minute of it."

Okay. Tough guy. Proud of the shitty things he's done. That was part of the thrill of being so close to Falling. Kind of like passing over the event horizon into a black hole, when one part of you accelerates faster than the rest. His soul was a ragged plastic bag caught on a tree branch, waiting for the last big wind to come along.

His heart had already flown loose. In his heart, he was a vampire.

Well, his body was still here, and his soul was still here, and I was still here. He was in for a surprise.

I surveyed his power, using Sophia-sight to visualize it. It was dark, like cooling lava, black and cracked and sullen red showing through the seams. The black crust was his resignation. He'd stopped fighting. But maybe he just needed the right sparring partner.

How did you get rid of hard, black cooling lava? Why, you heat it up, of course. Nothing got a man hotter than his temper.

Well, that wasn't exactly true. There were other things, but that wasn't my brand of therapy.

I pushed through his brittle ugly shell into the lava beneath, then through the lava to his inner core. It was tiny, but it was cool, and green, and still had the essence of who he used to be. His feelings were still packed away inside and I latched onto it, expanded it, examined it. Family. He had kids. A job. He'd been a lawyer, and a good one. He was proud of what he'd done—in the beginning.

Ah. That's where it started to turn. I sifted along the line of those memories and found the point when he started fighting for the bad guys.

"A dirty lawyer?" I snorted and rolled my eyes. "There's a shock. Your parents must be so proud."

He growled and dug his fingers into his thighs. "Shut up."

"No wonder you turned into this." I waved my fingers at him as if I were calling out a Coach bag knock-off at a street vendor. "I thought you were going to say you ate babies or something but a corrupt lawyer? That's sick."

Rage filled him like a burning warehouse, the fury consuming his power. If it weren't for my personal shields, I'd have been incinerated. The fire of his anger melted the hard shell of his former apathy and he became a miniature sun of murderous intent.

He wanted to end me, wanted nothing more than to get his hands on me.

I beat him to it.

With the flick of a mental finger, I opened the door in my mind where all the bad stuff went. It was like a vacuum in there and once it was open, it just sucked at his power, the ugly, the hate, and the agony he'd surrounded himself with. I pulled.

It hurt. It hurt me, it was like sandpaper on the eyes and it hurt him. He howled as I ripped away all the fury of his self-loathing and hate.

Normally, I did this in steps, gently, kind of a leeching away. Not this guy. I had to over-power him because at this stage, he could just grow it all back. Vampires were infinite wells of hate and evil and this guy was so damned close.

His howl became a roar and he made a lunge for me. I slid a ramrod of my shields at him and held him at a mental arm's length. He struggled to reach me, his clawed hands inches from my eyes and if he got to me, if he reached me, he'd tear my throat out.

No, he wouldn't. I was stronger than that. I bit down on my lips and tasted the tang of blood and continued to strip his agony away.

This little man wasn't big enough to break me. I continued to pull away the damage of his soul, and sent a simultaneous stream of the Sophia into him, a cool mist against the acrid hate. His soul had been dried and withered and it soaked up the Sophia's healing rain, swelling and anchoring itself once more.

The fight was going out of him. He dropped his hands, fighting to breathe. Part of my brain screamed to stop, this was too much, too fast. But a part of my heart was intent on pushing the limits, almost wishing to break because maybe then—just maybe—I'd break past whatever unknown obstacle had been holding me back. Desperation drove me just as surely as it had driven him.

So I was relentless. I continued the pull and the push and I found myself standing over his slumped body. He'd slid down in his chair, head dropped against the back of the cushion, his eyes darkening into a deep green, like spring grass. And I didn't stop.

I didn't stop until he'd fallen to his knees before me,

forehead pressed to my feet, crying and repeating words I couldn't hear because the Sophia was too much in control. My ears didn't work right when she was filling my head. I kind of got used to it.

When it was all gone, all the damage and the negativity and the self-hate, the Sophia pulled itself back, sealing the drain. Sound returned, and I could hear his labored breathing, his murmured chanting. My insides still felt raw. That would take a day or two to settle down.

I was aware the outer barrier was still up and I dispelled it. Another ear-pop and we were both submerged in a cacophony of applause and happy shouting. Several people rushed forward to embrace him, hugs for him, awkward hugs for me. I backed away from the jostling and let his family and friends bear him back to the seats. He beamed at me, incredulous joy and gratitude on his face.

And it didn't touch me at all.

I only had two thoughts. The first was: I had just gotten inside him, battled his demons, saved his soul, but I never learned his name. Maybe it was better that way. There were so many DV. I couldn't remember all their names and keep my sanity.

The second was: it hadn't been enough. He was, by far, the worst I'd encountered and it still wasn't enough. There had been no revelation, clue, no hint how to fix the one problem I needed to fix.

I'd come no closer to solving Marek's problem.

A terrible panic tried to grip me but I squashed it down. I swallowed hard and pinched myself and turned to the crowd. The entire group fell silent, hanging on my words.

"Another," I called. "Please. I need another."

And I continued to heal, and I continued to need, and I continued to fight the growing fear that in the end, I might save a million DV and still stand to lose the one I truly loved.

Another stepped forward, and after him another, and it was pushing dawn before I realized none of it had given me what I needed to save Marek.

I stared bleakly at the sea of hopeful faces. So many saves, so many solutions, all of it dwarfed in the shadow of my heart's crushing failure. All my exhaustion, all my despair, all of the raw edges inside me, seething with the scalds of so much negative energy, and all I could think was that I had to do this all again for the next envoy in three days' time.

Einstein's Definition of Insanity Sophie, that's me.

Rodrian was waiting outside the courtroom when the Conclave finally let out. The crowd dispersed fairly quickly; good thing, too, since the regular staff would be showing up for official court house proceedings. And by *regular staff*, I meant *generally-unaware humans*.

The sky was as dreary as my mood, and I was tired. I didn't complain when he suggested we make a brief stop. No sense in complaining when it couldn't be put off anymore.

Fifteen minutes later, a light rain drummed on the roof of Rodrian's silver Audi, mixing with the higher-pitched *tick-tick-tick* of the cooling engine. It would have been music had we been parked anywhere else.

Rodrian removed the keys from the ignition and bounced them in his hands, looking as uncomfortable as I felt.

"I'm sorry," he said.

I turned to him, a slight drawing of brows to question

why.

He scowled and peered out the windshield. "I didn't bring an umbrella. Damned weather is so unpredictable."

I shrugged and looked back out the window again, watching the rain stream down, collecting into puddles on the brick sidewalk.

He laid his fingers on my sleeve. "We can do this some other—"

"No," I said. "Today is a good day."

"You sure?"

"No, not really."

He nodded. "Right, then. I'll get your door."

Rodrian was a real gent. His manners came from a time when men bothered to have any. Sometimes his quaint gestures made me feel like an antique myself, even though he was nearly a hundred years older than I. He ducked out and came around to my side, pulling open the door. I stepped out into the rain and headed toward the red stone steps leading to Marek's townhouse.

I pushed the door open as soon as I heard the lock click. Rodrian had little patience for keys and usually compelled simple things like locks six ways to Sunday.

The air was close, that sense of damp neglect that rooms get when they'd been empty for a long time. The clouds outside tinted the available light a steel gray, bright enough to see where we walked but not enough to animate the details of the rooms.

I'd last been here perhaps two years ago but not much had changed. Marek probably hadn't spent the last few years playing Suzy Homemaker.

Actually, I had little idea of how he'd spent the time since we separated. Considering he'd assumed the position of master vampire (albeit in a non-vampire kind of way) I assumed very few of his evenings were spent with popcorn and reality television. Call it a hunch.

Rodrian thumbed through a thin stack of mail he'd picked up on the way in. "I've been by a few times to take care of basic things but I haven't moved anything. I wanted to wait for you."

"Why?"

He shrugged and tossed the envelopes onto the dining room table, where a pile of old mail had already begun to accumulate. "It didn't seem right."

"I don't see why not." I looked around at the shadows and vague shapes of furniture. "It's just a house."

"If you say so." He took a deep clearing breath. "So, what do we do with it all?"

"Can't we just leave it the way it is? He'll get mad if he knew we were messing with his things."

"I don't think it matters to him now."

"Duh, of course not now. But when he comes back, he'll be pissed."

"Sophie…" Rodrian's face was gentle, careful, as if he were afraid he'd hurt me. Didn't he know I couldn't possibly be hurt anymore? "He isn't coming back."

"Oh, ye of little faith," I replied lightly. "Does the water still run? I need to use the bathroom."

He nodded. "Upstairs to the right."

Sometimes, he forgot I knew.

Truthfully, I didn't need to use the facilities. I was simply tired of listening, but I was too polite to tell him to shut up. Rodrian had taken to treating me like a widow, which made me both depressed and furious.

I never had the joy of being married, the bliss of honeymoon, the opportunity for love's passionate fire to dwindle down to low heat. I wasn't a widow. Being treated like one made me feel like a shutter that had blown loose in a windstorm, banging ferociously against the window, impotent and helpless and raging against being stuck on a hinge.

I fooled around in my purse, flushed the toilet, and made a big business out of washing my hands before assembling enough self-control to walk downstairs.

"In here." Rodrian called from a room toward the back of the house.

I followed his voice to Marek's personal room, which served double duty as office and lounge. This was the only room downstairs that looked lived in; the front parlor was too formal and the kitchen was fresh out of the pages of Better Homes and Garden—all white marble and chrome accent, countertops suspiciously absent of respectable coffee rings.

For the most part, it looked like a museum. Hence my argument for keeping it that way.

This particular room was worn and comfortable and, in comparison to the rest of the house, downright cluttered. It seemed to be the resting place of anything important to Marek—books, photos, weapons (no, really. Weapons. Big scary weapons that looked too heavy to lift and left little to the imagination regarding their proper use.) The room took up a full third of the downstairs, which was huge considering Marek hadn't scrimped on square footage when he shopped for a townhouse.

I noticed a big book with spotty gilt edges, the cover having a textured design of knot work bordering the title. I'd seen that book before. Marek had once dumped it into my lap, then told me I was an almighty oracle, redemption of the DV.

Some redemption I was.

I flipped open the cover and turned a few pages. The text appeared hand-written. A thousand ancient scholars were probably screaming in their dusty graves because I wasn't wearing cotton gloves. I glanced over my shoulder, wondering why Rodrian had gotten so quiet.

Rodrian knelt before a tapestry that stretched from floor to ceiling, a frail-looking weaving of castle and mountain and men on horseback, and pushed it aside to reveal a very modern-looking safe. He punched in a series of numbers and I heard the mechanism grind inside.

"Why did you bother with the combination?" I figured he'd have just DV'd the lock open.

He cast a wry look over his shoulder. "Marek warded it compulsion-proof. I think he did it just to annoy me."

I scooped together a pile of strewn newspapers, judiciously avoiding looking at the date, and uncovered a chair. "I would do it just to annoy you, too."

"I know," he said amiably. He swung the door open and I could hear him shuffling through stacks of paper.

"What's that stuff, anyway?"

"Financials, for the most part. Private papers, journals, family records." He pulled out a stack of bound books and set them on the floor, before continuing to root through the safe's contents. "He asked me to finalize some paperwork for him before he... left."

The leather books caught my attention. "Those are his journals?"

Rodrian looked down at the floor where they lay. "Some, yes. I think others are in the family vault but these, I think, meant most to him. Why?"

"Do you suppose..." I bit my lip, unsure how to ask. It felt dirty, as if I were a nasty old lady scavenging through Ebenezer Scrooge's bedclothes.

The harsh comparison didn't stop my selfish thoughts. Marek's personal journals could hold valuable memories, thoughts, observations he might have shared with me, had there been more time. Denied his presence and his affection, I wanted those books.

Avarice had nothing to do with it. It was my due. I had loved him too completely to be denied those small things.

Rodrian picked them up and pushed to his feet. "Sophie, would you like these?"

Yes, I did. I wanted them with all my being. And even though Rodrian was closer to me than any living soul, even though he was one of the few I trusted and loved, I didn't know how to ask him.

When he placed them into my trembling hands, I took them the same way my mother had accepted the folded flag that had been draped over my grandfather's casket. He died when I was eight. I remembered how Mom jumped and squeezed her eyes shut when they fired the gun salute. I remembered how *Taps* seemed to reach inside me, grasp a corner of my soul, and tug it away as the notes wavered into thundering silence. Those images, so clear and so staggering, stole my breath from me now and left me feeling very unworthy and very, very small.

I poured my essence into my barriers and kept those raw images from Rodrian. If he knew—if he knew, it would be worse.

"You don't need to ask permission to take anything," he said. "Marek had a will, you know."

"Oh, no." I wrinkled my nose and swallowed down a stinging sensation. "Not this again."

"All I'm saying is, he named you beneficiary. I'm sure that under these circumstances the same would hold." Rodrian pulled me to my feet, the books between us; wrapping his arms around me, he pressed his lips to my forehead. "It's okay. We'll preserve the memory of who my brother was and honor him. Take the journals. They are an important aspect of Marek's life."

His touch was meant to be comforting but I shrugged

out of his embrace. It felt too uncomfortable, too wrong, somehow, to be near him here amongst Marek's things. I felt like Marek could see me; I knew he'd disapprove.

Rodrian knelt at the safe again, pulling several folders out before swinging the heavy door shut and allowing the tapestry to fall into place. He hesitated near the big dusty book, hefting it up and adding it to his pile.

We journeyed through the grey gloom once more. He took a big black umbrella from the stand near the door before we left, holding it over me as I got back into the TTS.

Rodrian treated me like a widow. I hated myself for feeling like one.

We stopped for lunch at Cordula's, although the meal was uncharacteristically small and quiet. At least it was too early for Caen to be on duty. Bonus right there.

Ever since Marek left, Caen was too nice. And by nice, I mean sinister and gleeful and not the least interested in pretending not to stare at me. I never understood why Rodrian didn't see it, or do something about it. Maybe Caen had been working with Rodrian for so long that it became hard to see flaws, or at least too hard to call Caen out on them.

When Rodrian's cell phone rang he only glanced at the caller ID before dismissing the call. I didn't have to see the name to know it was Aurelia. His power always took the same twist whenever she appeared.

Aurelia was Rodrian's mate. Couldn't call her a wife, really, since they never took formal vows. She was, however, the mother of all his children, even if only in terms of genetic ownership; Aurelia was more of a visiting spirit than a reliable partner.

The last time she'd come to town was the early nineties. She stayed long enough to bring Shiloh into the world before dashing off to a faraway corner of it again. There was probably something to be admired in her strong-willed independent ways. Rodrian absolutely loved her and feared the inevitable moment when she'll disappear from his life again—and that gave me another reason to not like her a whole bunch.

When she called the third time, Rodrian's power surged so desperately that I shooed him off. "Please, Rode. Take it before she hunts you down."

"I don't want to be rude—"

"She's rude enough for both of you. Please."

He stood up and opened his mouth but I cut him off. "And stop apologizing. I have to make a call anyway."

He disappeared in the direction of his office, which occupied a corner behind the kitchen. It wasn't at all pleasant like his old office at Folletti's; this one was loud from the kitchen racket, there was always someone in the hallway outside his door, and most days it smelled like the deep fryers. Cordula's was big on fried food.

As soon as he left, I called my girlfriend Dahlia, who answered just before it went to voicemail. She sounded just as miserable as I did. That made me feel better; at least I didn't have to worry about bringing her down. Being an empath meant I had to wear a happy face and prevent my mental touch from transmitting my real feelings. Some days, it was downright exhausting.

"What are you doing tonight?" I hoped she'd be willing to come over to watch a movie. I'd even let her pick one of her bloodier war epics, even though I barely made it through the last one we watched together. *Saving Private Ryan* had a lot less to do with saving than I'd assumed.

I just didn't feel like being alone and, after today, being alone with Rodrian would still feel like being alone.

"Toby's made plans, actually," she said. "It's werewolf business."

Ah. That explained the cloudy undertones to her voice. Dahlia had been adamant that her sweetie Toby join a pack so he could learn how to be the best Were he could be. Kind of like a Cub Scout, I guessed, and only a mild pun intended. But Dahlia was DV, through and through. Even though it was best for Toby, it was still difficult for her to reconcile their different cultures.

I guessed it was similar to an uneasy marriage of different faiths. Putting the Star of David on top a Christmas tree didn't mean everything blended.

Dahlia was a tough chick, though, and not one to let a little adversity deter her from what she wanted. She loved Toby and was determined to make everything work. "It shouldn't be that bad. Balaton's packs have arranged for some sort of music festival at the Philly Majestic."

"So you have to go to a concert? How bad can that be?"

"Not bad, if you're Were. I guess you don't want to go with?"

It had been quite some time since I've seen a live show. I've been so consumed with work and the Sophia and avoiding my issues with Rodrian that I hadn't even thought of a night out. "I suppose. Depends. You know who's playing?"

She recited a list of local rock bands, names I knew from small posters plastered on city fences and lampposts or mentioned on the radio. But the last one floored me.

Turn of the Wheel was headlining.

I must have misheard. "From Germany?"

"I think that's what he said. I never heard of them."

I could have spun in place. "You've never heard of *Turn*

of the Wheel? My God. And you've been around longer than I have."

"Metal's not my speed. I can't believe it's yours, either."

"Metal's not your speed? What about knives or chains or war hammers?"

She chuckled. "Music should soothe the savage beast. You know I don't listen to that stuff."

"Well, nobody said you were perfect. I'm going, right?"

"I want you to go because I don't want to be by myself but I have serious reservations about it. I don't know if this would be a good place for you."

"I've ended up in a lot of places that weren't good for me. But if I would get to see this band, who I've never seen live before—" I paused for dramatic significance. "Please don't make me stay home."

"Did I mention that this is a Were-organized event?" Silly girl. She thought she could convince me to forget about going.

Normally, it would have worked. "Do they forbid non-Weres?"

"No, of course not. After all, Toby invited me."

"And I'm going with you," I said, my voice brighter than six months of summer. "Finally. I get to see Dierk Adeluf sing. Oh, my God. Boots. I need boots."

"Well, then," she said. "You had better get ready. And I had better change into something more appropriate for saving your ass, should you decide to start trouble."

"Me? Start trouble?"

"You're right. You don't start trouble, you attract it. I'll dress for more defense than offense."

I hung up with a smile, feeling lucky to have a friend who understood me so well. Hopefully, Dahlia's wardrobe wouldn't get us brought up on weapons charges on the way to the show. I'd really hate to miss the band.

I corrected myself. I'd hate to see the band without her.

Dahlia wasn't kidding when she said it was a festival. We'd been to the Majestic for shows before but I had never seen the theater this crowded. The three of us stopped for a quick supper and arrived around seven. Dahlia said the first band had gone on around one o'clock in the afternoon, but since the Werekind were only mandated to be present for the last act and subsequent gathering, we could arrive later.

The Majestic was an old theater that had been converted into a concert hall and, like any good concert hall, the outer rim of the auditorium was lined with bars. After enduring the first set, I thought perhaps there was good reason for it. Metal had changed quite a bit since I was in high school. The rockers were seriously scary-looking, and there was a great deal more growling.

Or maybe it was a Were thing.

At nine o'clock, the under-21 crowd was dispelled, and the barriers that had corralled them away from the evils of alcohol were dismantled. By then, the serious fans had begun to assemble.

I had been prejudiced against werewolves since being introduced to their charms by an assassin named Tanner a few years ago. His "brother" Toby, who had since become my good friend, did a lot to redefine my idea of Were. Still, as I surveyed the crowd I wondered if this was a concert or a biker convention.

At first, the crowd wasn't too bad. I had room to move my arms, at least. Of the few times that I thinned my barriers, I realized that, while there were a lot of Were, the crowd wasn't completely homogeneous. I detected plenty of humans and, more surprisingly, quite a number of DV.

I saw no flashing eyes, anywhere. Even people as powerful as the DV knew which crowds were safe and which ones weren't. This one definitely was not safe.

As the crowd began to fill out with backs broader than barns and more leather than a Harley shop, I realized how many of them looked like wolves. They had dark, hungry looks. They snapped at each other over their shoulders. They barked with hoarse laughter. And all of them wore their pumpkin-colored eyes.

The full moon was maybe a week past, on its way to a slender crescent. At this point in the moon, the waning pull of power that bled Were eyes from normal to rust would have diminished so I suspected most of them wore them for fun. It was easy to figure out who the humans were— they were the ones wearing uneasy expressions and trying not to stare at the strange, animalistic eyes of the people around them.

Eventually the crowds became too unbearable. I, in the true spirit of the occasion, wore boots that looked dangerous and sexy but were next to impossible to walk in. When the first surge of crowd lifted me off my feet and threatened to carry me away with it, Dahlia found my hand, tugged me out of the mass of people, and motioned we should go upstairs.

A door in the foyer led to a side stairwell, an old metal thing that clanked like a fire escape when we climbed it. Our destination was the upper balcony; it was generally off-limits but I had floating permission to sit up there. The DV who ran the theatre knew the Sophia didn't like crowds.

Although this was a Were event, this balcony had plenty of DV guard patrolling it. The Majestic was owned by the DV and, although they were cool about letting the Were use the venue, their generosity didn't extend to letting them have free reign. Along the walls behind the lighting crews were dark shapes, the flash of bright eyes, and the glint of firearms. I hoped tonight would not be the night their services were needed.

Dahlia and I slid between the rows and made our way to the front of the balcony, and I perched on the edge of the seat, gripping the railing and feeling like I would burst with anticipation. The stage was dark, and shadows moved equipment from one side to the other. Soon.

And then over the crowds I detected an ethereal hum, growing louder, keyboards that expanded into a winding melody. Most of the crowd fell silent and still, turning one by one to face the stage. Dark figures took their places on the shadowy stage, evoking cries and whistles from the crowd.

Then, a voice. I closed my eyes and smiled, as a surge of recognition and pleasure flooded me. I knew that voice.

That voice wound itself around the music, a handsome tenor. A glow like approaching dawn grew behind the stage, and the silhouette of a man showed against the back screen. The music built, the voice built, and when they both peaked, the veil dropped.

Dierk Adeluf, standing atop a dais, spread his arms wide. The audience received him as a god.

Guitars and drums and keys joined his voice in harmony and contrast, a tidal wave of sound that crashed into me, leading into a song I've sung along with for fifteen years. I forgot everything else except the man on the stage. For the first time, my troubles and my trials melted into the background, all but forgotten.

Dierk Adeluf was thirty-nine and in the prime of his life. He wore a grey button-down shirt open over a black tee, black jeans, black shoes. His brown hair, shoulder-length and straight, fell back from his brow. Simple. Nothing glamorous, no leather or war paint, just man. Man, and his extraordinary voice.

I spent the next hour in a dream-like state. Dahlia could

have spontaneously combusted and I probably would have missed the whole thing unless my sleeve accidentally caught fire. I didn't even look at her until after the show, the bows, and the encore. By then, Toby had joined us.

Thank goodness there were DV with guns looking out for my best interest. I didn't even notice he'd appeared.

"I hope you aren't ready to go home yet," Toby said. "The Were have been encouraged to stay and mingle after the show."

"They planned a social event," Dahlia added. "It's part of an effort to improve interpack relations, which, I admit, are even worse than Were-slash-DV relations."

I jerked my head in the direction of the stage. House lights showed a once-more restless crowd in front of it. "I get the impression that Were just don't play well together. They hate the DV. They hate each other. They hate people. Why would you want to knowingly be a part of that, Toby? It seems like the packs are only put together so that they can hate in bigger numbers."

Toby looked away, leaving Dahlia to answer.

"He needs the contacts," she said. "Toby's never been a part of a pack. He needs to learn rules and traditions. Cultural ideals. I just hope he doesn't learn the bad habits."

She patted his leg and he smiled, a nervous flash of teeth. "DV security will compel humans to leave soon. Given the amount of booze they had tonight, their minds will be more than open to suggestion. Once they sweep the crowd, Were security will double-check and take over."

"Oh," I said. "Are all the DV going to leave, too?"

"No," she said. "Some, like me, will remain by invitation. You'll stay, too, as an extension of DV hospitality, although it's best if we keep your status a secret. If you leave your barriers up, you won't even notice the compulsion. Hopefully, the others will just assume you're plain human."

"Sounds like a plan. I'd like to keep out of the way, though."

"Not a problem," she said as she glanced down at the roiling crowd. "I really don't feel like trouble tonight."

On the way downstairs, Toby's demeanor went from tense to rigid with apprehension. His face assumed an odd tightness, his mouth stretching across his jaw. It looked about as natural as a smile in a funeral home.

He ushered me to a side bar, one closest to the front of the auditorium near the stage. I hadn't noticed this bar before but that was because it hadn't been open during the show. This one was classy—it had stools, for one thing, comfy ones with cushioned tops, and classy brass rungs, more along the style Rodrian would have in his lounges. A glance behind the bar showed the stock wasn't limited to the cheap stuff, either.

Then I saw why: tray after tray of cocktails and pitchers were prepared and whisked off through a thick door about twenty feet from the side of the bar, leading to what I presumed was backstage. Catering to the talent, I supposed.

Even the bartender was well-dressed compared to the tee shirts and tank tops the others had worn throughout the show. The white-shirted and pristine-aproned gentleman was joined by an elegant lady in similar garb as I took a seat. She smiled and made me the best pomegranate Cosmo I'd ever tasted but shook her head when I lay a ten on the bar.

"Compliments this evening," she said. "This is a sponsored party."

I wiggled my eyebrows at Dahlia and grinned. "If you can make another like this one, then consider it a tip."

"Tips are always appreciated." She grinned before leaving to take another's order.

"You okay here, Soph?" Toby's tension made his voice

sound frayed around the edges. Being Were, he couldn't benefit from a good Sophia session. Whatever business the Were had, he wasn't looking forward to it.

A glancing touch on Dahlia's power told me she was concerned but not nervous, although feeling a little stifled by all the Were. I sympathized easily—being in a room full of voids was unsettling. It was like walking in the dark. Anything could pop up and surprise the life out of me. I didn't like surprises, especially not Were ones.

"I'm okay if you are." I eyed him and reached out to take his hand, wanting to comfort him.

He pulled back from me, shaking his head. "Don't get your scent on me. It's not smart."

Enough said. I picked up my drink, sipping and looking at Dahlia over the rim of the glass.

"Just call me if you need anything," she said. "I'll be listening."

"And, hey." Toby laughed, a false sound meant to put me at ease. "Don't get loaded and go home with anyone."

The joke was a bad one but it worked. I winked at him and pretended to adjust my cleavage. "Party pooper."

Eventually, the bar area filled up, although no one appeared to have hunkered down the way I did. The entire auditorium had become a huge cocktail party, tuxedoed servers carrying silver platters of appetizers to quite a mixed crowd. Some parts still looked like a biker rally, but now there were just as many wearing suits and dresses and flannel shirts as there were wearing denim and leather.

Usually I was a big one for people watching. Not tonight. I'd gotten a smartphone for Christmas from Santa Me and had downloaded a new romance for my e-reader. Those who can't do, teach, and those who can't be with their soul mate read about the ones who are. I read between snippets of conversation with Glory, the bar maid, and paid no attention to anyone behind me.

I did notice, however, when Glory's eyes grew wide as she looked over my head, and I fought an urge to duck. Instead of a growl, I heard a very familiar voice ask for two lagers.

Dierk Adeluf.

He leaned forward casually, one outstretched arm against the bar next to me.

Without thinking, I turned to face him. "One for each hand, huh?"

He glanced down in surprise before grinning. "Actually, yes. It took all night to get this close to the bar. Who knows when I'll get close enough again?"

"Yeah, I guess." I wanted to sigh and flutter my eyelashes at him. His voice was so…sigh. "Great show, by the by. Reminded me a little of the Rotterdam bootleg more so than the last live album."

Dierk raised his eyebrows.

"An attentive ear," he said. "Very impressive. Hans is with us tonight, and he sings the harmony. Actually, we can't keep him from singing." He shook his head and laughed. "Rotterdam was the last tour he played with us."

Glory pushed two draughts across the bar to him, her gaze on the bar. He slid a folded bill toward her and she took it with trembling fingers. Another fan girl, I thought. I'll have to hug her later.

"It's an honor to know we have such an elegant listener. Usually our followers are a bit more. . ." His gaze roamed the room and he nodded toward a rough-looking assembly at the other end. "Organic. If you are inclined, it's less crowded backstage."

He pulled a lanyard pass from his back pocket and lay it on the bar next to my purse. "You are welcome to join us.

I'd love to speak with you further."

He bowed with a courtly dip of his head, picked up his glasses, and melted into the crowd.

I picked up the pass, turning it over in my hands before slipping it into my purse. Blood and excitement hummed in my ears. If I wasn't careful, I'd pee my pants with delight. With so many discerning noses nearby, that could have been problematic.

Of course, I had absolutely no intention to take him up on his offer. That brief snatch of conversation was enough for me. Hero worship was never meant to occur up close—it was definitely a from-afar phenomenon. Anything closer was akin to stalking.

Although, if I was going to stalk anyone, I supposed it would be Dierk Adeluf.

As I happily contemplated a fresh drink and the memory of his charming half-smile and honey-soft brown eyes, the last thing I anticipated was the physical removal from my daydream.

Someone spilled an ice-cold drink down my spine.

I spun around in indignant shock to see a tall blonde, big-haired and shrink-wrapped in black leather, staring me into the ground and waving an empty glass. The cruel smile that sliced across her mouth ensured me there was nothing accidental about the mishap.

"What's your problem?" I took a towel from Glory and tried to mop up the cold streak that soaked me from neck to waist.

"You owe me a drink, you clumsy bitch." Her voice was thick with European accent. Great. An out-of-towner. Obviously, they don't teach etiquette in Leather Land.

"I what? You dumped it on me!" I looked down at the towel, seeing it come away bright orange. "Oh, great. Kool-Aid doesn't come out, either."

She narrowed her eyes. At least her command of English included satire and reference to childish things. "Pay for my drink and get out."

"Pay for my blouse and kiss my ass," I said. Where was Dahlia? Here I needed protecting and she was off sniffing rears with Toby. I thinned my barriers and send her a query of power, noticing that the blond drink bomber had a distinct lack of power.

Great. A Were void. Just great.

"Kick your ass?" She smiled as she deliberately misquoted me. "With pleasure."

Note to self: never write a human check your sorry ass can't cash because you are in a room full of werewolves.

She stalked closer. I noticed that a semi-circle had formed around us. At least they weren't waving fists and chanting for blood. Still, they looked far too interested in what the blonde was doing. Too much smiling.

The circle broke and Dahlia pushed through, bouncer in tow. Of course, he was a nicely dressed bouncer, but his biceps stretched the sleeves of his polo and a tattoo snaked up his neck. "Trouble here?"

Blonde Menace pointed a red-painted nail at me. "She spilled my drink and insulted me."

"I did no such thing. Anyone here could vouch. Glory?" I peered behind me for the bartender but she was no longer behind the bar. Great again.

"Seeing she wears the drink and you don't..." The bouncer crossed his beefy arms at the other woman. "I will respectfully disagree. Separate at once."

Dahlia eyed the foreigner. "We should go, Soph. Toby doesn't need me to stay."

"Yes, you should," Blondie said, eyeing the bouncer with distinct disapproval. "And take your purse with you. I'd hate for you to forget it and need to return."

I glared at her, my face hot with futile anger. "Pity. We were getting on so well, too."

She stepped closer, ignoring the bouncer's growl. "Oh, you can stay, sweetheart. I can arrange for privacy and we could really get to know each other."

The sticky cold stream down my back turned my phony smile into genuine snarl. "As long as you don't serve Kool-Aid at our tea party."

"Sophie." Dahlia pressed her hand into my side before herding me away. "Passive aggressive doesn't need to be so aggressive."

Dahlia led me by the hand, zig-zagging around groups and clusters. Her firm grip was relentless and I clipped along behind her, worried that any minute I'd twist an ankle. She forgot I wasn't wearing running shoes.

My face still flushed from the encounter, I alternately cursed myself for not standing up for myself better and praised myself for not sticking my foot into my mouth when Dierk was there. I knew I'd eventually forget the almost-fight but that brief encounter with my rock-star crush would take a long time to fade from my memory.

I'd wear that pass like an Olympic medal every day for a year. By the time we reached the back of the auditorium, I had a week's worth of matching outfits planned. Including boots.

Dahlia let go of my hand to push open the back door. One of the bouncers stopped her.

"What's the problem?" Dahlia contained her irritation and chose a diplomatic tone.

"Her." One of the bouncers pointed at me.

"I did not spill that chick's drink." I didn't care if I sounded diplomatic or not. I still had a wet sticky mess dripping into the back of my jeans. "Just let me go."

"We don't care about some broad's drink." The bouncer curled his lip and flashed his orange rust eyes at me. "But we don't tolerate criminals."

"Her?" Dahlia rolled her eyes. "You gotta be kidding."

"Nope." The bouncer stepped forward and tapped my chest hard enough to push me off balance. I bumped into another guy behind me, who clamped his hands down on my shoulders. "We'd like to have a word with you. Miss," he added with snide emphasis.

The guy behind me gave me a sideways shove. The two of them pushed me backwards through the crowd to a side door and two others slid between me and Dahlia, cutting us apart. Her angry protests turned to sharp shouts. They'd called out the North Philly girl in her. The dangerous Demivamp was only a step behind.

"Dally!" Panicked, I thinned my barriers and felt for Dahlia. She wasn't following. Oh, shit. Don't get in trouble, she'd said.

The door slammed shut. Dahlia's voice continued on the other side, muffled by the thickness of the wall. We stood in what looked like a service hallway. The grey cinderblock walls and fluorescent lighting seemed harsh after being in the warm dim concert hall. I squinted to see another guard leaning against the wall, arms folded.

"This the one who stole his wallet?" He stomped closer and stared down his long nose at me. Were eyes glowered with contempt. "A pitiful weak thing, too. You surprise me, thief. Now give me the wallet."

"I did not steal any wallet. This is ridiculous."

"And I have a witness that says otherwise."

"What witness? I was minding my own business, then someone spilled a drink on my back, and the bouncer broke it up, and my friend and I walked away right after. I never stole anything."

"Except the wallet in your purse."

"Whatever." I yanked my bag open. "You've got real nerve."

I pulled my wallet free and held it up to his face. "Does this look like a man's wallet to you?"

"Yes," he said. "It does."

"You're blind then, because this is obviously—" I looked at it. And blinked. "Not Vera Bradley. Shit. Not my wallet."

He grabbed my hand, holding it aloft. "That's just what I was thinking."

He leaned into me, baring his teeth, and I arched my back to keep away. Not an easy feat in these boots—I had to descend steps backwards in this pair. I dangled from his grasp, off-balanced and helpless. The Were snatched my purse with his free hand and tossed it to his partner. "Hiding anything else, thief?"

I couldn't answer because I was still in shock. How the hell did someone else's wallet get into my purse?

"Only this," his buddy said, dangling the backstage pass by its lanyard in front of my face. "She steals passes, too. Going back for seconds?"

"I didn't steal that. It was given to me." I shook my head frantically. "Ask the bartender. I didn't steal the wallet, either."

"Oh. Somebody gave you that, as well?"

"Obviously, someone planted it there. Not me. The only time I took my eyes off my purse was when that girl picked a fight with me."

"Good excuse. Tell *der König* yourself. Who gave you this pass?"

I had absolutely no idea what a kernick was and really didn't care. I rolled my eyes, knowing they'd never believe me. "Dierk Adeluf."

He laughed. "Right. Dierk Adeluf roams through crowds, begging for company. Especially company of your sort."

I glared at him through slitted eyes. "Oh, you mean the intelligent, decent sort?"

"Picking up the trash, Stohl?"

I twisted my head toward the familiar voice. The guard

still had a crushing grip on my wrist and the light was dim but I could see it was the blonde that poured her drink on me.

"You." I bared my teeth. "I should have guessed."

"Quiet," Stohl said. He gave my captive wrist a shake before looking toward the smiling blonde. "Go backstage. This does not concern you."

She circled close and blew a red-lipsticked kiss in my face before sauntering off down the hall.

"Great," I said. "She's with you. Of course. That's the one who picked a fight. She must have planted it."

He turned his head toward my hand, which had begun to tingle from being held high over my head. He waved his face near it, eyes never leaving mine. "I only detect Dierk's scent and yours."

"Stohl, you worry too much about my scent," Dierk said from behind me.

My stomach dropped. I closed my eyes, the flush of my face turning damp and cold.

Reaching up, Dierk plucked the wallet carefully from my numbing grasp. "Thank you for holding this. Next time, wait until I ask you to do so."

"I didn't take it." Fear trembled my voice. "I swear."

"We will determine that. Let me see your face."

Stohl twisted my arm and spun me around like a puppet to face Dierk.

His eyes moved across my face as he tried to place it. He nodded, once. "You. Well. That's a surprise. I didn't think I passed close enough for you to lift this."

"That's because I didn't."

"No. I don't believe you did." He quietly looked at me for a long moment, a half-smile playing over his mouth. "Let her go, Stohl. She's no thief."

"But *mein König*—"

"I said, let her go." Dierk tilted his head toward me, his voice taking on a soothing and persuasive cadence. "You've already frightened her and I don't like my fans to be mistreated. There is obviously a mistake."

Stohl rumbled deep in his throat. "I saw her take it from her purse. I can scent no one but her and you. You need more proof?"

"Not proof. Just the missing pieces." Dierk's mouth played a slight smile but his eyes seemed genuinely contrite. "My dear, I apologize. You have been wrongfully accused. I wish to make it up to you. Will you allow me?"

Stohl growled and slapped my purse into my hands with enough force that I went back a step. I decided I really didn't need to be here any longer. "Thanks, Mr. Adeluf, but I've got plans."

"Such as?"

I opened my purse and cursed under my breath when I looked inside. "Canceling my credit cards since, despite the happy ending to your wallet's story, mine is still swiped."

His brows dropped shrewdly. "You don't say? Then I insist you come with me."

"Oh, no need." I took a wary step toward the door, pricking my Sophia ears to catch a thought from Dahlia. "It's easier to cancel and walk away."

Dierk shook his head slowly. "Easier for you, perhaps, but I have a proud sense of honor. My entourage has been up to something and it needs to be sorted."

I pivoted on my heel and headed for the door. "Sort without me."

"Let her leave, *mein König*," Stohl said.

"Please," Dierk said.

I knew he'd spoken only to me. I paused to turn back and look at him. The word had held so much.

"I insist." Dierk gave the other man a stilling look. "I

meant what I said before. I'd like you to come back. You'll be safe, I promise."

My purse on shoulder, I twisted the straps. My heart and my brain were arguing again, weathering my resolve. "Is that bitchy thing going to be there?"

Dierk looked a question at Stohl.

"Cacilia," Stohl said.

"Ah," Dierk said. He laughed, as if finding the whole bit charming. "I should have known. She won't bother us."

His easy laugh and personal nature had a thawing effect on me, making me linger when I should have been running in the opposite direction. Years of listening to his albums had given me a false sense of familiarity. Just because I knew who he was didn't mean I knew him.

And still. "Must I come back alone?"

"No, of course not. You said you were with friends. Bring them. Stohl, make pass for—three friends?"

I shrugged. "Two is fine."

"Two additional at the door, Stohl. She still has her pass, correct?"

Stohl didn't disagree but he didn't look happy, either. Hopefully he'd stay at the door and I wouldn't have to worry about him hitting me with those heavy glares again.

Dierk tipped his head at me. "I will see you soon?"

"I have to find my friends first."

"I'll be waiting." With a slight bow, he turned and left, walking off down the hallway in the same direction Cacilia had gone.

Stohl exhaled hard, a gravelly sound, and gave me a look to shrivel. "Two friends. No vampires."

I pouted. "Oh, darn."

He slapped the pass into my hand and pointed back to the door he'd dragged me through earlier. Didn't need to tell me twice. Dahlia's power was poking at me, inquisitive taps. I knew I'd better find her before she went nuts.

I followed the thin trail of Dahlia's power back to a corner bar and found her hunched over a Bloody Mary, looking both furious and guilt-stricken. Toby had his arm around her shoulder, and gave her a squeeze when I approached.

"See?" He grinned. "Sophie can take care of herself. You can stop beating yourself up now, baby girl."

Dahlia twisted and launched herself at me, hugging and apologizing for not rescuing me. "I tried. I even called down someone from special ops. They said they couldn't risk an incident."

She held me at arm's length, her voice taking on an unfamiliar oily tone. A lavender gleam simmered in her eyes, a reckless move in this potentially-hostile environment. "I really want to cause an incident, Sophie."

"Relax," I said, alarmed by her intensity. "It was just a weird mistake. I'm okay."

"So we can go. I'm over that drink, anyway. I thought you said it was tomato juice?" She glared up at Toby who just laughed at her.

"Ah," I said. "We can't go. I kind of told Dierk Adeluf we'd go back to meet him."

"Who?" Dahlia rubbed her nose.

"Dierk Adeluf." Toby swallowed, eyes widening. "You have to go."

"We all have to," I amended. I lifted the pass. "He gave me this."

"He gave you a what? Let me see!" Dahlia grasped the pass with two hands and pulled it close to her face to examine it, apparently not realizing that its cord was looped around my neck. "Oh, wow. He's with the band!"

Toby just grinned at her and wiggled his brows behind her back. Dahlia got drunk quickly and it was always a good time.

I freed myself from her enthusiasm before she choked me. "You can come with. I don't want to go alone. Psycho groupies and stuff. I hope it doesn't come to it, but can you still fight?"

"Don't need to," she said. "My compulsions are registered weapons in six states."

"Wow, Toby." I wiggled my eyebrows at him, trying not to laugh. "You, ah, got your hands full tonight."

"You ain't kidding." He gently reined Dahlia back and steered her in the direction of the stage door and I followed behind.

Anticipation began to cancel out the stress of the previous mishaps. Backstage with *Turn of the Wheel.* This might be totally worth cancelling a few credit cards, after all.

For nearly twenty years, I've known Dierk Adeluf's voice.

I learned it listening to CDs and watching videos. Smooth like a cello, desperate like a warrior's dying cry, ragged like a raging beast. Dierk Adeluf sang with tremendous range and I knew all of his voices.

Sitting an arm's reach from me, speaking casually about the last week, his plans for another music festival, some mix-up at the airport, Dierk used a new voice. No production tricks, no dubbing, no myriad of vocal lines. One voice, one sound. Simply Dierk, speaking.

The sound fascinated me; it needed no musical accompaniment. His laughter was smooth and full-throated, a superior sound that managed to include, rather than exclude, everyone around us. German being his native language, his accent gave odd emphasis to certain words, occasionally leaning heavily on first syllables and cutting off ending r-sounds.

Dierk wasn't a glorious rock star. Even back in the 80s, when wardrobe and hair were every bit important as the music, he tread the non-adorned path, settling for straight hair in a bangless cut, jean jacket and high top sneakers. He looked like a roadie, not a front man.

When he opened his mouth, all doubts disintegrated. His voice was his presence.

I started listening to *Turn of the Wheel* when I was in high school. They played a lot of thrash and speed metal back then, disdained by my head-banger girlfriends. They were more interested in Joey Tempest's supernaturally-perfect hair and the leather fringe on Don Dokken's jacket. (Have to admit, it was wonderful fringe. I still YouTube those old videos whenever I need cheering up.)

My then-boyfriend was the only one who seemed to understand me. Jared used to tell me I had more than one soul inside me, because no one person could possibly have so much vehement interest in such a vast assortment of styles. Ironic that he was sort of right; unfair that he didn't live long enough to learn the truth.

It was the progressive side of *Turn of the Wheel*'s music that attracted me and over time I was well-rewarded for my loyalty. During the nineties they polished their style. Many of their lyrics retold old legends and great Tolkienesque tales; they sang of battles and tragedy, bards and minstrels, heroes and villains.

If they tossed a bit of thrash in from time to time, I didn't complain. Music was supposed to be fun.

So while my best friends would try to sneak backstage when the big bands came to town, teasing her hair up and snapping on studded bracelets, I settled for jeans and great boots (yes, it had always been about the boots) and my cassettes, because *Turn of the Wheel* wasn't about raunchy glam rock and tour bus antics.

They were noble.

They toured once or twice in the States when I was newly graduated from college and work obligations kept me from throwing in for a road trip and a rock show. They kept playing, kept producing, and I faithfully bought their CDs, always impressed with the depth and the effort. Dierk had more youth and vivacity in him now at forty than I did back at twenty-five. Of course, that may be because he wasn't lugging around a dormant oracle somewhere in his brain or being oppressed by a burdensome career.

Considering my admiration for the band, I found it quite surreal to be lounging backstage with them. Could life have thrown me a more exciting slider? Although I was by far the least hip-looking chick in the room, I had to be the happiest.

Dahlia and Toby hovered close by. Judging by the power signatures there was quite a variety of species in attendance. Mostly Were-like voids, almost too many for my comfort; I reminded myself that many DV knew how to completely shield while many humans simply didn't "care" enough to emit a detectable vibe unless I really looked.

Tonight, I wasn't looking.

I was too distracted by Dierk's voice and the comfortable, familiar way he spoke to me. I was too consumed with not acting like a boring nerd. I was also all too mindful of the fact that not everyone loved the Sophia and I didn't want to advertise my presence any more than absolutely necessary.

After being presented with my wallet—found in the trash but completely intact—I'd joined a circle of people who lounged in a grouping of cushioned chairs and old couches. I ended up sitting closest to Dierk, our knees near enough to touch if I scooted a little bit to the left. Some of the band were there, too, as well as a diverse group: Were voids, plain people, me.

Dierk and his lead guitarist, Janssen, took turns describing humorous mishaps from their last tour. Dahlia slid through the crowd, sinking onto the couch next to me. Leaning close, she whispered so as not to interrupt the speakers. "You okay, Sophie?"

"Are you kidding?" I squeezed her leg. "This is amazing. I can't believe we're back here."

"Yeah, how 'bout it?" She grinned, but I knew something was weighing on her mind.

I thinned my barrier and brushed against her power. "What's wrong?"

"Nothing, I—I was wondering if you were ready to leave, actually."

I couldn't glean anything but didn't want to risk dropping my shielding any further amongst these strangers. Couldn't be sure who would be listening. "What's wrong?"

"Nothing. I just—it feels really crowded. I can't explain it."

"Oh." I didn't want to stay if she wasn't comfortable. She was probably suffering from Were overload. I glanced at Dierk, who caught me looking at him and smiled.

It was a nice smile.

I couldn't keep from mirroring it. Turning back to Dahlia, I wanted to heave a huge disappointed sigh but held it in. Fishing around in my purse, I dug out my keys on their Hello Kitty key ring. Throwback to the Eighties Sophie, that's me. "You know you come first, Dally. Wanna meet me at the car? I need to say goodbye first."

She squeezed my hand. "I'm sorry. I know I'm ruining your time, but…thanks."

She took the keys I held out to her and left.

Dierk marked her departure with a thoughtful glance and leaned close. "Everything all right? Your friend didn't seem to be enjoying herself."

I smiled an apology. "She's ready to leave, so…I should go. I just hate to leave this."

"And I hate for you to leave…but I understand. May I?" He reached behind him to pull out his wallet and slid out a card. "This is where I'm staying. Would you call me tomorrow? I'd like to see you again before we leave."

I tried not to swallow my tongue. "Sure. Who knows? Things might run a little smoother. That whole thing with the drink and the wallet wasn't my idea of a good time."

"All things happen for a reason. Sometimes the reason is petty. I apologize again for Cacilia."

"Don't mention it. Really. I'd be happy if I never had to see her again."

"You judge her too harshly but, then again, you are somewhat entitled this evening. She didn't flaunt any of her positive qualities. To be safe, I'll walk you out."

Oh, I liked the thought of that. "Deal."

Dierk stood and extended his hand to help me to my feet. Enjoying the courtly gesture and thinking how well it suited him, I slipped my fingers into his.

The moment we touched, a zing of electricity passed between us, a thudding jolt of shock that made me snatch my hand away.

"Yikes!" I shook my hand and rubbed my fingers against my jeans, feeling the tingle ride up my arm to my elbow. "A little static there. Sorry."

Dierk didn't reply. He gripped his right wrist, wriggling his fingers, eyes wide with disbelief. The people who'd been sitting with us were on their feet, conversations forgotten. Silence spread out from us like cracks on an ice-covered pond. Everyone stared at us.

"Um, what's wrong?" I thinned my barriers and skimmed, trying to pick up a clue without being too obvious. The few DV signatures were as clueless as I was.

Stohl pushed his way over to us. "Dierk, what was that? My hair stands on end."

"That was her." Dierk looked intently at me, his expression hard to read.

"What?" I backed up a step. "Oh, not this crap again. Dierk, can we just go?"

Stohl paid no attention to me. "Her? You must be mistaken."

"I'm not." Dierk glanced at him briefly before training his eyes on me once more. He looked at me like he had no idea who I was, as if I hadn't spent the last two hours sitting across from him. "You know I'm not."

"I can't believe this. Her?"

"What about her?" Cacilia squeezed between Stohl and the circle which had formed around us. "And what was that lightning I felt?"

"Quiet, Cassy." Stohl growled at her. "Now is not the time."

"Oh, yes, it is." I hiked my purse and stepped around Dierk, searching for the door. "It's time I left."

Stohl rolled his eyes. "Sit down. You are not going anywhere."

"Stohl." Dierk announced his name like a command. He seemed to shake whatever had spooked him and he raised a lone finger toward his friend. "Do not speak to my woman in such a manner."

"She's a groupie, *mein König*."

Dierk crossed his arms over his chest. "She's my mate."

"Mate?" Oh, hell to the absolutely no, I wasn't. "I don't know what you planned, Dierk, but whatever it is, you planned wrong."

"It is not I who has decided."

Cacilia glowered, rage spilling up in a flush across her

pale cheeks. "You can't mean—"

Dierk cut her off by turning his back to her and stood between me and the others. "Sophie, listen to me. Did you feel that shock?"

I looked around warily at the circle that had formed around us. Boots or no boots, I was beginning to hate being noticed. "Static. So what?"

"Not static. No carpet, and you are wearing non-conducting soles besides. Hold out your hand. I need to tap your hand three times. Be not afraid. It will not hurt."

I tuck my hands under my arms. "This is ridiculous."

Stohl appeared over Dierk's shoulder. "You are overreacting, Dierk."

Dierk closed his eyes. "Silence."

His voice carried to the ends of the room. There was silence. Instant, deafening obedience.

"Now." Dierk returned his gaze to me. His voice was gentle when he focused once more upon me but no less commanding. "Hold out your hand."

Trembling, I raised my palm, fingers splayed. As I did so, I pulled up every layer of barrier I could and tried to hold steady.

His expression was serene, the slightest hint of a half-smile on his mouth, as he extended his index finger and pressed it to the center of my hand.

The shock zapped down my arm once more and I jumped. Several of those standing closest flinched. Cacilia turned her face up toward Stohl, outrage in her eyes.

"Dierk." I decided it was okay to be frightened now, considering the circumstances. "What the hell is going on?"

He ignored me. "Stohl. Tap her hand."

I yanked my hand back with alarm. The big bully looked like he'd rather tap me with a sledgehammer.

"Do it." Dierk's voice had fallen to low notes that

rumbled over each other.

I summoned my courage and raised my hand again, staring defiantly into Stohl's face. He hesitated a moment before poking me.

Nothing happened. I smirked and crossed my arms, watching him skulk back to Cacilia's side. Dierk moved to stand in front of me again.

"Sophie, your hand. Once more, then this will be over."

More confident that whatever had been happening was just a bunch of nonsense, I lifted my fingers a third time. Dierk's hand descended and I held my breath. The tension in the room was palpable. Dahlia wasn't kidding; it was crowded. The sooner I got out, the better.

When our skin made contact, the shock that snapped between us made me cry out in pain and surprise. Dierk closed his eyes and bowed his head as he raised clasped hands to his mouth in a gesture of prayer. A hum of whispers and muttering moved through the crowd.

"No." Cacilia's brittle voice rose above the others. "Not her. I refuse to abide."

My nerves screeched as I passed my breaking point. "What is this, Dierk? What are you doing?"

"Not I. It is the moon."

"The moon? What does that have to do with anything?" Crowded turned to oppressive and the air became too thick to breathe.

"Everything. We are hers." Dierk lifted his head to reveal eyes the color of golden October glory. "We are Were."

Out. Out. Get out now.

All I could think about was getting out of there. Away from him, away from them, away from the horror of his words still hanging in the air between us.

I backed away, first one step, then another, before turning and fleeing. I had to get out. Now. The crowd parted, their heavy gazes pressing in on me.

The stage door banged open against the wall, echoing through the now-silent auditorium. The stage was black and empty, the concert hall devoid of life. My heels clacked, sharp desperate sounds that bounced up into the darkened heights.

Worry made me feel ill. It crept in, settling over my chest and my stomach. The urge to sit and wait for it to pass was almost as strong as the need to get away. By the time I got to the foyer doors, I struggled to keep my momentum.

Fear pushed me toward the bright lights of the street entrance, a promise of safety. Yet every step I took was accompanied by an increasingly leaden feeling. My insides were twisting. Stretching.

By the time I reached the street doors, my feet dragged. The sick feeling had spread like fog. I felt disoriented, lost. What could I do? I had to get out but how can I get home like this? Where was the car? I couldn't remember.

I pushed myself to the curb, praying for a taxi. I didn't think I'd make it to the bus stop on the next block. I couldn't even stand up straight.

I paced backwards to the theater windows and sank back against the glass, eyes closed, feeling the cool bite of wind on my cheek as a tear slid down. Never before in my life had I felt as I did now.

Cars streamed by in spurts as the traffic lights changed. The sound was rhythmic, as was the rush of blood in my ears. I measured time with the thunderous noise of my heart.

Gradually, slowly, the fog thinned, the wrenching inside lessened. I inhaled with relief, finding my feet, opening my eyes. I guessed I just needed to collect myself after the spook and the rush. Now, time to get lost.

I stretched out an inquiry, hoping against hope that Dahlia was close by. Not only was there no Dahlia, there was no DV, period. Long shadows on the corners surrounding this end of the block revealed individuals, and I reached for each one. Were. They were all Were. They'd set up a perimeter—a Demivamp-free one.

I couldn't even bum a ride. Public transportation it was, then.

Raking a hand through my hair, I turned to check my reflection in the glass to make sure I didn't look too disheveled before setting off for the bus stop.

Dierk stood behind me, the window between us, one hand pressed flat against the pane. There was a long space between breaths as we gazed across the glass at each other. He looked apologetic, his chin wavering with a slight shake of his head.

He pulled his hand away and his mouth moved. Although I couldn't hear his voice, I knew his lips formed my name. Stepping over to the door, he pushed it open with his left hand, silently entreating me to come back inside.

Somehow, I knew I hadn't a choice. With a heavy sense of resignation, I did as he commanded.

Not knowing what awaited, not knowing what mess I'd gotten myself into, I went back into the theater, to the Weres who waited for me.

"Are you all right?" Dierk's voice was quiet, almost tender in his concern.

"Now. For a moment there I thought—wait." I looked at him closely. "How did you know?"

"I don't like seeing you suffer. I knew it would be difficult for you but I had to be sure."

"Sure? Of what?"

"Of who you are."

Oh crap, I thought with a sinking feeling. Dahlia was right. *I'm screwed. The jig is up, Sophia.*

He still wore his usual look of gentle amusement. By now, I'd realized it was unintentional. Dierk wore that pleasant expression when he wore no other.

"Come back inside," he said. "We need to decide what to do next. This is a most unexpected turn of events."

"I really don't think it's a good idea," I said, my voice shaky. "I should go. My friends are—"

"Gone." He waved out toward the street, a dismissive gesture. "They know you will have a ride home."

"Yeah. A cab. Now."

"The door is there." His voice was mild. "I would never

make you do anything you don't want to do."

I watched him for a moment, unsure what to do. When I saw he would make no move to stop me, I backed up to the door and went out.

Once again, the sick feeling crept in, pulling my insides and slowing my steps at the curb. I wanted to march across the street, away from him, away from here.

I just didn't have the stamina to do it.

Once again, I turned around and saw him behind the glass, feeling a thin respite as I looked at his face and his gentle, expectant expression.

It wasn't compulsion. It was some kind of magic.

I didn't know what any of it meant. All I knew was that this werewolf had me and there was nobody, save him, that could help me.

What could I do? The only relief I'd find would be at his side.

I trudged back inside, clarity returning and with it, anger—anger I didn't dare show because it would just be another check to bounce. Right now, I had to focus on getting out of this mess. Somehow.

He raised his hand, gently urging me to return with him to the depths of the theater. "You will not be in danger. I won't allow it."

"I don't want to go back in there," I whispered. "I'm afraid."

"Of what?" His accent made him sound so sure, even though I suspected my words puzzled him.

"Of them. The werewolves."

"Sophie, they are mine. There is no need to worry. Do you fear me?"

I bit my lips, thinking for a moment and fishing around my gut for a reaction. "No. You make me cautious, not afraid."

"Well, then," he said with a chuckle. "If you do not fear me, then you shouldn't fear at all. I am the one in control here."

"About that," I said. "They keep calling you *kernick*. What is that?"

"*König*," he repeated. His careful pronunciation gave the word a subtle flourish at the end. "It is a title."

Vague. Maybe it was German for *front man*.

We crossed the darkened auditorium floor toward the side of the unlit stage, past the bar where we'd first met. A few hours ago the stage was alive with sight and sound and this man had prowled across it. I thought about how he'd sung, about the things I thought about while he sung them. I thought about his voice. He was accustomed to singing to thousands.

Now, in the empty theater I was his only audience and he sang only for me. He hummed a simple tune, a soothing melody. It was warm and brooding and I relaxed against my better judgment.

Humming became words. "Strangers were we before this night, two spirits meant to pass in the dark…"

I snorted. "My requiem?"

"Sophie, requiems are for the dead. You are alive."

"Yeah, well…" I swung my purse by my side, rubbing my shoulder. "My past experiences with the Were haven't done much to convince me I'd end up anything different."

"Then you have only met sad excuses for *Wolfenkinder*. My pack does not run about harming beautiful maidens."

I laughed, despite wanting to throw up on the floor and flee. "That's poetic."

"If a poet describes what he sees with his heart then it is not poetry. It is merely truth."

We headed backstage, passing through the long corridor. It seemed much less forbidding before when it was lined with crew and hopeful fans. Now, it was empty and the walls echoed with expectation. Voices carried from the rooms beyond. They ceased when we rounded the corner and stepped into the common room.

"Ah," called out a voice. Stohl rose to face us. "A change of heart, thief?"

"You might say that." Dierk answered for me. "Sophie has agreed to help us solve this charming puzzle of who she is. First, my friends. I think it is fair that we show who we are. My dear Sophie is fearful of *der Wolfenkinder*. I do not wish for her to spend time here with us worrying about which one of you will eat her. Gentlemen, if you'd be so kind. . ."

One by one, the men standing closest to us dropped backwards into the crowd, allowing room for sleek shapes to push through. Black wolves, bigger than German Shepherds, eyes glowing like Halloween lanterns.

Were. They were all Were.

Startled by their sudden change, I lost grip on my barriers and they wavered, wide open. That's when I felt it.

The few DV who had remained in the room were threatened by the Weres' manifestation. Surges of DV power erupted, eliciting growls from wolves throughout the room. The growls only made the DV more nervous. Tension was building, a positive feedback loop that would only end with an explosion of aggression. The DV's power squeezed at me, clawing through my barriers. If I didn't calm them, a whole lot of bad was going to happen and I'd be caught in something far worse than a mosh pit.

I reached out, locating each of my DV, draining their anxiety and their defensive anger, calming them, soothing them, getting them to withdraw their power. The growling ceased. The tension drained. Bloodbath averted.

At least I had thought so.

I turned back to Dierk to find him downright glaring at me.

"What are you doing?" He sniffed at the air around me, frowning. "You are human, yet you command these Demivampire. You wear their power. Are you a succubus?"

"A what?" I knew what a succubus was. At least, Syfy's version. If that's what he meant, I had better be hearing wrong or I was going to club him, superstar or not.

His lip curled. Apparently, that's exactly what he meant. "A vampire whore."

A condemnation if I ever heard one. I'd known vampire whores and being placed in the same category as Donna made me want to spit. "Is that what you think I am?"

He shrugged, seeming very comfortable with hurling insults. "Perhaps."

"How dare you!" I raised my hand, intending to slap off his smug expression.

He grabbed my hand before I could strike and held it firmly. Although it didn't hurt, I still didn't like it. I twisted, trying to pull out of his grasp.

"I do not mean to insult you," he said. "But I am *Wolf*. This is our world. Don't blame me because my brethren are not overly fond of your Demivampire pets."

"Look. Let's just agree to disagree. Okay?" I struggled to yank my hand loose. His half-smile made me furious. "You don't like my friends. I don't like yours. Let's just say so long and good night and let me go."

"I cannot." He lowered our hands to his chest and I could feel his heart beating. "There is still the matter of the *Leni*."

"Which is?" His tone made me wary. I was suspicious of foreign words and foreign traditions. I was still trying to figure out the DV, for crying out loud, even with the Sophia giving me an inside track.

"The *Leni* is a ritual of destiny. The sensation you experience when we are separated is the sign of the soul-bond. The *Leni* will determine if it is a true bond."

"A true bond meaning...?"

"It's a mating ritual, you stupid human. Honestly, Dierk, this one? She isn't worthy of *ein König*!" I didn't have to see the owner of the ugly voice to know it was my new BFF. "She is an insult to *Wolfe*. An insult to our *Leni*. She makes mockery of legend."

Not that I wanted to agree with the mean bitch, but still. "Dierk, I didn't come back here for a mating ritual."

"Can you deny what you felt when you walked away from me?" His tone was not bossy. It was tender, soft and gravelly. "I know what I felt."

"Dierk, you must be mistaken," Cacilia insisted.

"Cassy." Dierk's voice raised in dark warning. "Now is not the time."

"It's never the time," she said, her words running together in a growl. "I will not abide this."

Pushing aside the people who stood in her way, she stomped out.

"Look, Dierk," I said. There was something big going on with that woman. I more than suspected the entire drink-down-the-back thing was in retaliation for Dierk speaking to me at the bar. "I don't want to cause problems with your girlfriend."

He glanced in the direction she had gone. "Cacilia is not my girlfriend."

"Neither am I."

"True." His half-smile deepened and took on genuine expression. "But you may turn out to be so much more."

"Do I have any choice?"

"Destiny is not a choice, my dear."

Ugh. *Dear*? "This isn't my destiny. I've already got one."

58

"We will see." He half-turned and called out: "Clear the room."

Immediately, several large men, some of whom I recognized as the lovely gentlemen who'd asked me about a missing wallet, began ushering people toward the doors. Murmurs of disappointment trailed in their wake. Several DV spikes, questioning, suspicious.

It was the DV that were being shown out. The people I'd identified as humans, too, I noticed. Alarmed by this, I hesitantly peeked my power out.

Only Were remained in the room, and me. The sudden vacuum made me suck in a hard breath. When the doors closed with a boom, Dierk turned his attention back to me.

Gently, he raised my captive hand to his mouth and I felt the scrape of new beard mingling with the softness of his lips. It was a very courtly gesture and I didn't appreciate it one damn bit.

"Destiny…" His voice carried to the corners of the room. The gathered people and wolves held collective breaths, me included. "Determines the path of the stars and the cycle of the moon. We can deviate from our destinies no easier than the moon or the stars can from theirs. I, Dierk Adeluf, son of Schatten, *der König von Wolfenkinder*, invoke the *Leni* to determine if it is destiny that our soul-bond become life-bond."

Life-bond? My eyes must have bulged with the disbelief I struggled to contain. *Oh no, he doesn't—*

Before I could protest, he thrust our hands out and down to our sides.

A wolf bit into my hand.

The attack was silent. The pain was splintering. The stars and their destinies exploded behind my eyes.

I rocked on my feet. Heat traveled up my arm, filling my head and squeezing out my breath. My knees buckled once, twice. I tumbled forward into Dierk's open arms. He'd been waiting for me to fall and he caught me, gently sinking to his knees with me, cradling me to his chest.

As the room and the light and the sound faded into the haze of heat and pain, the last thing I saw was Dierk's face and his damnable half-smile.

Waning gibbous | *moon 10% visible*

I floated in feverish delirium. Consciousness evaded. Dreams evaded. I floated alone on a warm red tide.

Pain swam through me, pooled in my hand. I floated, rocked hopelessly by a tide I didn't understand. The red moon never moved, never waned—just hung in the dark as if painted there. Oh, uncompassionate moon! It didn't care if I sank or not. She talked to herself, a tumbling sound of murmurs and laughter, and gave no notice to my broken body riding the rising tide.

So I sank, letting the warmth surround me and pull me under. Why should I care, if the moon did not?

My hand throbbed with a dull restless ache. It wanted attention and got it; I could concentrate on nothing else. The pain came in a series of blooms, like drops of ink falling into water, falling and blooming and making everything hazy.

Never stopping.

Eventually, I could think past my hand to the rest of my body, which ached all over like the flu. My joints ached, my muscles felt bruised; fever and headache pretty much made applesauce of my head. Suspecting it would hurt to open my eyes, I kept them closed.

My ears rang with a zinging pitch, though, so I lay still and listened. I always thought tinnitus was cool. It drowned out everything else. I wanted it to drown out everything else.

Then I realized someone was singing along with it. Oh, dear.

Time and reality clicked into place when I opened my eyes, the way one slide advanced to the next during a projection show. Sight gave me anchor, even though everything, save the man, was completely unfamiliar.

Dierk lounged in a wide square armchair, listening to a music player. He sat forward the moment my eyelids moved, rising immediately to sit on the edge of the bed.

"Hey, sleepy," he said.

Sleepy? If I had to have a Seven Dwarfs nickname, it would be more accurate to call me Pissy. Or Doom. Because as soon as I could lift my arms, I'd kill him.

At the moment, however, I was hot, achy mush. All my anger came pouring out in a weak whimper of discomfort and fear. Way to enunciate, Sophie. Go on with your big, bad self.

"Shh. I know you don't feel well but you'll be better soon. I promise." He stroked his fingers along the side of my face, down my arm. Where his skin touched mine, I felt better.

His touch chased the ache away.

"Try to sleep." Dierk rose and smoothed the blanket.

"It's easier if you sleep through it."

"No," I mumbled. So much work for such an easy word. "Stay."

His half-smile almost spread but he seemed to force it down into a neutral line.

"Of course," he said, and lay down next to me, arm around me, our heads close together. He pressed along the entire line of my body and he kept the pain away.

Comforted by his nearness, I slept. And this time, there was no red moon.

I awoke with a clearer head, aware of how much extra skin was in bed with me.

A quick inventory revealed I wore only my camisole and undies; apparently Dierk was clad only in his shorts. Not modest enough for strangers, soul-bond or no.

I tugged my right hand out from under the thick blanket. It pulled free with difficulty. The large bandage was heavy, making my hand look like a freaking Q-Tip.

Great, I was done for. Bitten by a God-damned werewolf. Just what I never wanted.

I couldn't even cry about it. This was beyond the worst thing that had ever happened to me. It was like finding out how and when I would die. The bite might not actually kill me but it didn't matter. My life was over.

Dierk stirred beside me, sliding his free hand over my ribs and tucking his fingers under me, snuggling closer. I felt the scrape of new beard against my skin when he pressed his face against my shoulder.

"Are you awake?" He murmured to me, his face in my hair.

Stuff like that should only be for sweethearts. Not us.

"Yes." I couldn't keep the bitterness out of my voice. "They gonna take me away soon?"

"Are who going to take you where?"

"The Were. Are they gonna take me to a safe house?"

He withdrew his head from my shoulder and pulled away from me, resting on his own pillow. Cool air seeped between us where we gapped. "Are you afraid of safe houses?"

"Yes. I just want to go home."

"Why? Are you afraid, I mean?"

"I know what happens there." My nose started to stuff up, making me sound childish and small. "They're gonna bite me again and hurt me and I don't want to be pack-broken. I'm not an animal."

"Ah. I see." He dislodged his hand and gently rolled me over on my back so that I could look at him. His expression was sympathetic under his mussed hair. "That's an awful thing to think about right now, especially after how sick you've been. No one is going to treat you like an animal. I am here."

I believed him. What other choice did I have?

About an hour later I was washed as thoroughly as I could with a washcloth and a travel-sized bar of soap, while sitting on the toilet, draped in a towel. I didn't trust myself alone in the shower and I sure didn't want any company.

He had given me privacy and stayed out of the big bathroom, which reminded me of the ones in the better hotels in Philly. Marble and tile and shiny things. Fuzzy white bathrobe on the door.

I had privacy but at a steep price. By putting the distance between us, the achiness and strange stretchy I-don't-feel-good feeling seeped back in.

Staring at the bandage gave me enough resolution, albeit spiteful resolution, to keep from crawling out to him or calling him in. Mule-stubborn Sophie, that's me.

Damn him and his Leni and his werewolves. Damn him

for turning me into this. I threw the soap but it thudded against a stack of fresh towels, giving me little satisfaction.

When I wobbled back out, the bed was freshly made and turned down. He met me at the door, guided me to the bed and eased me back in like I was an old lady with a bad hip. The ache was slipping away again but the fever remained.

I exhausted myself by walking from the can. Shoot.

"That was some housekeeping," I said, as he pulled the blanket up. He'd opened the drapes, revealing tall windows and a city view I didn't recognize. The room looked like an actual bedroom, with matching suite, although it didn't appear to be a personal room. The top of the bureau wasn't cluttered enough to be anything but one in a swanky hotel.

He nodded, confirming my suspicion. "Efficient staffing."

"So this is a hotel?" I glanced around, seeking the usual rack of pamphlets and amenity guides. Nothing in the room offered a clue as to where I was.

"Yes and no."

Boy, was he being helpful. "Is the room service as efficient?

"Hungry?"

I nodded, afraid to ask.

He swiped the television remote from the bureau and closed the curtain behind the TV set. "That's good, because I ordered already."

That made me suspicious. "You don't know what I like."

He shrugged and crawled up on the bed next to me. Dierk lifted the remote and clicked on the flat-screen TV, flipping through the program guide. "I guessed."

"Thanks for this." I pulled gently at the T-shirt he'd given me. It was big enough to reach halfway to my knees, but it was fresh, unlike my orange-stained, grimy camisole.

Before he could answer, a knock sounded.

"Come," he called.

A fair-haired man opened the door and leaned in. "Our girl is awake?"

I didn't care for the rather possessive pronoun he used, but didn't waste the energy scowling. Besides, the only thing that alarmed me about the man was that he didn't alarm me at all. He kind of reminded me of a blond Henry Winkler with thin wire-framed glasses.

"Ah, Tancred. Good. This is Sophia Galen, my guest."

"Sophia Galen. An interesting name." He half-lifted a black leather satchel he held in one hand. "How well do you live up to the title?"

My stomach tightened into a solid lump and I gripped the covers around me, suddenly cold. What did he know about the Sophia? I stammered an uncertainty, unsure what to say.

He laughed gently and sat on the bed, reaching out to pat my leg. "I didn't mean to put you on the spot. It's not every day I meet someone who shares a name with a physician and philosopher of such high renown."

I let my breath leak out between my teeth. Galen. He referred to the Roman doctor of the same name. "I'm formally trained in nursing, although I haven't practiced in several years."

"Nonsense." He smiled and opened his bag, which I saw now was an old-fashioned doctor's bag. He pulled out a thermometer and shook it before placing it in my mouth. "Once a practitioner of healing arts, always a practitioner."

He chatted with Dierk about my progress during the night, making very little eye contact with me. Although Dierk accurately portrayed me as a hot mess, Tancred nodded as if pleased. He checked my pulses in my wrist and elbow but didn't unwrap the gauze.

"You rest, Sophia. That is the best medicine for you."

He patted my leg again before leaving, making berth around someone else at the door.

A big room service cart came in, pushed by none other than Stohl. Gee. Those warm fuzzy looks would smother me to death if he wasn't careful. I sighed and cleaned my nails to avoid looking at him.

I think he hated me more and more every time we saw each other. I guessed serving dinner to your least favorite person was a good reason to glare but it wasn't like I demanded his services. Instead of glaring back, I donned a neutral business face and tried to pretend I wasn't lying in bed with his best friend.

The two spoke briefly in German—I, of course, understanding nothing and not even resenting them for it. I was through knowing other people's business. It just brought me more trouble.

Stohl left but not before he favored me with another contemptuous glare.

I huffed out a sigh. "Really, Dierk, I had no idea your friends were so charming."

"Ah, they are protective. They worry for me." He rolled to the side of the bed and began opening the trays. "Now, you said you were hungry. Let's see, there's country-fried steak and Eggs Benedict here…"

My stomach issued an unladylike growl. "That was just what I was hungry for!"

Gratefully, I dug in. I didn't know how he guessed what would perfectly hit the spot, but he did. Sausage gravy with just the right amount of fresh ground pepper made a mouth-watering contrast to the creamy brightness of Hollandaise sauce. Mouth full, I eyed the carafe. "Tea?"

"No," he said, almost sheepishly. "Just coffee. Is that okay?"

"I guess." Inside I was jubilant. Wow. It had been so

long since I had coffee that I got a rush just thinking about it. I doubted it was decaf: no tacky orange lid. Screw my no-coffee thing. This was almost like a monster's ball.

I swallowed a chunk of steak and reached for the carafe. "When did Stohl get a job running room service?"

"He adapts to the situation. I won't allow anyone else in the room."

"So he's a guard?"

Dierk lifted his shoulders in a vague shrug.

Prisoners were kept under guard. Appetite forgotten, I let the fork slip from my fingers. I closed my eyes and leaned back against the pillows. The anxiety was stirring again.

"Tired?"

I nodded. Easier than telling the truth.

"Want me to leave you alone?"

"No." I slid down the pillows. I had a feeling that I'd only be safe as long as he was near. "I'm hot. Can I get some Tylenol, at least?"

"No, it won't help," he said quietly. He lifted the tray off the bed and set it on the desk. "The fever will pass soon, I promise."

"I want to go home." Then I realized: home.

Oh, no.

I never came home after the concert. Dahlia left before the shit storm started and I was confident no one had bothered to call my friends to let them know Sophie was bitten by a werewolf and was shacked up in a hotel under guard.

"Sleep. We'll talk more when you're rested." He smoothed back my hair and I closed my eyes, too weary to argue.

Rodrian. What would he think of me when he found out? I wanted to go home. But what if Rodrian didn't want me back?

Waning gibbous | moon 5% visible

I woke during the night to use the bathroom. Dierk steadied me and politely waited outside the door. I rested my cheek against the cool wall tiles and almost fell asleep again.

By morning I was sick of the bed, sick of the room, sick of being inside my skin. I squirmed restlessly through the morning news programs before pushing down the blanket. Swinging my feet over the side, my head spinning like a Tilt-a-Whirl, I reached for the phone and announced: "I'm going home."

"You can't even sit upright by yourself," he protested.

Outside, I heard the distant rumble of a trolley car, its rattle and ring. City noises. Foreign noises. I wanted my woods back. "So? I'll lay in my own bed. I want to go. Now."

"Soon."

"No." I shook my head once, afraid to stir up a headache. "I had enough."

"Eat first."

I wanted to argue, but the rumble in my belly gave me away. "Well. Fine."

"You have a tremendous spirit." He took the phone out of my hand and set it back on its cradle. "I never imagined a mate with such a ferocious attitude."

"First, I'm not your mate. Second, I wouldn't date, much less mate, a guy who holds me down and lets an effing werewolf bite me."

"It was ritual," he said, voice solemn and low. With a gentle hand he pressed me back into the bed, tucking my legs under the sheets.

I tugged the blankets closer around me. Hot with fever, shaking with chills. There was no happy medium. "No. I know a ritual when I see one. That was an attack."

"I'm sorry you feel that way. The bite is necessary."

"Great. Just great. Let's bite Sophie. I like my women hairy." I tried to mimic his voice but it came out more Schwarzenegger-like than I wanted. Tough shit. "What is it with you Europeans? If you wanted to date, you could've asked. But no. You get one of your mutts to chomp me and ruin my life forever."

Tension seeped into his voice, the sound of someone who was running out of patience. "How is it ruined?"

"I know all about how you get turned Were. I know all about your so-called safe houses. Don't try to lie. You're going to turn me over to them so they can bite me and hurt me until the full moon. You took my life from me."

He rubbed his mouth. "How can I convince you that none of that is true?"

I hugged my ribs and tried to stop shivering. "You can't."

Dierk paused, blowing out a breath. "Answer me this. Was the one who told you these things Wolf or Demivampire?"

I narrowed my eyes, suspecting a trap. "DV, of course."

"Of course." Dierk sat down on the bed, one leg tucked beneath him so he could face me. "So how could he tell you the truth if he himself didn't know it?"

"He wouldn't lie," I insisted.

"Look at me." He lifted my chin and peered into my eyes. "Do you know any *Wolfenkinder?*"

"Yes."

"Besides me or my men."

"Yes." I pushed his hand off my chin.

"Okay." He nodded. "Who is his pack?"

He'd said his pack, not their pack. I wondered how much he actually knew about me. "I—don't know, actually. I haven't really seen him much since he started running with them."

"Did he ever describe our rituals and traditions?"

Of course, Toby never talked Were junk in front of me. He tried to keep his otherness low-key. "I'm not sure even he knows them."

"Then how can you know the truth? Even if my brethren were desperate enough to increase their numbers—and I can assure you they are not—you are different. This is the Leni." He took up my unwounded hand, curling his fingers around mine. "We are allowed only one chance. If it is destiny that we are life mates then the moon will take you as her own and make you Were. It's fate, destiny. Not brutality."

His eyes were so gentle, so full of desperate wishes for me to understand.

Part of me responded to his plea, the part that still assumed a false sense of familiarity and softened toward him. I had to ignore it, because the bigger unknown was the bigger danger. "I can't believe you. I just can't."

"Why not?"

"Because I don't know you. I don't know who you are or what you all are saying about me when you speak German. I don't know what a Leni is or even a König—

"Leni is the word for moon. It's a traditional mate-selection ritual."

I snorted. "I find it a little hard to believe you need a ritual to get girls."

He toyed with my rings, twisting them and examining each one. "I have never had a problem getting girls. However, my mate will be selected by the Leni."

"So…Weres can't get married unless they do this ritual?"

"It is not a universal condition. Ordinary Were can marry as they please."

A dull dread settled into my gut like a weight. I leaned backwards into the pillows. "You aren't ordinary, are you?"

Dierk shook his head, a quick wag, and looked away, his Adam's apple jumping.

I took a deep breath, even though anxiety had tightened my chest to the point where the muscles had frozen, making each breath hurt. "Who are you, Dierk?"

"King," he said, his eyes downcast. His mouth twisted into a rueful smile, and he glanced around the room before finding my face again. "I am king."

I opened my mouth, but nothing came out. The gravity of my plight had just exponentially exploded into astronomic proportions. A Were—I had hoped to evade a Were. I had my entire population of Demivamps to hide behind if I couldn't evade him. But a king—I'd need an army.

It would take an army, and I would cause a war.

Suddenly, I felt more alone than ever. I wasn't worth a war.

"Look." He released my left hand to reach across my body. Dierk tugged my wounded hand toward him, unwrapping the thick white gauze.

Peeling off the dressing, I saw the wound for the first time. Ugly puncture wounds dotted my palm from heel to center. I gasped at the rawness, the greenish tint of newly-forming scabs. "Oh, my God!"

"Turn your hand over," he said.

The skin was intact.

But... how could the wolf have bitten so deeply without marring both sides?

Dierk held up his own hand to show me light pink marks on the back of his left hand. Scars. It was the hand he used to hold mine. "I heal much faster."

He lay his hand over mine until they were positioned the same way they'd been when I was bitten. The bites lined up perfectly.

I slumped against the pillow and tilted my face up toward his. "The wolf bit you, too?"

"It was ritual," he repeated.

"Ugh." I yanked my hand away. King or no king, I was skeeved. "Universal precautions, hello? You're a rock star, for crimmeny's sake! Who knows what's floating around in your veins? Now I need Hep titers and HIV prophylaxis rounds. Great."

"No, you don't. Wolfe are resistant to blood-borne disease. I won't give you AIDS, I promise." He shrugged. "I guess that lycanthropy is the ultimate vaccine."

"Yippee. Still not a fair trade." I winced when he reclaimed my hand and redressed the wound. "Not even Neosporin? Or a rabies shot?"

"That is funny, but no. It's a clean wound."

"Dog bites are full of germs. All that licking—"

"Not dog." He looked mildly offended, and narrowed his eyes. "Wolf. Now rest. I'll order something to eat."

"Order me clothes, too, 'cause I'm going home."

"Your jeans have been cleaned. Your shirt, I fear, was ruined. You are quite the bleeder. I did purchase fresh lingerie. I had to guess your size but…" He grazed his hand down my side, over my hip. "I think I guessed it perfectly. For now, you're staying in bed. Really. I am der König. Why is it so hard for you to obey?"

"I'm a spiteful bitch who doesn't take orders," I said, and rolled over. The fuzzy hot feeling was coming back, and it didn't take me long to fall asleep again.

Having the last word can be so satisfying.

Waning gibbous | moon 4% visible

I complained and nagged at him every time I opened my eyes. His patience was wearing thin, and every time I started the Going Home mantra his tone became a little tighter, a little more brittle. I'd grin when he wasn't looking because I wanted him to get so sick of me he threw me out.

But he didn't. He'd always get this close to losing his poo and he'd stop, reset himself, and end the conversation.

His self-control annoyed me and added more fuel to my resistance, which I continued even while he marched me into the bathroom and pushed me into the shower. I had only a moment to hastily disrobe behind the shower curtain before he reached in and started the water. The shower felt so good I couldn't complain.

Dierk stayed in the bathroom long enough for me to wash, leaving only after I turned off the water. When the door clicked shut, the ache came back. At least it was a double-shampooed ache. I dressed in the clothes he laid out for me—my jeans, new underthings, another of his t-shirts. It smelled like him—cologne, maybe? I couldn't define it, but didn't care.

It didn't make me angry. Part of me wished it did.

When I was finished in the bathroom, I came out to see Tancred waiting for me. His lips pressed in a thin line, he shook his head slowly from side to side at me. Okay, then. He wasn't happy, either. I wondered if I could get a third opinion before deciding I just didn't give a flying feck what any of these Weres thought about my departure.

Tancred took my temperature and redressed my hand with a petroleum dressing and clean gauze. He clucked his tongue. "You should know better, Sophia."

I lifted my chin and looked stubbornly away from them both. Nothing I knew mattered anymore. I just wanted to go home.

When Tancred left, I sat on the bed. Dierk helped me into my boots, which he simultaneously admired and chided for their impracticality. Both were taken as compliments. I put a lot of work into selecting my footwear. Good things took effort.

Dierk draped one of his jackets over my shoulders before we left the room. His arm around me, he guided me to the elevator, through the lobby, out to a waiting car. A man named Olberich drove, not Stohl. (Bonus right there.) We sat together in the back seat, and we did not speak. The leg room was amazing. I think the rear seats reclined, too.

The only part that worried me was that he didn't need directions to the Stocks. When Olberich slowed the car to a stop in front of the porch, I looked up at the front of the house through the window. Nearly a dozen cars lined the driveway. So many lights were on. Nearly the entire house was lit. I craned my neck. All except for my wing. That part of the house was dark.

Dark like my fate.

"A full house, *mein König.*" Olberich said. "You should not get out of the car."

"Nonsense. I won't simply drop her off at the curb. Let them worry. I do not." Dierk came around and opened the door himself, easing me from the car and guiding me toward the steps. "Are you sure about this, Sophie?"

The front door flew open before we reached the porch, the foyer lights spilling out in accusation as Dierk helped me up the steps, his arm around my shoulders. I was weary from the exertion of walking from the car. My head drooped and I leaned into him for support, too weak to hold myself up.

I knew what it looked like. I wanted to cry.

Rodrian stood in the doorway, a silhouette against the sharp light. I still had a low fever and a banging headache and the bright light made me wince. I hid my face in Dierk's chest. It only made things look worse.

"You," Rodrian said. It was the blackest word I'd ever heard him utter.

"*Guten Abend,*" Dierk replied carefully. "It is good to see you again, *Herr* Thurzo."

Rodrian advanced to the edge, towering over us. "If you have hurt her—"

Several men slid out, fanning out in an arc behind him. I didn't recognize any of them by their power, and their faces were silhouetted by the glare from the foyer.

Dierk tightened his grip on my shoulder. "I would never. She is a thing to be treasured, not damaged."

"Sophie," Rodrian said. "Are you all right?"

I could have wept for the worry and the concern in his eyes. I would have, if I wasn't preoccupied at the moment with remaining upright.

"Rode," I said, whisper-thin. "I'm sorry."

"Sorry?" He rushed down the steps toward us. "I'm just glad you're home safe and sound."

Dierk tensed slightly, bunching muscle and bracing, but stood his ground, holding me as I huddled under his jacket

Rodrian stopped in front of me and inhaled sharply. Without taking his slowly brightening eyes from mine, he issued a warning spike of power. His eyes glowed, a lion-esque shade of amber. His voice was angry. Deadly angry. "What have you done to her?"

"Nothing that destiny would not have arranged on its own."

"Rode," I said. "Help me. Take me to my room."

Rodrian pursed his lips and took the last few steps toward me and extended his hand. After a small hesitation, I pulled away from Dierk. His jacket slipped from my shoulder as I left the protective circle of his arm and the cold air found its way through the gap. Chills raced through me and I reached up to pull it back around me. As I grabbed the collar, Rodrian's eyes immediately spied the white gauze on my hand.

"Inside!" Rodrian hissed, his eyes fully ablaze. He unfurled his power like a tremendous flag, so territorial.

Dierk sighed as if he expected more than simple conflict with Rodrian. He gently fixed his coat back over my shoulders and urged me forward, still supporting me.

Rodrian cut between us. "Not you. You've done enough."

Dierk didn't back away from him. I wasn't sure it was a wise move, because I'd never seen Rodrian like this before. I also didn't need to be a Sophia to know that his men were hair-trigger-ready to jump at the slightest go-ahead.

Dierk had to know he was dealing with a volatile Demivamp, and he still stayed his course. "I will stay until I see she is settled. I will be assured that she's properly cared for."

"You will leave." Rodrian leaned into him, a flare of power behind the menacing gesture. "Now."

I got between them and placed my uninjured hand on his Rodrian's chest. "Back off, Rode."

"Stay out of it, Sophie." He stepped back but I didn't know if he backed off Dierk—or away from me.

I felt like a leper, dirty and tainted. "I can't. I'm ass deep in it. If I could've stayed out of it, this wouldn't be happening."

He stole a sidelong glance at Dierk. "Sophie, you don't know who he is."

"But I'm going to find out aren't I?" I laughed, but it was a bitter sound. "Don't make it harder."

"Sophie," Dierk said, drawing my attention back to him. It wasn't right that I should respond so easily to his voice, but I couldn't not listen. His voice had a gravitational effect on me, pulling me to him. "It is not my wish to leave you here. You'd be safer with me. I do this only because you ask. I am not comfortable leaving you alone."

Rodrian snorted. "She won't be alone."

"Thurzo, be rational. I don't have to point out the obvious. You see the bandage. You scent the infection. You know what is happening to her. Why not let her be with someone who can help her?"

Rodrian made to reply but I interrupted him with the palm of my uninjured hand before swinging toward Dierk.

"I am an adult, Dierk. He doesn't let me be anything. I asked you to bring me home because it's what I want." I looked him in the face to make my point but, when I saw his soft brown eyes, I softened a little inside. Dammit. "Look. It's one night. I need to be alone and sort things out. You dumped a shitload on me and I really need another shower."

"I'll say," muttered Rodrian.

I ignored him. This back and forth took more effort than I could spare. "I'll call you, Dierk. I promise."

"Tomorrow?"

"Sure. Whatever."

He reached up to cup my shoulders, making it an embrace. His touch bolstered me, strengthened me, rewarded me for allowing the contact. I was beginning to understand the power of this Leni crap; although I didn't crave Dierk's touch, I knew that I'd feel better for it. The Leni wanted us to stay close to each other.

His voice was tender, full of emotion. "It won't be easy, walking away without you."

"I know," I whispered back. I brushed my hands across his chest, smoothing his jacket. With a sigh I rested my head against him, just a moment. He pressed closer to me, not quite hugging me, his touch gentle but unsure. "But try."

I turned and walked into the house as quickly as I could, closing the door on all of them before the growing discomfort made me change my mind. I stumbled across the foyer and almost made it to the staircase before tripping. I ended up crawling up the stairs.

What a way to show Rodrian I was going to be okay. Overconfident Sophie, that's me.

Waning gibbous | moon 2% visible

The moon followed me.

Back when I was a kid, riding in the back of Dad's car at night, I'd watch the full moon slide along through the clouds, following the car. It was magic, Mom said. The moon only followed children because they were special.

Mom had been right. The few times I'd thought to look for the moon as an adult, it didn't do that magical slide through the clouds. It was always pinned to the dark sky, oblivious to my journeys.

Not now. The moon was keenly aware of me while I ran through the trees, looking for something. Every time I turned to look at the moon, it glided along, always over me, never letting me get more than a step ahead. It was like a shadow. All I could hear were my foot falls in the crisp leaves and the hum of a song I almost recognized.

Where? What? Why was I here and how long would I

run?

Suddenly, a wolf howled. I couldn't judge the distance but it was close and I smiled into the rush of relief that flooded me—

Woke up on the couch. The dream tugged at the corner of my brain, wanting me to drop back into sleep. I shook my head, feeling thick with vertigo. Door was open. People talking down the hall. Rode. The DV doctor that had run Shy's hypolution treatment. Clouds of doubt and helplessness that pressed at the edge of my Sophia-sense like a suffocating fog.

Those damned moon dreams.

I was hungry but nauseous. Tired but restless. Lonely but never wanting to see another damned person ever again because people did dumb shit to me like kidnap me and try to kill me because they were vampires and let werewolves bite me. I crawled to the guest bathroom and drank a handful of water from the sink, rubbing my wet hands over my face.

Didn't help much. I staggered back to the couch, vaguely aware that someone was in the hallway, calling my name.

I didn't know who it was. Didn't matter who it was. They couldn't help me.

Dropping onto the couch again, I panted with the exertion and closed my eyes, feeling the world swirl around me, waiting for the moon to reclaim me.

The moon was only too happy to oblige.

I had absolutely no idea how long I lay in the parlor but at some point, I heard a voice that woke me from my restless sleep. He kept saying my name, over and over. Insistent. Urgent.

"Sophie. Sophie."

I couldn't ignore it anymore. I pushed up onto my

elbows, grimacing against the taste of road kill in my mouth. Great. I even had wolf breath. I was screwed for sure. "What, already?"

"Sophie. Come out here."

I sank back on the couch, finally recognizing the voice. "Toby, I'm tired. Leave me alone."

"I said—" His voice took on a hard edge. Was it Toby? He didn't sound like that. "Get out here. Now."

Oh, whatever. I was going out there, all right, and I was going to breathe all over him when I did. I got to my feet and tottered to the door, noticing I still had on the same clothes I came home in, pretty much. Dierk's shirt was in a crumple on the floor but I still wore the camisole he'd given me. Shoot, I still had my boots on.

Walking in a straight line was difficult when you couldn't see right but I wasn't going for points. I made it to the door and leaned heavily on the frame, spying his shape halfway up the hall. He wasn't coming past the wards that protected my suite.

I squinted, trying to focus. "What is so damned important?"

"Come here, Sophie."

I started to slide down. Sitting would be so much easier.

"Sophie! I said, come here!"

His tone was so ugly I was afraid to disobey. I righted myself and pushed myself down the wall toward him, wanting to cry.

When I got close enough to see his face, I did cry. His expression wasn't angry like his tone—he was scared. Toby being scared reminded me how scared I was. I lunged the last few feet toward him and he caught me, pulling me up to him in a crushing hug.

"My God, girl. I thought we lost you in there." His voice was tremulous, breath in my hair. "We couldn't get in. You didn't answer—"

I hiccupped, holding onto the sobs. I just wanted to wail with the despair that filled me. I wanted to scream my rage at having been bitten. I couldn't, not while the only comfort I had was this desperate embrace from my friend.

He was a Were. I couldn't tell him the last thing I wanted was to be like him.

Toby didn't ask me to accept it. He drew back and cupped his hands around my head, holding my face to his. "How do you feel?"

I gave him the truth. "I'm sick. This is—the worst. Just..."

He pulled me back to his chest and crossed his arms around me. Traces of Dahlia's fragrance lingered in his shirt and I took comfort from that, too. "I can't even imagine how bad it is. The bite is bad enough, I know, but he said you'd be going through the other thing."

The other thing. What an innocuous term. This inescapable entanglement with Dierk—this curse, this seizure of my liberty and my destiny and my future—

Right now, it was the only thing. I didn't have anything else anymore.

"C'mon." He released me and helped me walk out to the staircase. The office door was closed.

I gathered my strength, lowered my barriers, and reached out through the house. All the usual inhabitants—the staff, the guard—but there was a looming omission. Rodrian wasn't here. I closed my eyes against the thin tears that seeped down my cheek. I knew it. He'd left me.

I had to wait for the painful spasm in my throat to subside before I could speak. "Where is everyone?"

"Dahlia said the Conclave is meeting. They call the Leni an act of aggression against the DV, and I guess a bunch of important people showed up."

The Conclave. They didn't get together for any old reason. The last time the Conclave met, it was because Marek had introduced the Demivampire community to their long-lost Sophia. Now, they met because their Sophia had betrayed them by getting bitten. "I'm in trouble, aren't I?"

"Depends on how you look at it, I guess." His voice was tame. I supposed for a Were this wasn't bad news at all. But he wasn't facing the moon for the first time.

He tried. I should at least give him credit for that.

Toby walked me down to the tri-suites where Shiloh stayed. Now that she'd cusped, she had a lot more freedom and stayed out a lot more. I had no reason to doubt her ability to take care of herself—she was stronger than the average DV.

A child of Marek's line, through and through.

So much for college and vet school. Shiloh was training to be a slayer. A killer. Of the undead, to be sure, but this is the girl who ironed her tee shirts and never touched a generic anything in her life.

The other reason she wasn't here much anymore was Aurelia. Shiloh's mother had been pressuring her to spend time with her at her place downtown. I guessed she rented an apartment; guessed, not knew, because I didn't ask. I always had the impression that she resented me, although hell if I knew why. She never went out of her way to be nice when I saw her, so it didn't encourage a lot of small talk.

The suites were empty. Toby led me to the lone vacant suite at the far end of the hall—by which point I wished he'd just thrown me over his shoulder and carried me. He steered me into the bathroom, where he handed me a soapy wash cloth before kneeling to tug off my boots.

"Just do your best, Soph." He picked up a hairbrush and

began to untangle my hair. His touch was clumsy but gentle as he twisted my hair up into a ponytail. "You need a shower but I can't help you with that. Here's a towel, though. Get out of those clothes and wash up. I'm bringing you fresh stuff."

He stepped out and shut the door. I did as he said, rinsing the wash cloth out in the basin he'd filled with warm water. Really. Why was turning into a werewolf such cruddy stuff?

I relished the chance to clean up, still wondering what day it was. The nausea, though, didn't abate, although sitting rigidly on the toilet seat and trying to hold my head level kept the vertigo to a minimum.

Until Toby rapped on the door. I jumped at the loud sound and nearly fell over. Holding onto my towel, I grimaced against the quick thump of migraine. "Yeah."

He opened the door. "Here, these were in the laundry room. They're clean. And I found these under your desk."

He lifted a pair of sneakers. "Want 'em?"

I nodded. "Got a toothbrush?"

"Shiloh's."

She'd flip her wig if she knew. "You can bleach it when I'm done ruining it."

Eventually I was dressed and decontaminated. Toby gathered me up and carefully walked me down the stairs and outside to my car. Depositing me in the front seat, he trotted around to the driver's side and together we pulled out of the driveway.

I had no idea where we were going and I didn't ask. I hoped alternately for either a Rita's or a firing squad. When he took a turn too fast for my stomach, I hoped for both.

He put the radio on, playing a CD that was already in. Turn of the Wheel. We'd been listening to it on the way to the concert. Dierk's voice surrounded me and, for the first time, I couldn't enjoy the song. I reached over and switched it off.

"I'm sorry, Soph. I forgot—"

I lifted my hand. "Where are we going?"

"The Balaton Lanes."

I groaned, letting my head sink against the headrest. "I have a headache and I don't want to bowl."

"You don't have to."

Okay, then. I guess I was just along for another ride. At least he was keeping me awake. Maybe I still had earplugs from the last concert.

The last concert where I got chomped by a Were. How many times will I have to kick myself for going out that night?

We drove toward the downtown area, taking an exit that led us south of Balaton's densest area. Toby took us through the suburban spread and pulled into an ill-paved lot. Balaton Lanes and Blue Moon Pool. Shoot. It hadn't been a bad joke.

Wait. I could read the sign. My vision had cleared a little. Part of me knew why. A sudden flare of anxiety threatened to choke me.

Toby took a spot at the edge of the parking lot, coming around to help me out of the car. "I know it's hard, but walk straight and don't attract any attention. I ain't supposed to be here."

I nodded and took a deep breath. Leveling my shoulders, I slipped my hand into his and, together, we walked into the bowling alley.

It was still very difficult to focus on our surroundings and the clatter from the alleys bounced around the inside of my head in a most unpleasant manner. A balding man leaned on the front counter, sliding a pair of rental shoes toward a kid. He pushed a long strand of iron grey comb-over out of his greasy eyes and watched us intently, his scrutiny getting under my skin. I concentrated on the tug of Toby's hand, tagging alongside him like an old drunk chick. At least my stomach was settling. Throwing up on the carpet would attract that unwanted attention Toby warned against.

We strode toward the far end of the alley, where a room was walled off with huge windows. A dated neon sign blinked Pool. The closer we got, the stronger the scent of cigarettes and body spray, with an under layer of sweat and old lockers. Uck. If that's where we were headed, all bets were off and I'd puke for sure.

I took my last gulp of comparably clean air before crossing into the pool room. Steel lockers spanned the near wall, and at least a dozen tables filled the room. I didn't notice that Toby had stopped walking and I bumped into his shoulder.

I leaned around him to see a brawny guy blocking our path, holding a cue. I guessed he'd been playing at the first table. A skinny guy with a long neck and a baseball cap sidled up and nudged the big guy. "You expecting company, Thorpe?"

A blurry group of people drifted closer and Thorpe pointed at us. "Who do you belong to?"

As if it was his business. I had enough of this belonging-to-people crap and I intended to tell him so but Toby side-stepped, eclipsing me.

"Bayridge," he said.

"Bayridge." Thorpe's voice deepened with displeasure, taking on dark colors. "Bayridge don't got business here."

Other people began to take interest in our pleasantries and one by one they left their tables, straying closer to form a casual but menacing group. Toby fanned his elbows out, putting me behind him.

"She has business here. I'm her friend."

"I don't care who you are." Thorpe smiled a mean I-don't-give-a-shit smile, full of long teeth. He dropped the cue on the table. "Get out before I throw you out."

"Just a minute, bub," I interjected in his general direction. Although I felt somewhat better that I had in the car, I was still operating with boozed-up dexterity and I had trouble focusing. "You don't own this place."

Boy, was I a toughie. Step back before Sophie puts the pow-pow on ya'll.

"Sophie," Toby said. "Be. Quiet."

The man stalked closer, and I could smell the beer on his breath. Talk about making a voice carry. "Your bitch got a mouth on her. She better watch she don't get it slapped."

Oh, no, he didn't. "How dare—"

Next thing I knew I was sprawled against the lockers, holding my mouth and seeing stars. The ugly brute stood over me like an abusive husband.

"Apologize to her," Toby said quietly.

Thorpe stepped into Toby, leaning into his face. "Or what?"

"Do it, or else. She didn't do nothing."

Thorpe smiled as if he imagined doing terrible things to Toby and would enjoy every single one of them. Reaching behind him without looking, one of his buddies handed him half a pool cue. The thick half. He swung the heavy end down into his palm like a club.

I wiped my nose and squinted at the blood on my fingers, all—fifteen of them. Great. More dizzy.

"I gave you a chance to leave walking, kid. Now you'll be lucky to crawl out of here."

I climbed to my feet, using the lockers behind me for finger holds. Toby grunted with pain. The Were drove the cue into Toby's stomach, cracking him beneath the jaw as he folded.

Suddenly, my focus snapped into hi-def. Toby was on his knees, his collar wadded into Thorpe's fist, who had the cue pulled back, preparing to strike again. The bigger man looked like a tennis player preparing to serve, and Toby's head was the ball.

No way was he hurting Toby again. I lunged at the man, grabbing his arm and scratching for the cue. "Stop it!"

He shook me off. "Still don't know how to keep quiet, huh? Maybe I need to break your jaw, too."

"Maybe not." A voice, as strong and clear as a tolling bell. "Things would not end well for you."

Dierk. Relief made my knees weak.

He stood with Olberich and Stohl. Demolition blazed in his golden eyes. "I don't appreciate men who flaunt their strength."

"I told you boys." The guy who had been handing out shoe rentals stepped into the doorway holding a shotgun. "Next time I had to break up a fight, I'm gonna break one of you in pieces."

Dierk raised a hand. "Put your gun down."

"And who the hell are you?" Shoe Rental Guy swiveled the gun in Dierk's direction.

One of the girls sidled up to the manager, rising up on her toes to whisper in his ear, rolling her eyes toward Dierk and the others. As she did so, his expression melted into one of worry, and he stammered, lowering the gun, bowing awkwardly. "I beg your pardon, I beg your pardon. I didn't know."

Dierk had already forgotten him and focused once more on Thorpe. "You have damaged the young *Wolf*."

"He's out of his territory." Thorpe sounded strained. It was a desperate excuse, now, not a conviction.

Dierk wanted none of it. "You are brothers."

"He's Bayridge—"

"We are not curs. We don't have turfs or run in gangs. We are civilized." Dierk tilted his head. His tone had remained level and firm, but his hands balled up into white-knuckled fists. He was seething inside, and I could see his struggle to remain in control. "You are not."

The brute hung his head. That he would receive punishment was definite and understood.

Dierk's gaze darted over me. "Sophie, he has hurt you."

I looked at Thorpe and saw the whites of his eyes. He stared over at me like I'd become his lifeline—and he knew he'd all but severed it.

With a single word, I could condemn him. I could end him. One single word would find the king's ear and resolution would be swift and severe.

I had real power over that man, the one who had backhanded me and hurt Toby for no good reason. If I wanted vengeance, it would be mine. All I had to say was one single word.

That realization frightened me more than the Were's cruelty.

"I am unhurt." I wiped my nose as surreptitiously as I could. Tough to do when the whole room was watching.

Dierk closed the distance between us and seized my hand, prying open my fingers and displaying the blood I tried to conceal. "People do not bleed when they are unhurt."

He released me and stalked back towards Thorpe. His chest rose and fell with each breath, his nostrils flaring. His voice dripped lower, coiling and angry, rage in each word. "I should like to see how he will fare against me, now that he's proven himself against a young wolf and a woman. Fair matches, no?"

"Please, Dierk—" My chest tightened, a hum of kinetic

energy stretching me to capacity. I had to do something. This was my fault—if I hadn't come here, the confrontation would never have occurred and Dierk wouldn't be at the edge of his self-control. My mouth ran dry and the words faltered in my throat, unspoken.

Dierk gave me a quelling look and signaled to his men, who stepped forward. Stohl and Olberich each grabbed one of Thorpe's wrists and twisted, joint-locking him and driving him to his knees between them. "This doesn't concern you anymore, Sophie."

I didn't want to see this. The Were were capable of terrible things, the same as everyone else, but their culture operated on a totally different level. The *Leni* may have tied me to Dierk forever. I couldn't stomach seeing him resort to savagery, common or royal, just because some asshole slapped me.

There was only one way to stop this madness. I put my heart, my fear, my desperate wish for peace into my voice and I cried out the only word that could stop him from being the thing I feared worst: "Majesty!"

The word disarmed Dierk, every muscle stiffening. Dierk abandoned his predatory stance and stood straighter, taller, even though he never moved his glare from the man on the floor. It was as if he had suddenly remembered his nobility. Up until this moment, he had been a man championing his mate.

Oh, God. It wasn't an act. Dierk really thought of me as his own.

"Majesty." I spoke in a low voice, trying to sound unshaken. Hard to do when I knew I had to make my words carry. "Please. He was only doing his job. He didn't know."

"It is no excuse for his loathsome behavior."

"It was instinct. This is their place. He didn't know I

have business with you. Spare him." Dierk crossed his arms but I couldn't let him block me out. I went over to him, sank down to my knees, and reached for his hand. "Please, I beg you."

He looked down at me, still angry, still intent on punishment. "He wouldn't have spared you."

"No one should ever pay the ultimate price for a mistake."

Long moments passed. The brute looked crazy nervous, his eyes darting back and forth, perhaps desperate for a clue as to the manner of his fate. He wouldn't find it looking at Dierk, whose expression was difficult to read.

Dierk looked off-balance, as if he had to find a new definition for me. He took my hand in his and helped me to my feet, then bowed from the neck, granting my boon. This wasn't an act for him.

"Tell your man to learn diplomacy." Dierk jabbed his finger at the chest of the skinny guy in the cap before striding back through the doors of the bar. Olberich and Stohl flanked Toby and me, and we followed behind.

Once inside, Toby and I were taken to a table at the back of the pub, which was uncomfortably full of Were. All those voids felt like a vacuum, and my Sophia struggled to breathe. It felt stifled.

Is this what I would feel like forever, denied the mental touches of the DV? I sat amongst the laughter and sounds of clean bar fun, the muffled sounds of the pool hall, the steady thump of the jukebox, and felt completely isolated.

Dierk was somewhere close by, judging by my level of comfort, although I couldn't see him. Seeing no other alternative, I took the chair that seemed furthest from the others and dug a mirror out of my purse.

Toby stood awkwardly to one side.

"Hey," I said. "Why don't you sit?"

He grimaced and shook his head. Crap. I'd forgotten. Dierk said they'd hurt him. I dropped the mirror and went to examine him. "Is it bad?"

He shook his head, but I noticed the odd angle at which his arm hung. "Elbow or shoulder?"

"Shoulder," he replied. "It's jammed."

"Let me see." I lifted his collar and slid his jacket down, trying to avoid moving his left arm. His shoulder looked oddly square. "Dislocated. You need to go to a hospital."

"No, I don't. It'll right itself."

Right itself, my Aunt Fanny. While I didn't doubt werewolves had some genetic advantage when it came to moving limbs around, I was fairly certain that, when it came to human shoulder injuries, I was still the expert. "You'll need an X-ray to make sure it's back in."

"Ah." He looked apprehensive. "X-rays are expensive. I'll heal. I patch up really quick."

"Not on your own, you won't." I rubbed the back of my neck, knowing what I had to do. Damn. I'd assisted with closed reductions plenty of times when I still practiced nursing, but never in a bar and never on a friend. "I have to unbutton your shirt."

Dislocated shoulders are creepy to look at. The knob at the top of his humerus was a visible bump near his collar bone and his shoulder looked like a bony ridge more suitable on a gargoyle. I gently pressed my fingers to the bend of his elbow, the underside of his wrist. Pulses felt okay, so I figured there was no vascular emergency. Still. It had to be fixed. "Stand against the wall."

I lifted his hand and bent his arm at the elbow, studying his face. Although I knew Toby had a high tolerance for pain, a doctor would have loaded him with a heavy dose of opioid first. He closed his eyes and exhaled through his nose, his jaw tightening as I maneuvered his forearm. I paused, waiting for the spasm in his arm muscles to stop before continuing. He endured a few starts and stalls until I got his arm in the position I wanted. Now the tough part.

"I'm sorry," I whispered, then bounced up on my toes to kiss him on the mouth. His eyes went wide with almost horrified shock and, before he could recover, I rotated his arm. The head of his humerus slid back into place.

Toby cried out once before biting it back. After a moment, he bent his arm, flexed his wrist, rolled his shoulders. "Hey. It's in."

"Stop that." I quickly re-buttoned his shirt before taking off my belt, wrapping it around his chest and upper arm. Tight fit, but it was the best I could do. "It needs to be immobilized. And I still think you need an X-ray. Something might be fractured."

"That's less than nothing to worry about." He looked down at me, the signs of discomfort nearly gone. "You ain't half bad, Soph."

"I have my moments." I dropped into a chair and opened my purse. Time to tend to the disaster that was my hair.

"Sure do. By the way…" He licked his lips and grinned. "Is your lip gloss cherry or strawberry?"

I stuck my tongue out in reply.

"See?" Dierk's voice came from behind us. "Sophie is a compassionate and talented caregiver. A fine choice for a king's mate."

"Knock it off, Dierk." I rolled my eyes so that only Toby could see, but he'd become stiffer than a back brace when Dierk walked over.

"What happened to Majesty?" He drew up a chair next to mine. A waitress set several glasses and a pitcher on the table.

Oh, hell. I reached for a glass. "We were in public."

"This is public."

I glanced around and saw faces of his entourage people, interspersed humans. Cacilia stood away from the group, speaking with strange girls who looked scarier than she did. Great. More bitches. "No, it's not. Anyways, you're their king, not mine."

"Perhaps now. The moon is two weeks away. What will you call me then?"

"Long-distance, I hope." I took a big mouthful. Ugh. Lager.

He chuckled, apparently enjoying the banter. "You are all right, young *Wolf*?"

Toby nodded, but didn't look at Dierk. He kept his gaze on the table.

"I'm okay. Sophie took a wallop, though." He pointed to the side of his nose. "You need a tissue there."

I had forgotten about my bloody nose. Checking my mirror, I saw the sticky blood smear and rummaged for a tissue.

"Come, let me see." Dierk called out in German, and one of the girls from the bar brought him a cloth. When he touched it to my skin, I shuddered from the icy dampness. Gently he wiped away the blood and, after folding the soiled edge inside, pressed it once more against my nose.

His other hand cupped my jaw, his thumb stroking the side of my face. I wanted to rip him apart because it was exactly the touch I needed after that ordeal. I felt better being in the same room with him, being cared for by a man who made me a priority. Little things like that made it increasingly hard to remember the great big thing I hated about him.

His voice was mild, as deceiving as his half-smile. "When I saw you on the ground, the blood on your fingers, knocked down by that *Hurensohn*..."

"Shh." That word didn't sound like a nice one. "I appreciate your chivalry and what not, but hurting him wouldn't make things better."

"I am *der König*. My judgments are fair and well-deserved."

"Right. And Toby will live here after you take your royal behind back to Europe. I don't think you can mandate those guys to treat him nicely for playing the King's favorite."

His brows scrunched, making horizontal lines across the bridge of his nose. "That is why you begged me to spare him?"

"Partly." I drank again. The lager really wasn't as bad as I'd originally thought. It had flavor, unlike the light beer I ordered out of habit. I just hadn't wanted to be the first one to order a Silver Bullet in front of a bunch of lycanthropes. Who said I wasn't insightful? "And partly because I saw how mad you were. I didn't want to see how much madder you can get."

"You dislike violence."

I set my jaw and gave him a curt nod. "Very much so."

"Even if it is part of nature?" Dierk glanced up at me through his cinnamon-colored lashes. He ran his finger along the base of the pitcher, toying with it. Toying with me.

Too bad for him, I had a long-standing grudge against nature and its deviant behaviors. Wouldn't accept it from a Demivamp, so there was no way a Were would get away with it. I expected better. From everyone.

I frowned and crossed my arms. "Especially, then."

"Sometimes violence, like nature, cannot be avoided."

"And sometimes people use nature as a convenient excuse to do shitty things."

Dierk blinked and reached for a glass. "Granted. But

some things can only be cured by using violence. It teaches harsh lessons."

"Unfortunately, you talk about teaching people who don't want to learn."

He poured a drought but didn't drink. Instead, he drummed his fingers on the table, the cadence keeping time with the tension I read in the lines around his eyes. "I wouldn't say that about everyone. But yes, I agree. Many do not learn. And that's what frustrates me so much."

"Why? I thought you were Mr. Traditional."

Dierk reached for a third glass, pouring before holding it out to Toby, who had been leaning against the wall. Toby took it, but remained standing apart from us, clearly uncomfortable about approaching our intimate conversation.

"Traditional," Dierk said. "Yes. But even I do not deny that we can better ourselves. Better what we can. It is slow progress."

"I believe it." I patted my nose with a clean tissue, but the bleeding had stopped. "Especially with jerks like that."

"How do you civilize a man who has a beast inside? The Were have vast limitations. I am not a preacher, and I am not a politician. I am only me. God made me king, my heart made me a bard, and my intellect tells me I don't have to settle for less."

His statement had a profound effect on my opinion of him. It was as if another veil had been lifted, allowing him to come into better focus. However, not every man was born a king. One man's ideals didn't flip hearts over like a line of dominoes. "They weren't always animals. Once they were just men. They were men until someone changed that for them."

"Not all," he said.

I shook my head. "But lycanthropy is spread—"

"Mainly by bite, yes, but not only by bite."

"How then? By sneeze?"

Dierk tilted his head back and laughed, a wonderful sound that moved his entire throat. He loved to laugh, I could tell, because he was so good at it. "Fortunately, no."

"There's a relief. I can't imagine what the world would be like if a pandemic ever hit."

He took a long swallow seeming to think that over. "You don't think a world of Were would be a better place?"

"Are you seriously asking? I think it would be horrible. Not that there's anything wrong with you all," I amended with a no-offense kind of shrug. "I'm more of a people-people person. And considering my connections to the DV, I like variety, too."

"You wouldn't have so much variety if the *Leni* binds us." His expression stilled. "My court is not as diverse as you might hope."

I scowled and looked away. "All the more reason to hate you for dragging me into this mess."

He leaned forward on his elbow and reached for my chin, tugging my attention back to him. His brown eyes, rimmed in espresso, contained starbursts of champagne, giving them a golden light. Those eyes danced with mischief as he peered into mine. "So, if you despise me so much, why are you here?"

"I brought her." Toby startled me when he spoke. "She don't feel good when she's separated from you. I wanted her to have some relief."

I snorted. "Some relief. I get to listen to his Highness over there."

"And is your head still pounding? Still feel like you're gonna throw up? Still feel like every piece of your body is being pulled like taffy?" Toby leaned forward and leveled a stern gaze at me, humbling me with this unaccustomed show of forcefulness. "You're a stubborn lady. I didn't bring you here so you can fight and get more miserable. I brought you here so you can get a little peace. Now get it."

"It's a risk he took, bringing you here. He ventured into a literal den of wolves." Dierk's gaze flicked toward Toby, who lowered his head under the scrutiny, forcefulness forgotten. "Do you always put your beloved in danger like this?"

"Toby isn't my beloved. He's my friend."

Dierk's expression darkened, his half-smile taking on a condescending slant. "He smells of your lipstick."

"So?" My cheeks grew hot. At least Dierk didn't accuse me of ripping open Toby's shirt and pawing at his bare chest. "I had to distract him from a painful procedure."

"You cherish him," he insisted.

Nothing wrong with that. "Sure I do."

"Then he is beloved." Dierk shook his head, idly fingering his glass. "Americans have a habit of confusing sex and love. No wonder they forget things like honor and loyalty."

I wanted to argue but couldn't. "I'd never put him in danger."

"But you have. His loyalty to you and his concern for your well-being encouraged him to pass scent boundaries and tread onto no-trespass lands, as it were. Had I not come out when I did, that pack would have destroyed him. You too, after they finished with him."

I grabbed Toby's hand. "Did you know that? I didn't—I had no…"

Toby pulled his hand free but wouldn't look at either of us now. "Yeah, I knew what could happen. I was sure it would work out. And it did."

"Toby, you can't do stuff like that," I said. "You can't put yourself in harm's way. You're still getting used to your pack. You're still learning the rules."

"So, what. I should ignore you? You couldn't even get out of bed. Rodrian's a wreck 'cause he can't even see you or do anything about it when you're up in your room. I had to do something."

"Toby is your protector." Dierk's half-smile crept into his voice, setting off warning bells even though I hadn't the faintest clue why.

"No, I'm not." Toby's reply was quiet but firm, his eyes fast on the floor.

"You take risks, make choices for her. That is assumption of dominance."

I didn't like the look on Toby's face, or the odd shade of pale it had become. He obviously understood the point Dierk was prodding at, but I was still in the dark. "What's going on, Dierk?"

"Nothing." He cleared his throat and reached for his glass, draining it. "Your friend won't be bottom rank for long. I think your damsel-in-distress act has borne a knight."

I huffed a breath through my nose. "Tobe. What's he trying to say?"

His voice sounded like there were two fists around it, squeezing. "He's saying that I think I'm ready to go and fight my way out of the bottom ranks. But I'm not. I'm still getting used to my new family. They were nice enough to take in a stray, and I'm not out to bite the hand that feeds me."

"Your actions speak clearly, *Wolf*," Dierk said.

"Then something got lost in the translation. I can never be Sophie's protector. I can never dominate her." Toby raised his head to meet Dierk's eyes, holding his gaze without wavering. "She is second only to the moon."

Dierk opened his mouth but shut it again without saying

a word. He only nodded, once, and released Toby's gaze. The younger Were's exhalation was audible, even in the ruckus of the bar.

The waitress brought a fresh pitcher, interrupting their cryptic exchange. Dierk motioned toward the corner where several of his entourage circled the lone pool table. "You've been watching them. You are free to join them, if you'd like."

Toby's expression lifted at the prospect, but darkened again when he glanced at me.

"It's okay, Toby. I'll behave." I stole a glance at Dierk. "You should get to have a good time, considering the trouble you took to bring me here."

"If you're sure…" He shrugged out of my make-shift sling and placed my belt on the table.

"I'm sure. Beat it."

I watched him approach the others tentatively, and after a moment of them sorting out their wolfly differences, Olberich tossed him a cue and racked the balls. It wasn't long before Toby relaxed, unhunching his shoulders and kidding around with the others, laughing. Dierk's eyes followed each of his wolves, surveying the room and his pack as he evaluated each one.

"Thanks," I said.

Dierk tilted his head toward me when I spoke.

"Oh. That?" He jerked his head toward Toby. "Nothing. He needs to be socialized. He will benefit from it. He'll grow confident, better able to care for himself."

Those were my biggest fears when it came to Toby. Dierk surprised me by telling me exactly what I needed to hear; considering I never confided in him about Toby, I could safely assume it was the truth. I pulled up my steadiest poker face and kept my thoughts to myself. I'd hate for Dierk or anyone else to try to use Toby against me.

"He's young. He could use an ego boost."

"He is welcome within my pack and will always find shelter in our den."

I smiled in spite of myself. "There you go, all poetic again."

His eyebrows lifted. "How so?"

"Things you say, the way you say them. It's not modern. You sound like an old king." I regretted it as soon as the words left my mouth.

Dierk grinned and stretched his arm along the back of my chair. "Thank you for noticing."

"Jackass," I muttered, and chuckled in spite of myself.

"That's King Jackass to you."

I laughed and picked up my glass. "Anything you say, Majesty."

The rest of the night passed faster than usual, probably due in large part for the alarming number of lagers I'd consumed. At ten of two the overhead lights pulsed in a notice of last call. Way past time to go.

"I think…" Dierk steadied my chair when I nearly toppled it in an effort to stand. "I will drive you home. Olberich will follow in my car."

"No, that's not necessary." I'd dropped my purse and had to fight through my hair to find the damned thing when I bent over to retrieve it. Standing straight again, I pushed my bangs back and blew at the straggling strands. Drunk hair sucked. "Toby will take me back."

"You don't drink bier very often, do you?" Dierk watched me struggle with my jacket for a few moments before intervening. I didn't want his help, but then again, I feared someone might have sewn the sleeves shut for all the trouble I had. He eased it up onto my shoulders and straightened the collar with a deft swipe. Gallant jerk.

"I drink plenty. I'm just no good at it. Unlike some people, apparently. How many did you have?"

"Not enough to join you in your antics, but more than enough to enjoy watching them."

I huffed out a breath again and swatted him. "What a prince you are. Where's Toby?"

He steadied me with a hand on my back, steering me toward the door. "Toby has found friends. Let him stay with my pack tonight."

"Uh-uh. Not after that crap with the other pack earlier. He needs to go home."

"Don't you trust me?"

I spun on my heel, armed with a pointed finger and a witty retort but when I saw his patient expression, the words disintegrated. I felt small and alone, except for him. My gut instinct still functioned, and it spoke up without hesitation. "Yeah. Yeah, I trust you. I definitely trust you."

"Do you trust my pack?"

I peered around him to see Olberich. He reminded me a little of Chewbacca, big and good-natured but capable of pulling off someone's arms. If I had to hide behind someone, he'd be the guy I would pick. Janssen was shorter and had a more formal air to him but he knew how to laugh. He also had a fairly nice backside so I guess hiding behind him wouldn't be so bad, either. Then there was Stohl. Cue the retching. "Most of them."

The corner of his mouth curled downwards in disapproval.

"I can't help it." If I had to face becoming a Were, he had to face the fact that Sophie doesn't play nice with everybody. "I'm sure you trust them, but I don't ever want to have to depend on people like Cacilia or Stohl. They suck."

He must have realized that any type of response, no

matter how carefully worded, would lead to a loud ranting on my part and decided to dead-end that little opportunity. He scored another point by doing so. "Your trust in me is well-founded. I pledge to you that Toby will be safe from harm in my keeping."

Did I have a choice? I wasn't sure I'd be able to find the door on my own, let alone make him change his mind. "Whatever. But he's got my keys. I have to get them back."

"No need." He held up my key chain, dangling Hello Kitty by her poor neck. I grabbed at them but he dodged my tipsy lunge with ease. "Oh, no, you don't. I will drive."

"Fine. Whatever. You're the boss."

"Not yet, but soon enough." His half-smile held a world of secrecy, but I wasn't interested. I aimed for the middle door and determinedly swayed my way through them, marching like Lucille Ball in all my drunken defiance.

He poured me into the front seat before getting into the driver's side, pushing the seat back to accommodate his long legs. I almost fell asleep on the way home. I supposed it was a mixed blessing that he already knew where I lived. At least I regained enough sobriety to punch in the correct alarm code and make it upstairs. I think I even remembered to take off my coat before flopping down in the middle of the bed, still fully dressed.

At least I didn't barf. Bonus right there.

I cracked my bedroom door, peering out into the parlor. I felt fresh, like line-dried linen and spring water. My head was clear. Even my morning breath was less potent than it should have been. For the first time since Dierk brought me home with The Bite, I was able to tolerate getting out of bed without wanting to wilt into a sagging, nauseous pile of please-shoot-me.

That could only mean one thing. He was still here. But how did he get past the wards?

Dierk slept on the couch, rolled toward the back with his forehead pressed to the cushions. He wrapped his arm around himself, hand lying loosely upon his ribs; black boots off and tucked against the side of the couch, he drew his knees slightly as if he wanted to curl up on the narrow cushion. Too small a bed for a man of his build, I thought.

He still slept, the sounds of even breathing washing

through the quiet room. It was perfect accompaniment to the slivers of sunlight that glowed along the edges of the closed blinds.

I crept forward, one toeful of carpet at a time, relishing the freedom to move without the illness that plagued me in his absence, until I reached the armchair. Making as little sound as I could, I lowered myself into it. He never stirred as I curled my legs up and tucked my bare feet under, taking him in.

Looking at the sleeping man made it hard to connect him with the moon dreams. I remembered the mournful howl, the lonely call, the tag-along moon. I remembered the swift run and the blur of branch and bush. I remembered the taste of fur and earth and night air.

He rolled over and my breath caught on an exhale. Eyes closed, he wriggled to a comfortable position, the sounds of sleeping keeping an even cadence. I eased out the rest of my held breath when he settled once more.

Dierk looked so much younger—eyes closed under straight brows, gentle arcs of dark lash against his cheeks, now shadowed with dusty morning growth. He must be a twice-daily shaver. I wondered if all Weres were.

So this was the man who made me a werewolf. This was my mate. Or something.

I sighed, catching myself halfway through the sharp breath so I wouldn't wake him. I smelled wind and crushed leaf, even though I knew had he spent the previous evening in a bar and driven me home in my Cavalier that definitely didn't have a Wolf Pine air freshener dangling from the mirror. I was pretty sure no one sold perfume like *eau du loup*. But I smelled him, or at least his power. He was still a void like every other Were, but I smelled him and knew it was him, knew he was there.

I blinked against a sting of hot tears, feeling them hang

on my lashes before sliding down my cheeks. If I tried to keep them in, they'd go straight to my nose and then my sniffling would wake him for sure. Here in the darkness of my warded rooms, no one would see my tears. No one could comfort me, even if they had.

I didn't have much hope to come out of this and remain human. The dreams, the scents…already the infection grew. That seed would grow like a vine and strangle out every other part of my life until only what he meant for me to have remained. I still had a low-grade fever, even though the bite on my hand had almost closed and didn't appear infected. But something was there. Maybe not a raging strep colony, but something just as potent. Something more. Something that allowed him to get past the strongest of wards when no one else could.

I looked at him, seeing nothing unkind or sinister in his peaceful face and wondered how deep a man he was, to cleverly conceal such things.   His arms wrapped snugly around his chest, Dierk kept his secrets to himself.

I'd learned how to get inside the DV, although it had taken time. There was never any risk to it; I wouldn't become DV by simply immersing myself in their power.

Risk. Funny word. The only way to catch lycanthropy is the bite. I'd been bitten already. There was no other risk. What would be the harm of trying now?

I considered the void sleeping on my couch. Even when living with Toby, I didn't really push too far past the event horizon. Then again, I still hadn't been bitten. I had never gotten too close to Toby for fear of changing that little fact. Now, the game had changed.

Closing my eyes, I dropped into the Sophia and raised my barrier. The shimmer of my pattern had grown deeper, forest green and navy night sky, jewel-toned. It had to be due to the poor lighting. I couldn't stop and consider my colors had changed. Not yet. Not now.

I slipped up the curtain of power, leaning into it and making it thicker, bulkier. I wanted a good layer between me and whatever lay within the void. Peering with Sophia-sight and a pinched brow, I saw nothing remotely like the DV power signatures I'd learned to "see."

But—I saw something.

I thinned the barrier, layer by layer, and with each removal Dierk's power came sharper into focus. I sat and stared and tried to decipher the puzzle. Dierk wasn't void. I'd just never looked deep enough to really see.

His power wasn't light and emotion. Those were qualities of the DV. Those were qualities by which I'd learned to identify and measure and respond to the Demivampire around me. Those things were not Were.

This was...different. Wind and scent and force, a pull from an ever-changing pendulum that swept the night sky, dragging lovers and slaves behind in her wake. Instinct. Instinct to obtain. Instinct to protect. All these things were Were.

No malice. No deceit. Honesty and integrity, bound by the pull of the moon. Even in sleep, Dierk was these things. I let another layer slip down. Now wearing the thinnest layer of shielding like a silken sheet, I reached for him.

The scent, stronger. Leaf and water, cool and crisp, a cold press upon my tongue. The solid earth against my hands, digging and connecting with primal forces deep below. Knowing it felt good, felt right. The urge to run. The need to run—

I pulled back, shaken. The dream. It was real and I was awake and I drew up my barrier, strained to find my familiar pattern, chasing away the colors of woods and night. Cobalt. Gold. My colors. As they bled back into the walls of my mental barriers, I wanted to weep with relief.

My colors did little to warm me, though, and I huddled in the chair, shivering with the after-thought of having brushed against Dierk's power.

The darkness remained at the edges, content to let the sun shine while it was the sun's proper time to do so. But night would fall. It always did. The sky turned, the wheel turned, and eventually, we turned with it.

I returned to plain old eyeball sight, and once more, Dierk was just Dierk, sleeping with his hair falling over his eyes. After experiencing that little sensory rush, I didn't want to try again. I feared I would be pulled in. Seal my own fate.

The thoughts lingered, though. Dierk was a good man. He was pulled by the moon. He was bound by traditions. Now that I felt it myself, I knew it wasn't a cop-out.

I knew something else, too. Something entirely human. I didn't want to dwell on it yet, but nonetheless I lifted myself carefully out of the chair and tugged an afghan from across the back. Gently, quietly, I draped it over him, smoothed the edge with a hesitant touch, and turned to go back to bed.

"Sophie." His voice, thick and gravelly with sleep, sounded pleased to let my name be the first word he uttered for the day. Pleased I was nearby and pleased I'd heard.

I stopped, not turning, hearing all he'd put into my name. I felt valued. God help me, he'd only said my name and I felt valued.

When I turned, he raised a hand out to me. Blinking lazily, sleep not entirely banished, he smiled, pillow-soft and dreamy. "Please?"

I waited for something inside to resist. My gut-instinct never even twitched. Closer to him would be better. Closer would be much better.

I found myself at his side. Closer was wonderful.

When I sank onto the couch, he urged me to stretch out along the front of his body. Deeper relief spread as he wrapped his arm over me to tuck his hand between the couch and my ribs. Our legs found a comfortable tangle almost instantly, as if we'd slept next to each other for years. My head rested on his other bicep and, with his breath against the back of my neck, I drifted into deepest, safest sleep.

When I dreamed of woods and hills and sky, when I ran with the moon on my back, I didn't run alone.

"Is this necessary?" Dierk squirmed under my ministering fingers.

"It is if I want to keep my job." I straightened his tie and smoothed the white dress shirt down. It was tucked into belted jeans, not Haggars, but it would have to do. I didn't exactly have much to work with. He and Marek weren't the same size, not by a long shot, but at least he didn't swim in the large shirt. "Hold still."

"You won't have to work when the Leni completes." He raked back his damp hair and unbuttoned the cuffs, flipping the too-long sleeves into neat, flat rolls just below his elbows.

I slid my bag off the bar, peeking inside for my wallet and keys. Wallet check, keys...I checked the coffee table and the floor before spying them in Dierk's hand. "I have to work today. Today is as far ahead as I can think right now."

"You still consider it a curse." His quiet voice held a measure of apology.

I knew he'd never apologize for something that seemed so right for him, his kind. Yet, I didn't doubt the sincerity in his tone. He apologized that I struggled to accept it, that I felt such pain.

I knew that his eyes would sway me the last measure of resistance so I avoided looking at his face. "I don't consider it a choice."

"It usually isn't."

I blinked, my eyes dry and tired. "I gathered that. Let's go."

We headed downstairs. He insisted on carrying my messenger bag for me and tucked my hand under his arm. The contact comforted me and I didn't argue. I needed to be as close to the top of my game as possible.

I flipped open the alarm panel and punched the exit code. It responded with a flat tone instead of a bright yes ma'am! beep-beep. Ducking back to peer at the display, I saw it was already disarmed. A throat cleared behind and above me as Rodrian revealed his presence.

He stood at the rail in front of the open office. I'd been so self-absorbed that I hadn't noticed his presence. My stomach tightened when I looked up. Rodrian had watched us walk down together.

I could taste the disapproval on his power. He didn't bother to mask it.

We still hadn't had the chance to talk about any of this. After everything we'd been through together, this had to appear like the ultimate betrayal—and I had never meant for things to turn out this way. I wanted to run to him but his pointed feelings kept me at an agonizing distance.

"Good morning, Rode." I spoke with as much neutrality as I could. I didn't want to provoke his temper.

"Going to work?"

I nodded. "I have to try. God only knows how pissed Barb will be. I haven't even called off for the time I missed."

"And him?" The question held a hint of condemnation.

"He's coming with me. He's responsible for how I feel today."

"Glad you admitted it." His power took on a blade-like edge that pressed at me, slicing at my barriers. He wanted me to hurt the way he hurt inside. He wanted me to feel the same.

Rodrian got what he wanted, every time. I had to lean into my shields to hide the flash of guilt, the streak of new agony that swelled up like a welt on my heart, and I twisted my face away. He couldn't see how truly his arrow had found its mark. I feared he'd only aim again.

"I don't mean to interrupt," Dierk said.

Rodrian sniffed, a disdainful echo of Marek's gesture. "Then don't."

Dierk stiffened slightly as Rodrian's rudeness. "But I will insist we speak together, you and I. Privately. This evening, here."

"If I'm here." Rodrian faked a disinterested look, his power betraying his real reaction. That reaction was Oh, I'll be here, all right. And I'll be ready for you.

I glanced at Dierk, wondering what he was able to pick up.

Whether or not he got the DV message, Dierk was through playing games. He turned to face Rodrian, his shoulders squared, feet planted. There was no cowing this man when he was set on a course. In a tone that sounded more despotic than diplomatic, he spoke louder than he needed. "You will be here. It is a formal request."

"I don't have anything to say to you."

"And yet, you still have so much to say. We will speak like honorable men. We will confront our differences and embrace our common interests."

Rodrian's gaze slid toward me and his power pulled

back, locked in once more. "Fine. I'm glad to see you're feeling better, Sophie. Have a good day at work. TGIF, right? Be careful."

He went back into the office and closed the door, shutting me out. Blinking did little to keep my eyes from stinging, and I gritted my teeth. I would not cry. It wouldn't fix anything.

Dierk and I headed out to find his Mercedes parked in front of my car. I guessed Olberich followed Dierk, and someone followed Olberich. He insisted on driving, so I stopped to take the parking pass out of my car first.

Before opening the passenger door, I glanced back toward the house, wondering if Rodrian would wave goodbye, like he always did. The gesture was one that had become sort of tradition for us; after losing and nearly losing so much, goodbyes were precious last looks, always shrouded in a sense of an unspoken What if?

But this morning the windows were empty. There was no wave, no smile, no touch of affectionate power.

Resignation dried the well of potential tears, leaving a numbing fog to settle in my chest. I was leaving with the Were who had spent the night in my warded rooms. Why would Rodrian see me off?

I wasn't too keen on being driven to work by a European. No offense, but I wasn't sure he knew what side of the road to stay on. Much to my relief, however, he drove like a normal person, even if he wasn't exactly human. If anything, he took things on the slow side.

When I realized he wasn't going to drive us head-on into a tractor trailer, I relaxed enough to speak. "I'm surprised he acted reasonably when you went all kingly on him. Rodrian doesn't take orders from anyone."

"'Kingly'? How so?"

"I heard the authority behind your request."

"I'm surprised you discerned it," he said.

"I know your voice."

His eyebrows lifted. "We only met on Sunday."

Was it almost a week? I kept forgetting. Time had been a bit mushy for a while there. I could have caught birds, let alone flies, when I'd heard the newscaster announce it was Friday earlier. "I knew your voice long before that."

He looked over at me. I guessed he was trying to understand what I meant.

"Hello? Turn of the Wheel fan, remember? You sometimes use that tone when you sing. Like in 'Kinsman Take Arms'. I guess the song's about the tension between Were and DV."

His eyebrows lifted quickly. "I've never spoken publicly about that song."

"It's evident now, after seeing you and Rodrian this morning."

He raked his hair back with one hand and rubbed the back of his neck. "It is more than a difference of species. Thurzo and I have known each other for many years now."

"I meant to ask how you recognized each other the night you brought me home."

He flexed his fingers on the wheels, cracking his knuckles with a series of soft pops. "Long history. Short explanation. He knew my father and assumes I am the same man."

"You mean, he didn't like your dad, so he doesn't like you, either."

He nodded. "The summation suffices."

"What did your dad do to him?" I couldn't imagine a crime heinous enough to create such a long-standing grudge.

Dierk looked insulted. "My father was *der König* before I.

He did nothing but act as such."

"Was Rodrian in Germany at the time?"

He mulled the question before answering. "Yes."

I only knew of one story when Rodrian was in Germany. His son had evolved and was exterminated as vampire. The vampire, formerly known in life as the Demivampire Boxer Thurzo, had died on his uncle Marek's sword—a detail Rodrian didn't know. Didn't take a genius to gut-jump this one. "Mannheim."

"You are full of surprises. What has Thurzo told you?"

"He never said he knew you or your family..." I hesitated, reaching for a neutral word. "Business took him to Mannheim once, he told me. It was a lucky guess."

"Hmm." Mild sound that said I don't believe you but that's okay. "My family is in Mannheim. My home is there and will always be there."

"Do you live in a castle?" I didn't smirk, although it certainly was meant as a joke.

"Yes."

Joke flopped.

"There are many castles throughout Germany, many great historic estates. However, my home is not open for tours. The family home is an official court. I have other places throughout Germany, other properties. I travel extensively. Our success as musicians is usually viewed as the cause of the extravagance. The family home, however, is not publicly associated with me."

"So you don't get parades or ride around wearing a crown?"

"I'm not sure how to answer." He glanced at me, searching my expression for a clue. "Are you serious or trying to be humorous?"

"I don't know. I just—don't know anything about you." I twisted the strap of my bag into a knot, letting it flop loose before twisting it again. "I guess being a smartass makes everything I say come out like a joke."

He nodded and concentrated on the road for a few moments. "I don't wear a crown or ride in parades. The existence of the Were is a secret, no matter the country. No human civilization would welcome us."

"Oh," I said. "That's not really fair."

"That is reality. Being Were is not exactly about having choices."

There was that word again: choice. It was quickly climbing my list of Sour Grapes Words. "Did you have a choice? I mean, I assume you succeeded your father. Did you have a choice in the matter? Could you have walked away? Would you have wanted to?"

He laughed, delighted at my inquisitions and curiosity. "You will be disappointed by the answer."

"Maybe not."

"Does any child choose his family? They are my point of reference, the only world I ever knew. And they are all Were. Now, humans who Turn grow up in different realities. Many times the Turning is accidental. Sometimes it is chosen. Sometimes it is inflicted." He glanced at me, but I schooled my expression into one of polite detachment. "But kings are not made, Sophie. They are born."

"Well, I assumed that much. Born a prince and trained to be king."

"More than that. I was born Were."

Sudden horror made my throat painfully dry. Several mile markers passed in smothered silence. We'd turned onto the parkway by the time I found my voice. "So. Born Were."

"Yes."

"You changed with the moon. . .as a baby?" I once saw Toby change. I didn't want to envision an infant exploding in a shower of werewolf glue. I didn't think I could survive that single thought, because the next thought would be: I could be his mate, future mother of his children. My children—

It suddenly felt too close, like a closet full of winter coats. I cracked the window and started counting cars.

"No," he said. "Not as a baby. The first moon of a princeling occurs on the harvest moon following his fifth birthday." He patted my leg, letting his hand linger for several long moments before pulling his hand away.

The comfort was lost on me. "That doesn't make it easier to accept. Kindergarteners shouldn't erupt into claws and fur."

"I wasn't a schoolboy at age five. I was future *König*, who grew up in a caring den of people who were blessed by the moon, who shifted in front of me because it was natural. I looked forward to my first change. I remember the anticipation."

I remembered Toby's change and the shower of mess I endured by standing too closely when it happened. Retching would be very uncool at this particular moment so I squelched the memory. "I'll take your word for it."

"My mother held me in her arms, surrounded me with love and support. She guided me through the pain. She nosed me to my feet, cleaned my paws, reminded me to shake. She helped me face my father as a strong cub, and I remember the pride in his eyes when he called my name. I remember the sound of the pack when they echoed him. When we ran, I remember how they flowed around me and helped me find the wind. I will never forget my first moon."

Dierk's voice was soft and sweet, full of childhood joy, the memory of perfect acceptance and absolute love. The car was full of the scent of woods and wind and earth despite the crawl of rush hour traffic all around us. No diesel fumes. Just Dierk and his spirit. I was surrounded.

I wasn't afraid.

I wasn't afraid, not until we pulled into the parking garage next to my office, where my job as columnist for The Mag most likely hung in the balance, if it still existed at all.

"Hi, Amanda," I said as I passed her desk. Just when I raised my hand to rap on Barbara's door, Amanda stopped me.

"Hi, Sophie. Wait—" She stood up and reached out. "She's with someone. She'll call you when she's free."

Amanda's voice sounded a tone or two higher than normal, a sure sign of tension. When she was really upset, she squeaked. Something was up. My hope sank.

"Um, sure, I—" I glanced through the window but I couldn't see anyone inside. "I'll just head on over to check the mail then."

"Glad to see you back."

"Yeah, Amanda. Glad to be back."

She took her seat again, but watched me. Discomforted by her strange behavior, I slinked back to my office and dreaded the sound of the intercom.

Dierk busied himself by examining the photographs on the file cabinet. Mostly they were pictures from work and work-related gatherings; Barbara and others at work, at the Expo (which I staunchly refused to attend anymore), at various conferences. Among them I'd slipped in my family—Rodrian, Shiloh, Dahlia and Toby. The non-humans. The ones who lingered among humans without really being recognized for what they were.

Rodrian's picture was the one that got noticed the most. Funny, though. No one ever said, "Ooh, who's the hottie?"

They always said, "Where'd you get that frame?"

People assumed his was the picture that came in the frame when I bought it. That's what happened when you looked like an underwear model—nobody took you seriously.

Dierk turned away from them as I shut the door behind me. "Well?"

I sighed and slumped into my chair. "I'm screwed."

His expression clouded. "Was your editor angry?"

"I couldn't even get in to see her. Her secretary said she was with someone, but I didn't see anyone. I didn't feel anyone, either. Not even a wisp of people."

"So you think she was delaying you?"

"Something, anyway. Probably waiting for Tom to come over so they can ambush me and send me packing."

"Don't be pessimistic. Maybe the one in her office was Were. You wouldn't have detected him."

"I looked in. There wasn't anyone in there with her." I snapped off the rubber band bundling a fat stack of mail. "All I can do is get to work and look like I still deserve my job when she comes in with the ax."

"Will I disturb you as you work? I can go downstairs for coffee."

"No," I blurted. "I mean, stay. I'm fine. You're no bother unless you start talking about mating and being king and junk."

His half-smile deepened, perhaps going three-quarters. "I will keep my junk to myself."

"You better." I reached for a letter opener and began to deftly harvest the morning mail. Too bad this wasn't an Olympic sport—I'd gotten pretty good at separating the mail. Silver medal, at least.

What would I do if I got canned? Full-time writing was tough. The market was awful. Living on freelance paychecks wasn't dependable enough.

I supposed I could renew my license and go back to medicine. I'd left my nursing career years ago when the stress had gotten overwhelming, but now I could depend on good ole DV compulsion to tap that vile anxiety—

Or not. I couldn't depend on DV compulsion if I wasn't with the DV anymore. If this *Leni* thing had its way, I couldn't depend on DV anything ever again. I'd belong to the Were. But then, I wouldn't need a job.

I glanced at Dierk, who wore his earbuds and leaned back in his awkward chair, sunlight on his closed eyes. He seemed to be dozing, looking nothing like I'd pictured over years of knowing him only as the front man of a rock band. And though front man was the only title he'd worn for most of the past fifteen years, over the last week he took on another definition, causing his front man image to crumble as if it had never meant anything at all. His current definitions were overwhelmingly distracting.

A tingle of bitter red emotion caught fire in the pit of my stomach. I knew better than to let it unfurl, even though I wanted nothing more than to be angry right now. I wanted to slap him, hard, for wrecking everything that mattered to me. My job, my friends, my Sophia—all of it could be swept away like voices in a storm. All because of him, his tradition, his toothy bastard buddy Stohl. If only he—

No. If only I.

If only I had gone home instead of sitting at the bar, I wouldn't have met him. If only I left after Cacilia picked that fight, I'd only had to have cancelled my credit cards and bought a new wallet. If only I had left when Dahlia asked, instead of lingering just one moment and one moment and one moment more—I'd never have gotten bitten.

Enough "if only". It was done. If I wanted to lay blame, I'd have to slather it all over myself first.

Time to face the music. I might only have a few weeks of my life left before it all went away, but that didn't mean I should stop living now.

I took one last glance at the man who might come to define me, and I got down to business. Today, I was still me.

The *knock knock* shook me out of my Sophia zone nearly two hours later. I was submerged in a stack of petitions, on my first decent roll since The Bite. Quickly I dispelled the mood, urging the Sophia to retreat and take her Oracle-blue eyes with her. Still staring at the paper in my hand, I waved Barbara in.

"Well, Sophie." Not even a hello, hello. Barbara's voice was thin and subdued, as if she wasn't sure she knew me anymore. "Making any headway on that stack?"

"Yeah. Actually, it's going great. I've picked some great letters for the column, and think I can even do a theme thing here—"

She glanced at Dierk then back to me again. "The theme that involves bringing friends to work?"

Oh, I wasn't sure I would like where this was going. Barb was using a new tone, one I hadn't heard since I first started here. It was the *I'm Your Boss Tone*. "Yeah. Barb, this is Dierk Adeluf. He's…"

"Helping with research, actually." Dierk had risen and extended a hand, wearing a full smile that made him look boyish, charming, and enigmatic. He wasn't holding anything back. "You must be Ms. Evans, her editor."

"Barbara." She took his hand, unable to keep the line of her mouth straight. "Research, how?"

"Well, Sophie told me about her column's unique position on the US market. The syndicated-but-not-duplicated scheme." Dierk let his accent work its magic on her. Shoot, it had a spill-over effect on me. The way he thickened and flattened his words made me want to pour gravy on his voice and just dig in. "I was telling her about a few projects we've done at our own publication."

Barbara's interest became keen. If I wasn't paranoid about losing my job, I would have ventured a guess to say she forgot why she came in. "Your publication? Where are you based?"

"Frankfurt."

"Sophie." It was still a scolding tone, but at least it was warming up to our customary climate. "You didn't want to fill me in?"

"I—ah—"

"Was extremely distracted. She's been kind enough to show me the city, and I admit my own enthusiasm for a potential syndication contract has kept her from meeting her obligations here."

"And you met…?"

Dierk rubbed his temple, ducking his head and letting his charm swing to the sheepish side. "Blind date, actually. Fortunately for me, she didn't flee when the blinders came off."

"Not yet, anyway." I smiled harder than I needed, and frowned once Barbara looked away from me.

"Well. I really don't know what to make of it. Sharing of

ideas are always a good thing, especially from two distinct and separate markets..." She trailed off and gave Dierk a significant nod.

"My thoughts exactly." His smile deepened. I'd swear he dimpled at her.

"Sophie, I have time before our editorial meeting at three. Stop by my office, will you?"

I showed all my teeth, a well-practiced but no less phony smile, meant to anchor my quivering chin. I was being called to the office where she could shred me in private. All the king's men wouldn't be able to put me back together again.

Damn the king.

I decided to spend the rest of the day working on schedules and queuing up emails. Thankfully, I'd been able to stagger submission dates throughout the month so it was simply a matter of opening the right template, attaching the right files, and hitting send.

My filing system was organized, but the work was still time-consuming. I dreaded this part, the non-writing end. The business end. This was the work part. And I'd missed four days of work.

When I opened my spreadsheet for the week, the first thing I noticed was that each of the week's submissions were marked *sent*. That couldn't be right. I didn't send them.

I switched over to email and looked in the "sent" folder. Sure enough, the emails and their files had all gone out.

Puzzled, I decided to get that meeting over sooner rather than later. This time, Amanda didn't stop me at the door.

"You got an intern this week. You'd know that that if you had called in." Barb stirred her coffee with a stern swish of her spoon. "You'll have to wait until Monday to meet her, though. She's down with HR for the day."

Barb pushed her cup to the edge of her desk and rocked back in her chair, flipping her pen between her fingers. "Lucky to find someone familiar with your column. Lucky too that you are such an OCD record keeper of what needs to go out and when. She stepped in and covered you."

"That's impossible. I don't keep a paper calendar. Everything was stored in my—"

"Computer. Yes. She sat in your chair, she logged into your account, and she saved your job. Stop choking on your tongue, Sophie. She did what was necessary to keep this column moving forward."

"But—" I was completely aghast. What if she'd gone through the Sophia records? It's not like I was blogging about the secret life of a single oracle but still. Those letters were special letters. They didn't get sent out to the papers and the publications. What if she was mucking around in my private stuff?

"Don't be looking at me like that. She's not a whistle blower. She's an intern who simply looked at your ridiculously detailed schedule and followed it to the letter because that's what she is paid to do. By the way, I need to remind you to get a life."

I needed her familiar ass-busting right now. I needed to feel normal because lately I felt like an alien in my own world, a transplant into a parallel universe. Everyone looked the same but all these tiny differences, these weird alterations kept reminding me that life could never be the same.

Maybe an intern would be good for me. I couldn't argue with Barb—my methodology was ridiculously organized but it was the only way to do both my column work and my petition correspondence without ending up drooling in a straitjacket. As long as I answered the letters, queued the submissions, and wrote the schedule, I supposed an assistant could take care of the sending and logging stuff. That was just time-consuming work.

This could kind of like having a mini secretary. A secretary would be cool.

If only the control-freak part of me would stop screaming in the back of my head. I hated relinquishing control and I hated thinking about it and I hated the certainty that I needed to do it.

I scrubbed my brow with the back of my wrist. Barb had that no-nonsense look on her face. I hated that look. It reminded me she was my boss and I needed my job, for financial as well as emotional and perhaps oracular reasons.

"Yes. I do need a life. And, yes." I nodded my concession. "An intern would help with a lot of the non-composition work. And it would help keep things going when I kind of miss work."

"Kind of miss work." She said it with a grand flourish. "That's definitely one way to put it. Even if you were off doing something work-related. Ever hear of calling off? Giving a head's up? Sending a smoke signal?"

"It's not like he gave me a lot of space. He's a little pushy and a lot over-bearing and he's pretty much taken over my life. Geez. It's been a rough week." I didn't have to fake my irritation.

"Then give him the heave-ho. Or work with someone else on his team, if you don't want to walk away from the project. He's got to have directors. I searched his company, Sophie. It's legit and it's worldwide."

He was worldwide, all right. "I wish I could but…it's pretty much set. I'm stuck with him."

"Can't be all that bad, hon. He's handsome in that rugged-boyish European way."

I stuck out my tongue. I really didn't want to hear

compliments when I was bent on hating him.

"And he has a wonderful voice. I bet he'd be great at karaoke." Barb leaned over her coffee to take a quick sip off the top. "And he is charming. Is he married?"

"I'm pretty sure he's single right now."

"Then just be nice. There may be a really good opportunity here. You can break into the German market with this. You don't have to marry him."

I chuckled weakly and got up to leave. "Not today, at least."

Dierk drove me home but didn't take off his seatbelt when he shut off the car.

I paused, my hand on the door handle. "What?"

"I'll see you later, when I return. I have business."

"Business?" Not that I cared what he wanted to do. I just didn't like the thought of him leaving. "Aren't you staying? I really don't feel like another night of delirium."

He laughed. "You'll be fine. The process has nearly ended. New moon this evening. The need to be close fades with the new moon."

I must have looked like he was speaking German because he reached for my hand.

"You see, the beginning of the *Leni* is about bonding. Spending time together. Becoming familiar with each other. It is a courtship. The ill feeling when we try to be apart is a reminder that we should be with each other instead. I think we have satisfied the requirement, don't you?"

"So..." I looked at the front door, wondering who

would all be home. I saw Dahlia's car, and Rodrian's. Might be a full house again. Maybe that's why he didn't want to stay. "I can stay here and not be sick as a pig?"

He grimaced at my terminology. Dierk seemed to find distaste with many of my turns of phrase. Well, sorry, bub, I thought. I never went to Princess School.

"You will be fine. I have all your phone numbers in my contact list, if you need to call. I will only be gone a short time."

I nodded. "Um. But you're coming back?"

"Yes." He raised my hand to his mouth and pressed a kiss to my skin. "I will be meeting Thurzo tonight to discuss the situation and our expectations."

I got out of the car and he waved as he drove off down the driveway. He would meet with Rodrian tonight? That should be fun, in a sarcastic way. I wondered if they'd do battle. I half-expected they would.

Once inside, I was greeted by Toby, who delivered a nice chunk of news: he and Dahlia decided to move in for a while. He'd come over to drop off a few things while she was at work.

Toby said she felt really guilty about the whole thing, since she was the one who dragged me out to the concert in the first place. I didn't say much, especially when my initial reaction had been *Don't worry about it, you can't change fate.*

That would have sounded Dierkish and I would not give Dierk or the moon the satisfaction.

Euphrates couldn't be happier about the whole arrangement. After giving me hell for being away for so long, he disappeared from the suite. I followed him down the hall, watching him streak down the stairs and go right into the guest wing. Well. That's good. He liked Toby. I wanted my cat to be happy.

And Fraidy was happy. At one time, I saw Toby carrying him like a baby. The cat's tail waved along from under his arm, long contented swishes.

Toby caught me looking and blushed.

"Not my fault," he said. His protests were unnecessary, though. Fraidy's half-closed eyes and rumble-strip purring gave me all the evidence I needed. He had that wolf wrapped around his little paw.

It was the first thing that actually made me happy inside.

I hadn't really thought about what would happen to Fraidy. I doubted he'd be happy if I changed. I mean, I see him with Toby and they are like birds of a…nah, bad comparison. But still. I'd swear my cat would happily run away with the boy.

Dahlia, different story.

It's not that she hated the cat. I just got an unmistakable sense of mistrust between the two. It was the same thing with Rodrian. Cats and DV just didn't mix.

But what about me? It had taken Euphrates a long time to learn to trust me when we first met. If I suddenly changed my entire nature, I'd be a totally different person to him. He might not know me anymore.

It was perfectly plausible. Rodrian had the same trouble, after all.

After I'd washed and changed and grabbed a microwaved burrito (I had a mean craving for beef and beans) I went downstairs to the guest suite. The door was open so I knocked on the frame. "Toby, got a second?"

He'd been sitting in the kitchen table, where he'd been putting in new laces in his tan work boots. "You look tired."

I rolled my eyes. "Thanks."

"I didn't mean—"

"It's okay, bud. Just—never say that to Dally. It's pretty

much the meanest thing you can say to a woman."

He hung his head a second in obligatory penance. "Okay, but sit down anyway."

I dragged a wooden chair from the running board. This suite was the oldest part of the house—it had started as a simple colonial cottage, a beloved home that Marek never wanted to relinquish. However, Marek was a living-large kind of man and eventually a huge estate grew up around it.

The estate was formally named Black Oak Stocks, largely in part of the trees that filled the woods on the sprawling property. Marek wasn't a materialistic man, though. He called it *the cottage*.

Marek had preserved these rooms in their own style, along with the furniture and the trappings of the era. It was a museum in its own right. I'm pretty sure the shocking union of a Demivamp and a Were wasn't something he'd foreseen frolicking in his carefully-preserved cottage. Oh, the scandal.

I took a deep breath, hoping I already knew what he'd say. "I'm really glad you guys are here. The house has been so empty."

"I thought Rodrian was here all the time. And Shiloh— where is she, anyway? I haven't heard a door slam since I got here."

I crossed my arms around my stomach. "They were, pretty much, but then Shiloh cusped and Brianda thought she'd benefit from…physical training."

"You mean, drinking blood."

I raised my hand between us. "Don't know, don't wanna."

"Right, so?"

I shrugged. "Shy drives now so she doesn't depend on me. Some days I'd wake up and she'd be gone, car still in the driveway."

Toby reached for the other boot and tugged a lace out of its plastic wrapper. "Dally said Shiloh's been different since the whole procedure thing."

"She is. I just don't know how different. It's like she woke up one day and *kablam*, she became Brianda Junior. I mostly see her when she stops in for new clothes. She packs a bag, dumps her laundry off for the staff—oh, by the way. There's new staff."

He made a teasing noise. "Look at you, Miss Sophie and her maids."

"Nuh-uh, not mine. I get along on my own, thank you. Well, I don't cut the grass or dust the den, but I cook my own food and take care of myself. It's not like I'm living like a princess."

"Well, you're gonna be queen. Might as well start living like one. Oh." He leaned forward, peering at my face. "I said the wrong thing again, didn't I?"

I laced my fingers and concentrated on them. "It's okay, Toby. I'm trying to keep a level head about the whole thing. But that's the reason I stopped down. I need to ask a favor."

"Anything for you, Red. Name it."

I smiled at the sound of his silly name for me. I was Little Red Riding Hood and he was the Big Bad Wolfboy. I liked the fairy tale part of it. And the ridiculosity. Toby wasn't Big Bad Anything. "If something happened to me...would you keep Fraidy?"

"Oh." His demeanor changed, like, just fell. All the goofiness just drained away. "Oh. I don't know, Sophie. I mean, I live with Dally now. You know how she feels about your cat. If I agreed without her knowing..."

I hadn't expected anything less than a huge *YES!* and maybe even some jumping around. I mean, who wouldn't be thrilled? Euphrates was quite possibly the coolest beast on four feet. And really, all I wanted was a little reassurance that at least one of us would be okay.

For seven years, it had been me and Euphrates, orphans against the world. Occasionally, it was a lonely world and sometimes it was a crazy dangerous world but it was always ours, together. I needed to know he'd be okay if I—

Swallowing hard and wanting to get out of the room before my eyes began to sting, I nodded. "Oh, yeah, of course. It's a big responsibility and I have no right to ask. Maybe you can talk to her."

"Sophie, you don't need to worry. He'll be okay. He'll get through this." Toby dropped the boot and knelt in front of me. "He's a tough old cat and he's a little worried that something is up but he knows that he's got people who love him very, very much."

Toby reached up and untangled my arms, seeking my hands and holding them tightly. "He is a most beloved creature and a member of this crazy family and he knows that he should remember that, even when it gets real hard. If our family situation changes…he knows he won't be forgotten. This family will adjust."

My vision blurred and I clamped down on my trembling lip.

"You know that, don't you, Red?" Toby released one of my hands to rub the side of my head. "You are loved and we will get through this."

I dropped my gaze to my lap for several long moments, just trying to chase down my breath. "I'm trying to remember it. It's just that…this thing is so big. I can't see around it."

He patted my leg and stood up. "It's just another thing, Sophie. You'll get through it."

"You've talked with Dierk's people, haven't you? What are they saying? I mean, every Were bite doesn't result in the Turn, does it?"

Toby retreated from me and busied himself with his bootlace again. "This one seems like a done deal. The *Leni* stuff...I don't understand it all the way because they talk funny and they leave a lot out but most of the others have already accepted that it's gonna happen."

I puffed out my cheeks with a hard exhale, surfing a sudden swell in my chest. Just when I thought the anxiety might pass, a new surge would roll me. "But some don't think so, right?"

He shook his head. "Nah, some just don't want it to, is all. Don't feel bad, Sophie, you know there's always going to be at least one jerk in the crowd."

"Yeah," I said with a snort. "Except in my case, the jerks try to kill me. What the hell?"

"You're just special, I guess." Toby shoved his feet into his boots and yanked the laces tight. "But don't worry. I think there's gonna be plenty of people around to protect you this time."

"Toby, one more question before you go. The Turning thing—is it going to hurt? I mean, I watched you change. It looked like it hurt. A lot."

"Yeah, about that." He peered into an antiquated mirror near the door, ruffling the front of his hair, smoothing back the sides. "I don't always shift like that. I was kind of...well, pissed off at the time and I wanted Rodrian to see something fierce. That's why it hurt so much. I was pushing out instead of pulling in and the energy was fighting me—you don't really follow me. Okay. But long story short, it's a little bit easier than that whole jump-out-of-my-skin thing."

"A little bit?"

He shrugged. "It's a big thing, Sophie, to change your body."

"You aren't making me feel better about it."

"I don't know how to. I want to, but you know I'm no good with words. Just—don't worry. It won't be anything like what happened to me that night when you guys had to watch me. The others said it's blessed or something. And, after the first time, your body doesn't forget what to do and it happens again on the next moon without thinking too hard about it. So, don't think about it."

He stepped near a china hutch and picked his wallet and the keys to Dahlia's car. "I have to go if I'm gonna pick her up on time. I promise we'll talk about Fraidy-Man and I will do everything in my power to charm her into submission. Stop worrying about it."

I walked out to the foyer with him, half-listening to his change of topic. Something about dinner and a game up in Philly and what all, I didn't know. All I could think about was the hum of power that had come into the house as we'd sat in the cottage suite, the hum that had drifted into the den and was now waiting for me. I felt it. That much was still me.

Toby waved goodbye and pulled the door shut behind him, leaving me in the foyer. I hesitated before turning to look toward the den. The doors were open. There was a fire going, even though the afternoon wasn't cold. I looked into that warm room, its burgundy carpets and dark oak and comfy couches and thought, *how perfect.*

It was easy to disregard the single memory of badness that had happened in that room, the day we lost Marek. That was the only bad thing. Lots of good things happened. A couple awkward things, too, but mostly good things. And just about all of them had something to do with Rodrian.

That last thought made my heart thump a bit. A throb of power from within that room responded. It was an invitation I could not ignore.

I processed into the room, careful steps. Only once I was all the way inside did I see him. Rodrian sat at the far end of the bar, carelessly thumbing through a screen on his phone. He didn't look up right away.

I took a long moment to look at him, to preserve the sight of him. He was in his work clothes, yet—dress pants, pressed shirt. No tie, no cufflinks (which, I think, were always my favorite part of his suited-up look), no jacket. Just dress casual. Sitting there, chin on his fist, he looked like an Armani ad with a Calvin Klein ad lying just beneath the surface. Oh, if only I were bold enough to snap a picture. But tonight wasn't the time.

"Hey," I murmured. My shields, bullet-proof and at the ready, kept me from discerning his disposition. I had to play it by human ear.

He picked up a bottle and finished the contents. Although the lighting was dim, I recognized the shape of the container. It was an emergency unit. Shiloh's treatment was over and done with for months, now, but for some reason he kept shelf blood around. I had assumed it made it possible to avoid asking me for mine.

He leaned over the bar and dropped it into the trash with a clatter. Very slowly, deliberately, he altered his seat until he was facing me, then raised his gaze to meet mine. His eyes were everyday-hazel, devoid of his inner light.

"You look better." His voice was polite. Too polite.

I shrugged. "I guess I feel a little better. Not—not much. But I can walk."

I tried to follow it up with a little bit of a laugh and a Sophia push of *Hey, I'm fine* but I stumbled. I couldn't pretend. My edges crumbled.

He pushed off the stool and came over to me, his hands running up and down my arms as if to warm me. Truth was, I felt so cold inside. I desperately wanted his warmth and I wanted him to chase away the foreign threat within me.

"Oh, honey." He wrapped an arm around my shoulder and steered me toward the sofa. Sinking to the cushions, he tugged me down with him, cuddling me up to him like a beloved plush animal.

I didn't resist. I just wanted to feel him. I wanted him to want me near him. "You're here."

"Why wouldn't I be?" He stroked my hair as I rested against his chest.

His scent encircled me, Brut and cherries, the faint metallic tang of blood. Those were the flavors I used to define him, everything I knew about him. "After this morning, I wasn't sure you would be. Because you hate me now."

"I could never hate you. You're—" He paused, maybe looking for the right word. "I just couldn't."

"Why not? I hate me."

He sighed, a deep regretful sound. "You can't do this to yourself. It's pointless."

I sighed and fidgeted with the buttons running down his chest. "But I have to do it."

"Why?"

"I have to do something." I tugged myself out of his warm embrace. "I have to feel like I am doing something."

"Sometimes, you can't."

"Well, I don't accept that." Scooting down to the other end of the couch, I drew up my feet and hunched into a stubborn ball.

"I know. I want to just throttle you for it. Which reminds me…" He reached into his shirt pocket and pulled out a business card holder. After pulling out a card, he slipped the case away again. "Here. This is the guy you want to talk to at the lab. He'll expect you."

I took the card he held out to me, glancing at the name. Kevin Somebody-or-another, Aerogenetek Laboratories. Marek's biotech labs, where he ran his clandestine hybrid research.

I'd asked Rodrian for a contact a few weeks ago. I wanted to see the research for myself. I wanted to see what they were missing because I wanted to bring Marek back.

Now what? I might soon be gone, too. Who would save him now?

"It's okay," he whispered. "I know you want to do something. You want to fix Marek. You want to fix yourself. I get it. Sometimes, though, you just need to sit back and not do anything."

"But, why?"

"Because these might be the last weeks we have. This might be it. Don't waste it for us, Sophie. Don't waste it for me. I lost my brother. My little girl grew up overnight and I hardly see her these days. And now you. You want to leave me."

I stared at the fire. *No, I don't. I don't, not at all.*

"The damage is done. You can't do anything about it," he said. "So I want you to do nothing about it. Live. Live these last weeks with me. Just live with me and let's be happy and if everything works out, we'll laugh about it and I'll take you someplace nice for your birthday."

May suddenly seemed half a lifetime away, instead of a matter of weeks. "And if it doesn't work out?"

"You spend your birthday in Germany with that son of a bitch." His voice tempered into solid steel, dark and pointed. "And I will spend the rest of my days taking my revenge."

He tilted his head, as if distracted.

"Speaking of the Devil," he said. His lips curled into a

smile that was far from cheerful.

The doorbell rang.

I let Rodrian sit and went to get the door. Dierk wore a suit, iron grey, his hair combed back into a tight tail bob. The fedora and Tommy gun were missing.

The henchmen weren't: Stohl, Janssen, and Olberich stood behind him. Their suits were not as slimly tailored. I suspected they were packing. Good little bodyguards.

However, I didn't think Rodrian would be pleased.

Without a word, I showed them in to the foyer. The den was shut, as were the office, the guest wing—every door was closed and I never heard it happen. Rodrian stood, one hand gripping his other wrist, in front of the den. He, too, was spruced up. Jacket, tie, cufflinks. All in a matter of a minute.

I shuddered, at a loss for what to think. Rodrian didn't do much hocus pocus around me and this was off the abracadabra scale.

Rodrian lifted his chin. "Dierk Adeluf, son of Schatten. I welcome you into our home."

He managed to sound congenial, yet his greeting didn't have a congenial effect on Dierk, who stiffened and curtly bowed from the shoulders.

"Rodrian Thurzo. My thanks for this...hospitality."

"I have no men here, Adeluf." Rodrian tilted his head toward Olberich. "Do I need my men?"

Dierk still hadn't looked at me. "I see no reason we cannot speak with civility."

He lifted his hand and his boys went back outside.

When the door had clicked shut, Dierk smiled. It was just as phony as his half-smile. And he still didn't look at me. "Now. I assume we will speak in private?"

Rodrian nodded and did his restaurant bow, one hand sweeping to indicate the formal parlor. I rarely went into the parlor or the adjoining dining room. They were stiff and unaccommodating and straight out of a showroom. "We will be comfortable in here. This way."

Dierk stepped off with a click of heel on the tile and passed me without a glance. I trailed behind them but, at the threshold, Rodrian paused and turned, blocking me.

"I will call you when you may rejoin us," he said. Spreading his hands, his gaze on mine, he grasped each of the pocket doors and tugged, thumping them shut between us.

I retreated to the office upstairs, dutifully dragging my black cloud along. A hotter emotion brewed deep down, taking the energy from my constant anxiety and giving it a fierce head. I stomped from one side of the room to the other, trying to blow off that steam.

It had been a long time since I had paced. It'd been even longer since I did it cracking my knuckles and imagining new ways to clobber Rodrian.

What made the pacing torturous was the fact that this

mood would have called for music, loud music. Metal music. Most notably, *Turn of the Wheel*'s second studio release, third track. And I refused to give that song or its creator the pleasure of being played.

The bastard.

And that other bastard.

At length, I gave up. I couldn't sustain a good stomping without the soundtrack accompaniment so I just went out on the balcony. It was still light out, and a balmy breeze swept up from the field, fragrant and full. Deep breaths of the sweet air calmed me. Bird song and bug droning drifted up from the yard.

When a familiar cry sounded overhead, I smiled, despite a very different emotion hovering right behind.

Watching the falcon make its swooping passes overhead—so hard to describe in a word how I felt. I'd always admired the grace of a large bird in flight, always saw the art and the magic of every drop of wing, every tilt of steering. In another life, I would have been blessed to see this bird every time I walked outside, this magnificent creature that always appeared out of nowhere and took flight just for me.

In another life, it would be just a bird.

The French door clicked behind me, startling me. Dierk stepped out, looking at me for the first time. He'd taken off his jacket and loosened his collar and sleeves. Well, I was still pretty miffed at the whole thing from earlier so I ignored him. Taste of Your Own Medicine Sophie, that's me.

"Thurzo asked me to convey his regrets." Dierk sounded like he had no clue he'd landed himself in the dog house. "An urgent matter required his attention."

Figured. Rodrian had to know he'd be in for a stiff ranting so he chickened out and scrammed. "Did he say what the matter was?"

"No, but she was tall and very...persuasive."

Aurelia. Of course. Bitch came for her puppy. Oh, wait, that's more of a Were insult. Let me think about it a while.

"He told me you would be up here and to, ah, tread softly." Dierk eyed me and tapped his palms together. "He was generous in his advice."

"Don't worry, pal." I refused to look at him. "I'm not one to commit treason."

"Nice choice of words. You sound like you have come to an acceptance of sort."

"Didn't say you were my king. However, your boys might not appreciate me giving you a tight slap."

Dierk walked to the edge of the balcony, a few feet away from me, and rested his forearms on the rail. Bird song came to us in layers: the sharp whistles of robins down in the yard, who always seemed to be complaining about something; the rapid-fire rapping of a woodpecker in the trees to the left of the house; the back-and-forth chirps of a pair of cardinals who claimed the patio area as their own and frequently gave the grill hell for being too shiny.

Sometimes, it was a downright racket. A pretty one, but a racket all the same.

The yard was a cacophony at the moment. He surveyed the yard, the field and trees beyond, eyes crinkling as he did. "So, you are taking advantage of this fine weather. Bird watching, hmm?"

Wouldn't it just blow his mind if he knew, I thought. "How'd you guess?"

"I apologize for earlier." He bowed his head slightly. "I could not acknowledge you at that particular moment. It was protocol."

"Stuff your apology. It was rude."

He leaned on one arm and faced me. "You will learn to

accommodate the times when business is business. It is simply a necessary thing."

"Hopefully, I won't. All this king garbage is annoying."

He chose not to answer. Very diplomatic of him, since it wouldn't have gotten either of us any closer to peace.

The falcon called out, close by. Dierk looked up and searched the skies. A familiar shape crossed overhead, soaring over the open fields.

"Can it be?" He pointed. "That falcon—too large to be peregrine. Wings too broad, tail too long. And the spotting—"

He looked at me, mouth open in a delighted *ah*. "That's a gyrfalcon. See the lazy wing beats? He owns the sky. King of falcons. Falcon of kings."

He tipped his head, his brows drawn. "But—gyrfalcon aren't abundant here, are they?"

"I don't know much about birds." To myself, I added: not even the ones who used to be people.

He turned his gaze back to the bird, which paced the sky over the field across from my balcony. Its *hyaik-hyaik-hyaik* calls were sharp and full of warning.

Dierk just laughed. "He's mad, that one. He is threatened. Something distresses him and he wants to scare it off."

Yeah, I silently agreed. Like maybe the werewolf standing next to me.

"Is there a falconry nearby?" he asked.

Another noncommittal shrug. "A place closer to Philly has an observatory."

"Gyrfalcons are noble, noble birds. I wouldn't mind hunting with one again. My father hunted, his father before him. Sport of kings. Looking at that bird makes me long for the past. I wonder—"

My muscles locked at the curiosity in his voice. I

followed Marek uneasily in his progress, arcs that brought him closer with each pass.

Dierk pointed toward Marek's memorial. "I see the great perch down in the yard. I wonder if that falcon could be persuaded to land."

"Oh," I said. "I don't think that's a good idea."

"Why not? It is not unheard of to train a wild raptor. Stohl would know. Our fathers hunted together."

"No!" I tucked my hair behind my ears. "I mean, not Stohl. I don't want him back here."

Dierk lifted his chin at me. "And?"

"And, what? Sorry if I don't get the whole bromance thing."

"You are anxious. Your scent changed. What else? More than afraid of Stohl. You are—you're concerned about the bird. You want it left alone."

I bit the inside of my cheeks. I watched Marek and tried to smell like it wasn't true.

"Sophie." He gentled his voice. "Tell me. I would not hurt you. I would not harm whomever or whatever you loved. There is a story about this majestic gyrfalcon that flies the skies to which he does not belong."

I laced my fingers together, wondering how to persuade him. "Will you protect it as you swore you'd protect me?"

"With my life." He placed his hand over his heart. "Kings owe fealty to each other."

I nodded, believing that he believed what he said. "Do you know who Horus is?"

"Egyptian god of the sun. Head of a falcon."

"Do you know why he is significant to the DV?"

"Of course." Dierk stepped closer, his gaze following the falcon. "Our legends share the same origin."

Well, that was a relief. "So, you know that if DV and Werekind blood mix—"

He pointed at the falcon. "Him?"

I nodded. "You understand."

"Yes, yes. *Wolfram*. Wolf-raven. We have our own version of the legends. Can it be? How do you know this?"

I shrugged. "I saw it happen."

"You saw it." His jaw dropped. Dierk gaped at me.

If I wasn't feeling so desolate inside I would have enjoyed his loss of composure. But I didn't. This was too important. "Yes."

"No one has ever seen it happen."

"I kid you not."

To my amazement, he laughed, an open-mouthed, wide-eyed laugh of boyish disbelief. "Amazing! Tancred will be speechless!"

He chattered on, his accent clipping the syllables into mouthfuls of excited unintelligibility. His voice droned and I zoned, finding it hard to enjoy his enthusiasm.

His hand, a soft touch upon my shoulder, brought me back. "Are you all right?"

"I'm fine." Actually, I felt irritable again and I felt like showing it.

"You didn't hear what I said."

I stepped over to one of the patio chairs and flopped down. "Okay, so I didn't. Your German was invading. What did you say?"

"I asked, who was it?"

I'd been expecting the question; I'd even expected direct delivery. Even so, I felt like I'd been slapped hard between the shoulders.

"Did you know him?" he persisted.

"Yes," I said.

His expression darkened, as if he understood the reason for my reluctance to answer. "Do you—not want to tell me? Was it someone you cared for?"

I met his gaze and took several breaths before answering. "Yes. Very much."

"Ah." He shifted uncomfortably, joyous curiosity gone. "Explains much."

"What do you mean?"

"Your fascination with birds. It is just one bird, I see, that holds your attention. The *Wolfram*, I think, knows you, too."

I closed my eyes for a long moment, feeling an odd dry pain behind the lids.

"Explains much about you and I, as well," he said.

"This has nothing to do with you."

Dierk's posture changed. Gone was the easiness of our familiarity. It had been replaced with dissatisfaction and rigid formality. For the first time since meeting, he held himself away from me, like a stranger. "It has everything to do with why you do not accept me."

"I don't need a bird to tell me I don't want to be Were."

"True. You have your own valid reason why my people are such a repulsive mass. But always I have felt the presence of another." He crossed his arms and scanned the sky, trying to conceal his clenched fists. "The *Leni* would never have selected a woman with a mate."

"I have no mate." I shook my head, irritated that I could use the word so easily.

"I see, and I understand much more now." He strode over to me, leaned to grip my arms and pull me up from the chair. He held me up to his face, fingers tight with anger. "And if this is why you make misery of what should be a time of discovery and wonder—"

A piercing scream sounded startlingly close and the bird dove, skimming our heads and making me duck. The falcon, its plumage a breath-taking pattern of black checks on white, pulled up in a spread of dark-tipped wings to land on the rail a few feet from us. It had never come this close before. Its hooked beak looked deadly, its talons like weapons.

It screamed its rage, a guttural *kak-kak-kak*, finding purchase even on the curved stone rail. I jumped in surprise.

But not Dierk. He nodded and calmly released me, stepping backwards away from me.

The bird quieted, clicking closer, one dagger-like talon at a time.

"See," he said, his voice taut as a fist. "The *Wolfram* protects his mate. It would have attacked me if I hadn't moved away from you. That I would live to see a myth made flesh—that it would be here, where I kneel in front of yet another myth. That I would be trapped between the two."

He fell silent, half-smile disappearing for the first time, his face taking on weight and his shoulders sagging. Dierk looked more man than king. "I am already slave to one unstoppable force. I refuse to be subject to another."

"What's that supposed to mean?"

"I am following my destiny." He jabbed at his chest with one thumb, anger in every line of his body. "The moon has chosen you. Not me. The *Leni* is not a choice. But I give the moon more credit than this."

My temper had started to creep upwards. Did he dare reprimand me? "You make it sound like I'm doing something wrong."

"You are and you aren't. You cannot help what you are. Nor can I. I was born to this life and this rule. Finding my own mate has never been an option. I put my trust in tradition and destiny."

"Yours isn't the only destiny at stake here. It takes two mates to. . .well. You know."

"Two mates. One destiny."

"Wrong. Hello? I had my own destiny, thank you very much, your highness, before you came to town."

"The *Leni* involves both of us."

"Because of you. I didn't need a mating ritual to decide who and when I love. Your *Leni* doesn't get to cancel my life."

"It's not cancelling anything."

"Oh, no? So I get to grow a fur coat every month and what?" I sliced at the air between us with my palms. "Keep being Sophia? Keep my job at *The Mag*? Live here? That's lovely, isn't it, a mate who lives on the other side of the ocean. Can't you see? It might be your destiny, but what if it isn't mine?"

"Do you believe your destiny is to be with the *Wolfram*? Is that more satisfying? Quite hypocritical, in my opinion. You disparage my people because we are not human enough. The *Wolfram* isn't human at all! I shift. I am not trapped in an animal's form. How is that creature better?"

"I never said it was."

"Yet your heart is bonded."

That was it. I decided to drop my veneer, my careful shield, and let him see me for what I was—a wretched well of agony. With a belly breath, I relaxed my barriers, not knowing what he'd sense but knowing this was the only way.

"My heart is frozen." My throat hurt, wanting to wail but forced to form intelligible words. Each word was carved in that pain. "It's trapped in this form, it's unforgiving and unchanging. I'm stuck on the past. The present keeps taking me further and further away and I am powerless to stop it."

I saw something register in his eyes, their quick shift as he sought a way to process it. He reached out and ran his palm against my arm, long strokes meant to comfort. "That is what destiny is."

My hands fisted. "Stop talking about destiny!"

"That *Wolfram* is the reason you won't love me."

Didn't he get it yet? It wasn't only about my desperate wish to escape this Leni. I just wanted all the bad to undo itself. I wanted to rewind back to the day I faced the Conclave, the day the Sophia first manifested. That was the first time Marek had smiled at me. I wanted to go back and live in that smile forever and I wouldn't ask for anything else ever again.

But I couldn't go back, could I? I wasn't holding onto a bird in the present. I wanted to hold on to a happiness in the past. It was selfish but I could never outrun it. How could I love someone else when I couldn't let go of Marek?

I couldn't tell him he was right. It would shift some of this onto him when Dierk had absolutely no role in this tragedy. He deserved more than *It's not you, it's me.* I tried to soften my voice so the words wouldn't land as hard a blow. "That bird is the ghost of something that never stopped haunting me."

Dierk shut down on me. His mouth a thin, pale line, his eyes wooden, he'd taken in more than I had intended. A flash of regret turned into a lingering burn as I watched him distance himself from me. What had I expected? I had let my heart and my words articulate my feelings as accurately as I could. I couldn't have possible expected him to say *Sure, I get it, we're cool.* Not when I had basically just told him that I had never wanted him in my life.

"He must have been a hell of a man if you are still bound by the pains of losing him." He turned away, taking a few steps before sweeping out his arm toward the falcon. "Can I at least know the name of the one who is turning my life into quagmire?"

What would it hurt now? "Marek—"

"Thurzo," he finished in a stony voice. "Of course. It would be him."

He cast a contemptuous glance at the bird, which ruffled its feathers and lifted its beak in a dismissive gesture. Dierk raked back his hair and shook his head before stalking back inside, leaving me alone with a rather smug-looking falcon.

After a moment, even the bird took off, leaving me alone.

Completely alone.

New moon | 0% visible

A slamming door jolted me from an uneasy sleep, the force strong enough to send a tremor through my bed.

Groggy, I sat up, stretching out an inquisitive finger of power, trying to identify who was making all the racket. It didn't take a genius. The Demivamp's signature was full-blast and self-secure, and would have glittered if it could.

Shiloh. She didn't know how to temper her energy yet. Who needed an alarm clock when you lived with Shiloh Thurzo?

As if I needed an alarm set for the middle of the night. Her nocturnal habits had gotten real old, real fast. Sleep was a sacred institution for me, and Shiloh had become a heretic.

When she made noise at this hour, there was usually a story behind it. I drew a deep breath and shoved off the blankets, much to the dismay of my sleeping partner, who'd stretched and hooked his back claws into my arm when I reached down to settle him. Sheesh. Cats were so high maintenance.

I slipped on my robe and padded out, grabbing my cell phone from the charger on the way out. Once in the hallway, I detected another pulse of power, this one subtle and guarded, just as the sounds of voices echoed from the foyer.

"Fine!" Shiloh's voice was shrill enough to raise the hair on my neck. "Enough already, I said I'd go!"

I couldn't quite catch the quiet response. When I stretched out my senses to inquire, I came up against a wall of power. Solid and impenetrable. I could have powered through it, but then I'd have to give up my curiosity. I knew who it was.

That voice didn't have a calming effect on Shiloh. "Well, considerate people leave notes when they disappear in the middle of the night. She's driving me to school tomor—"

Her companion cut her off. This time, the speaker made no effort to conceal her voice—or the hint of aggression behind it. A shove of mind-your-own-business made me teeter on my mental feet.

The message was unmistakable. A stranger in my own home. Don't belong here. Get out.

Shiloh's power flared. She released a wave of energy that I felt all the way upstairs, as strong as getting socked in a pillow fight. Every door in the house slammed simultaneously with a floor-shuddering thump.

Every door, that is, but mine. I spun, seeing the door to my quarters had closed gently behind me. Shiloh shielded me, even as she lost her temper.

Her voice rose in a conversation-ending roar. "I said, okay, Mother!"

Another slam, this time from the front door, echoed into

the sudden silence. I heard the sound of a familiar high-pitched engine and tires scraping on pavement as their car took off down the driveway.

I wilted as the flash-flood of adrenaline subsided. Hooray. Aurelia was here. No wonder Shy was so shrieky. Hell, I knew I was thrilled. I wrapped my robe tight, my shields tighter. I hated how Aurelia got to me. She was a razor-sharp wedge, slicing between me and the people I loved.

And I knew one day, the razor's edge would tilt and take it all away.

With a sigh, I continued down the hall toward the kitchenette in Shiloh's suite, too awake to think about going back to my room. I stuck a mug of water into the microwave before swinging the cabinet doors open wide. Decisions, decisions. I scanned the shelves crammed full of Keurig boxes and hot chocolate before reaching for a can of instant chai.

When the microwave beeped, I took out the mug and carefully measured the prescribed amount of powder into the water. After a moment of deliberation, I dumped an extra spoonful of chai powder into the cup. Really no need to go back to sleep so soon.

Giving the cup a half-hearted stir, I turned toward the snack bar where I'd dropped my phone. I stumbled over something, biting back a curse when pain lanced through my toes. The offender was a pair of black army-type boots, scuffed and stained. Despite the lack of a designer label, they belonged to Shiloh. Her new look: slayer-in-training.

Little Miss Prissy was out learning how to be a vampire killer.

You'd think I'd find it a tad bit more objectionable but honestly, I was all for it. I knew what she was learning how to kill and, knowing they were dead already, I had no moral complaints.

I just worried.

I felt the same way about Shy following in her sister's footsteps that perhaps parents do when enrolling their children in martial arts classes. They'll learn to defend themselves. They'll learn courage and self-confidence. It's for their own good.

Except kids didn't usually get killed in judo class.

Up until now, Shiloh's greatest weapons were her teen-aged disdain and her ability to spot a fake Louis Vuitton at fifty yards. Now, she was adept at Filipino stick fighting and knew eleven different ways to use a garrote.

I didn't worry all the time, especially not when she was down in Marek's gym. I watched her idea of a workout. She was just as twisted as Marek had been. God, I shudder to think how proud he'd be.

I didn't worry when she came in at three in the morning on a school night because sleep didn't seem to be a requirement anymore. Apparently, her cusp was a permanent caffeine high—she had become utterly tireless.

I only worried when Aurelia was with her.

Whenever Aurelia came around, Shiloh's power took on a different tint, a gun-metal edge. Admittedly, I'm just a human and a wussy one, at that. I knew next to nothing about what Brianda and her patrols actually did. But I knew aggression when I saw it, and I knew it when I felt it. And I felt it around Aurelia.

Aggression could have been a positive factor when training to be a slayer but Shiloh was new to the emotion. She wasn't focused enough yet to use aggression as a driving force. It made her reckless, impulsive. I didn't know if it was lack of control, an inability to harness a strange new source of power, or if she pushed herself to try and impress the mother who had suddenly re-appeared after a lifelong absence.

I tried not to judge Aurelia, even though Rodrian was not the same since she showed up on our doorstep. Whatever was between them was unequivocally their business, even if it seemed it was spilling over into Rodrian's relationship with me. I tried to remain aloof and not give Rodrian more grief than she already gave him.

I didn't like Aurelia. But for Rode and Shiloh's sake, I tried really hard not to hate her.

Rubbing my toes, I decided I hadn't broken them. Just to be safe, I looked around to make sure she hadn't left a sword lying around. Next time I tripped over something, I might not be so lucky.

I was on my way back to my room when I paused in front of the office door, a voiceless command to stop, wait. I tried to peer into the inky darkness. Usually, moonlight would spill through the French doors, diffusing into a cool glow in the sheer curtains. Tonight, the office was as dark and still as a coat-filled closet.

And I went in, anyway. Something was outside, and it wasn't DV.

I stepped out onto the balcony, fingers of cool air slipping beneath the collar of my sleep shirt. The black sky was dotted with punctuations of starlight, blending seamlessly with the row of trees beyond the field. New moon tonight—a dark sky, dark and unforgiving. I had a vague recollection of someone calling my name but, reaching out to survey the inhabitants of the house, I sensed no one whose power matched the timbre of that voice.

Whoever it was, she was invisible.

When I subconsciously identified the speaker as female, a presence began to unveil itself much like a blush, a soft glow of somethingness. Standing on the balcony, I saw no one. I heard no one. I felt no one.

And yet, she was there.

Sophie.

I tilted my head, hearing my name but not. It was directionless, a shadowy echo. It came from somewhere outside my head. Or did it?

A light plucking along the back of my neck made me jump and swat at my hair. It wasn't an insect. It felt like fingers. "What do you want?"

The air pressure changed.

Who am I?

I shook my head and hugged my waist, feeling chilly and bare. The scent of earth was strong, earth and the unfurling oaks beyond the field. "I haven't the faintest idea."

Yes, you do. There was a smile in that mind-voice, a teasing tone. *You've always known.*

"Vampire?"

Nothing so trivial. I am more. I am nearly all, and you know me.

Suddenly, I remembered a similar cryptic exchange I'd once had with another female I'd never quite figured out. But this wasn't Dorcas, either. Whatever it was, it was massive.

The air pressure increased, pressing my eardrums and thinning my breath. The mental bear hug threatened to take me to my knees, and I reached out to grasp the rail of the balcony.

"Stop!" My voice clacked against the stone of the house, a slight repeat against the trees. "Just leave me alone."

You don't understand what has happened to you. The voice was coy, patronizing. *This is a process you cannot hope to deter. The wheels have been set into motion.*

"What are you?"

You know. You can never truly forget. No one escapes a destiny. The voice took on darker tones. *Not even in death.*

A shrill scream lit the night air, close by, and I staggered back toward the door. An owl. That's all.

And that's all I needed. I ducked inside and slammed the door shut, whispering a breathy prayer that, whatever that voice was, it couldn't follow me inside. I hurried back to bed, trying to forget how dark that voice had become, and how I'd swear I could still hear its smile.

Saturday morning, and I couldn't sleep. What a crime. I spent an hour cleaning my rooms wearing little more than my bathrobe and a pair of flip-flops and argued with the cat. Apparently, he'd been having no trouble sleeping at all. No matter what I did to occupy myself, I kept hearing those words from the night before, a crystalline repeat.

No one escapes a destiny.

Not even in death.

I wasn't sure if it had been meant as a threat but, paranoid as I'd become lately, I sure took it as one.

As I carried my laundry basket out of the bedroom, I spied the books I'd brought back from Marek's place. I hadn't even looked at them since bringing them home. Tucking Marek's journals into the pockets of my robe, I lugged my linens down to the laundry. Once back upstairs, I went to sit in the tri-suites, reading while I waited for a pot of tea to brew.

I spread the books over the top of the snack bar, not even knowing where to start. Rodrian had given me the stack of hard-bound journals, the covers worn, the corners abused from being tucked into pockets. Marek had dated his journals, perhaps as a reference, in the inside of the front covers. Did he ever go back and read what he'd written, many years later?

I saw the years he'd written inside those covers and refused to believe them. The earliest was dated 1863. My immigrant ancestors hadn't even arrived in America and Marek was already keeping a diary.

At first, I tried to joke it away, a slight comment about hot older guys, but when it came to Marek's age, I had a truly hard time wrapping my brain around it. Someone who had been so warm, so alive, couldn't possibly be that old.

His penmanship was an even scrawl, if not overly flourishing. Like Marek, the letters were lean and constant, the words precise and objective. One journal described business transactions and a subsequent purchase of land in Balaton village. The street references made me smile in recognition and I realized he described having bought large plots in outlying Chaucer's Square and downtown. If he'd retained ownership of all that land—

I shuddered. It meant he owned huge interests in Balaton, at least at one time. Since I couldn't imagine him giving up—or (perish the thought) losing—anything, it meant Marek's estate went far beyond a cottage and a townhouse and a biotech company.

Closing my eyes, I pinched the bridge of my nose, willing the looming headache to keep away. Rodrian said I'd been granted his estate. Oy.

I shut the journal with a snap. Enough of that one.

Picking up one that looked newer than the others, I peeked at the date. 1981. Whew. Practically yesterday. Flipping to a random page, I noted his handwriting hadn't changed much.

July, 1981

Amarisa returned from the north today. She left a fortnight ago after receiving a letter from her superiors. She has a haunted look in her eyes, one that I've seen before.

Pain, for another. Someone she loves is suffering and she is powerless to comfort them.

We spent the afternoon in the city, she feeding the bold squirrels that have come to recognize her. Amarisa insists on shelling the pistachios for them. The little scavengers are spoiled and complain loudly when I toss them unshelled nuts. I tell her she makes wasted efforts, but she pays no attention to me. She says that a kindness offered, even if it isn't returned, still increases the sum of goodness in the universe.

I admit I don't understand her position on kindness. I might have once, but those days are rusted and gone.

Times such as these, I admit I am not the companion she needs. Our past binds us, secrets and all, and within her light she makes much room for my shadow. All I can do is listen to the truths she is permitted to tell and pretend that I understand why she would chose a vocation that lends itself to such tremendous grief.

I know I would never be one to bear such pain. That would require a soul, and I'm perfectly aware I do not possess the prerequisite qualities. Times like this make me glad my own fosterling is grown. I am not a compassionate man.

Not now. Not for a very long time.

I lowered the journal and closed the page on my finger. Marek's words were difficult to read. They called up the memories of when we first met; he was so dark, so tortured, and although I only caught glimpses of his shadows, I knew they must have run deep.

His journal entries provided insights to the terrible past he'd hinted about, those peeks when his somber shell would stretch full and the cracks would leak his darkness. Who was Amarisa? He called her a companion. Was she a lover? A friend? All I could do was send a desperate prayer to Heaven that she had been a source of comfort to him. Reading that entry made my heart ache, knowing he'd suffered so much in the past and I had been not there for him.

I was in elementary school when Marek wrote this. What would a skinny kid with freckles and a frayed ponytail have done? Especially not a skinny kid who, at the time his journal entry had been written, was still trying to deal with the loss of her little brothers.

With a sigh, I closed that journal, too, and dropped it on the snack bar. Silly me, thinking Marek's diary would distract me in a happy way. He had a funny way of reminding me of all the things I'd lost.

Tea brewed and poured, I went into Shiloh's room to strip her bed while the tea cooled. Although she didn't spend much time here, I wanted her room to be ready for her when she came home.

I seemed to be going through a lot of motions. All these little tasks, chores to pre-occupy myself, taking care of people who really didn't need to be cared for.

What if I was just treading water? I was being carried along on strange currents. Wouldn't it be easier to swim along with it, and perhaps find a resolution further downstream? As it was, I was in completely over my head, and eventually I'd exhaust myself with the mere effort to stay afloat.

And why was I doing Shiloh's laundry, anyway? She knew each of the household staff, seemed comfortable with their duties and their position. Rodrian was always scolding me for not letting them do their job. He hated wasted money and he swore every load of wash I did on my own cost him unnecessary payroll dollars.

Don't you have enough to do? he'd ask.

I wasn't sure I did. Not anymore, anyway.

Swiping the journals into a stack, I picked them up and lay them on top of the bed sheets I'd retrieved from Shiloh's room. Perhaps for now I'd tuck the books onto a bookshelf in Marek's tiny library. That's when I thought about the other book Rodrian had brought back for me. The canon.

I passed one of the staff on the way to the staircase. She noticed the wash basket on my hip. "I can take those for you, Miss Galen, if you'd like."

Any other day I would have said no, thanks and scurried off but the image of Marek's big dusty book wouldn't budge from the front of my mind. Maybe just this once. I nodded and took my books off the top before handing the basket over to her. She smiled, perhaps thinking she'd made a tremendous breakthrough with me.

There was a breakthrough, all right, but the maid would be very disappointed that she couldn't take credit for my sudden ability to let something go.

Waxing gibbous | 2% visible

The afternoon sped past while I pored over the old tome. In fact, I may have even added a new butt-grove to Marek's ugly armchair. Once I sat down and started flipping pages, I didn't move until Fraidy came in to holler at me. I'd forgotten to feed him. A rumble in my own belly reminded me I'd forgotten to feed me, too.

How could I even begin to figure that book out? That it was a volume in a sequenced set was certain, as long as the crude table of contents was correct. The list described a five-book set of which this was the second. *Scriptura Semideis.*

Each chapter was in a different language, with hand-drawn images and woodcut pictures of every conceivable type. I alternately used an online translator and a magnifying glass, trying to pick out some kind of clue. What this book needed was a scholar, maybe a college department full of scholars. Not some broad with a smart phone app.

I flipped through the pages, translating what I could and skipping what looked as impossible as Organic Chemistry. Eventually, I came across a picture that looked very familiar. I'd located the page Marek had originally shown me, the spindly drawing of a Grecian-type woman in robes, holding a lantern that emitted a cloud-like plume, under which was the word SOPHIA. The text surrounding the image was in Greek. There'd be no way I could translate it unless I downloaded a Greek keyboard.

A thin scrap of velvet still marked the page. Instead of hanging free, the end was tucked into another page near the back of the book. Curious, I turned to the other page.

The language was completely foreign to me, and there wasn't a single picture to give me a hit as to the nature of the text. It was footnoted six ways to Sunday, though.

Someone had made hand-written notes in the margin. Although the pencil was faint, I recognized the even scrawl of script.

And, the notes were in English. Thank you, Marek.

Although the printed text was foreign, I could read Marek's notes with ease. The phrases "Horus equation" and "hybrid machine" and a few other equally curious terms, with references to other sources, presumably the other canons.

Where did Marek get this book? And why did he make these strange notes in them?

I turned a page and noticed a thin sheet of yellowing paper tucked inside. Unfolding the paper, I looked at the pencil drawing that had been hastily drawn upon it. A triangle, each corner bearing an odd symbol and one of three terms: *puer lunae, puer solis, filia oceani.* Large letters below it: *Divinum Coniunctione.*

What struck me as the oddest part was that the first

corner, *puer lunae*, was crossed out and in a different hand, were the words *enfant de la magie*. In bigger letters, below the original title, same hand as the previous alteration: *L'appareil.*

I pondered this picture a moment. Marek had drawn it, someone else had added to it. Who? And what did it mean?

Most of all, why did it make me think that badness was coming?

"Sophie?"

My attention was broken by the sound of a young woman calling me from the hallway. I shut the book with a thump and left it on the chair before running out to the hall, mysterious diagram forgotten.

Shiloh was home.

After a barrage of hugs that only left my ribs bruised, she half-carried me to the tri-suites. She needed to check out the fridge, she said. She'd been worried I had neglected it.

I grabbed a can of sweet tea and perched on a stool as she fixed herself a snack. First thing I noticed were her duffle bags. The second thing was that the door to the empty bedroom was closed. "What's up with that? Somebody come home with you?"

"Just my mother."

I paused mid-swig, unsure I heard right. "Aurelia?"

"Mmm hmm." Her voice was muffled while she peered through the fridge. Standing up and shutting the door, apparently disappointed at the holdings within, she scowled. "I'm supposed to be with Bree this weekend and instead she made me bring over some of her stuff. I get that she wants to bond, okay? But I'm almost eighteen. I lived this long without her. I don't know why she wants to push so hard. She said we need girl time."

"Shiloh, why do I feel like you are leaving out the one clue I need to understand what you're talking about?"

"I just told you. Mother is going to start staying over. She doesn't want me to be alone. I guess she reconsidered the position she maintained for the last seventeen years."

"Stay here?" That was a horrifying thought. "Why would she do that?"

She shrugged. "I guess some kind of latent nurturing instinct."

"You're fine here with me."

"But you won't be here anymore." She clung to me, suddenly, burying her face in my neck. "I know all about it."

"Your dad told you? But he said—"

"He didn't have to. I knew something was wrong for a while now. I came home a few days after you met that Were. You felt different. You feel different, now. It's like there is another person under your skin. Like a parasite. Maybe something less gross, but still." Her eyes unfocused, and I felt her power sweep across me, the way Greco's did whenever he scanned me. "You have a hitch hiker inside you."

What exactly could she sense? Apart from their enormity, Shiloh's cusped powers were a mystery to me. She didn't like talking about them with me, and I always got the impression that she was trying to protect me somehow. It never left me with a peaceful feeling. Still, maybe now was the time to come clean, about her and about me. "We should talk about this."

"I don't need to. Mother told me everything I need to know. Look, I don't blame you. I know who he is. You have his CDs all over the office. But I never thought you'd hook up with a Were."

Whoa, Nelly. I held up both hands and pushed the thought away. "I didn't hook up with anyone."

"It's okay, I get it. Everyone needs a mate. It's all I hear about from mother, anyway. Sometimes I think she's trying to arrange my marriage or something."

"It's not a done deal, Shy. There is still a chance—"

"No. There's not. Mother says I have to accept it. When the full moon comes, you'll be gone." She took a deep breath and hugged me again. "I just want to spend time with you while I can. While you're still you."

I was stunned. I'd been written off. Is this how Rodrian felt, too? Like I was already gone?

I tried to shake the feeling of being packed up and ready to ship. She chatted while we ate dinner together, after Shiloh had run downstairs to whip the kitchen staff into a frenzy. She told me all about school and cross-training with Bree and all about the amazing creature Aurelia was.

Shiloh didn't love her, exactly, but admired her, without doubt. Aurelia was a woman of means—style, wealth, ambition, although Shy didn't mention the fights I'd overheard. Shiloh didn't identify her as a parent—there was no affection, no parental protection. I got the feeling Aurelia was fostering a peer-like relationship.

Just great. Aurelia was the last role-model I wanted for Shiloh, what with her egotistical obsession with herself. I wanted Shiloh to have a better chance at learning how to grow into an emotionally-balanced woman.

Not that I was capable of providing an ideal example for relationship development. But I did want her to be happy. At least I'd encourage her to learn from my mistakes, instead of Aurelia's desire to encourage making those mistakes.

I wasn't comfortable voicing my concerns, though How I felt about Aurelia was my own personal opinion. Shiloh wasn't my daughter. I didn't have the right to influence her.

Or did I?

I was still Sophia. I still had a duty.

And I was failing at it, more and more, with every new sliver of moon that shined each night.

Waxing gibbous | moon 12% visible

King Pissy Pants didn't call me once over the weekend. He
didn't show up Monday to take me to work and he didn't
call me at lunch. By two o'clock, when I had thoroughly
enough of Jasmine—

Oh, yeah. Forgot to mention. I met my intern, Jasmine.
Joy to the freaking world.

First off, I didn't like the way she already knew her way
about my office. She knew what files went where, she knew
how to log into the column account, and she was extremely
adept at following my submission schedule. Jasmine knew
the office layout, knew each department and their purpose,
and knew who to circumvent if I wanted something done
in a hurry.

She was a good intern. God, I hated her.

I hated the way she wore her hair—a tight gelled-back

bun that gave her a phony plastic doll appearance. I hated the way she made condescending little noises as she read through the column work. I hated the way she'd dump out my mug every time I left my office (oh, I thought you were done with that, she'd say). But the worst of it?

I hated the way she'd make suggestions because they were good suggestions that I hadn't thought of first. She stirred my territorial instincts and sent them clawing to the surface. At two, I sent Jasmine out to the supply room for something I didn't need and I dialed Dierk's mobile number, keeping a hawkeyed lookout for her severe dark-blonde bun and her dark-rimmed eyes and her probably dark-intentioned pit of a soul.

"Yes?" No hello, no hi, Sophie. His voice sounded clipped and precise, more so than usual.

"Dierk? It's me."

Stiff inhale through his nose. "Yes. Sophie. Something you require?"

"No." His abruptness caught me off guard. I figured he'd be thrilled that I called. "I just…"

"If you do not need my urgent attention, I apologize but I am attending business. May we speak at a more convenient time?"

"Are you blowing me off?" I almost pulled the phone away from my ear to stare at it, I was so incredulous.

"Nothing of the sort. I am simply—preoccupied." His voice deepened at the end, curling itself around a secret. That throaty chuckle he added at the end infuriated me. It made absolutely no room for me.

I started to protest when there came a noise as if his phone rubbed against something, a clacking, then a new voice, close to the receiver.

"*Mein König* is busy, human. He'll call you when he has time for you. Maybe." The line went dead.

I knew that voice, although it took a second to penetrate. Cacilia.

Kind of killed the impulse to hit the redial button.

I moped all the way home. I don't know why his brush-off bothered me, but it did. I guessed part of me had pretty much decided I was stuck with him and he had just given me the heave-ho.

The TTS was in the driveway when I pulled up. That brightened my spirit. What did Rodrian and Dierk talk about Friday evening? Dierk had stormed off without saying anything and Rodrian left before I could ask. Maybe he'd share.

Rodrian was in the den, trying to look busy. Funny how he still thought he could fool me after all this time. His center was a coil of agony and conflict, and he expected me to believe he was only distracted by a stupid budget.

I lingered at the door, hesitant. "Hey."

He didn't look up. "Oh. You're here."

"Yeah, I—just came in. Are you busy?"

"Well, I have to get these documents to a courier but—" His briefcase was open on the bar, and several folders had been spread out. He stopped shuffling papers around and looked at me. Kind of. He wouldn't look me in the eyes. "I guess it can wait a minute."

I took a deep breath and ripped off the mental bandage. "You know I love you, Rode."

He flinched as if I fired a gun. "But?"

"But nothing." I spread my hands and ventured closer. "You're my family. I never wanted you to feel the way you've been feeling."

"It's not your fault." Rodrian shuffled his papers in a new order, a senseless pre-occupation of hands. It wasn't like him.

"Part of it is." I gently drew the papers out of his hands and lay them on the bar. "I didn't have to go out that night. I certainly didn't have to go backstage."

"You can't think like that."

"Trust me, I know that but, when I look at you, I do. I think I should have stayed here with you."

Rodrian backed away a step. "Your place isn't here with me."

"And Aurelia loves nothing more than to remind me. But I can forget her, Rode, because I remember what it was like before she showed up. You were willing to put me under glass and protect me like I was a fragile thing. I should have let you keep doing that but truth is—that's what made me go out that night. I was tired of being treated like a fragile thing. I love you and I know you feel the same—"

"No." His voice took on the hard edge I'd come to recognize. It was the sound of him trying to harden his heart against vulnerability, disappointment. He almost always used that tone when he talked about the way he felt about me, as if it was the source of his greatest pain. "Not the same way, and you know it."

Yes, I knew it. It shamed me because I also knew I had exploited that love in the past, just to feel wanted. I would exploit it again in a hot second if I thought it would solve any part of this mess. His pain should keep me from such selfish thoughts, but the depth of his feelings only enforced the conviction that I could keep doing it without consequence.

I pulled my hair back, wanting to rip it, tear it, punish myself. I didn't deserve to be Sophia. "So what? We can't have it. You said it yourself, my place isn't with you. For a little moment, I thought that I might actually have something on my own."

"Well, you found it." He didn't say it in a mean way. It was just a hard truth.

"Dierk says…" I glanced at him, hoping the name of his adversary wouldn't set him off. "Destiny has its way and we can't change it. Well, I think it's a load of horseshit."

He began to laugh but smothered it behind his hand. "And do you plan to do something about it?"

"Like what? I can't even get the cable company to give me free HBO for a week. Full moon is coming, Rode. I feel—wrong, like something is sliding around under my skin. I don't know what I can do to stop it from happening. I keep having weird dreams and my joints feel tight and—"

I didn't want to tell him about that woman's voice I'd heard the night before when I was out in the moonlight.

I didn't have to tell him.

"So." His throat moved, a painful-looking swallow. "It's really happening. I'm losing you."

Hearing it out loud from the person I trusted most in the world had a strangle-hold effect on me. "Don't say that."

"I have to. I have to say it so that it sinks in. It's the mistake I made with my brother. Maybe if it sinks in, I will accept it and it won't hurt so much."

I just gazed at him, my heart torn asunder by the pain in his power, and covered my mouth, peering over my fingers through a wave of tears.

"Maybe it still will hurt, all the same," he said. Pulling me against him, he tucked me under his chin and hugged me, tighter than he'd ever held me. I pressed full against him, wanting to feel as much of him as I could. He pushed his fingers into my hair on the back of my head, encircling me.

The sensation, so solid and real, gave me anchor once more. As long as I had him, I could find the strength to face another day. A temporary reprieve from the horror.

The front door slammed and he jumped, the shock causing him to release me. He ran his palms over his thighs and peered through the door toward the sound of clicking heels.

"Let yourself in, why don't you?" I glared at Aurelia when she posed herself in the doorway.

"You were busy." A tint of cold amusement colored her voice. "Didn't want to disturb such a tender moment."

What a liar. Her smile, that slit of ice, said it all.

Rodrian patted his pockets. "I need to run upstairs for my keys. Meet you outside, Aurelia."

His voice was low, heavy with something more than suggestion. I wondered if bossy jerk worked on a woman like her. She blew a kiss at him as he stalked past her, earning a stern look from him in reply.

I just pinched my lips together to keep from commenting and walked out.

"Where are you going, Sophia? Don't you want to chat until he comes down?"

She'd never been openly hostile toward me before. Now, I could hear the heat behind her words, her longing to burn me and cause me pain. "Don't you have someone better to torment?"

"No, I don't." She crossed her arms and smiled.

"Well, I don't hate myself enough to linger." I headed upstairs, intending to lock myself in my room.

"Rodrian doesn't need you, you know."

I froze mid-step. I should be running from confrontation like this. But no one came between me and my Demivamps, especially not that one. I gripped the bannister until my fingers paled beneath the strain, feeling a motion inside me kick up like a jet engine.

"For some insane reason," she continued, "he wants you, and I am getting tired of the energy I have to put into showing him his folly. He thinks he needs you, but I am happy to say that he is beginning to remember why he is my mate, not yours."

I twisted and dropped a contemptuous look on her. "Rode and I aren't like that. We don't—"

"Mmm." She waved her had at me. "Don't waste your time trying to convince me. He lusts after you with his heart, Sophia. He has a vulnerability, a weakness for sentimentality. But when you aren't around, he remembers his true nature. You aren't one of us, Sophia. You aren't even one of your own kind. You are only you. Sad, lonely you. And soon, Rodrian will forget you, just like Marek did."

A knot of flame tied itself around my stomach and I squeezed my eyes closed, holding my mouth shut with every ounce of constraint within myself. The jet engine was primed and waiting for a flip of the switch.

"You should be glad the Were have taken you." She strutted out into the center of the foyer and kept on. "You are not much of anything on your own."

I couldn't take anymore. I shot a shielded strike toward her, wanting to smack a Sophia-sized hole in her attitude. My touch was met with a blunt rebuke of sharp power when she slapped my intention aside.

She placed her hands on her hips, leaning into her stance. "Stop trying to tap me, or whatever nonsense it is you do. You cannot diminish my strength and you cannot weaken my position."

She wouldn't take a touch of Sophia? Fine by me. I stomped down stairs, readying a fistful of good ole fashioned Galen. I'd knock her on her stilettoed ass if it was the last thing I did.

Three feet from her, I realized I had no idea what her DV strength was. I could be fatally outmatched and not even know it. I hovered at the edge of my self-control and took a caustic tone. "You remind me of a bitch I once knew."

"I should hope I remind you of every bitch you ever knew." She bent her neck, bringing her that much closer to me, taunting. "I'd settle for nothing less."

"Aurelia, out." Rodrian hit the top step at a jog and hurried down the stairs. "Next time I tell you to wait outside, you will do it."

"Yes, darling." Aurelia waved her fingers at me before she sauntered out, leaving the door wide open in her wake.

"Soph..." Rodrian paused near me, licking his lips.

"Go, Rode." I rubbed my eyes, feeling like I'd overthought my place in his life again. "She's waiting for you."

He turned and doggedly walked out, and even the thump of the closing door wasn't enough to make me believe he'd actually done it.

He had really left me. To be with her.

Work sucked, if it was actually possible. I believe it was the first time I said that about my job at *The Mag*, which was pretty much the only constant good thing in my life.

It started the moment I walked in to my office.

My morning ritual never changed: I sat down, fired up the PC, opened my desk drawer, and took out my coffee mug. It was a bright purple monstrosity that had a cat's tail for a handle and the words CRAZY CAT LADY on it.

Today, I needed the comfort of my ritual more than ever because I craved a moment of normalcy. My home life, my anti-love life, everything was about as screwed up as it could get. I walked into my office, I sat, I punched the power button, and I reached down for my mug. But the mug wasn't there.

My mug was always there. I always cleaned and stowed away my mug at the end of every working day. It was my equivalent of punching a time card.

Looking around the room, I spied it on the window sill.

I got up and stomped over to the window snatching up the cup. Half-filled with Dr. Pepper, flat and sticky and definitely not mine.

I clenched my teeth at the sacrilege. Jasmine. I'd choke that girl. So much for punching in on time, I thought, as I stomped all the way to the break room so I could clean out my cup. When I passed Jasmine on the way back to my office, she looked at the cup and didn't say a word.

But she smirked at me, with her beady dollar store-cosmetic painted eyes and that smug look.

By lunchtime, I'd had all I could take before resorting to violence. Well, maybe not violence, *per se*. But definitely a lot of angry exhaling and slamming things around. I was pretty sure I could give her the ass-beating I couldn't give Aurelia but that would be bad for business.

Lucky for Jasmine, she left on her break without telling me where she was going. I would have had to respond to her, and it would have sounded really pissy.

I made sure she had completely left the office before walking over to Barb's office. By the positioning of her eyebrows and the way she chewed the cap of her red pen, Barb was having just as shitty a day as I was. Good. That made me feel a little better.

She didn't look up when I flopped into the chair. "Something on your mind?"

"Why, yes." I feigned a sweet tone and smiled. "My boss hates me, because she gave me an intern from hell."

"Now, Sophie. She's not that bad."

Not that bad? We weren't talking about biscotti from a vending machine here. Not that I wouldn't have minded if someone jammed her up inside one, sideways. "She's a little witch!"

"Oh." She sat back and put her glasses on her desk. "I was wondering if you were going to react this way."

"What way, disgusted? I dread coming here just because I know I'm trapped in close confinement with her for eight hours a day."

Barbara tapped her thumb on her desk, her gaze lowered. "I'm really disappointed in you, Sophie."

"Me?" I choked on spit and almost needed a slap on the back. "How about in her?"

She folded her hands in her lap and gave me the soberest stare I'd ever seen coming out of her eyes. "I never took you for a bigot."

"A b—what?"

"I've never asked you to hold back anything, but this is not acceptable in the office. You can't disparage someone on their choice of religion."

"Religion? Being a bitch is a religion now? Who knew?"

"You knew. Wiccan practitioners are to be given the same consideration as any others. Really, I am surprised to find out you have something against witches."

I just stared. Agape. "She's...a witch."

"Yes, and if she or anyone else comes in with a report of your anti-wiccan views, I'll have no choice but to call human resources. Please, Sophie, don't let it come to that."

I sank back into the chair, feeling utterly deflated. Over the last few years, I learned that my city and my world and my life were crawling with people who weren't actually people or who were only people some of the time. I'd been hunted by vampires and chased by werewolves, one of who wanted to marry me. Or something. All this time I'd been hiding it from my oldest friend because I didn't want her to find out I had a psychic entity living in my brain.

And she was accusing me of bigotry? Holy fricken wow.

That was it. I was clearing the air. I wasn't going to keep up this charade any longer. I hated keeping secrets. I'm too lazy to be good at it and I talked way too much to keep up my guard. And besides—I loved Barb. Not just *I-love-working-with-her* but *I-love-her-as-much-as-I-can-love-another-person-without-it-getting-awkward*.

She was my friend. She was my foster family. She always told me the truth, she always gave me what I needed, and she always made me feel a lot less alone in the world.

And all I'd done, since the night Marek pulled me off the top of a skyscraper, was lie to her.

I couldn't let these days pass with her possible last memories of me being a bigoted liar.

"Barb, I—" I steeled myself, wondering where to begin, ready to tell her everything. I wasn't even afraid of losing her because I felt like hiding my life from her was more like pushing her away, even if she didn't know it.

That's when I looked down at my hand. Two scars. One Rodrian's, the other Stohl's.

Damn it. I couldn't tell my secret without telling theirs.

This was not the time to come clean, not when I wasn't certain of the ramifications. "I didn't know she was Wiccan. I mean—I really meant—she's a mouthy whore who keeps looking in my desk and she spills out my tea without asking and she spends a lot of time snap chatting when she could be typing and I can't stand the way she talks at me. That kind of witch."

"Oh. Oh. I—" She rubbed her eyes. "Sophie, I thought you meant—"

"Forget it." I leaned forward, begging her with clasped hands. "Just reassign her? Please?"

"I can't. I'm sorry, but I can't."

"Because…" I prompted, sliding forward on my seat. Any closer and I'd have to hang on to the desk to keep from falling off the chair.

She bit her lips a moment before pressing the intercom. "Amanda, I'm going out for lunch. Send everyone to voicemail."

Her eyes were tight, brow as furrowed as a week's worth of bad copy. "You ready for lunch, Sophie? We should probably talk."

Suddenly, I wasn't worried about the secrets I tried so hard to keep. I had the distinct feeling that Barb was going to be handing me some new ones to worry about.

We walked uptown to the courtyard deli that Marek had often chosen for our lunch dates. It wasn't as crowded as it normally got in warmer weather; April was a free-for-all as far as weather went. Today was one of the chillier days, dim-skied and dull. We found a corner table where we could talk without worry of being overheard.

My stomach had lurched when she chose the spot for us to sit. Privacy often heralded bad news. And, in my case, sometimes dangerous news.

"I know all of this is going to sound really weird and foreign and bizarre but—I need you to know, even if you can't possibly understand." She took a deep breath and paused, perhaps reconsidering whether she should tell me. "I'm kind of under orders."

"To give me a witch for an intern?"

"It's not like that at all. Tom's request. He wanted to try out intern placement and thought your department was a perfect place to start."

"But I don't need help—"

"Yes, you do." She unwrapped her sandwich and took a bite, tipping a finger at me while she chewed. "You know, two years ago you were a part-timer with a home-made column. Now, you're full time and nationally syndicated. They've had to hire two new slush readers since New Year's just to keep up with the email."

"Slush readers?" My eyes flapped open so wide I thought

I sprained one of my eyebrows. "You mean someone is screening my email? What aren't I seeing? I could be missing—"

"See?" Barbara cut me off with a point of her finger. "That's what I mean. You are trying to do everything single-handed. You do an amazing job, hon. You know that and I know that. But you have to work nearly seven days a week to keep up with it all. That's fine, really, if that's your choice but I know it isn't. And then there's the status of your health."

What, did I have the consumption now? "I'm fine."

"Now, maybe. But I think the stress is really piling up, Soph. Your sick day usage is a little extravagant. Not that you aren't entitled, of course, but when you aren't here, everything stops. You are the only one who knows what is going on in that office and that's bad for operations."

God, I wanted to tell her so badly that what she thought was sick time was more like on-the-job-injuries from being Sophia. Or being bitten by a werewolf. It wasn't like I had a weak constitution. "Fine. I'll use an intern. Have Tom send me a different one."

She shook her head and reached for a potato chip. "She's the only one."

"Ugh. Why?"

"Budget. Besides, I'm the one who gave her the position. She needs this chance, Sophie. I've known her mom a long time and I can't fire her."

What a load. I couldn't believe the bum deal this intern business was turning out to be. "But you'd fire me for acting like a bigot?"

"No, I'd publicly reprimand you and send you for sensitivity training."

I glared at her. "Do you not see the irony in that?"

"Yes." She broke rank from her Evil Boss persona and

chuckled. "But I'd do it."

We finished our lunch with no more talk of interns or witches. As I walked back to my office, I glanced over to the section where a certain Stapler Nazi once sat. I hadn't had trouble with any co-workers since the inimitable Donna Slate. For a swift but terrible second, I was glad she'd ended up slaughtered by the vampire she'd whored herself out to and wondered if Jasmine…

Nah. That was too rude, even for me.

But I wasn't above hoping a natural disaster would befall her. I couldn't be blamed for acts of God. Fingers crossed, it would be an extremely localized event.

Since Jasmine was such a pro at getting the column work done, I left her with a list (and with an annoyingly patient voice explained each item, even though she didn't need the explanation. Bad Ass Sophie, that's me) and left early. I wanted to hit the expressway and get to Bluebell before rush hour.

Traffic was a bear, but it was a steady-moving bear. I followed the GPS to the address Rodrian had given me and pulled into the mostly open lot. The building itself looked like many others in this area; angles of concrete and colored glass that made one picture the original concept sketches, right down to the placement of bushes and decorative trees.

The company was identified only by its address over the main doors; the entrance sign listed a realty agency rather than the actual name of the company. *Aerogenetek Laboratories.*

Thinking it a prudent move, I reached out and did a DV headcount. Perhaps twenty. Not so bad then, for a building this size.

Rodrian said to look for a keypad by the door. I punched

in the code that he'd given me and waited for the door to slide open. Once inside, the door closed behind me. A second keypad and a second code got me through it.

The foyer was as sleek and as sketch—conception perfect as the outside. No reception, I noted; didn't think that was weird though, as I imagined Marek would have little use for a bright-eyed operator to wish him good morning every day. Instead, thought, there was a lively waterfall wall and fountain, its watery music filling the pristine space. The air seemed charged, an ionic freshness that made each breath tingle.

A thin man with short auburn spikes and big brown hipster glasses approached from the left side, where I noticed a hallway. A matching hallway came into the foyer from the other side and a glass elevator shaft rose straight up from its position behind the waterfall wall. A double door mirrored the front entrance, as well as another keypad.

Boy, Marek had liked his toys kept on lockdown, didn't he?

"Sophie Galen? You had no trouble with the access code, then." As he drew nearer, he took a sharp breath. "Sophia."

"Yes, I'm Sophie."

"No, sorry, it's—" He stammered and rubbed the top of his head. "I just never met a—you know, Sophia before."

"I know, it's trippy." I sincerely hoped this wasn't going to turn into a cow-eyed swoon fest. Sometime, a Demivamp had difficulty acclimating to me, or at least my reputation. Trouble was, I still had yet to become clear on exactly what that reputation was. "You're Kevin, I hope?"

"Rodrian told me to expect you." His composure restored, he waved me to follow and walked back down the hall way from which he'd appeared. Offices and conference rooms lined the hall and a broad staircase stood at the midpoint. "We'll take these stairs here. I'm not sure why you wanted to come out, though. Are you assuming an interest in the lab?"

I guessed that was his way of asking if I was his new boss. "Not in terms of leadership, no. I'm hoping you can share some of your research, though. On the Horus Bird Phenomenon?"

"Well, I'd be the one to talk to. I'm the senior research coordinator. Although I'm not sure what a Sophia wants to know about hybrid mechanics."

I recognized the phrase from Marek's big book. "I was very close to Marek Thurzo. This operation was very important to him and I just want to make sure that his work continues."

"And?" At the top of the stairs, he prompted me along with a wave of his hand. "Sophia or not, I can tell when a human is being completely honest. What else do you hope to get from this?"

I was taken aback by his directness, the almost physical weight of his assessment. "Well, I have a certain level of investment in the DV. Any loss—whether to death, or evolution, or this Horus Bird shift—is a personal loss to me. I'm trying to explore all avenues to see what can be done to serve the DV better."

He must have bought that because the sense of scrutiny had lifted. "My office is near the end there. Why don't we take a look around before we head back there?"

The upper floors were laboratories and equipment rooms. I noticed that, just as it was on the first floor, a set of keypadded double doors faced the elevators. Kevin walked us down to those doors and punched in a number. "Might as well start at the beginning."

The doors slid open to reveal a thirty-foot tall chamber,

the ceiling open to the sky in a glass dome. The center was a tremendous enclosure with an oak tree in its middle, lesser trees and contrived perches at its circumference.

Oh, the birds. I'd never been up close to raptors, from smaller peregrines to several red-tailed hawks, so common in the local skies. Every size, every shape, each one bearing a sharp intelligence in its eyes and a cuff around one leg.

"Are they...hybrids?" Although I'd been calling Marek the *Wolfram* in my head, I wasn't sure it would be an acceptable term to use with one of the DV.

Kevin scratched at his head. "Unsure, actually. According to samples we've taken from them, we know they are a little different from typical examples. We keep them for comparison."

I frowned. "Experimentation?"

He shrugged. "Nothing inhumane. Blood draws, skin and feather samples. That sort of thing."

I thought about the *Wolfram,* who was undoubtedly the sample that would become the gold standard. "Marek said there's been a lot of *in vitro* testing."

"In the past, yeah, but it's getting harder to obtain Were subjects. Ethical complications."

"Why not just kidnap a werewolf and bite him? That would work, wouldn't it?"

He looked at me with shrewd suspicion. "Are you actually Sophie Galen?"

"Yeah, why?"

"I can't imagine a Sophie would put a Demivamp at risk like that. We're not Mengelian monsters."

I covered my mouth. "I didn't mean anything by it. I just thought—"

"It's okay, Sophie." He steered me back to the door. "Everyone has thoughts when they get desperate. It's just important to avoid acting on thoughts like those."

My shields up and back to him, Kevin couldn't see my expression. I knew then that I wouldn't have to worry about ethical issues with this guy. Silently, I thanked Rodrian for putting me in touch with the right kind of person.

We walked back down the hallway to a set of small offices near the end. The door at the farthest end was closed. A plate next to it had been engraved. *M Thurzo*. I curled my fingers and pressed my arms to my sides.

Kevin opened the door next to it. A broad desk was covered with folders, while a second desk bore an elaborate computer set-up that made me a teensy bit envious. He lifted a jacket off a chair and indicated I should sit down. "Rodrian said you were interested in the research here. But why? Is it because of Marek?"

I blinked a few times, marveling at the clinical levelness of his voice. Then again, I reminded myself, Marek hadn't been his soul mate. "This was a very important cause to him."

"It's important to all of us. We're grateful Rodrian saw fit to continue the work here."

"Do you know what happened to Marek?" I ventured.

He shrugged and flipped on his monitor. "Came close enough to Falling that he doesn't exist anymore. It's a risk we all face. You know that, right?"

He didn't know, did he? I slid the knowledge away in case I need an ace from my sleeve later on. Shields still up, I nodded and continued playing the role of Sophia, Hybrid Research Ambassador. "Which is why I want to know about every aspect of this—transformation. I don't like the thought of losing another Demivamp."

"Well, then you came to the right place. I've been Marek's senior officer here since he began the study. But why you—and why the Horus Equation?"

"I have a degree in nursing, you know. I'm not clueless. Besides, Rodrian thought maybe the Sophia could figure something out."

"No offense, Sophia, but it's a longshot." He drummed a pen against his leg. "There is nothing we've seen or collected or observed that we haven't pulled apart a hundred different ways. I appreciate your education and I admire your religious work, but there's nothing you can figure out that we can't."

I was offended, and I wasted no time in letting him know it. Thinning my barriers, I expanded my power outward, swelling like a room full of smoke. Hovering just a few inches from his own power, I hung a moment before suddenly reaching out for him, engulfing him. His eyes flashed, gunmetal gray, and his power tasted like urgent fear at my sudden manifestation.

Remaining still, my expression as clear as the synthetic foyer down below us, I titled my head. "Are you sure about that? I have a really weird ability to look at things in a way most DV can't."

He swallowed hard, his forehead looking shiny. Good. I pulled it all back, leaving him reeling in his seat. Kevin shook his head to clear the sensation of having his arse handed to him by the Sophia. "I upset you. I'm sorry, it was insensitive—"

"It's fine." I smiled, gently, a balm to the trick I just pulled. "You don't know me. It's okay. But know this— finding the answer to the Horus Equation is the single most important thing to me right now. I want to help. It's what I do. And I can't sit by, doing nothing."

I let my voice drift off and dropped my gaze, hoping he'd take the bait.

After a moment, he rocked back in his chair and opened a desk drawer. Pulling out a flash drive, he stuck it into the side of his computer and began to open files. "These are executive summaries of each of the main studies conducted over the past fifteen years. If you decide you need actual data, we'll have to arrange for you to come back in."

After a few moments, he disengaged the flash drive and handed it to me. "I hope you do find something. We can all use a fresh perspective. Just call me if you have any questions."

I took the drive with a grateful smile and stood to leave.

"I'll see you out, Sophie. Sophia or not, you smell too good to go walking around on your own here. My guys don't, ah, socialize enough. They'd forget their manners."

"Yikes," I said, pulling a comically aghast face.

"No, I'm serious."

I gulped, believing him. He followed me to the doorway and flipped off the light switch, jingling through a key ring as he locked the door behind him.

Out in the hallway, I stole another glance at Marek's door. "Is his office open?"

Kevin shrugged. "No one ever goes in."

"Can I?"

"I guess, I mean, we wouldn't but—you're different. You're really different. Forgive me if I just wait for you here."

I stood in front of Marek's door, my hand over the latch. A quiet zing of energy. A ward. It hummed on my skin, alive, recognizing. How, when I was tainted by a Were bite? It didn't matter, did it? I just know it recognized me.

I pushed the door open, stiff on its hinges. The office was bright with sunshine, streaming in through two huge windows. Corner offices were so classy, even abandoned ones.

A hook near the door held a long white lab coat. I leaned into it, inhaling the faint scent of Marek's skin, closing my eyes against the memory that came away with it. Leather and sandalwood, lingering after so long an absence. Like so many things, it was haunting, a trigger object.

Marek's spaces were sparse, by nature, and this room was no exception. It could have been a generic office space, a stock photo. Few things personalized this office; the lab coat was one. I walked to the window and looked out over the trees lining the lot, the other office buildings further off. When I turned, I saw a photo, propped up against a pen caddy on the desk. The picture wasn't visible from the door.

It was a picture of me.

A candid shot, I looked off-camera. Maybe I didn't even know he took the picture. That tiny photo revealed a sliver of sentimentality I never knew Marek had. Seeing it resolved the twinge of guilt I felt at having plundered his office, seeking another connection to the man I had lost. It made it worthwhile.

I should go. I shouldn't linger where even he does not. I saw what I'd hoped to see and it was time to close the door once more.

I walked around the desk but, on my way to the door, my eyes caught something else.

Off to the side, on top of a filing cabinet, I spied a brown leather-bound book. It was half-familiar, though I couldn't place it. It was perhaps six inches long, small enough to fit inside a coat pocket. The dark leather had been rubbed pale on its corners. It looked like it wanted to be touched.

I ran my fingers over the worn smoothness of its cover before picking it up and opening it. Like all his journals, Marek had dated it on the inside front.

This one was the most recent yet.

I flipped to a random page for a peek. What would his

mindset be? Would he still be the same dark soul? Would there be some flash of light in his eternally dark sky?

Should I even hope it was possible?

I found her. It staggers this unworthy heart to even form the words in my mind, let alone set them down.

I know it as surely as I know that I am damned. Although I've only spoken to her once, I know once is enough. So many failures have paved this lonely road, and it takes one brief brush of her spirit to illuminate each and every previous fault. Now that I have found her, I see clearly what every other woman lacked.

And though I know I am damned, I know that if anyone could change the mind of God, it would be she.

I lost all thought of simply skimming and continued, reading each word carefully, as if trying to memorize the text.

I'd returned from an extended stay abroad only a few days earlier; although business is largely unfinished, I cut negotiations short when I received a missive from Amarisa. She said it was time to come home.

I admit I'd had mixed feelings. Home was an idea that belonged in someone else's mind. Not mine.

However, she had warded her letter with an under-current that made it impossible to remain away any longer. I established our interests and tied up what issues I could before returning home.

Balaton had changed greatly in my absence, but the underlying pulse remained constant. Persistent. I craved the familiarity that my old city provided, even though long gone are the days when wagons drove ruts into the muddy earth and my journals were feverishly filled by candlelight.

Yet, for all the light this city shines forth, I saw none of it. No light, no heat, no color—the heaviness of my spirit and the hopelessness of my many years had kept me behind a wall of glass, isolated from life.

Until now. To think of her makes me pause in my writing, so dumbfounded am I.

It all started with a scent.

Odd, I know, to describe that touch of power as scent but, the more I think upon it, the more I know it to be so. I knew it could never be power like that of Demivampire. It was too...multidimensional.

This power had depth, a nuance of subtle strength that played like a flavor upon my tongue. This power tinged my grey world with a wash of gentle color. This power caught my attention and drew me to it, not knowing what it was but knowing I had to find it nonetheless. I needed to find it.

And I found her.

She has a subtle beauty, this woman; chestnut hair that falls in waves upon her shoulders, deep set brown eyes brimming with compassion for all the sadness they hold. It took all my strength to keep from reaching for her. I could not frighten her away, not when I may have caught a glimpse of my own salvation.

Another word that staggers me. I'd forgotten how it felt to hope for salvation. Though her eyes were not oracle blue, I knew the Sophia was only a heartfelt hope away.

I found her. I would not lose her, ever. I could not survive if I did.

And when I turned the page, I found a collage of sketches, the face of a woman with dark hair. Sometimes she smiled, other times she frowned hard enough to create deep creases between her brows. That same face, over and over, from every single angle with every gesture, every expression.

And they were all me. Younger, perhaps, but unmistakably me.

I stared at the sketches until my vision swam. He'd been talking about me.

I hastily looked back to the beginning of the entry for

the date and saw it was dated in the late nineties. But—when did he ever speak to me? It was more than ten years before I met him, yet he had spoken to me, watched me, captured my image in his journal.

He'd found me and known me long before we'd ever met in the museum.

And this was the journal he'd been carrying that day. Not fate, not happenstance. He'd simply decided it was time.

I nodded, my mouth set. I didn't know if I should laugh or cry. Both would have been appropriate. Such was the duality of my love for Marek. Pain and joy. Love and loss. Grief and completeness.

He was my everything. This entry made me think that maybe I was his everything, too.

I couldn't read anymore, not here in his abandoned office, surrounded by unfamiliar lab techs and bird specimens in cages. Tucking the journal into my purse, I took one last look around before closing the door.

My resolve was set. No matter what happened to me, I owed Marek the last full measure of my devotion.

Thankfully, traffic was lighter on the trip back home. I was grateful to put real distance between myself and Kevin's hoard of probably rampaging DV biologists. There was only so much geek I could handle at once, even without all the DVness.

As I drove home, I frequently reached over to my purse, just to brush my fingers against the journal. To make sure it was real. I kept seeing those sketches in my mind, those stolen glances Marek had inked upon those pages. They were the signs of an obsession—and it validated me, in a way. It proved that I wasn't crazy, or over-attached, or desperately hanging onto something that I'd blown up to exaggerated proportions.

Marek had been hung up on me, too, not just the other way around. It made my determination all the stronger. I'd see him back, somehow. It wouldn't be fair to let him down now. He'd loved me for too long.

Heat bloomed in my cheeks, though, when I reminded myself of my current predicament, caught up with a man who professed to love me despite not even knowing me. I couldn't help but feel like this *Leni* thing cheapened what Marek and I had. This insta-love, this out-of-the-blue courtship with a man who should have lived out his existence in rock magazines and on CDs and upon far away stages. I was all for fairy tale love stories and happy endings but the one I seem to have ended up with felt way too Grimm.

But it wasn't simply the *Leni* that made me ashamed of myself. It was remembering how it felt to be blown off by the guy I swore I didn't want.

And, even as I stroked the leather cover of Marek's journal, I spent the ride home working out what I planned to do about it if I didn't hear from His Highness by Friday night. Part of me really wanted to take matters into my own hands.

Not The Same Old Sophie, that's me.

And that might not be a good thing.

Waxing gibbous | moon 46% visible

The Expressway traffic was lighter than I expected, but then again I always expected the worst when travelling into the city on a Saturday. A few exits before center city, I turned off toward West Philadelphia. Before long, I pulled into the lot of the Windwood Hotel, which looked more like the parking lot of the budget supermarket in my old neighborhood. Grass growing in the cracks of the pavement, the hedges looking like they needed a stiff spraying.

Stop it. Stop finding fault with everything.

Really, the hotel was decent as far as I could tell. The fact that this one had on-site parking should have put it higher in my opinion because street parking sucked and I was too cheap for valet, or even a garage. I supposed that under more normal circumstances parking wouldn't have been a concern at all because Rodrian would have been driving.

I backed into a space and turned off the car, my hand paused on the seatbelt release. It was difficult to appreciate effortless free parking because the Windwood Hotel was the safe house where Dierk and his entourage were staying.

Enough with the unanswered calls already. We hadn't spoken since Cacilia took the phone. If he really wanted to blow me off, he'd better have the stones to tell me to my face.

Getting out, I got some looks when I slammed the car door. The lot wasn't empty. Not strange to see people coming and going in a hotel lot, but standing around in twos and threes, especially when they weren't smoking or holding luggage—that was weird. Hanging out in a hotel lot was weird. And the way I felt them watching me was weird. Paranoid? Who, me?

I had at least three dozen reasons to get back in the car and leave. Dierk was blowing me off, so if he was the King of the Pack, then by definition, all the other Weres would blow me off, too. With the Weres out of my life, things could go back to normal. I could get my life back. I could smooth things out with Rodrian, get my focus back on the hybrid research, become Barb's favorite employee and friend again. My life. My family. That's what I wanted.

So why didn't I get back in the damn car?

I balled my hand. The bite had healed, more or less, more scar than scab. A string of shallow pink dents where the front teeth, needle sharp, made clean pits. The scar itched sometimes, especially after I got out of the shower, so I rubbed it with vitamin E oil. It helped. Soon, it would fade like every other scar and memory that went with it.

Pressing my nails into the healing wound reminded me it was there. The sensitive skin in turn reminded me why I'd come here. There was only one reason why I wasn't driving away.

Shouldering my purse, I walked into the hotel and marched over to the reception desk. Bright smile, yellow ponytail, skinny tie softening the effect of the receptionist's starched shirt and stiff collar. She looked pleasant enough, although I didn't think I'd expected a hairy raging beast answering the phone and swiping room keys. Still.

She met me with a polished ultra-bright smile. "Do you have a reservation?"

"No." I smiled back. "I'm visiting a guest."

"Shall I call their room?"

What a relief. This would be even easier than I thought. For the duration of the ride out here, I worried I'd have to pull a scheme of Mission Impossible: Sophia magnitude. "Yes. That would be great."

"Room number?"

"Oh, I'm not sure. It's Dierk Adeluf."

Her gaze slid sideways and a dark-skinned man who'd been typing at the other end of the desk glided closer.

"I'm sorry, we don't have a listing." His voice sounded like water over rocks. Smooth, powerful, dangerous if I wasn't careful.

"Then look for the listing he is using. It's a suite, only a few doors down from an elevator."

"Is he expecting you?"

"No. No, he's not." In my periphery I saw another person get in line behind me. He stood too closely behind to be a guest waiting for reception.

"Your ID, miss," the second clerk said.

I pulled it out of my wallet and gave it to him, who handed it to Yellow Ponytail. She took it to the back corner of the office and picked up a telephone, speaking quietly to someone on the other end. I stowed my wallet in my purse and shouldered it again, twisting my waist with enough force to whack the man hovering over my shoulder.

I turned with wide eyes, faking an apology. "Oh, dear. Didn't see you there. Sorry."

"No answer in his room. Sorry." The receptionist had returned and held out my ID. "I'm happy to leave a message. Phone number, please?"

I was pissed. No answer. Right. The jackass was refusing me again. Well, two can play that stupid game. "Sure, I said. 382-5633."

She wrote it down, apparently not realizing those were the numbers for F*** OFF. Her loss. I couldn't care less if she was that shallow. I turned to leave, feeling bad (again) for whoever actually owned that number. Another casualty of my spite and vulgarity. Oh, well, wars were messy.

I smiled like a snap of the fingers at the man who had been breathing down my neck and left.

Fine. Done. Fine. It was official. I could just go home. I had lab reports to get through. This whole stupid Were business only kept me from figuring out a solution for Marek. And Marek—if Dierk was out of my life I could sit down with Marek's journal and submerge myself guilt-free in his pages. That was what I wanted—I was a step closer to solving that wretched equation.

I reached into my purse to grab my keys. The metal key ring caught my palm the wrong way and woke up the nerve, sending a winch up my forearm.

No. I couldn't. Maybe the old Sophie would have taken the hint.

I wasn't her anymore.

All this *Leni* and Dierk's mate business and treating Sophie like a trophy oracle. Baloney. I'm me. For all I knew, everyone around me was a figment of my imagination and my whole life was only a dream and dammit, I hated passive voice and weak verbs and clichés.

I was a writer, dammit again. I owed myself a better ending than—than whatever *this* was.

I got into my car and left the lot, driving around the block and parking it out of sight behind a rusty panel truck. I pulled off my hoodie and stuffed it in the backseat, grabbing my black leather jacket instead. Then I pulled the elastic out of my hair, shaking out my messy bun. Jogging back to the hotel, I fooled with my phone while walking up to the pool entrance.

Humans inside. A few ladies left and I walked up to the door just as they came out. The last in line held the door, even.

My barriers were up as thick as I could make them. Dierk said the top floors were safe house only, the bottom two public. I could start at the top and walk the hall, scan each room until I found him.

Or look for a guard detail posted outside. That would be a big giveaway, too.

A couple and their children were using the pool. No one even glanced at me as I crossed the deck and exited the pool area. Elevators might have a camera. I'd take the stairs.

Ugh. Five stories.

No rooms on this floor, just business center, conference rooms, hotel laundry, pool. Turning the corner, I saw guards. Olberich and Janssen.

Could be good. Could be bad. At least I hadn't had to walk up any stairs. That was probably the good part.

Other people milled the halls, lounging, slouching, but Dierk's guards stood at rigid attention. That's where he was. I knew it. Very determinedly, I headed down the hall, not looking around, not trying to catch anyone's eye. I knew they watched me, but a practiced flip of hair over my shoulder allowed a glance behind that showed nobody followed.

All they did was watch and scent the air as I walked by. That was precisely what I had hoped would happen.

The bad part was that I didn't have time for a story. I just had to wing it. Both their heads turned as one when I passed the wide staircase leading up to the lobby, bringing myself into their section of the hallway.

Too late to turn back. I marched up to them, licking my lips and hoping I didn't wear my fear like a cologne.

Janssen inhaled deeply and grinned. "What took you so long?"

I tried to smile but anxiety kept it short. I zipped my coat up all the way. "Oh, you know. This and that."

He pulled the door open and held it for me. "Pay up, *Alda*," he said over my head.

I paused before walking through. "What?"

"Not you. Him. We had a bet." To Olberich, he said: "Told you she'd show."

"Unfair," Olberich said. "You couldn't have known she'd show up dressed like that."

The door shut behind me. A last glimpse showed a disgruntled Olberich slapping money into Janssen's open hand. Wow. Glad I made someone happy.

My back to the door, I surveyed the room, filled to comfortable capacity. Two guards flanked the doorway on this side as well. These were dressed in a sort of uniform, holding tall metal poles with vertical flags on them. Heraldic banners.

Uh, oh. I had just barged in on Dierk's court.

I unzipped my jacket half-way and pumped the lapels, feeling stifled. The guards, looking more like Olympians than bouncers, marked my sudden appearance but said nothing.

There were groups of well-dressed men and women that

stood in quiet dignified circles. There were clumps of adults, all ages and manners of dress, who laughed and very clearly enjoyed each other's company. And there were wolves.

They were not dogs—dogs would have barked and their noise would have announced their presence. Sleek shapes, mounds of muscle and fur, clustered together, just like the people did. The creatures nosed each other, lounging on the floor, some displaying throats or teeth, behaving every bit as social as the people. Some wolves sliced through the crowd like shadows, pausing to touch, nose to nose, nose to hand, meeting, greeting.

And they were beautiful—not a single Teen Wolf or American in London in sight. Just beautiful creatures.

Not all of these people were entirely strange, nor were all of them strangers. I recognized several people, even if I didn't know their names. One of them was my last mail carrier. Were it not for the constant playing of magic tingling on my skin like a facial peel I might have laughed. Imagine, the mailman that bit back. So not appropriate.

And there were others—a girl who worked in the deli that I frequently visited for lunch, the older lady from the bank whose line always moved the fastest. A man who worked in my office building and often shared my elevator. These were people I knew. Faces to the nameless Were I feared and dreaded. They were people. It wasn't a pleasant realization. I wanted to fear monsters. Children grew with the inherent ability to fear the strange and loathsome.

The Were were people. All of them.

I knew I had to find Dierk before my luck ran out so I began to weave my way through the crowd. However, persistent trouble found me first, giving me a rough shove with her shoulder before she spun me around.

"How did you get in?" Cacilia's lips curled, revealing

teeth I hadn't noticed during our last exchanges.

"I walked through the door when they opened it."

"I doubt it. I'll bet you slithered under it."

You will pay for this insult would come off so cliché. I bit on my tongue and tried to sidestep her. She blocked me, hands on her hips.

Movement in my periphery made me snatch a glance over my shoulder.

One of the door bouncers stood just behind me. He cleared his throat, his voice as deep as his chest was wide. "Be civil, Cacilia. The *Leni* may not have completed but she still belongs to him."

Cacilia stood her ground. "Remove her at once. She has interfered with *der König's* business one too many times."

The guard shook his head. "I suspect she is our *König's* business."

"She is human. Not his mate."

"You." His hand on my shoulder, he tugged me around to face him. "What is your business here?"

I looked at him, swallowed hard. "I only wish to see your king, that's all."

"Then you will see him. For where is the harm in the looking?" He released me and held out the crook of his elbow, indicating I should take his arm.

I slid my hand into the bend of his arm and nodded, indicating that he could escort me when he was ready. Suddenly, he looked more royal guard than bouncer. That was the difference. The responsibility of a gentleman. Now instead of meandering through the crowd a path opened for us.

Of course with a man that big, a path would have little choice but to open for him. It didn't keep the guests from leaning in, though, and sniffing at me. It was always subtle, of course, but I didn't think that it was coincidence that each and every person would suddenly inhale through their noses as I passed.

Good.

As we reached the front of the room, the crowd thinned and I could make out a chair, set atop a wide carpeted platform that raised it a foot off the ground. High backed and upholstered, baby blue fabric accented with gold, red, gilt. Sitting in that chair was Dierk, decked out in a black brocade vest over a deep burgundy shirt. He watched me make my way through the crowd and lifted his chin from where it rested on his fist, his eyes the color of pure gold.

I couldn't register anything else once I saw his eyes. His eyes held me, a fluid yet tenuous touch that sent my heart stretching out toward him, feeling miles away until he spoke my name and brought me back.

"Sophie, you surprise me. Truly I did not expect to see you here."

"I had to see you," I said.

The guard released my hand with a gentle pat and backed away.

Dierk remained motionless, except for his eyes. "Is something the matter?"

"There must be." I crossed my arms and locked my sight on him, half-fearing to look around at the Weres surrounding me. "You aren't returning my calls."

"And is he slave to your call?" Cacilia had followed in our wake and now competed for Dierk's attention. "He answers to no one."

"And no one answers for him." Dierk's gaze flicked toward Cacilia, pinning her into silence. "I received no calls from you."

"I called you six times," I said. "Six times. It didn't even go to voicemail. You rejected each of my calls. The least you can do is talk to me."

Dierk clasped his hands over his mid-section, his voice slightly louder, edgier. "I received no call."

I pulled out my cell phone, wanting ever so much to bean him with it. Room full of werewolves, I reminded myself. Won't like it if I give their king a concussion.

"This is ridiculous. Do I have to go over my call log and show you all the times I tried?" I started thumbing down the list of calls. "Here and here and eleven o'clock this morning and four o'clock yesterday afternoon."

Dierk made an exasperated noise, leaning forward to tug his phone out of his back pocket. "And I tell you. I did not receive a call from you. At those times only came calls from unfamiliar numbers. I do not answer unfamiliar numbers."

"They were my numbers, you jerk."

Heads turned when they heard the insult. Warily I tried to keep them all in my periphery, wondering if the king would have my head.

He, however, seemed to have forgotten there was anyone in the room with us.

"No, they are not! I have all your numbers saved. You called me from your cell? Let's see. This is who called, not you." Then he rattled off my cell phone number.

I rubbed my eyes, feeling familiar defeat, and glared at Cacilia. "Meddling bitch. Why not?"

She growled.

I gave her the hand. "You changed my numbers in his phone so my calls would come up unknown."

She laughed, spreading her hands wide and twisting to look at the people closest to us. "Do you hear this, *mein König*? I can't believe this woman, Dierk. How she lies."

"Honestly, Cacilia? You did have my phone when she called." He tapped his mouth with his fingers. "Did you do this?"

She rolled her eyes and parked a hand on the angle of

her hip. "Are you going to throw her out or not?"

"No. She has something I need." In a fluid movement, Dierk stood up and stepped off the riser, stalking toward me. He raised a hand, and I thought for a moment he might strike my cheek.

But he didn't. He grabbed the zipper of my coat and yanked it down, unzipping my jacket all the way and spreading it open. "I thought I had lost that shirt."

"That's it?" I smirked at him, looking up through my lashes. "You rip open a woman's coat and all you say is I *thought I lost the shirt*?"

He shrugged. "It's a good shirt."

"Well, glad to be of service. You could just have your shirt back and I'll go." I shook off my jacket and dropped it on the floor. I grasped the bottom of the shirt, lifting it as if I would take it off, giving him and the room a glimpse of my belly.

Which, might I add, is not at all a bad looking belly. I'm not saying I'm ready for a piercing but a half-shirt, sure.

His eyes wide, he pushed my shirt down in a hurry.

"No, no, no," he said, his words stumbling out in a rush. "That won't be necessary."

I grinned over his shoulder, only half-meaning for Cacilia to see me. "I'd rather trade shirts in private anyway."

"Well, that will have to wait," he said. "You are invited to stay."

"You are not *Wolfenkinder*," said someone near us. The nice bank lady. "You could have been killed, dear."

"I have learned Sophie is a very determined woman." Dierk stepped back from me. "She knew exactly what she was doing."

"Walking into a den of wolves, where she would not be able to defend herself?" Her brows lowered, dubious and scolding.

"Walking into a den of wolves wearing the king's shirt and wrapped in his scent." Dierk glanced down to look for my hand and took it, entwining our fingers. "I'd say, that was a very smart thing to do."

We left the conference room through a single door behind Dierk's dais. This new room was smaller, windowless, and had a long craft table laden with food on one side, a healthy grouping of gear boxes on the other. In between paced Stohl, engaged in an intense telephone conversation.

Maybe it was the German, the unfamiliar words and inflections that sounded terse. Maybe it was Stohl—could be he talked that way to everyone. Either way, he paced and talked and stopped when we came into the room.

Dierk waved at him to continue. Stohl did so, albeit in a softer tone.

Covered trays and plastic wrapped desserts lined the table, and an impressive coffee service lay at the end. Looked like an industrial strength barista contraption. I knew Barb would go nutty for one and briefly considered texting her a photo. Dierk passed the coffee station and reached instead for a simply glass tea pot next to it. The pot was full of a honey brown brew. He poured two mugs.

"Sugar?" he asked.

I nodded. He reached for a rectangular decanter and drizzled a stream of amber syrup into each of the glasses, giving them a stir before handing one to me.

I sipped cautiously. This was no Lipton. It was—not indescribable, because if I had the time I could describe every nuance of the flavor, from the deep earthy base to the delicate fruit essence that lingered on the tongue after I swallowed. I wanted to say indescribable because it was so complex in its simplicity—a perfect snapshot of a summer's walk under a canopy of flowering trees—it didn't defy description. It simply didn't deserve to be described with words.

All that from a single sip of tea.

Dierk grinned while he watched me take that sip. "This is one of my favorite reasons to visit the US. I can only find this particular flush of Darjeeling in a shop in New Jersey."

"So, you weren't really avoiding my calls?"

"Of course not. In fact, I was disappointed you didn't call. I admit, I was too proud to call you myself. I paid a heavy price for that pride." He cast his gaze downward, regret in the lines of his face. "However determined you are, Cacilia is three steps ahead. She has much more to lose, and she has desperation driving her. It is hard to compete against a woman like that."

I couldn't help but scowl. "I didn't think I had to compete against anybody. I figured destiny, and all that, kind of gave me a leg up in the game."

"You forget." He pointed to the black boxes in the corner, heaviness and regret replaced by childish youth, insolent and fresh. "I'm a rock star."

I whacked him in the arm. "I can't believe you just said that."

He ducked his head and grinned. Raising his mug to his lips, he blew across the surface of hot tea, leaning against the table. "Destiny, huh? Is Sophie coming around then?"

I paused to sip the tea again, relishing that bright taste of sunlight in trees once more. "I'm in it until the moon. Then…we talk."

He growled deep in his chest. Normal guys didn't do stuff like that. His eyes dripped down into the King's gold again and he pulled me against him with his free hand. "Maybe…there won't be much talking."

"You're right," I said. Leaning toward the table I set

down my mug before returning to his rugged embrace. "You'll be too busy chasing rabbits."

Stohl ended his phone call abruptly—or, at least it sounded abrupt to me—and marched toward the door, briefly saying something to Dierk before leaving. Not my business. Happier this way.

"Come." Dierk released me and tugged me by my hand toward the door. "I still have some business to take care of in there. Come sit with me."

"Won't that be…offensive to them?"

"Another thing you forget. I'm king. No one else has the right to take offense if I do not."

Returning to the conference room, Dierk escorted me behind the dais to a second smaller chair that had been placed beside his. Seating me first, he then took his own. Stohl appeared on the other side of his chair and announced a man, who was escorted forward.

It was very weird to be sitting there, and I really didn't like being the subject of such scrutiny. Although the people closest to the throne paid strict attention to Dierk and his subjects, the people to the sides and rear of the room carried on their conversations. Plenty of heads craned to look in my direction. No friendly eye contact, but nothing outright hostile, at least. Even the wolves avoided me. I folded my hands on my lap and kept my eyes down.

Anywhere but here. I'd been saying that so often lately, I might have to get it inked.

As the man finished up and went back to the crowd, a voice sounded at my side. A woman in hostess uniform held out a small tray. On it was my tea cup, rose lipstick and all. I took it with a grateful nod, glad to have something in my hands again. Dierk glanced down and nodded, a slight drop of his chin. Then Stohl announced another person and the whole bow-and-greet thing started all over again.

Sitting down and doing nothing was tiring work. After nearly an hour of sitting still and fighting the impulse to pull out my phone and play a game, Dierk raised his hand and announced a break. He stood and the crowd bowed their heads. Stepping off the dais, he raised a hand and gestured to me with a spread of his fingers to precede him.

In the rear room, he refreshed our tea cups before consulting a clipboard with Stohl. Four more speakers scheduled, from the sounds of it. Then adjournment.

"Supper in your rooms tonight, *mein König*?"

"That won't be necessary. I'll be going out." Dierk tilted his head in my direction. "Think about where we should dine, my dear. You've accommodated me greatly today."

They spoke a brief while in German so I helped myself to a brownie. The last two speakers who'd approached Dierk had taken up much of the past hour so I figured on two more hours, at least. One little brownie wouldn't put me off dinner, not even one with gooey icing and a generous sprinkle of walnuts.

I saved the last bite for Dierk and, once Stohl walked out, I held it up. "Hungry?"

He glanced from my hand to my eyes.

"Yes." With slow steps, he paced over to me. "But we need to go in presently. I shouldn't get my hands dirty."

"That's what you've got me for. I don't mind wearing a little icing." I popped the fudgy bite into his open mouth, sparing him the mess. Oh, these men were such high maintenance. Rolling his eyes, he smirked as he chewed, wiggling his eyebrows.

He caught me by the wrist as I turned away for a napkin. "Not so fast."

Dierk raised my hand, inspecting my chocolate-covered fingers. "You weren't going to waste this, were you?"

Very deliberately, he leaned over my hand and slid my finger into his mouth, licking the chocolate off. I felt the slip of his tongue on my skin, the fullness of his lips as they pursed around my fingertip.

"Mmm. Best I've ever tasted. I'd like more." With a golden gleam through thick sable lashes, he eyed me, not the plate of brownies. "But it's time we go back."

He spread his hand to urge me out and I hurried out, fluffing my hair, keeping my head down.

It was in vain, though. I could tell by his throaty chuckle that he'd noticed my flushed cheeks. Damn that man for making me blush.

Just as he promised, he spoke with four people before standing and ushering me out again. Through the closed door, I could hear Stohl's voice as he announced the court's adjournment, and the subsequent chatter as the attendees filed out. Dierk prepared two travel cups of tea while Olberich gave him a recap of the day's business. He kept a straight face when he recounted my arrival, leaving out the drama of Cacilia's objections, but ruined it when he glanced over at me and winked. "Even if it did cost me a hundred."

Dierk laughed. "That will teach you to bet against her."

Once they were finished, Dierk took our jackets from a rack in the corner. "Shall we? I hope you have something decided for us."

"Sure do." I hoped he was in the mood for street food. "Shall I run it by your posse first?"

"Your evening, your choice. I am sure you have excellent taste in cuisine." He bowed like a gentleman before helping me into my jacket. "Do we need to change for dinner?"

"You do," I said. "Unless you want people to chase you. That vest isn't street smart."

He laughed and unbuttoned it, removing the vest and

then the burgundy dress shirt. He tugged at his white t-shirt. "This is acceptable?"

I nodded. "Much better."

He took me by the hand and led me out to the lobby staircase, pausing and nodding toward Olberich and Janssen, who had stopped to lock the conference room. "I want this to be just us tonight but…I don't go anywhere in the city alone. You understand that?"

"I figured. They'll drive a second car though, right? They won't fit in the back of the Cavalier."

"I'd like to see Olberich try to get into your car. He is humbled by average-sized vehicles. But seriously." His laugh dwindled. "I'd prefer to go alone, but this thing is not practical. They will drive us but I promise they will remain a discreet distance away. Philadelphia is a big city with many unpredictable elements."

"Is this what life is like for you all the time?" How sad. I loved my alone time, or at least my voluntary alone time. "Always being followed?"

He shrugged. "It's necessary. No sense to complain about what cannot be changed."

I smiled wanly. No sense, but something I did, nonetheless. I tended to waste a lot of time, these days, complaining. Maybe it was time to conserve energy and effort.

He must have sensed my change in mood because he squeezed my hand. "Come. Let's enjoy ourselves tonight. The work day is over."

We ended up on South Street. Olberich parked off the main drag and we walked a few blocks to my favorite cheesesteak place. The guys kept their promise to remain aloof, even changing their voices and thinning their accents to be less conspicuous.

I looked forward to being in a normal crowd, invisible

once more. We were invisible, for the most part, but every now and then a passerby would seem to recognize Dierk. I'd catch their wide eyes and head bows, or an occasional subtle fist-heart salute. Did they recognize him as a Were, a rocker, or a king? Being with him was a little intimidating, knowing he was a celebrity to so many people.

By contrast, I picked out plenty of DV, every single one of them locked down and impassively hurrying by without incident. Maybe they wanted to protect me by not calling attention to me. Or maybe they were disappointed to catch me slumming it with a Were.

The restaurant was packed, the line stretching outside and around the corner. I ordered our sandwiches to go, but someone tugged on my sleeve as Dierk paid.

A twenty-something punk in a Sons of Anarchy shirt stood next to me and gestured to a group near the front window. "Our table is opening. We'll hold it for you."

Dierk looked over, then, and one of the men at the table did the fist-heart thing. A thin woman in an unseasonal halter top too short to hide her back tats hurried to put their plates on a tray, wiping the table down. They hadn't been done eating. They wanted to pick up and move to make space for him, just like that.

"You don't have to do that," I said, my face heating up.

Dierk reached out to him, and they clasped hands. "Your hospitality is appreciated. She has never seen me try to walk and eat at the same time."

They walked to the table together, and I trailed behind with our order, watching as he thanked each person and chatted. The group left, each face beaming as if they had a brush-in with royalty.

I suppose they actually did.

The boys, as I was beginning to mentally call Janssen and Olberich, managed to grab a spot at the outside counter next to the front window, where they kept an eye on us. Janssen, I noticed, had an eye for redheads, and made sure to talk to each one that walked past. I caught Olberich's attention, now and again, and he rolled his eyes in exasperation at his partner.

We took our time with our subs, chatting and people watching. Dierk had one thing that was firmly in his favor—he was wonderful for conversation. He listened, too, responding and letting me know each minute that I was the focus of his attention. Unlike Rodrian, whose DV power spoke as many volumes as his words, Dierk had only his physical expressions to remind me we were on the same page, and his body language said everything I needed to know—he was with me, not the other way around.

Under regular circumstances, I would have said he was the ideal date. "Date" would have been too trivial a word, though, because I knew he was courting me.

After dinner, we walked down to Penn's Landing, a leisurely stroll. He took my hand, entwining our fingers as he had before, and we enjoyed a lovely evening out together. I can't say I was disappointed. And I can't say I was surprised, either.

It was well past midnight when we got back to his hotel. I let him come around to my side to open the door and waited until the boys walked away, giving us some space.

"I had a nice time tonight," I said, rather glad for the shadows, so he couldn't see evidence of my contentment. I didn't want him to know how much I enjoyed the evening. It might give him the wrong idea.

"So did I." The lamp light was full on his face, illuminating the sincerity of his smile. He stroked my arm, a brush of his fingers that beckoned a spread of goose bumps. "I could get used to you."

"Oh, really. Don't struggle with it, now."

"I won't if you won't." He tugged me a little closer. "Don't drive home. It's too late. I arranged a room for you."

I gave him a look of playful shrewdness, narrowing my eyes but wearing a slight grin. "Is it guarded like the last time?"

He only shrugged. "It is next door to my suite, so I suppose it is."

"I didn't pack a bag, though—"

"And once again, you forget that I think of everything. Come."

Once upstairs, Janssen opened a door for me and let me and Dierk inside. It was a spacious suite, a king sized bed with a mountain of pillows decked in a cream-colored satin duvet set, nothing at all like the economy poly-blend mustard-yellow bed spread of a plain old room. The windows were high and arching, as had been the windows in his room. The view was vaguely familiar, so I trusted he was serious about being right next door.

Dierk leaned against the door jamb, arms crossed, watching. "Get some sleep. I have court again tomorrow. I'd like you to be there for it, if you would not mind."

"Do I have to sneak in again?"

"No." He smiled, a full-faced smile that matched the sparkle in his eyes. "You'll be with me."

I nodded. "If you want me to, I will."

He raised my hand to his mouth and kissed it, lingering over the touch. "If you need anything, just call. Or knock," he added with a laugh. "I will be just on the other side of this wall."

"Okay," I said, my voice a whisper. "I'll count on that."

He kissed my hand again and left. I watched the door for a full minute, waiting for it to reopen.

When it appeared he wouldn't change his mind and

came back in, I went into the bathroom. On the vanity, a pink nightie and silk dressing gown had been laid out. I held my breath as I lifted the gown, pressing it up against me in front of the mirror. It was sweet, just really sweet.

I took a few minutes to change and wash up, appreciating the details he'd organized for me. He seemed to have noted what soap and toothpaste I kept in the guest bath of my own rooms because they were arranged on the sink, and the nightie was a perfect fit. I wasn't surprised.

I wondered what else he had gleaned about me from the little time we've known each other. Either he was Sherlock Holmes or—

Or he actually cared enough to learn all he could about me.

I slipped into bed, enjoying the luxurious touch of the sheets and the perfect softness of the pillow and turned out the light. After a moment, I sat up in bed and rolled onto my knees, looking at the wall between us. Reaching up with my hand, I hesitantly knocked, two soft, slow taps. Just to say goodnight. It was the least I could do to thank him for a wonderful evening.

As I got back into bed and pulled up the sheets, I heard his reply. *Knock knock.*

Good night.

I fell asleep wearing a smile, my heart at rest for the first time in a very long while.

First Quarter | Waxing gibbous | moon 50% visible

I woke early, completely rested, and took a quick shower. After getting dressed, I rolled my hair into a wet bun and opened the door. Janssen stood at ease, more or less, arms in front, one hand around the other wrist.

He half-bowed and took on an easy smile. "Early riser, Miss Galen. Shall I wake him?"

"No, I just want to run to the lobby. Do you have the key to let me back in?"

"I do."

"Good. Let him sleep, then. I'll be right back."

I hurried downstairs and called Dahlia. She answered on the first ring. "Where are you?"

"In Philly. Listen, I need a huge favor."

A half-hour later, I saw her car pull into the lot and I dashed outside. "Did you find it?"

"Yes." She waved a dress bag at me. "Hanging in the

laundry room, right where you said. But you were right. No shoes, not even up under your desk. And I don't think those boots are going to go with this."

"That's where you come in. Come on."

We went back inside, up to the room. The guard stiffened as we turned the corner together, but he relaxed when he saw me, only eyeing Dahlia with suspicion and not flat-out pinning her against the wall or frisking her for weapons.

Janssen lifted his chin. "What's in the bag?"

"A dress." I lifted the bottom of the plastic and offered it to him for closer inspection. "Don't tell him, okay? I want to surprise him."

He shook his head. "*Der König* doesn't appreciate surprises."

Janssen was going to be tough to persuade. "Okay...how about tell him my Demivampire female friend came over. But don't mention the dress, okay?"

"I have a duty," he said, with a firm shake of his head.

I pouted. "Can I order you to forget the dress?"

The guard's gaze bore into my own for several uncomfortable moments before flicking over to Dahlia. "You smell of *Wolf*."

She nodded, carefully. "My beloved is *Wolfenkinder*."

That seemed to do something. He pulled out a key card and popped the door open. "I saw no dress. Go inside."

I waited until the door was shut. "Smooth move, Dally. You went all Germanic on him, what with the *Wolfenkinder*."

"Classic concept in communication. When you want people to know you are on their level, you speak in their own language. And, don't think I didn't notice you, either. Ordering the King's Guard around came awful easy to you."

"Don't look at me. He only did it because you sleep with a Were."

"So do you." She grinned at me but after a moment, she lost the smile. "You do, don't you?"

A prickly heat scalded my cheeks as I dropped my purse on a table.

"I knew it," she said. Her voice was softer, but chiding. "You haven't. You still are true to Marek."

"Please." I held up my hand. "You know I can't think of him now. It's wrong."

"But why is it wrong? He'd want you to be happy."

"And I will be," I said firmly. "But I won't give up everything in order to do it."

"Sophie." Dahlia shook her head at me and put her hand on my shoulder. "What do you have left? This thing you have with Dierk—it might be alien but it is something more than what you have now."

"I have my humanity. I have my Demivamps—"

"And Toby has those things, too."

What did I say to that? She was absolutely right. I sat down and pulled off my boots, tossing them aside with a double clunk on the hardwood floor.

"You're lucky you called when you did." Dahlia set the hanger on a hook in the bathroom and began stripping off the plastic. "Another thirty minutes and we would have been gone."

"Plans this early?" I yanked off my shirt and chucked it onto the bed. Parading around in my bra with my potential mate right next door made me feel downright brassy. Sliding the dress off the hanger, I ducked into the bathroom to get changed.

Her reply sounded strained. "Just packing our things."

I stuck my head back around the corner to look at her, but her expression was closed, her eyes lowered. "Why?

Where are you going?"

"Anywhere Aurelia isn't. We're going back to my place downtown."

I flexed my fingers, fighting the urge to punch the door. "Is she giving you guys grief about staying there?"

"Not grief. More of an ambience thing. Feels like a power struggle going on, even though she's the only one fighting. Put that dress on and let me see it."

I kicked off my jeans and slid the dress over my head, tugging it into place before glancing at my reflection. It was a ruched black knee-length dress that I'd worn the day of Marek's memorial. I'd told myself I never needed to see that dress again and left it in the laundry room.

Too bad, because it had been a great little dress. I just never wanted to need it again. Maybe if I never saw it, I'd never end up needing it.

Now, it was the only thing that I could get at short notice on a Sunday morning, when no shops were open and no person could get into my rooms because of the wards.

Dahlia eyed me, tapping her lip. "A little somber, isn't it?"

"Yes, but you can fix it, can't you?"

She laughed. "I'm not a seamstress."

"No, but I saw you make a sweatshirt for Toby once." I twisted and turned in the mirror, trying to see the back of the dress. "Can't you—I don't know, add a little trim?"

"Oh. Right! How about..." She rolled the neckline between her fingers and tugged, a line of white piping appearing. "And..."

After ten minutes of tugging and folding, she'd given the funeral dress white trim and a skinny belt and lightened the black material to a navy color, even altering my hobo bag into a matching clutch. Although it was a very tough decision, I gave her the go ahead to change my boots into heeled navy pumps—but only after taking a dozen different pictures so she could change them back.

I stood in front of the mirror and surveyed my new look. "Thanks, fairy godmother. I'm pretty sure I can go to the ball now."

"Prince Charming is one lucky guy." She rubbed her eyebrow and turned away. "I just wish—"

"Me, too," I whispered. "I just wish being happy didn't have to suck so much."

She toyed with a left-over piece of material. Weird, since the dress was a lot lighter before she started adjusting it. I sincerely hoped it wasn't like putting an engine back together and having a piece left over. A wardrobe malfunction in court could be disastrous. She rolled the cloth between her hands until it became the head of a zipper. "Yeah. I'm really going to miss you guys when you leave."

I chuckled. "I didn't know Dierk grew on you so much."

"Not Dierk." Her voice was thick with sadness, and I opened my shields a tiny bit to get a better sense of what she meant and bit back an oath.

How could I have been so insensitive? Her sadness was true grief, deep and swift like a midnight river after a hard rain. She worried she would lose Toby.

Taking up her hand, I tugged her over to sit on the bed with me. I had no words with which to comfort her. All I could do was use what God gave me. I drew her into my shields and eased her pain, as temporary a fix as it would be. She rested her head on my shoulder, holding my hands in hers, while I did my best to let her know that I treasured her as my dear friend, and that if the worst came to pass, I would take care of Toby.

Next door to the Wereking's suite, in the middle of a

Were safe house, I didn't dare make overt use of my Sophia. I was no champion at sending secret Sophia messages, but she nodded and squeezed my hand. I guessed I did a good enough job.

She left quietly, and I spent the rest of the morning getting ready for Dierk. I even took a good while blowing out my hair and getting the ends to flip. I wanted classic and professional, with just a touch of whimsy. Something worthy of a day in court. I was still twisting in front of the mirror and practicing how to carry a clutch when a rap sounded on the door and Dierk walked in.

He stopped dead in his tracks, eyes wide, as he gave me a once-over, finishing up his assessment with a smooth whistle. "Wow. You did this for me?"

I nodded, shyly. "Couldn't wear an Ozzy shirt two days in a row, no matter how good it smells."

Dierk laughed and took my hand, encouraging me to spin around for him. "But how?"

"I have my resources. And a best friend that I'm sure your man told you about before you came in."

He only gave me his half-smile. "It is a comfort, this understanding you have of me. I don't have to explain many things."

"Not understanding, I don't think." I let go of his hand and opened my newish purse. "Just expectation."

"And do I meet your expectations?"

I leaned into the mirror to apply my lipstick. "I guess. I never thought too hard about what an actual king should act like."

"And what about me as a man?"

The hesitation in his voice disarmed me. Finding his reflection over my shoulder, I met his gaze. "You exceed every notion I've ever had of you."

"Except in one way."

I couldn't lie. "I try very hard not to think about that."

"It is enough, for now." He backed out of the room, rubbing his hands together. "Shall we breakfast in your room or mine?"

Smart guy, distracting me with food. Another point to the exceptional man, hoping to put one more step between the man and the beast.

Janssen briefed Dierk while we ate, the day's schedule sounding just as droll as the day before. My only comfort lay in knowing I wouldn't have to squirm under the scrutiny of his court, as I sat next to their splendid majesty decked out in jeans and a concert shirt. At least I could pretend I was an executive assistant or something. I was great at pretending.

An hour later, he escorted me back into the conference room and led me to my seat. When his back was turned to the room, he grinned and mouthed some encouraging word to let me know I had nailed the entrance. I smiled back and took a steadying breath.

Once seated, I glanced around the room, wondering if I'd know anyone. To my tremendous relief, Toby was posted next to the craft room door behind the dais. Suddenly, it was easier to breathe. I had a connection to my outside life there with me, and the vague sense of alienation disappeared.

The first session went by smoothly, despite the conflicts brought before Dierk; interpack relations were tense and full of power plays as the local packs struggled to acclimate to Dierk's new vision for his wolves. He was intent on opening the eyes of his people, getting them to obey the men and the wisdom they had within their beast. Dierk wanted his people to embrace both natures, man and wolf. It occurred to me that most of these Were had let their human sides go slack with disuse.

He would bring them back. He praised those who tried and encouraged those who faltered. He had harsh words for those who disdained his vision and, while I instinctively knew he had the power to break them if they fought, he guided them and pointed them in the direction he wanted.

Dierk was truly a ruler. My respect for him grew in those hours, and little by little I re-defined him...yet again.

By the time he paused the session for a break, my brain was full and my stomach was empty. I was more than ready to head back into the craft room.

Only a few joined us. Thankfully, Cacilia wasn't one of them. Dierk pointed to the table and whispered in my ear. "Chocolate cake looks good, doesn't it?"

Oh, I think I could learn to like that man. He really got me.

I served a great big slice onto a plate and took it over to a loveseat, setting the plate on the armrest before heading back for a fresh cup of tea. I caught Dierk watching, half-smile on his lips, and gestured to an empty cup. He bowed and shook his head slightly, mouthing "thank you" to me before returning his attention to a woman speaking to him. Tea sweetened, I went back to my comfy chair, pulled out my phone, and enjoyed my cake while reading on my ebook reader.

I still had Marek's journal inside my purse, but I didn't feel it was the right place to lose myself in him.

The icing was delicious but super thick. I could have used a knife to cut it into slices. It was sweet without being overkill and I was truly enjoying it until I had difficulty swallowing the third bite.

Yikes. Death by chocolate would be so awkward here.

I took a sip of tea, but it didn't help it go down. Dropping my phone onto the cushion, I stood up, hoping it would stretch my esophagus. Not enough. I raised my hands over my head, looking ridiculous but it sure beat choking on icing.

Still nothing.

Toby perked up, alerted by my discomfort and came over to me. "Are you all right?"

I shook my head. I couldn't swallow. It was like a mound of putty in the back of my throat, immobilizing the muscle. Breath squeezed past it a teaspoonful at a time.

Anaphylaxis. I started to panic, a wave of hot washing out through my limbs. Everything trembled. I waved frantically at my throat, my breath a ragged gasp, a squeak. I leaned on my hands over the table, unable to sit.

When the edges of my vision faded, I closed my eyes. Fight for control. Fight it. Forget that you're going to die. Focus and fight.

I didn't know I was collapsing until I felt the table under my forehead. I didn't know Dierk was next to me until I heard him scream for help. And then, I didn't know anything more.

I opened my eyes and sat up, not knowing why I was lying on top of a long black gear box. When I jerked awake, I almost fell right the hell off it. Honestly, who puts a sleeping person on top of something that narrow?

"Easy!" Toby grabbed my waist and anchored me. "Lay down. Are you okay?"

"I'm fine. Get me down. Why am I up here? Who's that? Toby." I looked at him hard, wishing I could feel more than his hands. My shields were skin-tight against me and I couldn't get them to relax. "What is going on?"

"You almost suffocated." His brows were drawn together, and his forehead glistened.

I pushed off his arms and sat up. "What the hell are you talking about?"

"Don't you remember?"

"Toby. I think I'd remember almost dying."

"You started to breathe funny, then you pointed at your throat—you don't remember anything?"

I felt my neck and swallowed. Nothing wrong as far as I could tell. Nothing. "Where's Dierk?"

"In another room. They're questioning someone. You said a name before you fell down. Can you think back and remember why you said it?"

"Toby. I don't remember. But I am getting a little pissy. Please get me down now?"

He took my waist again and lifted me down, easy as picking up a plate. Totally a big-up there, considering the depression binging I'd done. At least he didn't groan and stagger under my weight.

Toby pulled a radio out of his back pocket and pressed the chirpy button. "Stohl."

The radio chirped back. "*Ja*, go."

"She's up."

The radio fuzzed out with a spark of static. "We'll be in."

"Roger that. Over." Toby stuck the radio back into his pocket and walked over to the door, crossing his arms and waiting for the others to arrive.

"Wow," I said. "You really are the security guy, aren't you?"

"I never expected to be royal guard, but yeah. I like the job. He trusts me in here alone with you. That says a lot. I should have a good job once he leaves, if I don't leave with him."

"You'd leave with him?"

"Depends on you."

"I can't tell you what to do, Toby. I wouldn't make you give up a royal guard position."

"You don't understand. I'd only take the job if you were

going back with him. But if you stay, I'd stay here. Nothing's been decided yet."

It took my breath, hearing him say he'd give up his life here just like that, just to follow me to Europe. The value of that sacrifice—was I worth such a price? "But...what about Dally?"

Toby's mouth became a thin line, his lips going pale under the pressure. He inhaled hard through his nose. "Dally will keep on being Dally without me. She won't be going with me. It's just—not going to happen."

"Does she know yet?" I didn't want to tell him that she had already suspected something was going on with him.

He shook his head.

"I can't do that to her," he said softly. "I don't want her to suffer with the uncertainty. It still might not happen, you know?"

But, looking at the heavy line of his brows, the cloudiness of his expression, I knew he didn't believe it. Neither of us did.

A month ago, Toby had been content to go along with whatever Dahlia set out for him—meeting with packs, learning his estranged "heritage" a little bit at a time. Now he stood in front of me, royal guard for the king of all Werekind—it didn't get any further from his old reality than this. And he took it all in stride, unfazed by the earth-shaking changes our worlds have recently undergone. He acted like he'd been born to this life.

That wasn't the Toby I thought I knew.

"You've really changed," I said.

"Life is all about change." He ran his hand through his hair before letting his arms rest at his sides. "You change with it, or you stop living."

The door opened and Dierk came in, closing the distance between us in a streak. Searching my face, he held my face in his hands, his thumbs tracing tiny circles on my cheeks. "You are all right?"

"Everyone keeps asking," I said. "Yes. I'm fine. What happened?"

Dierk's brows were upturned. "It looked like anaphylaxis."

"I don't have allergies." Especially not to chocolate. I'd have been dead a lifetime ago. By my own hand, if necessary.

"We know," he said. "Tancred drew blood and analyzed it."

That's when I noticed the bandage on the crook of my elbow. I traced it with a finger, noting zero discomfort from the needle puncture. Not bad, Tancred. Not bad at all. "Analyzed it? What, does he have a travelling lab in the back of the tour bus?"

"He has resources," he said. "At any rate, we know it was not anaphylaxis. There were no cellular markers left behind."

"So…compulsion?"

He half-nodded, half-shrugged, looking all around at a complete loss. "Or magic, at least. We are questioning some people but nothing has turned out yet."

"Great. Who's after me now? Last time, it was vampires. Before that, it was a werewolf. Did I join a Hitman of the Month club?"

Toby cleared his throat. "Last couple of times, it was vampires. You forgot Eirene."

"Oh." I wagged a finger in exaggerated realization. "You're right. How could I forget her? Wow. Oxygen deprivation."

"You are not the least bit amusing," Dierk said.

"Sorry, Dierk, I have an inappropriate sense of humor." I began to giggle. I couldn't stop.

He hugged me, wrapping me in his solid arms, his scent and his heartbeat cancelling out everything else.

"Hmm." A young woman with long, coal-black spiky hair had been escorted into the room. Bedecked as she was in a lace top and denim capris, I assumed she hadn't been present for court. She flicked a penlight in front of my eyes, peering into them. "Hmm."

"Hmm, what?" I still had no idea who she was. Apart from human with very interesting hair, I was clueless.

"I need you to hold your breath and not blink."

What did I have to lose? "Okay."

She looked in, gazing intently, as I did so. My eyes started to sting and I grimaced to keep my eyes wide open.

"Quick blink," she said.

Ah. Blinking. That felt so good.

Twenty seconds later she patted my leg.

"Okay, breathe. I saw what I needed to see." She got up and walked over to the table where her purse lay and tucked the penlight inside.

"What did you see, Alise?" Dierk hadn't moved from

where he stood over my shoulder, arms crossed, chest inflated with an imperious air.

"It wasn't a compulsion," she said. "It was magic that choked you. Someone used a spell."

I stifled a groan. "You can tell that by looking in my eyes?"

"Magic leaves a residue in the blood." She handed a tube back to Tancred, who tucked it into a slot in a small metal case. "The vessels are visible on the retina, so you can see it if you know how to look."

"Can you identify the strain?" Tancred sat down, crossed his legs, and pulled his glasses off. I couldn't imagine a wolf in glasses. The closest I could picture was Beast from the X-Men but Tancred wasn't blue.

I'd read comics in high school. Sue me.

"I can narrow it down," she said. "It wasn't human, exactly."

Tancred folded his fingers over his chest. "Vague."

"Not green enough to be fey magic. Too small to be human witchcraft. Baffling, actually."

Dierk dismissed her with a scoff, clearly displeased with her analysis. "Tancred. Is there someone else you can call?"

"You don't need anyone else." She put her hands on her hips and turned on him with a shake of her dark head. "I'm the best there is."

"This is the best? 'Baffling?'"

"Not my fault." Alise pointed at me. "What is she?"

Someone else was treating me like a specimen. Joy, joy. "Who," I said. "I'm a who, not a what."

She hurried back over, very much like a little bird, and peered at me. "You're a what, all right. They said you were human."

"Last I checked, I was."

"She's bitten," Toby said.

"But not yet changed?" Alise eyed me.

I shook my head.

"Then it doesn't matter. You're human until the moon. But you're not human."

"Yes, she is." Dierk and Stohl spoke in unison.

"If you were human, I'd be able to tell who set this spell." She shook her head. "You're not human, or else there is something else in your blood."

Wisely, no one clarified the problem. She looked hard at me, then up at Dierk. "No? Not going to tell me? Fine. But I can't decipher these strains until I know what kind of medium her blood is."

"She's human." Dierk voice was pleasant and flat, his half-smile telling nothing.

"You can't keep her a secret. If she's other—"

"Other? What other?" I asked, although I had a feeling I didn't want to know. She obviously knew about the Were and the DV and yet, the word *other*.

"You aren't like anyone else here, and you aren't of the Fey. You aren't plain old human, either."

"Thanks for noticing." Smart ass was unavoidable. "I like to think I'm special."

She didn't laugh. "I want to know. Show me."

"Huh?" Suddenly I was holding my breath again. I tried to exhale, but the impulse passed. She leaned closer and I felt a weird tugging in my face.

"Show me what I need." She slid a vial out of her back pocket and unscrewed the cap.

"Stop, witch," Stohl said.

She smiled, open-mouthed, and gently shook her head. "I will know."

"No," Dierk said. "You will only be disappointed. And you will die if you don't stop now."

My eyes felt tight and suddenly the light changed. The

room took on a pink tinge. I blinked twice and everything looked normal again.

Alise's mouth pulled into an angry curl. "You can't keep this a secret."

"It's not my secret to share." Dierk placed both hands on my shoulders, drawing me against him. "She is not a threat. But, should you draw another drop of her blood, you will die. I promise."

I heard a quiet *snik* from Stohl's direction.

Alise blinked twice. She'd heard it, too. The tugging stopped and I remembered how to breathe.

"Now, leave with Stohl," Dierk said. "He will take you someplace to rest until I am ready for you."

Stohl smiled and gripped her arm, leading her away. She wouldn't take her gaze from me.

Dierk pulled a handkerchief from his pocket and patted my tears with it before folding it and putting it away again, but he wasn't fast enough. I saw the blood.

"Who was she?" I hesitantly touched the corner of my eye, scrutinizing it for a hint of blood. Nothing. It didn't even hurt.

"A witch."

"Seriously?" A thousand thoughts stumbled through my mind, tripping up every time they brought up Jasmine. Great.

He nodded, opening a bottle of water and pouring it into the tea pot. "Apparently, she's a pretty high ranking one, too. There will be a problem keeping her quiet."

"Great. That's perfect. So now I'll have witches after me."

"Not after you. Exactly," he amended. "But they'll want to find out all they can about you. It's their nature."

"Ugh." I buried my face in my hands. "Here we go again with the nature."

"They are witches. Researchers. Scholars. Scientists of the metaphysical."

I looked up when he sat next to me. "Friend or foe?"

"Neutral, I suppose." Dierk stretched his arm across the back of my cushion. "Were and *Witchkinder* coexist with no prejudices. In fact, we share common interests."

"What about witch…*kinder* and DV?"

He shrugged. "I confess I do not know."

"I suppose we better find out." I sat back, into the arch of his arm. "Can I call Rode down? Will he get a hard time if he shows up?"

"Here? Of course not. Common ground."

I looked up at him. "I mean from you."

He patted my leg. "If he can help you, I will not keep him away."

I was halfway through a mug of Darjeeling when I picked up Rodrian's power signature. He wasn't happy, and he wasn't alone.

"They come in with me." His voice carried through the closed door. Dierk lifted his chin, wearing a piqued look and Stohl opened the door, motioning for them enter.

Rodrian walked in wearing a Marek attitude, and six other DV followed. Stohl made no trouble and simply shut the door after they were inside. To my relief, Gian Greco was with them; I caught his gaze immediately and felt him scan me, his eyes blazing with his inner light. His expression relaxed somewhat, so I took it as a sign that I wasn't too effed up and let myself relax as well.

Caen, on the other hand, seemed rather disappointed I was still alive. Hmm. Must be Sunday. Or April.

"Adeluf." Rodrian tipped his head and sounded more civil than he had all week.

I gaped. Respect? Oh crap. This was really bad.

"Thurzo." Dierk got up and extended a hand, which Rodrian took without any major hesitation. "Thank you for coming so quickly."

Rodrian looked over in my direction, a darting glance. His power had a coiled-up feeling, like he was trying very hard to contain himself. "What happened?"

Dierk explained the attack and subsequent examination by the witch. He had a marvelously patient way of relaying details with logical precision. Usually I'm the type who has to butt in when someone doesn't get the story right; shoot, I can't re-tell a joke without improving it.

With Dierk, I didn't have to, although Rodrian kept looking over at me as if he expected me to interrupt.

"So," Rodrian said. "The problems are these: Sophie was a target of a magical attack, a witch investigator couldn't determine the strain of magic, and the witch community have been alerted to Sophie's uniqueness."

Dierk answered with a curt nod. "That is my assessment."

Rodrian looked very much like he'd developed a headache. He rubbed his temple and gave me a look that read like he was starting to think I was more trouble than I was worth. "She'll be put under guard, obviously."

"It is done," Dierk said.

"Not yours. Mine." Rodrian's confrontational attitude seemed to be surfacing again. I crossed my fingers and prayed they wouldn't resort to fisticuffs. Or, whatever fru-fru word royal people used to mean a butt-kicking contest.

Dierk inhaled deeply, stealing a quick glance at me, but didn't object. "We will work out the details presently. Of more pressing concern is that of the *Witchkinder* relationship with DV."

Rodrian shrugged. "DV would not prey upon them without invitation, since they are magic-sensitive. The amulets are the warning."

"Can they be compelled?"

"Persuaded, perhaps, but I do not think they are swayed by compulsion. Their mind-magics are highly disciplined from communicating with their deity."

"Do you think the Sophia, being demideity to the DV, could be in danger from *Witchkinder*?" Dierk took his seat again and crossed his legs, his ankle on his knee.

"They are women who worship women." Rodrian glanced over at Greco. "I don't see how Sophia can be a threat. If anything, the Sophia are a manifestation of the Goddess."

Funny how they could have such a revealing conversation right in from of me. I was pretty sure I wasn't under a glass dome, but anyways. Demideity? I could have so much fun with that, if not for the pressing problem.

"Witches, Rode?" I interrupted. "Didn't you think I should have learned about witches sometime over the last year or two?"

"Not now, Sophie."

"Okay. Not now." God, I wanted to slug him. "Let's just wait until someone else tries to kill me. Maybe an elf assassin with a crossbow and a Crystal of Destiny will be waiting by my car."

"Don't be ridiculous," Dierk said. "There's no such thing as elves."

"Why not?" I waved my hands over my head, looking almost as crazy as I felt. "Did they all perish in the Great Cataclysm?"

"They don't exist." He looked at me as if he suspected a head injury. "Where do you get these strange ideas?"

Rodrian swung a heavy lidded-look at Dierk.

"She's a writer," he said, as if it would explain everything.

"Ah." Dierk nodded sagely. "Overactive imagination."

I treated each of them to the dirtiest look I could muster. "Will you two stop cooperating? It's getting on my nerves."

They exchanged a smirk. I was *this close* to throwing my shoes at them.

"We will have to bring her back in," Dierk said. "The witch will have to be handled with delicacy. It would be wise to avoid incident."

Rodrian nodded his agreement. "Personally, I think the time for diplomacy passed when she used her will on Sophie." He looked at me. "I can smell your blood, Sophie. I can guess what she did."

"Tancred drew blood for testing," I said.

"And he deposited it into a handkerchief in Dierk's pocket?" He tilted his head back and looked down his nose at me. "Unless you mean to say Dierk is the one who hurt you."

"Of course, he didn't."

"And yet, you keep ending up in harm's way. How many attempts have been made upon your life since that man has come to town, Sophie? I want you safe. Just come home."

I felt the weight behind the words. He missed me. Home. Sounded so nice when he said it.

I turned to speak but Dierk answered first. "She is home. She is with me."

Rodrian responded snakebite-fast, as if he'd been waiting for the opportunity. "I didn't ask you, Adeluf. I asked Sophie. You may be a ruler in your own court but here, you're just another guy with a hot eye and a sharp bite. Now back off."

A low rumble of a growl started somewhere behind me. This is why I preferred standing against walls. I looked frantically around, trying to locate the wolf so I could plan where to dive should it decide to spring.

There was no wolf. It was Dierk.

His eyes had bled to true gold, the wolf king's eyes, and he lowered his chin to his chest. In four strong strides he crossed the room, stopping right in front of me, hands out slightly as if to better block me. "You act as if she is yours."

"She *is* mine." Rodrian rose to his full height and met Dierk, glare for savage glare. "Is that your way? Parade into another man's land and city and randomly decide whom to steal? You obviously have no respect for the privacy of a man's home. Do your people make a habit of carrying off women into the night? Is that a Were thing or a German thing?"

Dierk's voice dropped down into a growl. "You go too far."

"Not nearly far enough. You've no honor. You make covenants with criminals and vampires. You encourage the destruction of the weak and the innocents. You bar the way for justice and resolution. You stole my son. You will not steal her!"

The temper that had been rising in Dierk seemed to level off and his lips parted in a silent *Ah*. "I did none of those things, Thurzo."

Rodrian's temper was still climbing, his power pulsing with a seething red rage. "You did."

"I did not," Dierk insisted, his voice calm. He was doing that whole I'm-not-overreacting thing. I knew it would drive Rodrian nuts. "Where is your daughter?"

"You leave Shiloh—"

"Not the child. Where is Brianda?"

"Why? You want her to slaughter you instead? She'd have no qualms kicking an old man's—"

"We are the same age." He shook his head in contempt. "You DV are all alike. Why do none of you count the years? Do you have so many that you do not need to treat them like the precious commodity they are? My father,

Thurzo, was not as honorable as he could have been."

Rodrian seemed to take a reluctant pause, as if remembering. "Sins of the father. . ."

"I cannot make up for what he did to you, but I am not the same man."

"Then show me your honor." Rodrian lost his angry stance and took on a vulnerable tone. He rubbed his mouth, gestured to the door. "Leave. Just leave us alone. Leave her alone."

"I cannot." Dierk's voice was softer, dropping to a regretful tone. I knew he felt for Rodrian's agony, sympathized with his losses. Dierk did not wish to cause pain. "I will not leave her. I don't expect you to understand and I will not explain. Sophie and I have a road to travel. Together. There is no separate path for each of us."

"Sophie." Rodrian pulled me away from Dierk, blocking the rest of the room. His eyes were pools of copper, his voice anguished. "Please. Send him away."

"I can't, Rode." My heart ached for the desolation I felt in his power. I wanted to comfort him, to drain away every last wave of pain. If he felt anything like I felt, though, his pain was near bottomless. We would drown together. "I know it hurts you, but I can't."

"You want him." His voice sounded strangled. Rodrian looked stricken, felt stricken.

I didn't want to be the cause of his pain but I didn't want to string him along, chasing a resolution that might never materialize. I know the pain of chasing hope when hope was only a ghost of a wish. Taking his hands, I pressed them between my own, feeling the familiar touch of his hands, rough and tender at the same time. "I want a happy ending. Somehow."

He snorted, a quick, disgusted sound. "Being one of them is a happy ending?"

"Maybe it's not fairy tale-worthy, Rode, but I wouldn't be alone."

"You weren't alone before." He curled his fingers around mine and drew me closer, holding my hands up to his chest. His heart beat steady, persistent, a reminder of every time I'd been this close to him.

It wasn't enough. Lately, too much had come between us, and the situation made it all too easy to pick out the differences.

"Yeah, I was. Even with you right next to me, I was alone." I sighed. I really didn't want to think about Aurelia right now, not when I had all this other crap to process. "Things have changed. You just haven't noticed. It's not your fault. Aurelia's kept you busy."

I waved off his retort before he could start. "Whatever my ending is going to be, I have to believe I won't be alone. I don't want to fight anymore."

I stood close enough to Rodrian to feel his breath on my face. He stared me down with a desperate look.

"Oh, honey," he murmured. Tears welled, catching fire from the fleck of copper heat that smoldered in his eyes. "What did they do to you? You aren't the same."

"I know," I whispered. "But I love you. That won't change, not even when you give up on me. I will love you, and Shy, and...But I can't fight nature. It's easier to let it run its course."

"You're serious, aren't you? You're giving up."

"Not giving up. Just. . .letting go. I'm so tired of fighting, Rode. So tired."

"Let me take care of you." He ran his palms up my arms, drawing me in, breathing me in. I tried not to see the disappointment in his expression. "I used to love doing this. Just your scent was enough. Knowing you were close, that the possibility always existed that. . .You're not the same Sophie."

There. He said it. He *used to love*. I guessed that implied past tense.

I blinked rapidly and raised my hand up between us, turning the palm so the light licked across the slick scars. It was the same hand that once bore a faint scar from the first time he'd tasted me. That was so long ago.

Now the imprint of Rodrian's bite was eclipsed by another's. "How could I be?"

Before he could get angry again I stepped backwards, breaking his hold on my arms, and blinked away the sting of disappointment before it could manifest into tears. "I would still love you, even if you changed. I've proven that change in physical form can't change what I hold in my heart. Not even when Marek…"

I pressed my lips together, unwilling to speak the words in front of Dierk. Some things were too private. Nobody understood that, despite the Weres and the attempts and the Aurelias and Cacilias, I still walked around each and every day with a black hole where my heart used to be. Light and hope circled and drained before they could take hold of me, and nothing but grief filled the event horizon. I felt like that every damned day, and I had to seize the tiny joys wherever I could find them just so I could claim I still existed.

Guessed Rodrian wouldn't be one of those joys for me anymore. "I'm sorry that you have to decide whether you feel the same for me."

Rodrian's gaze shifted, the copper glints hardening into cold steel. "I will never forgive you, Adeluf."

Dierk exhaled through his nose, a sound of resignation. "You will never know me, Thurzo. You will never see me for who I really am. I cannot expect you to open your heart when you won't even open your eyes."

"Rode, try to understand." I raised clasped hands to my mouth, begging. "For me."

His eyes had turned to stone, dull and dead. Something vital had been extinguished. "I don't have a choice, do I?"

I took a deep breath, praying for forgiveness, because I knew I killed something in him. God help me. I had hurt my best friend. I'd dealt a mortal blow to the tender ties that kept us from being alone in this world and I did it because I thought it was the best thing to do.

I looked from him, to Dierk, and back to him. "None of us do."

"Olberich, have Stohl bring Alise back in. We need to get in front of this." Dierk brushed his hands together. "Unless we still need to discuss the obvious? No? Good."

Just before Olberich closed the door, Dierk stopped him. "Wait. We will wait for her in the other room."

"Why? It's not as secure."

"But I am tired," Dierk said archly. "I wish to sit."

Hmph. He just wanted his fancy chair. Kings were so pompous sometimes.

The conference room seemed so empty, now that the Weres had all been cleared. Only part of Dierk's entourage had been retained. Thankfully, it was the security part and not the Cacilia part. The two guards who had stood at the doors also remained, although the heraldic banners were gone.

Instead, they both had forced a partial change—clawed hands, a bunching of the brows that dehumanized their faces just enough to be unsettling. I tried not to look at them any more than I absolutely had to. Instead, I focused on Alise.

The black-haired witch stood alone in the center of the room. Her upper arm was still smarting red from Stohl's grip. She was sullen and resentful, her jaw jutting like a grounded fourteen-year-old.

Once she was brought in, Dierk came in from the back room. He marched over to his special chair and seated himself. "Let us discuss how we are going to cooperate."

"Why should I help you?" Alise crossed her arms. "You were a jerk before."

"I'm also a reasonable man," said Dierk. "You know she isn't ordinary."

"Blatantly obvious." She glanced behind her, where Rodrian and the Demivamp six-pack lined the wall behind her.

Dierk occupied the only chair in the room, and Stohl had moved into place behind his right shoulder. I'd drifted opposite to his left. It was automatic, and only after the three of us faced her from our new positions did Alise seem to realize that Dierk had pulled rank. Her eyes darted from face to face, mouth twitching into a straight line.

Dierk steepled his fingers. "You also drew her blood without permission."

"I—I didn't hurt her." Still, a wallop of defiance, although caution was seeping in. Caution, or self-preservation.

Dierk's voice was like stone. "She is my mate."

The young witch paled beneath her powder. "I didn't know."

"It would make...quite an incident."

She passed pale and went emo-white. "We wouldn't want that," she whispered.

"I agree." Dierk half-smiled and leaned forward. "But incidents don't happen when people are silenced."

A tight hum of panic started like a ringing in my ears. She was terrified, and I felt it. Seriously terrified. Her whole body tensed, arms drawn in, shoulders hunched.

"Majesty." I used my gentlest tone, leaning to place my hand on his arm. "I'm sure she'll help us. Won't you, Alise?"

"Yes." She swallowed and stood up straighter. "Of course."

Dierk patted my hand without looking at me. "It would avoid incident."

"And—and I'm sorry for what I did. I got carried away." She knelt, pleading with her eyes. "Please, Lady. I meant no harm. I was weak. I would not shame my Goddess again."

I smiled, pouring benevolence into my voice. "I know. And perhaps we can help find what you seek. All I ask is that you help us find out what happened."

"Of course. There is a question to be answered, and answers to be found. Of course, I can help."

Fear had a funny way of helping people see reason. I smiled, hoping I looked sincere.

Dierk only raised a hand. "Bring me the hotel manager. I require a conference table."

Within minutes, a table was brought in and set up, and a young man in hotel uniform brought in refreshments, setting soft drinks and iced glasses at each seat. I was parched. All this getting attacked and playing wounded future-Queen stuff had made me very thirsty.

When he came to Dierk, he set down two mugs of Darjeeling.

I got one of the mugs. And a brownie. #WIN.

Dierk sat across from Alise. I sat across from Rodrian, who wore his power like an egg shell—strong enough to conceal, thin enough to crack if need be. He alternatively stared at my mug or at the girl or at the ceiling. Anywhere but at me.

I would have noticed if he did, because I didn't look at anyone else.

I directed my first question to the center of the table. "Who uses magic?"

"Witches, of course." Rodrian answered. I guess he'd noticed I was staring and felt pressured to answer. "Not DV; we have our own power. Were?"

"Possible, but I can't see why." Dierk had his fingers laced before him. "Magic, per se, is anti-nature. *Wolfenkinder* are a part of the earth and wind. We have all the power in the world."

I shook my head. "All that proves is that the DV and Were do not prefer magic, but can perhaps still use it. Who else, Alise? You said it wasn't 'green enough to be Fey.'"

"The Fey are ancient," she said. "They keep to themselves, preferring the green lands away from cities. They aren't human. They usually aren't even corporeal. So many stories and myths and lies about the Faerie make it difficult to know the truth anymore."

"Fairy?" I tapped Dierk's foot with mine. "I thought you said they don't exist."

"No, my dear. That was elves."

"Elves?" Alise rolled her eyes and giggled. "You're kidding."

Looked like I was the last in the room to know something. Again. I wagged a finger. "Don't even start."

"Anyhoo… fey magic is a green strain." Alise started ticking off her fingers. "Demon is red. Hellfire is more than just a cliché, it's a stain."

"Angel magic?" I hoped I wouldn't get harangued again.

"Angels don't use magic. They are only messengers. God doesn't use magic, either; He has Will. Capital W, in case you missed it. Lesser divinities use magic because they don't have enough faithful to supply divine willpower. Other strains…orange, silver."

"Black." Rodrian's voice was mild, but I caught the

power behind it. *Black* made him nervous.

"Yes, black." Alise nodded, her bangs waving like feathers. "But it's rare."

"Black magic is rare?" I asked.

"Not the same thing." Dierk interrupted. "The black strain is dragon magic."

"Elves are fake, but dragons aren't." Really? Just really? I wished there was a way to bang my head off the wall without having to get up. I swore, these people lived only to make me look like an idiot.

Rodrian finally looked at me. "The kind you are imagining are. Dragons are weather entities. Occasionally they manifest in other forms."

"Orange is *djinn*. Silver is…" Alise trailed off. "Dead. Dead magic. Magic wielded by a non-living thing. It could be anything."

"Well," I said. "What color did you see?"

"There were two, but one faded as I watched. It was in pieces, I couldn't tell. I don't know any magic that does that—magic is stable and lingers. That one wasn't, I don't know. Right. See? That's why I had to know. That magic strain was an anomaly. The other…" She shook her head. "Blue. I'll swear it was blue."

"Which is?" Dierk and Rodrian exchanged significant glances, and I caught a pulse of surprise from Rodrian.

"Nothing is blue except the Sophia, and they're just a myth. Oh." She looked from me to the men and back. "That's it, isn't it? You're one of them?"

She pushed back her chair. "Oh, my Goddess. Oh. Oh. You didn't tell me."

I reached for my tea. "I didn't say a word."

"You didn't have to. You have the eyes. You flashed at me when I said the word." She got up and began to pace, pressing fingers into her temples as if she had a headache.

"I beg your forgiveness."

"This is what I feared would happen." Dierk crossed his arms. "You wanted to know. Now you know. Now you know how important it is I feel that information is safe with you."

She shook her head, dark spikes trembling like great plumes. "You shouldn't have kept that a secret. I—I can't go back—"

"Why not?"

"I pulled your blood. My Goddess will be displeased. I must go. I must—"

Dierk reached out his hand. "Sit down. Alise, dear, relax. The Goddess knows all that you do."

"Yes. She does." Her complexion took on a greyish tint. Poor kid looked like she wanted to throw up.

"And she knows when you intend harm. Did you?"

"No, I swear." Her eyes were anime-huge, liquid with tears. "I only wanted to know."

"Then she knows. And if you genuinely want to help my mate, and not lead her to further harm, your goddess will know."

She said nothing.

Neither did Rodrian, who had shut himself off when Dierk called me his mate. He looked at me then, flat-eyed and thin-lipped. My insides crumpled.

Dierk paid him no mind. "Alise, answer me, and answer Her. Do you intend to bring harm to my mate, directly or indirectly, through your words, actions, desires, or thoughts?"

"No. She's...really?" She looked at me through tears. "You are?"

"Yeah." I wondered if I should hug her for comfort. I've never encountered anyone who reacted this way before. "'Fraid so."

She drew her shaking hands up and crossed them over her chest, below the base of her throat. "With all that I am, and all my Goddess has granted me, I will serve. You are hers. I am yours."

A clank of air puffed past me, causing me to blink.

"Your oath is accepted," Dierk said. "We are most pleased."

"What happened?" I whispered.

Dierk stood and moved to pull my chair out for me. Apparently, we were done here. "She has bound her word in magic. You can fully trust her. She is ours."

Alise smiled up at me like a fan girl. Hoo boy.

Waxing gibbous | moon 76% visible

Rodrian drove me back to the Stocks that night, despite numerous unhappy protests from Dierk. Going with Rodrian had been the right thing to do. He'd been so distressed over the whole witch attack that I worried he'd go over the edge.

He seemed to have recovered somewhat from our earlier conversation, but it was too hard to tell. He was shut up tight against the touch of the Sophia, and his mouth didn't let me get a word in edgewise.

I would have thought that scoring a big point against Dierk in the Great Battle for Sophie would have made him happier, but no. All he did was complain about my car the whole way back.

No keyless remote. Automatic transmission. Windshield wiper on the wrong side of the wheel.

It had a tape deck and no MP3 player. The seats were

too lumpy. The steering column didn't adjust. The windshield was a dinged-up mess and the rear window was a bird strike disaster. And, gasp! The side mirrors had to be manually adjusted.

I doubted he'd make it back to the Stocks with his sanity intact. Even worried he might require smelling salts at one point.

At length, even the Cavalier's countless short comings weren't enough to sustain the conversation. We were still several miles from the Stocks so unless he dove from the moving vehicle, I figured it was time to tell him something I didn't think he wanted to hear. "Rode, are you sure she's the one you want to be with?"

He didn't ask me to clarify who she was. "She's my mate."

"But she's—"

"My mate, Sophie." His voice held the same dead weight his eyes had earlier. "I don't expect you to understand, but I don't need you to berate me over it."

I was starting to get the whole mate thing because I was facing a slight mating issue of my own, thank you very much, but I didn't feel it to be a prudent choice to argue. I wanted to tell him how mean she'd been to me—in my own home, no less—but I didn't want to sound like a whiny kid.

I had to give an objective assessment, to offer him logic. "But she's a disease. I feel it in her. She's pushing for a fast end, Rode, and she'll drag you down with her."

"Nobody forces my hand, Sophia, not even you."

Sophia. For some reason, his use of my title instead of my name pissed me off. We were closer than this, despite all the Leni crap. I had an overwhelming urge to seize him, shake him, slap some sense into his stupid head. I opened my barriers, full wide, and blasted him with an unadulterated rush of *Listen to me, dammit!*

He just side-stepped it. I felt my intentions glance harmlessly off his shields, as unheeded as a lecture by a teenager.

So I grabbed his arm and pinched him, hard. Anything more might make him drive off the road and I didn't want to get into an accident just to prove a point. "I have not endured all that I have endured, just to see you shredded by a woman like her."

"At least she's putting me first." He set his jaw and said no more.

I was glad of it. If that's all he had to say, I didn't want to hear any more.

Dierk arrived to drive me to work the next morning, just as I expected he would. I appreciated the dependability. Some men should take a lesson from a gentleman like that. Not naming any names.

He also surprised me by saying he'd arranged for Alise's high priestess to visit me at work. He suggested I would benefit from a human perspective as well as a chance to ask my own questions without him hovering or influencing me.

It was exactly what I wanted. Once again, he fulfilled a wish without my having to ask. It was becoming a pattern with him and I wondered who else had benefited from the sweetness of his intuition. Was there anyone else?

Before I got out of the car, he placed his hand on my arm.

"She is an important person, my dear. Just remember that she is powerful. We need her to be sympathetic."

"I'm not sure I follow. Can I get you in trouble?"

"Not me. Perhaps just keep in mind one thing—you were very noteworthy even before the Leni. She will be a curious person. Don't overshare."

Unsure of what to make of that, I waved him off and spent the rest of the morning feeling like Fraidy in a cat crate. Confined and hyper-anticipatory. Each rotted on its own. Both together, well, that was worse.

The witch arrived just before lunch and waited patiently while I finished up a few column letters. She busied herself looking through the picture frames (and wasn't immune to Rodrian's photogenicity; I heard her tiny appreciative mmm), but I knew she watched me with keen interest.

Nakia Hopkins was probably the oddest woman I've ever met, and that's saying something.

She sounded British, but said she had been born in Wichita. She was ginger, but didn't have a single freckle in sight. Completely gaga for gadgetry, hands calloused from hard work, yet the carriage of an empress. She wore men's tweed trousers with the cutest of heels (seriously cute heels. I kid you not) and a pearl necklace over a pentacle that had been tattooed below the hollow of her throat. Smaller matching tats danced across the inside of her wrists. Her ears seemed gaged, but instead of the hollow tubes favored by the majority who pierced that way, she wore enormous pearls tucked inside. And she was eloquent, even when she fell to using the vernacular.

I'm not trying to say that any of her traits or characteristics should have identified her with one particular social group over another. I'm just saying that the first impression she made on me was, well, kaleidoscopic. I didn't know what the hell to make of her.

Two minutes into our conversation and I had a new impression: extremely likable.

Nakia had been briefed by Tancred (whom I mentally referred to as Chief Science Officer) as well as, I assumed, the young witch Alise. She confided that, although she trusted both of them, she wanted to check me out herself.

Once again, I sat through the hold-my-breath-and-stare test.

Didn't need a tissue afterwards, either. This lady had finesse.

"Um, can I ask you a question?" I pressed the corners of my eyes, wondering what she saw.

She clicked off her pen light and motioned at me to sit back in my chair. "Sure."

"This Leni...what do you know about it? I mean, not just the Leni, because that's all I hear about. But you're human, right? You're not half-something magical, right?"

She laughed. "We're all magic. Even you. Especially you. You are the Sophia. Isn't that magic?"

"I don't know, I mean. I'm just regular people."

"Regular people, right. That's funny. I heard your eyes change color every time a Demivamp sneezes."

I scowled. That really wasn't my fault. And it only happened once. "I'm not Were."

"Oh, I see where you are coming from. True, you are not Were yet."

"I hate that word."

"Were?"

I shook my head. "Yet. I'm so sick of this will-I-won't-I crap."

Nakia put the penlight into a side pocket of her purse and sat down. "Full moon is almost here. You don't have long to wait."

"Isn't there a way to tell if I'm going to Turn? Like a Werewolf EPT?"

"No." She tried to suppress a snort. "No, it either happens or it doesn't."

"But why, though?"

"Well, it has to do with the lunar cycle and star alignment. See, there are thirteen full moons in every year.

Regular people will call a moon full for hours, if not days—but that is so inaccurate. Each full moon has a zenith, just like the sun does each day, when it seems to be hung in the sky, perfect and unchanging. That's when it's one hundred percent full, just those few minutes. And that's when the change would occur. Up until that moment, it's just waxing full, still climbing to that magical moment."

She leaned to dig her phone out of her purse and started tapping the screen. "And that's not all. Each of those thirteen moons is accompanied by a unique star pattern, and each one has its own unique divinatory significance. That means the blessing is slightly different from moon to moon."

She leaned to show me a chart she'd brought up on her phone. It was complex and ornate, but didn't make any sense to me.

I took the phone and turned it sideways. Oh, there it was. "Like the Chinese Zodiac? Except every year is the Year of the Wolf."

"Yes!" She clapped her hands. "Brilliant, that. I can see t-shirts with that logo on. But, getting back on track—it's not just mystical, like the Were will have you believe. It's science. It's the power and the energy of the universe, the pull on the tides at its most powerful. It's dependent on location and altitude and a thousand exquisite variables. We have the tech to calculate and triangulate the precise moment the Were element in the blood will respond to the fullness of the moon. See?"

Yeah, I saw. I saw a lot more than I wanted to. Suddenly, the will-I-won't-I option seemed better than knowing the exact second. "So you can tell me the exact moment I'm going to turn into a werewolf?"

She nodded. "Well. Plus or minus twenty-two seconds. To account for altitude, humidity, other factors. You want me to send you the calculation? Where are you mooning? Lancaster, right?" She held out her hand for her phone. "Turn on your NFC and I'll send it to you."

I took my own phone out of the desk drawer and handed it over to let her do it. "Why is humidity a factor? Do Weres frizz up a lot?"

"No, it's water. The moon affects the tides, right? Well, not just because of gravity and the fluidity of a large moveable body. It's the water. When you look at the moon, what do you see? A white ball with black smudges. Those smudges are called seas. There are lakes covering the surface, too. But where is the water? The moon's surface is devoid of water and spends the majority of her cycle trying to pull the Earth's water up to herself, to fill her empty seas. If it wasn't for Ocean—with a capital O—and his children, who are sworn to protect the Earth, all the water would simply fly up to be with the treasure of the night, the pearl that hangs amongst the diamonds of the sky."

"That sounds like legend, not science." I'd also noticed the shift to a feminine pronoun when referring to the moon.

"It's...murky. Sometimes, things are easier to describe using legends and stories. There's no scientific basis for water flying off through outer space. It's preposterous, really."

She handed me my phone. "I installed an app on your phone. When you click on it, it will open up to your time point and use the GPS to calibrate itself. I even added a little countdown to it. Check out the live tile. It uses a full moon graphic like a clock face."

"Not yet. I want it to be a surprise." Only half of me meant it. "So, there's no little prodrome to it?"

"No. Why? Are you experiencing something? This is a Leni. It's not a regular change so you might be able to shed a little light on the whole thing. This is scientifically relevant." She scooted closer. "What exactly are you experiencing?"

"Last night, when I was outside, I could feel the moonlight on my skin. It felt as heavy and as real as a cotton shirt. And—I heard a voice. A woman's voice. My friend Toby said the moon talks to Weres—"

"—but you are not yet Were."

"No, but still. What if it's the moon telling me that it's inevitable?"

She shrugged and thumbed at her phone.

"I really want to study you. I mean, it's so hard to sit here and not just seize you and examine you, inch by inch." She said it with such strained control that I didn't doubt the seizing part.

She stayed in her seat, though. "But I will tell you that we don't only work with the Were. We are ourselves daughters of the moon. Diana, Celeste, Isis, Astarte--every aspect of the feminine divine. And *Wolfenkinder* aren't the only ones who hear Her. I think what you heard was something different. Something older. The Goddess who shines upon us with Her silver blessing has taken note of you. It may mean something to the Were. But then again…it may not. You may be in a class all your own. Maybe She is threatened by you. Keep your enemies closer, and what not. This Sophia…what is it?"

"It's me, I guess." I paused for a swig of tea. "An instinct. It feels what the DV feels and knows what the DV has to do to straighten their heart. It eases their sorrow. It takes up the burden of their pain so they can act judiciously."

"No, no, I don't mean what does it do. I mean, what is it? Is it an entity, a separate existence? Do you experience a possession by another force?"

I made a fugifino face. "No, it's just me."

"Are you sure?"

"Not one little bit."

"Well, the obvious answer is research and documentation."

"Marek was the champion at that."

"I know. I also know he was last in possession of an ancient text."

I had a feeling I knew what text it was. Didn't think that telling her said text was sitting under a lava lamp in my parlor was a good idea, though.

"That text is the last of a set, the set long gone. There are rumors that a secret society holds them, but there is no such thing as a secret when it comes to society. Somebody always knows something and is willing to spill. We'll find it. It is essential to add to the common knowledge. Of my association," she clarified. "I don't mean putting it on a billboard."

"Last year, I spent a lot of time with a vampire. I didn't know she was a vampire, though," I added hastily when I saw her reaction. "She was with this—weird thing. Dorcas. I still don't know what she was. What's an Unseen?"

Nakia just shook her head, a tiny quiver, her mouth still open. I really had to learn how to deliver the v-word with a little more care.

"Whatever. This vampire was pretending to be a Sophia with the help of that Dorcas, right? But she told me things. I don't know what's true or what's not. I mean, she taught me how to raise my barriers—really, she did. That much, I know she didn't lie about. But what about the rest?" I sat back in my chair and swiveled it, bouncing back and forth. "I don't know. But she said there were canons—books that Sophia used. And there was a group of people who kept them."

"Hmm. The books are real. The barriers are real, because you use them. Maybe that group is real, too. I don't know, but I'd be sure they existed. And, why do you keep saying she? There are no—"

I smiled my tightest. "Yeah. Well. She had help. That Unseen thing."

"Oh, my." She sat a little straighter, pulling away just the slightest bit. "If you have witnessed one of the Unseen...I really need to spend more time with you. What does your schedule look like this week?"

"I'm full up," I said. "*Leni* and all. Speaking of which..."

I wanted to get her off the Sophia subject and back onto the moon. "What kind of moon is this?"

She titled her head and frowned, as if not understanding.

"You know—the zodiac thing."

"Oh, it's very auspicious. Fifth moon following Winter Solstice is called a Kingmaker's moon."

"But Dierk said he didn't change until the harvest moon."

"The Kingmaker's Moon is named that because it is the only moon of the cycle during which the *Leni* might occur. The full moon comes on the fourteenth day of the fifth moon. Those are significant numbers, we believe, that are connected to the *Leni* phenomenon. So. Why Kingmaker, you ask? A King is born, a happenstance of that Y-chromosome. But a King is made...by his mate."

The way she emphasized the word made caused me to grin. "That's both feminist and lurid."

"Innit, though?" She winked at me, the sassy broad. "The *Yin* and *Yang,* the wax and wane, the swing of the pendulum. All is part of an endless cycle. Balance. See, a king can rule, and rule well, all the days of his life. But a king's rule ends upon his death. A king's mate provided him with offspring. A future ruler. An endless cycle.

"You've been feeling terrible about this. I can feel it in your energy and I can see it in your eyes. You feel raped, victimized. But Sophie, you are no victim."

Rape. I'd never once considered the word but, hearing it now, I wondered why. "I didn't choose this—"

"And there are a lot of things you don't choose. You don't choose for a street light to turn red. You do not choose when it rains. You do not choose when to stop being thirsty halfway through a glass of water. You do not choose 99% of the things that occur to you, near you, behind you. But you adapt—you react. And how you react is what determines if you are the conqueror or the conquered.

"And in the *Leni*, you are the conqueror. You become the ruler of the king himself. That's why this is a Kingmaker moon. This is why the *Leni* has happened here, and now, and with you. The moon sees something in you that is worthy of a king—a strength, a resilience, a power. Yes, a power."

"That's the trouble. That power isn't for the Were. It's for the DV."

"Says whom?"

"The DV—"

"Right. The DV. Because with whom else have you shared—or tried to share—this power?"

I never thought about that. "You sound like Dierk."

"I'm playing Devil's advocate, sweetie. Before you manifested as Sophia, what other types of magic users, for lack of an easier term, have you known? You don't even need to answer because I already know. And need I say that Demivampires are slightly biased against *Wolfenkinder*?"

"You'd say that because—"

"Because I knew Marek." Her voice was gentle but firm, her eyes darting back and forth across my face. "Ah. I knew that would have an impact. I meant nothing unkind. I am simply saying there is a bias because one that was close to you had such bias. No?"

I bit my lips. It took a moment to summon the courage to answer. "Oh, hell, yes."

"Yes." She echoed me and gave my hand a sympathetic squeeze. "And if Marek were here, I'm sure he would be voicing his disagreements most vehemently. What's wrong, dear?"

I knew my regrets showed plainly upon my face. "If Marek was here, there would have been nothing to voice. I'd have been with him. I wouldn't have been near a Were King or his *Leni*."

"Would you have?" She eyed me. "If Marek had not become *Wolfram*, would he have been with you?"

"I would have been with him."

"That is debatable. I know what business he had kept near the end of his days. You would not have been together. But one thing is still certain—he would have made his opinion known. And he would not approve of this union. Not because it was you—but because he would thwart the *Wolfenkinder* at every turn, and none would give him more satisfaction in the thwarting than the son of Schatten."

I quietly absorbed this terrible proclamation. How had I become the repository for dangerous intel? Even if what she said wasn't high up on the List of Expensive Secrets for Sale, it was risky. They had the potential to cause pain to any number of people close to me and that made them dangerous, indeed.

Dierk had warned me not to overshare with this woman. I wondered if I'd disobeyed him, and what price I would be called upon to settle in the days to come. Without doubt, it would be a staggering one—Nakia had knowledge of the tension between Marek and Schatten. I could only imagine a king's ransom would be demanded when it came time to pay.

And I was simply a beggar in Sophia's robes.

It occurred to me that I should behave as one and hope it would endear me to her.

"You have been so generous—on so many levels." I reached for her sleeve, bowing my head. "You feel like the first friend I've met in all this."

She patted my hand where it lay on her arm. "Political move—you may be the Queen of *Wolfenkinder.*"

My hand slipped, as did my expression, I was sure. "Really?"

"Just teasing. It is no trouble to be kind. I know how immersed in the mythology the Were tend to be, and no one likes to explain why they believe in what they believe. It's faith. You just have to have it to understand."

Well, with all the talk about a Kingmaker's Moon and what not, I believed that things would end up in Dierk's favor. "A number keeps popping up. Five. Why five? I thought three was the magic number."

"Blame the Egyptians. Did you know the Egyptians calculated the year out to 365 days? Brilliant work, that. Oh, if only I could have been alive back then...well, there's always the hope for time travel, right?"

She sighed, clearly chasing down a geeky thought before picking up where she left off.

"The original calendar had twelve months of thirty days, based on the inundation of the Nile and the planting cycle. That left five days, called the yearly five days, a time for great feasting and ritual. Those days fell at year's end, and the final months were called the Season of Harvest, which went from February 22 to June 21. Your eyes are glazing over."

"I'm fine," I said. "I was just thinking. Funny that the calendar was based on the sun, not the moon."

"Previous calendars were based on the moon. Many still are. But the Egyptians were the intellectual force, the ones to set the trend. It was so influential it ended up in the Fifth chapter of Genesis. The Five Books of Moses. The five stones David used against Goliath. The five pointed star, symbol of Mars. The five wounds of the Christ on the cross. The five elements: earth, wind, fire, water, and spirit. The five fingers that close into a solid fist—five is everywhere. Five is fundamental. Five is powerful."

She rose to leave. "I'm meeting with Tancred later. I know he is just as curious about you so don't be surprised if we steal you away for a while. There is still the matter of that strange magic that attacked you."

"Tancred. He seems to have a lot of influence over Dierk." Which meant, I thought, he may have it over me, as well. "What sort of man is he?"

"Tancred is an interesting chap. He's rather progressive for a Were, despite being the epitome of traditional. I suspect the royal family indulged him. He holds several degrees, including medicine and physics. Can you imagine? When would you have time to practice medicine?" She winked at me.

I couldn't help but grin. "Are you trying to seduce me with your geeky ways?"

"Oh," she said, her voice suspiciously light. "It's just a matter of time, Sophia."

She shook my hand as she left, leaving a tingle that traveled up my arm. Time had a funny way of working against me. I just didn't need a smart phone app to remind me.

During the week, Dierk called on me at home, taking me out each night. Dinner, sightseeing, a movie. No pressure, just dating. Every day, I'd tuck one of Marek's journals into my purse but I never found time to read it.

Rodrian must have decided that he wasn't so interested in our remaining time together. He was never at the Stocks when I was.

I got my passport, too. A passport was probably the last thing I thought I'd ever get, with a vasectomy coming in at a close second. I never had been a traveler. My entire world had been lived in a two hour radius from where I stood, which is truly sad, considering the Jersey Shore is like, right there. As I filled out the passport application, I noticed the turn-around time was four weeks, at the soonest. Four weeks. I at least had that long before I left town forever.

At least, I'd thought I had four weeks. Unfortunately, Dierk had diplomatic ties and a good friend at the consulate. He handed my papers off to a guy in a suit who promised to have my passport by Friday.

Stupid kings and the expedience with which they did everything.

I was so pissed off at the whole thing that I made him stop at a drugstore on the way back to the hotel because I wanted one of every vaccine that they stocked. All I ended up with was a tetanus booster and a Were who laughed himself silly over it because he thought vaccines were a waste of time.

He chuckled about it the entire drive back, even while I rubbed my arm getting out of the car. Damn, but that pharmacist had nailed me with that shot. Hadn't he ever heard of putting a little TLC in the needle? I tugged up my sleeve and peeled off the bandage, expecting to see a wicked bruise the size of a fist, if the pain was any judge. Dierk carried my purse for me and steered me onto the sidewalk leading to the hotel entrance, shaking his head and murmuring nonsense about how stubborn I was.

I felt it then, like a round of cannon fire, a pressure that thumped at my ears, my lungs, my mind. It felt like sunfall times a thousand. I staggered in my step, tripping, feeling the world turn a hazy shade of muffled. I reached out to catch myself, catching the corner of the building with my hand, tearing the flesh of my palm. The sharp bite of concrete was nothing to the rawness that crowded me. I gulped for breath.

I knew that feeling. And I knew that power. One of my Demivamps had just taken a human life, pushing his soul a tick forward on the clock of evolution.

My Demivamp. Rodrian.

I screamed Rodrian's name, spinning my power out, seeking him, knowing he'd feel the burst of Sophia power that carried it.

There was no response. Wherever he was, Rodrian

ignored me.

Hate for that woman, that demon, seethed in the pit of my brain. She drove him to it. She laughed while he did it, coaxing him and smothering him with the promise of a lustful release when he'd finished sating himself in the blood rush.

I knew those things because she made sure I knew. She'd bundled the images up and sought me out, using my desperate cry to Rodrian as a homing device. She wanted me to know.

And I swore I'd kill her for it.

I spun in place, bruise forgotten, reaching out with all the strength of my being. I'd find them. I'd find them and go to him and stop him, and I'd fucking stop her once and for all. So intent was I that I found myself at the edge of the road, Dierk grasping my shoulders, shaking me and repeating my name. It wasn't until he growled that I shook free of that terrible desire to find and avenge Rodrian.

Dierk's eyes were sallow gold, twin specks of bright blue reflecting in them that faded as I watched. My reflection. I'd gone full-on Sophia in front of him and hadn't even realized it.

"What is happening?" His voice strained, little more than whisper.

I shook my head, reaching out, not finding Rodrian's power. He'd completely withdrawn. The knowledge and the loss drove me to sobbing.

I stood in the street and wept, and the king himself was powerless to console me.

The evening didn't improve. I called Rodrian's cell, over and over, cursing every time it went to voicemail. Dierk endured it, silently, for quite some time before drawing a heavy breath and taking the phone from my limp fingers.

"I can't do this, Dierk."

He sat down next to me on his bed and pulled me closer. What can you not do, my dear?"

"This. Any of this." I rubbed my face, holding my head. "If he Falls, it's on me. I abandoned him. I have failed. I know that, for you, I began when the *Leni* told you to sit up and take notice of me but I started long before that, with them. With Marek, and Rodrian, and..."

"Life doesn't always keep to one path." He released me and scooted away so that he could see my face better. "I, too, have had other relationships. But I can't fight the present just to keep hold of the past."

It had never occurred to me that Dierk had a life before I walked through the doors of the Majestic, before I sassed him at the bar or felt the shock of the *Leni*'s power rip along the nerves in my arm. Suddenly, I wasn't facing a certainty, which up until this exact moment, I assumed I had been. I figured there would be no one but Dierk in my life from here on out.

What if I faced a future with no one?

Dierk was handsome, attractive in too many ways to count, inside and out. His eyes, those mixture of coffee and champagne, represented what I felt when I was with him—common, graced by unreachable nobility. His character had earned my good graces a hundred times out and every time he revealed a new corner of his soul, he awoke another echo inside me. He resonated with me. There was only one thing I could not reconcile and even that was quickly becoming familiar to me, if not remotely embraced.

He could have any woman he wanted. I'm sure the world was lined with a queue of them long enough to keep him from ever thinking about me again.

"I wouldn't blame you if you did," I said. "I have more baggage than a man like you deserves."

"Oh, don't say that." He reached for me. "You are not baggage. You are a blessing."

"You say that now, but…"

He lifted my chin, holding my cheek. "I won't desert you, Sophie. I won't abandon you. You won't be facing this great magical change all on your own. Do you worry that, at the moment when you need me the most, I will turn and walk away?"

I nodded. "Yes."

"Why? Why would I do that?"

"Because Marek did. He loved me. He brought me to myself. He showed me the Sophia within me. He awoke this essence inside me that would forever change my life and then he left. He loved me, and he left me anyway. And, the thing is, he loved me because he wanted to. Not because I gave him a shock on the hand and the moon declared us to be a couple. See? You call me yours because of the *Leni*. He called me his because of his heart. And he still left."

"Do you think that—if the *Leni* had not begun, and it was just you and I backstage, and I wasn't *der König*—would you have seen me the next day? Would you have called me?"

He had me there. "Yes. I really thought I'd call you."

"Then there was a basis for us as man and woman. No *Leni*. Just us. Do you talk to me now as a Were? As *ein König*?"

"No. Just—*ein* jackass who proved his point well over."

He clucked his tongue. "Terms of endearment. You are fluent with them."

"So. What now?"

"Moon begins Saturday. My hosts have secured a running ground west of here, I believe. Privacy and safety. We will leave about three in the afternoon."

I nodded. Looks like he had our weekend planned out.

"Would you like to spend Friday night at home? With the younger Thurzo?"

Ah. There was that. I did want to, if I could convince Rodrian to stay with me. But I had a terribly sinking feeling that I would have to chase him down. How did I do that without hurting Dierk?

Because, looking into those amazing eyes, those eyes that picked up every day light and spun gold within them, I knew: I never wanted to hurt Dierk.

He leaned to kiss me on the cheek. "Do not worry about making me feel badly. I will bring you home after work on Friday and retrieve you Saturday afternoon. You need time with your loved ones."

"Thank you," I whispered, my heart tight with gratitude that, once again, he seemed to know just what I needed.

"Do not thank me." He traced my jaw with a tender touch. "I would do anything for you."

I believed his every word.

Waxing gibbous | moon 96% visible

Thursday we went to Chinatown for dinner. I treated him to my favorite restaurant and a double order of pan-fried dumplings and a pot of the house special soup. It was the simplest way to show my appreciation.

Despite the nearness of the moon, Dierk's manner was as easy-going as it was the night me met. He hadn't had to work hard to persuade me to spend the evening at the Windwood.

"Tell me about your castle," I said, curling up on the bed and hugging a pillow to my chest. I'd tested his room service skills by asking for popcorn. I got it. With butter sprinkles to boot. "Do you have a big throne room?"

He sprawled across the bottom of the bed, resting on his elbows. "Of course, I have a throne room. What a poor example of a king I would be had I not."

"And a jester?"

"No, sorry. No jester. But you, you are very amusing and quite entertaining. You can have the job if you like. I'll let you skip the application process."

"Another job? No, thanks."

"It pays quite well."

I threw popcorn at him. "Now I know you're rubbing it in."

"I rub nothing in." He picked up the pieces and ate them, wearing a smirk. "I am *der König*. I can afford an extravagant payroll."

"Like guards—"

"Of course, guards. You already know that I have security."

"What about ones that wear uniforms and carry pikes?"

"What about them?"

His expression was so serious I almost choked. "No, really?"

"No. Have you ever been to court? Not mine, of course, but any European court? It's very civilized. I am not Henry the Eighth. These questions, they are very odd. I wonder if you are making fun of me."

I rolled my eyes and grabbed another handful of popcorn. "I'd never."

"You'd never. Okay. I will take you at your word."

"I just want to know. You said I could ask you anything I wanted."

"I did. I apologize. You just come off sounding...so..."

"Smart ass."

"Yes. Thank you for saying it. I wouldn't insult a lady."

"It's not an insult, it's a skill I've practiced for a long time. So. To skip all the questions in order to avoid the risk of sounding smart assed—just tell me. What do you do at court?"

He slowly swayed his head as he searched for words.

"We just—sit, I guess, and talk. Much like what we did here. Sometimes it is more formal, sometimes less. Catch up on what is going on in the other regions. Many use the time to visit, see old friends. Take news. Meet new mates. Feuds. Deaths. All the usual. We talk business, taxes, ventures, partnerships. We talk about the band. I give free concerts."

"Aw. No fair. Can you bend the no-human rule for me?"

"I might not have to."

I stifled an ugh. "Can you tape it, then?"

"I was only kidding. Of course I don't perform in court. And I never give free concerts. I, too, can be funny."

I thought about how to word my next question and decided it would be better to just ask. "Do you wear your wolf form?"

"Some do. Usually they are either the weaker ones who change at the moon, young Were who cannot shift on their own will. Many times they are forced into their *Wolf* form. It is not shameful; it is nature, and the *Wolf* mingles amongst the man. I myself only hold court in human form."

"Why?"

"Courts are for men. Wolves have no need for thrones. We are dual-natured. Just as the sun belongs in the day and the moon shines the brightest at night, there is a time and a place best suited for each of our forms. Nature."

"Nature."

"Many of the older Were are more comfortable as wolf, and they will spend as much time as possible in that form. I am happy to accommodate them. Wolves are singularly beautiful animals, and I would not be unhappy to be surrounded by them all my days. My court is safe from the eyes of other species. We do not have to assume our roles on the world's stage. We are among our own kind, free to choose our form, to be bare of pretention."

"A secret?"

"Not a secret. We have nothing to hide. We do not express ourselves freely amongst the other publics. It is simply not your business. One does not flaunt gifts in front of people who do not appreciate them."

He reached into the bowl, picking out the less-buttery kernels. "Being *Wolf* is a blessing. A gift. And the rest of the world does not understand or appreciate our views. Being *Wolf* is release from the corruption of being human. We have instinct. Natural law. No corruption, lying, deceit. No backstabbing, no stealing, no moral decay. We are ruled by nature, honest nature."

He chewed a few moments. "That is our religion. The moon. The power it unlocks in us. That is beauty. That is honesty. We may not polish a pew in church every Sunday, but do not think we are without faith. Our gods are older than your church."

"I may not polish a pew in Church every Sunday either, but I am still Catholic."

"You might change your mind."

"And I might not."

"You are stubborn. You don't have a very open mind, do you?"

"Nope. I don't. I'm about as one-track as they get. Don't like to change, mind and species included."

"And what if you have no choice?"

I curled my lip, admitting that my stance wasn't the optimum. "I don't bend. Unfortunately, that means I break. And I have been broken before. And I don't learn. I accept my lot and move on."

"This may be one more lot to accept."

I toyed with a handful of kernels, considering. "Then...I guess I break."

"It doesn't have to be that way. There are benefits."

"Like. . ." I looked up into his eyes, sincerely hoping he had all the answers.

"Being with me. Come now. You don't hate me nearly as much as you did when you got bitten."

"But I don't like you nearly as much as I did before I was bitten."

"You mean you liked me more before you actually met me?"

"No, jackass. Backstage the night of the show. I liked you a lot that night."

"You did?" He smiled. It was a nice smile. It was the smile he won me with, that very first night.

I thought about how superficial our relationship had been before the *Leni* business started. I thought about the shallow connection I would have been satisfied making with him. It made me wonder exactly how honorable his intentions had been. "Not in a groupie way."

"I understand that. But you did like me."

I nodded. "Yeah. I did. You were easy to talk to. I admit I was a bit star struck at first. I mean, music video junkie here. You were everything I imagined you might be, and a bunch of great stuff more."

The smile deepened. I never realized how full his lips were. "I am getting a swelled head."

"Well, you shouldn't. You have more than enough negatives to balance you out into Completely Not My Type."

His expression lengthened, lost its boyish cheer.

I couldn't lie, even though at this moment, I might have done it, if only to save his feelings. "You're Were. It still isn't top of my list of qualities for a dream guy."

"How did you feel when you stood to leave, when you smiled so wistfully and told me it was time to say goodbye?

271

What were you thinking?"

"That I..." I chewed my lip, remembering. "Okay. I didn't want to say goodbye. I would have liked another hour, another day maybe. I was thinking that if things could be different, maybe I'd let myself be happy. I haven't been happy in a long time, Dierk. I don't know if I could be. Now, it doesn't seem to matter. Happy might be over for me."

He shook his head and looked away. "Happy was over for you when you lost Thurzo."

I exhaled, harder than I meant to. Just that thought was enough to take my breath away, so far away I worried every time that it would never return. "Yeah. It was. I've had moments since then. I have friends. I have Rode. But Marek left me hollow, and no matter how happy I get now, it doesn't fill the hollow. It never fills. All the happy keeps leaking out. It takes so much effort to fill it."

"You are trying to fill it with substitutes, that's why. You cannot replace a loss like that. Loss reshapes us and teaches us to fill ourselves with something new. If we resist, we feel as you do. Hollow. Empty."

"Loss reshapes us." I nodded. "I like that. Wish I thought of it."

"Take the words. They are yours. It is no bad thing to be inspired by another. Our best work is inspired by others."

Dropping my head, I rested my forehead against his chest. "I wish you wouldn't be so likeable. I don't want to like you."

"But you do." He placed a gentle hand on my head. "You just don't want to bend."

"No. I don't."

He stroked my hair lightly, a pleasant tickle on my scalp. "This doesn't have to break you. You are stronger than that."

"Why do people keep telling me that?" I rolled away and sat up, drawing my knees to my chest. "I'm not."

He sat up as well and reached out to cup my calf in his hand. "You are. You are very strong. I've seen you in action."

"Then why does it hurt?"

"Pain is not a voluntary thing. We don't choose to hurt. The world, the circumstances hurt us. It is the definition of victim. Strength of heart and strength of will is shown by our willingness to continue despite the pain. Pain should not be the victor. We should always strive to have the last word."

"Okay." I took a deep breath and held it, wondering if I were strong enough to know the answer to the next question. I had to ask. "What if...you decide you don't want me?"

"What?" He laughed as if I were a silly girl and scooted closer to for me, drawing me against him. The touch comforted despite my misgivings.

"What if I Turn and you take me home and you get tired of my smart ass remarks or something else and you don't want me? I'll have nowhere to go. I'll have lost all my friends. I don't know German so I won't even be able to call a cab."

"Do you truly worry that I won't want you?" He lifted my chin. "Do you want me?"

I didn't answer. Not because I wanted to say no, but because I was afraid to say anything else.

I don't know what he thought at my silence, but he didn't seem angry. Instead he wore his half-smile and used his default pleasant voice. "You shouldn't worry. I will mate for life. That's a promise, an oath, a vow, a contract. I mate for life, and I will value my mate all the days of my life, and I will make my mate's happiness my first priority because my mate will come before all others, *der König* or not. And if need be, I will die for my mate. On my honor as *der König*, as *ein Wolf*, and as a simple man."

Then, with a gentle but perfect touch of his lips upon mine, he kissed me.

And the funny thing was, I let him.

Waxing gibbous | moon 99% visible

Early morning. I didn't often sleep past sunrise anymore. Especially not after spending the night with someone. We hadn't done anything I'd regret later; we simply talked until we were too tired to talk anymore. Sleeping next to him felt natural and safe, and, God help me, I didn't regret that, either.

I rolled over to face him. Boy, was Dierk a sound sleeper. He didn't even stir when I moved.

I ran my index finger along his jaw, back and forth in lazy strokes, noting the difference between the rough stubble of overnight growth and the soft fullness of his trim goatee. Trailing my fingers down his thick muscular neck and full chin, all the time chasing vague thoughts.

I let my finger wander toward the edge of his bottom lip, while letting my mind wander back to the kiss we shared.

He'd approached me with such—not demand, *per se.* It

wasn't a bossy kiss. He simply had declared that he would be mine and I would be his and that kiss was a completion of the oath. A sealing of the pact. That was as close to getting his honor in writing as it would get.

When he bent his head toward mine, it was because it must be so. Not bossy, not possessive, not a rough seizure of what he decided would be his. It was simply the right thing to do at the right time.

And yet, it wasn't a boring, stately, proper old peck on the cheek. I felt my face warm and was glad he still slept because I wanted to duck my head to hide a grin.

The kiss started off chastely enough, a meeting of lips, an intimacy we had yet to share. His lips were so soft, so warm—and I was surprised, for some reason. Had I assumed it would feel like dog lips? I didn't know, I never had really thought about it so I couldn't be sure why I'd been so surprised but I was pleased, and I smiled against his kiss.

He'd noticed, and smiled in return. He chuckled softly, just a little. Was he surprised, and pleased, too? He kissed me again, treating me to his lower lip, a bit more mouth that time, the kiss sliding deeper when he brushed my lip with the tip of his tongue.

By then, I'd been ready, and more than willing. So easy to get lost in that kiss because I had been slowly getting lost in him.

He slid his arm around me, pulling me closer, and we lay heartbeat to heartbeat. We beat in time with each other and I began to thin my barriers without thinking. Once more, I was treated to the sense of his power, seeping into me like darkness seeped into the sky at twilight. The wind, the scents, the pull of the moon—I felt them, I enjoyed the rush of it because he was only a heartbeat away. I wasn't alone. I was partnered. I was half of a whole.

Connected by a kiss, an embrace, a whisper of power, a promise. There was no other thought than being half of that whole. I did more than allow that kiss. I delighted in the sensory explosion it caused and encouraged more.

And I remember the guiltlessness of it all. If anyone would beat themselves up for feeling like a treacherous adulterer, it would be me. Considering it had been sometime since I'd been in church, all those years of a proper Irish Catholic upbringing would have been there at the door, waiting for the slightest hint of an invitation.

Yet, there was none. That kiss had been immutably decreed. It was expected. It was owed. And it was long overdue.

Pulling my fingers away, I scolded myself, although I didn't put much scold in it. Perfectly plausible I could lounge here with him, toying with his facial hair as if I had the right to do so.

I realized then that I'd more or less accepted my fate. Although I didn't want to grow fur or a tail every month I knew I didn't have any choice. It had been taken from me the moment that zap of electricity passed between us. The last few weeks I've done nothing but fight and scream as if I could change anything.

I turned my hand, looking at the scars from Stohl's teeth. For the first time, I didn't get bent out of shape over them. In twenty-four hours the moon would reach full. If I turned, I'd lose a part of my freewill forever.

But I'd gain a king.

I thumbed the edge of his jaw, the patch of beard under his lip, the stubble and the beard. His heartbeat beneath my cheek, strong lopes of life as he slumbered. He shifted around in his sleep, tipping into a more comfortable position and tugging my arm more securely under his.

As far as prisons went, this one wasn't as bad as it could

have been.

Later that morning, I went to work, wondering if it would be the last time I sat at my desk, the last time I flopped down in Barb's red chair and laughed at her frown lines, the last time I'd open a letter that began with the words "Dear Sophia."

I looked around my office. It wasn't big, or even moderate—I had a desk, a filing cabinet, a triangular shelf filled with photo frames, an antiquated olive green love seat-sized couch of sorts, and just enough room to maneuver without getting bruises. But there was a window, and a door, and it was my kingdom.

And this may very well be the last day I step foot in it.

What would happen here if I Turned tomorrow? I highly doubted Dierk would allow me to give two weeks' notice. Doubtlessly, he'd pick up my furry ass and toss me onto a plane and I would just vanish from this world. No goodbyes—not to Barb, not to Rodrian, not to my Wolfram or my DV.

Sophie Galen, the Sophia of the North American Demivampire, would vanish.

I strode solemnly to my chair and sat down at my computer, setting down the thermos of tea Dierk had made for me before I left. I would make this day count. I would leave my mark and I would never forget this final day.

Reaching to open the bottom desk drawer, I saw my mug wasn't there.

I sat, hands folded, seething with an indescribable rage that boiled below my skin. All I wanted for this day was a perfect snapshot, a postcard to remember my life by. But no. I sat, and waited for Jasmine, who, by ten o'clock, didn't show.

Whatever. That might have been a good thing. Wouldn't

do to get fired for assaulting a coworker on my last day.

When it appeared that my full frontal obliteration wasn't going to happen, I decided to head to the break room for a pack of crackers from the vending machine.

Good thing I did. My cat mug was in the sink, half-full of flat soda.

Take the blessings where they lay, I told myself. But it was on, now. If I was here come Monday, it was war.

At four o'clock, I closed the door to my office, mug tucked in my purse instead of the bottom drawer. I also had spent the last few minutes rearranging my picture frames, taking out a few of the photos and slipping them into my bag. I had to be choosy—wasn't like I could walk out with a box. I made a lot of sacrifices and had to leave a lot in there.

Well. Maybe I'd be back on Monday, deliriously glad I hadn't destroyed my carefully-constructed *feng shui*. That was something to look forward to.

Barb was still at work when I walked by her office. I rapped on the glass and waved, like I usually did. She waved back.

Goodbye.

That was all. It couldn't possibly mean anything more than it did.

Swallowing down the urge to call out, I put one foot in front of the other and headed for the elevator, anticipating the sight of Dierk in the lobby.

Instead I was treated to Caen, who stood imperiously, arms crossed, watching the doors slide open. He frowned upon seeing me, and presumably my unrestrained expression of—well, more than disappointment, but falling short of yelling "You've got to be effing kidding me."

No mistaking that he was waiting for me, and that the feeling was mutual. Still. He was Rodrian's man and I had to accept him as part of Rode's world. Caen would never sully himself by standing amongst the plebeians of Balaton's workforce so no doubt he was here for me. I looked at him, saying nothing, waiting for him to explain.

I tried not to grimace. Over the years, I'd come to equate the man with the all-encompassing definition of unpleasant.

Once the majority of people had exited, he graced me with a glance. "I am to take you to Rodrian. My car is outside."

He turned immediately and strode for the doors. I more or less shrugged and followed him to the sidewalk. "Does Dierk know? He said he would pick me up and take me home himself."

"Rodrian's orders." He opened the back door of a black sedan and pointed.

I don't know if it was the word "orders" or the way he said it. Regardless, I didn't like being bossed around, not by someone who had never seemed to hold my best interests as his highest priority.

"Tell him I got my own ride." I scanned the sidewalk, still seeing no sign of Dierk. I reached into my purse for my cell phone and swiped the unlock screen. "After he calls me and tells me where to meet him."

"Sophie." Caen huffed out a breath and put his hand over my phone, looking me full in the face. Actually made eye contact. "Rodrian is fearful another attempt will be made. Just get in."

Eyes wide, I ducked my head and got in. Enough of the attempts. Sooner or later, one would succeed. It was statistically imminent.

I slammed the door and he shot away from the curb like a rocket, throwing me against the door. Shaking my head and thinking all sorts of rude thoughts, I pulled my seatbelt across me. That's when I noticed a person in the front passenger seat.

Dirty blonde curls, tousled against the headrest. She, too, swayed with the car's sudden movements, head lolling as if she were asleep. I sent out a tendril of inquisition to touch her, but she wasn't DV. She was empty.

Not Were, not that kind of void. This was different. The emptiness felt contrived.

And she felt—familiar.

Caen rounded a corner and I had to hold onto the door to keep from rolling over. My purse slid over and off the seat, landing on the floor behind Caen's seat. My phone and wallet dumped out. "Geez, Caen. Take it easy, will you?"

He lifted his chin to glance in the rear view, hooded eyes shifting slightly. "We must go with urgency."

"Okay, then. Just don't wreck us. I don't know what attempt you are expecting, but the last thing I want to do is die in a crash with you." I tried to reach my things but they were beyond my grasp. "Who is she? She asleep?"

"Don't worry about her. She's a little drowsy. We were busy."

The way he said it made me sick. I'd never spent a second trying to imagine Caen and a blood date. He could never treat a person the way Rodrian treated me those times he'd tasted me. Caen was too callous, too indifferent to the feelings of others to be tender.

Suddenly, I worried for her. That empty feeling—what if he'd done it to her? "She looks weak. Is she okay?"

"Sure, she is." With a final surge, Caen got onto the highway that led north out of Balaton. She drooped against her seatbelt. He reached over and pushed her back against the seat. "Right, honey? Hey, look alive there, Jasmine."

"Who?" Unsnapping my seatbelt, I leaned over the seat and turned her face toward me. That's why she was familiar. I just didn't recognize the hair, free of its usual severity. "What are you doing with her? Jasmine! Are you all right?"

She roused a little and looked up at me, a scowl spreading across her mouth. "I'm fine. Quit it."

"Good," Caen said. "It's about time. How about taking care of our guest?"

Jasmine turned around, looked me full in the face, and raised her hand.

A wave of power thumped into me, stealing my breath like a blow to the stomach. I couldn't get my breath all the way back. I couldn't move my arms. I was constricted by an invisible fist. The lack of air made me dizzy.

"Finally. She's speechless." He tromped on the gas and we sped along the highway. I couldn't focus on anything outside the window, not a sign or a familiar building.

"Rode," I gasped. I couldn't even say his full name.

"Sorry." Caen's mouth parted with predatorial glee, teeth gleaming. He sounded positively jovial. "I lied. We aren't going to see him. I have other plans."

"Caen." Jasmine's voice trembled. "I need power. I can't sustain this spell much longer."

Spell. I struggled to concentrate. Caen had a witch. But witches didn't cleave to the DV.

"Can't...breathe," I mumbled. Then I let myself fall back against the seat, eyes closed, and clamped my barriers down.

"She passed out," he said. "Loosen it."

Immediately I felt the weight on my chest diminish. I still couldn't move my arms, but I could breathe. And I could think.

I assessed the situation. Caen was an even bigger d-bag than I'd thought. He kidnapped me and said he had plans. He had a witch, whom he's using to control me with magic.

The car slowed and swayed to the right. We were getting off the highway.

"I did. She still isn't moving."

"Let her sleep," he said. "I cannot abide the sound of that voice."

I bunched my shields, chomping down on my flash of hate for him. He thought I was out cold. I had to use that as an advantage.

As I drew in my barriers, I felt an intrusion, like a splinter under the skin. Her spell. It was a line that had perforated my shield and kept its grip on my will. The spell gleamed like new razor coil and felt just as solid.

My phone rang. I opened one eye enough to see Dierk's picture came up on the screen. A picture I took that night at the bowling alley. I'd doodled on it, adding a lopsided crown on his head. It rang until it went to voice mail.

Find me, Dierk. Please.

Then it rang again, a loud insistent *brrrrring*. Not my usual ringtone. It rang three times without a contact or caller ID before it stopped.

Caen growled. "Get that damn thing and throw it out the window."

I shut my eyes just as she reached over the seat. If I had control of my legs, I'd have kneed her in the face.

She strained her hand toward the floor but to no avail. "I can't reach it."

"Fine. Just—here." Caen sent a compulsion to her, a stream of power I felt even through my thickest barriers. Her empty feeling subsided, and she momentarily pulsed with his essence. He must have given her a wallop because she laughed, giddy on the sudden surge of power.

I braced myself for a squeeze but instead I noticed I could shift my elbow. She'd been distracted by Caen's transfer of power. I remained still, waiting for a plan to show up and save my behind.

"Do you think this will really work?" Her voice was stronger now.

I heard the unmistakable sound of a soda bottle being opened, the hiss of fizz. She paused and swallowed noisily. I wanted to pinch her. Her and that damn Dr. Pepper.

"Of course it will. You've felt what happens when we focus together. And you remember how easy it was to do it before, even without her help." Caen laughed. "I never imagined I'd experience such strength."

"And—" he added, "once we get to your priestess, we can salvage the oracle and complete the machine. It will work. It will not fail."

The machine. I'd heard that before, didn't I? Where, where, where—I filed back through my recent memories, like flipping pages of a book—

A book.

A dusty old book with spotted gilt pages.

A hand-drawn diagram that had been altered by unfamiliar handwriting.

L'apparreil.

A new dread seeped into me, like cold ooze sliding down my neck, chilling me inside and out. I no longer felt my heart beat—instead, I was filled with an odd calm, a certainty, a destiny foretold.

Badness wasn't coming. Badness was here.

"I don't know what she'll say." Jasmine's voice was shadowed with doubt. "I still don't think she'll go along with it."

"Listen, she is just as hungry for knowledge and information as we are for the power itself. She'll be wetting herself to get in on this."

"If you say so. But there has to be another way to salvage the oracle," she said.

"Why should there be?"

"Because your way is savage. It's going to come back on us, in a big, bad way. I took a vow, Caen. "

"Listen, sweetheart, you left your vows scattered all over my bedroom floor when you offered yourself for this." His voice was dark and oily. Caen stretched his arms along the back of the seat to massage her shoulders, kneading the muscles. He seduced her with another pulse of compulsion. She made a tiny sound and laid her hand against his.

Ew. And, what a dick.

She keened. "But this is wrong. I know what I did with you and I accept those consequences. And I'll do it again and again. But her—it's wrong. There has to be a way to extract her power without causing permanent damage."

I did not like the sound of that. I knew Caen hated me, but what was he planning to do to me? My heartbeat thumped along an adrenaline surge. Damn my autonomic nervous system.

"Quiet," he said. "She is waking."

I cracked my eyes and took as deep breath as I could. Still pinioned, although not as tightly.

"Caen." I mumbled, trying to sound weak. "What are you doing?"

"Just what I've longed to do since the day I met you." He smiled once more in the rear view at me. "I'm going to kill you."

The deafening thump-thump-thump of a helicopter passed overhead. Were we near the air base? How long—or how fast—had we been driving?

Jasmine craned her neck to look out the window.

"That's only a traffic chopper." Caen spared only a glance upward. "Don't get distracted."

The chopper circled back over toward our direction. It sounded like it was directly overhead. I hoped it really was a traffic chopper and that cops would jump out to give him a ticket. And an ass-kicking. Did the police still carry batons? I hoped so. The sounds of *Stop resisting me!* and the crunches of Caen's nose against a billy club would be really awesome just about now.

Caen took another turn as if he believed we rode on rails. Blowing the stop sign, he sped to an underpass and skidded to a stop.

The chopper made several passes. No doubt they were very interested in us.

"Who is that?" Jasmine's grip on me wavered.

"I don't know, but I'm not waiting to find out." He took off, the sun over my left shoulder, onto a stretch of road, winding and tree-lined. "Contact your priestess. Tell her we will be delayed because I was forced to detour."

The chopper found us once more. I squirmed as much as I could so I could look out the back window. It hovered only a few stories above us. A man hung out of the open cabin and pointed at us.

I couldn't wave my arms, or do anything but wiggle my eyebrows at him. Not knowing who they were, I sent a desperate pulse of power, hoping someone would realize I was in danger. Hoping they weren't out to kill me on their own.

I wasn't sure if Caen saw the man. "Holy crap! They're going to crash into us!"

"Shut up!" Caen shoved at Jasmine. "Hit her, now!"

She obeyed. I felt the impulse of her curse, a squeeze around my throat. It was the same sensation I'd felt before, when I thought it was anaphylaxis and Dierk called in the witch to examine me—it was her, all along.

My sight dimmed. Their words came through in muffled waves. My pulse pumped in my ears.

"I can try a spell to confuse the pilot," Jasmine said.

"Let them follow. They can get tangled in the trees."

A heavy object crashed down on the roof of the car. Jasmine screamed and ducked, completely dropping the spell. Free of her hex, I bunched my barriers before she could reestablish her grip. No bullshit witch would ever spellbind me again.

Whatever hit us wasn't stationary. Something pounded over and over. With a crunch, the blade of an ax crashed through the sunroof.

Caen cursed and swerved the car, jerking the wheel side to side in an effort to dislodge the assailant. Who? I didn't dare stretch the tight shell I'd coiled around my essence. I might weaken the wall I tried to keep between myself and the witch. I dropped to the floor, putting as much distance between my head and that ax.

The sunroof shield was torn back and we were pelted with chunks of glass. The hands that reached down in weren't hands.

They were elongated claws, the hands of an animalized human. I'd seen those claws before.

The witch screamed and cowered against the door. Caen swerved again to the far side of the road. When he crossed over onto the berm, the front wheel caught in the soft earth and stumbled the car. I knew with perfect clarity what would happen next.

This is what it feels like to crash, I thought.

Everything lurched to the right, inertia at its finest, and I slammed into the door, sliding up to see the ground rush up to meet the side of the car. Air bags exploded into fluffs before deflating into white puddles. Unrestrained, I was tossed like a lottery ball. I couldn't brace for impact. I crashed and rolled right along with the vehicle. It all happened so slowly I noted every detail and so fast that I never had time to be scared.

The car abruptly stopped, balanced on its side.

Dazed, I watched Caen disappear out through his window. He slipped up and out like a serpent, just slithered out. His screams sounded like a wild beast—rage and destruction and so much power. Namesake, I remembered. He had been aptly named Power and his DV power burned at me, scalding as it always did, hot and sharp. My shields, weary but intact, kept my soul from being shredded by his lust for pain. But it still burned, leaving my mental nerve endings raw. Caen wanted to kill.

And then—

He just disappeared.

The girl lay crumpled and drooped over her shattered window. I reached for a pulse. Weak. I scrambled to reposition myself trying to see her better.

Jasmine coughed, pink froth collecting at the corners of her mouth.

"Ray." Her voice was paper-thin. "A ray."

"Oh, no you don't, Jasmine," I said. "Do not go to the light. Stay with me."

She seemed to see me then, her eyes wide and rolling. She coughed again, a wet sound. More pink foam.

"Don't talk." I tugged her hair away from her face. "I'm going to get help."

"Leah…" Her voice rattled, and she stilled.

"Leah? Who is that? Do I have to find Leah?"

Jasmine didn't answer.

I shifted my knees and stuck my head out through the missing sunroof. My shoulders would fit. I pushed my way through, scraping my legs, and used the car to pull myself up.

Searching, I looked for someone, anyone. The car had gone down into a ditch and we were half-hidden by bushes. I wanted to call out but I didn't have a voice. It wasn't a curse. It was the aftermath of trauma.

The road above. Had to get there. I tried to scramble up the hill but slid with each step. It was steep and my head hurt and my arms were bleeding and I saw Caen's body. A quick glance told me there was no point feeling for a pulse, even if I managed to identify a pulse point.

Mangled. He had been ejected from the vehicle and must have gotten shredded when the car rolled on him.

No. Wait. He wasn't ejected.

A loud rush of sound drowned my thoughts. Confused, I sat down in a heap, avoiding looking in the direction of his body. I felt helpless and worried and I needed someone. I should to call someone. 911. There's been an accident.

My phone was in the car and I just didn't even want to get up to look for it. I panted, trying to catch my breath.

A voice called out, conquering the pulsating noise. "Sophie!"

My head wobbled like a new-hatched chick. My someone was here.

Footsteps crashed through the brush on the far side of the car, crunching through the dried leaves. Dierk, running to me, dropping to his knees, feeling my limbs, checking my head, pulling me against him as if he'd decided nothing was broken.

I sagged against him, my knight, my savior, and laughed. Just laughed until the tears came.

"You found me." My voice was muffled by his shirt.

He drew back and held my face. "I'll always find you."

"I had an accident, Dierk. I'm sorry." I pointed without looking at Caen's remains. "Caen was driving. He's over there."

"I know, dear heart," he said. "I put him there."

I shook my head. "No, not you. There was a witch. She's inside."

Dierk stood and walked over to the car, looking through the windshield. Then he reached in. I couldn't see what he did. Finally, he came back to me.

"Here's your purse. Your phone and wallet are inside it. I didn't see anything else of yours."

"Oh." I took my purse with numb fingers, fumbling at the straps. "I should call 911. Right?"

"No. Our help is here."

That weird pulsing noise grew impossibly louder before I saw what made it. The helicopter passed overhead and came to rest beyond the rim of trees. Dierk scooped me up and carried me over to the whirly bird. Janssen and Olberich slid open the hatch. Leaning out, they each hooked an arm under each of Dierk's and pulled us up into the cabin. They slammed the doors shut and we took off. The dip and the tilt combined with the dizziness from the accident and I leaned over, away from Dierk, and was gracelessly sick.

I wiped my mouth and tapped the pilot's shoulder with my clean hand. "Sorry about your bird."

Dierk pulled me back up onto his lap, cradling me against his chest. The noise was crazy loud but I could tell from the rumble in his chest that he sang to me.

I fell asleep, feeling utterly and completely safe.

Saturday morning. Full moon day.

I slung my beach bag over my shoulder, wincing when the strap slid against a tender spot on my back, and closed my bedroom door behind me. It was a difficult moment. Was I closing a door to my life forever?

Maybe I already had.

The night before, Dierk had delivered me home, just as he'd promised, literally handing me over to Rodrian on the porch. I'd still been half-asleep and Dierk had carried me from the car. As tired as I was, I felt the gentleness with which he'd carried me and placed me into Rodrian's safe embrace. Dierk had leaned down to brush a tender kiss on my forehead before turning away.

Rodrian didn't stop him from doing it, either.

Rode and I slept together on the big red couch in the den, his arms snug around me, holding me close. No talk, no sass, no smexy teasing. We were both too tired and too far past those things. Tonight was a night for healing and for shelter and for taking comfort from the ones that loved us best. I awoke several times during the night, headachy and disoriented and he gently shushed me, stroking my hair until I settled.

When I woke, the couch was cold. He was gone.

Maybe it was better that way.

I padded down the long hallway, pausing at each window to open the heavy drapes. If I didn't come back, they might stay shut forever. What a terrible thing, for a hallway to hide from sunlight.

Dierk hadn't told me what to pack. He said it was just a night in the woods and I wouldn't need more than whatever I usually lugged around in my purse. He also used a tone that implied I normally carried enough for a long weekend. Men just don't appreciate the convenience of big purses.

I stuffed it just in case. I also left Euphrates' cat crate by the front door. Were or not, my cat was going if I was going.

At the top of the stairs, I paused. A rift of power had rolled across me, thick and unfamiliar. And huge.

Suddenly, I wasn't worried about what I had in my bag.

The power was large and roiling, like a barrel of fish. It churned, it moved, and it was looking for me. I could sense the expectation that crowned it.

And it was coming from the front of the house.

An incoming text alert made me jump. Dierk. Come out to the car.

Really? Here I was, on my way to meet the end of my humanity and he couldn't even walk to the door?

Please, came a second text.

With a huff, I marched back to the window and looked

out. Between the weird power and the weirder text I wondered what other surprises I'd find.

I certainly didn't expect to see what I saw.

I ran down the steps, yanked open the door, and stared in disbelief at the crowd standing on my lawn. Demivampires, all of them, filled the entire yard—and I'm talking arena sized here. There had to be thousands of people out in front of my house, pressed up against the edges of the porch, standing in the fountain, wrapping around the sides of the house, down the driveway—everywhere. Dumbfounded, I paced out onto the porch.

A murmur rippled through the crowd. I heard them say my name.

Sophia. Sophia.

They'd all come to see me.

Several people close by reached out for me. The power swelled, pressing on my barriers. I drew inwards, a reflex, before catching myself. This might be the last time I stood here with the ones I'd come to call my own. I couldn't remain apart from them.

Taking a deep breath, I let my barriers slide down, disrobing my core, letting the Sophia slip free. I unfurled my essence and spread it out, touching each one. I recognized some of the DV when I did—not their faces, but the timbre of their power. I opened my arms, closed my eyes, and touched each one.

Their sorrows, their regrets—I drained it all away, replacing it with a glow of my own. That glow sprang from a well inside, one they themselves had unknowingly filled—these strangers who validated me simply by needing me, these Demivampires who had given me a place in their world when I'd completely forgotten how to fit into my own. If this was the last time I could give something back, I was going to give every last piece of me.

And I'd do it the right way—standing here with them, looking into their faces, brushing my fingers against those outstretched hands. Not hiding behind a pen and paper or a magazine column, through words and wards. No substitutes.

Gratitude and genuine love for the DV created a glow of power that I poured into each person I touched. I blinked back a wash of tears, knowing that this was the proper way to honor Marek—to do what he'd only dared to dream about. If I did this for anyone, I did this for him—because without him, I might still be a lonely part-time bleeding heart who had never learned to love again.

Marek had made me a survivor. I had to do the same for each of these Demivampire who believed in the Sophia and her redemption. I would show us all that Marek did not live in vain.

I took what was hurting them and left each one in comfort, as best as I could. Unlike the first time I'd gotten submerged in Rodrian's power, I didn't become overwhelmed—I didn't drown under the massive force. I swelled with renewed strength because I was taking one last shot at the destiny I thought had been mine.

My spirit found buoyancy and I glided upon it, a crest upon the wave, and I sought every last Demivampire who had come to see me off, perhaps the last chance to see their Sophia. I spun my barriers out and cast myself into their essence, spreading my Sophia far out from my body. The power breathed and I breathed with it, an inhale upon the exhale, symbiotic, seamless. I was one with my Demivampire. This was where I should have been all along.

The crowd opened up, and I walked down the steps. They parted as I moved, closing behind me, leaving me in an empty five-foot radius. I kept walking, slowly, continuing to reach out to touch as many as I could. That's when I bumped up against a power I'd come to know very well and my breath caught, my heart seized the next beats with a wrenching grip.

It was one thing to play the Sophia and walk amongst a crowd of strangers. It was a completely different thing to face my family.

The crowd parted to reveal Rodrian, his arm around Shiloh. Tears glistened on her cheeks, and I ran the last few steps to them, wrapping my arms around her and bathing her in the glow of the Sophia. Her tumultuous power steadied, but I couldn't take more than the edge off her grief. It had all the strength of her sheer unrefined power behind it. And Rodrian—

When I released Shiloh and looked up at him, he smiled a sad smile and held open his arms. As I leaned into his embrace, he opened up his heart to me and let me inside. It was the closest we'd actually been since Aurelia showed up. Such a myriad of feelings—joy that we had been family, even if only a short time; sadness that this could be the end. And every shade of every feeling in between.

But no anger. If anything, there was hope.

I could not bear to be the one to kill that tiny spark. I exhaled deeply and, with the next breath, I siphoned away every negative vibe I could, until I'd reached the center of his essence. That was locked away, still a secret, shadowed and dark. I needed time to break down that final wall, just a little more time—

There was no more time. The desperate realization stole my breath—

He pulled back and sought my eyes, a tiny shake of the head, a wordless apology. *Do not remember me like this, his power said. Remember what we had…*

Rodrian reached for my face, drawing me to close to his own. "Remember me," he whispered, and kissed me with the touch of a feather, the press of his affectionate power eclipsing the press of his lips.

Shiloh took my hand in hers, giving me a squeeze, and tugged me away from him. Once more the crowd opened and flowed around us. Though we'd only gone a few steps, I turned back to look at him, only to find he was gone. I reached out my essence, looking for his, but met only strangeness.

Shiloh lowered her gaze and kept walking. A new presence opened up in front of me, an empty space.

A void.

The crowd parted to reveal Janssen's white Mercedes, Dierk behind the wheel. Shiloh leaned to kiss me on the cheek. Her nose pink, her eyes bleary, she backed away, one step, another, our arms stretched between us. I turned for a last look at the Demivampires, took in their faces, the essence of their power. Just one last look.

Shiloh released my hand. "Live long, Sophie. I love you."

I had to wrench my head away. If I didn't get in the car now, I never would, and I didn't have a choice. I reached down to the handle of the car door, pulling it open. A gust of wind flared and I looked up.

They were gone, just gone. Every last Demivamp had vamoosed. I stood alone in the driveway next to Dierk's car. No evidence that anyone had ever been there, not a gum wrapper, not a single bent blade of grass.

I searched the front of the house, the window where Rodrian stood in the morning to wave goodbye. An empty window. The only movement was the blur of a curtain falling closed.

My farewell. I nodded, more to myself. This had been a farewell worth saying. If I never saw my DV again, at least I felt like I'd given them something, even if it hadn't come close to what they deserved.

I slipped into the front seat, tucking my bag down next to my legs. A strange exhaustion seeped into my limbs, almost the opposite of an adrenaline rush. Dierk handed me a travel cup full of tea but didn't utter a word about what we'd both just witnessed.

I was grateful for the tea and his silence—I had gotten a final glimpse of what his *Leni* was taking me from, and right now I felt like I'd been stolen all over again. As hard as I tried, I couldn't keep the bitter thorn from sticking into my tender heart.

Dierk let me pick the CD to play on the way out to Lancaster. I spited him by not choosing one of his. Instead, I chose a late eighties Rush album because it made me remember the kid I used to be before I went to college and got engaged and got unengaged and left my job and lost a bunch of people I can't believe I'd managed to live without. If one called this living.

I almost found myself singing along a few times but at the last moment I'd see him out of the corner of my eye and the song would die in my throat.

We drove for about an hour and a half, before the train of cars turned off the Turnpike. Main roads turned into local roads as he headed into the country, eventually taking a road with no lines painted on it, and then a private drive that disappeared ahead into thick pines. Gravel and tree root made the ride too bumpy for the CD to play without skipping. I switched it off. Wouldn't want it scratched.

Heavy ruts, carved into the road by rain and wear, made Dierk slow down for fear of leaving part of the transmission lying in a ditch. The trees stood thicker still, stretching high overhead to block out the sunlight.

I didn't need to see the sky to know it was sunfall. Closing my eyes, I rapped my knuckles against the window, needing a different sensory stimulation than the tingles that nipped along my barriers, reminding me that somewhere, a DV was losing his battle against evolution. Maybe, that DV was one of mine.

The thought was too much. I whimpered in my throat. Dierk reached over and anchored me with his hand over mine. "It's okay."

I shook my head. He mistook my Sophia Fail to mean something entirely different.

Reaching up to stroke my hair, he made comforting sounds. "But it will be. It always will be."

We finally broke free of the trees to find ourselves overlooking a valley. Broad fields sloped down toward thicker woods. The cars pulled one by one onto a dirt spot, kind of a country parking lot. People emerged from their cars whooping and laughing and, if I didn't know better, I'd swear we were here for a bush party.

Dierk turned off the ignition but didn't remove the keys. We sat in silence, watching the others drift past. Someone banged against the car and I jerked my head, catching a glimpse of two guys hefting a keg.

He chuckled. "Despite the significance of tonight, the others are still here to enjoy themselves. You should, too."

"Eh." I twisted my hair around my fingers. "I'm too old for drinking beer in the woods."

"But just the right age for a party in the moonlight." He patted my leg. "Come. Stohl is getting anxious."

We joined the line of people travelling down a path through the patches of last year's grass. The sun had abandoned the valley, painting the ground in blues and greys. Farther ahead, the first ones were already disappearing into the woods. By the time we reached the tree line, I heard their laughter echo through the new foliage, along with intermittent crackles.

I sniffed the air. "A fire?"

"April nights are chilly in the mountains."

I hadn't noticed. Hooray for adrenaline.

It wasn't long before I saw the fire, a healthy-looking blaze with a large clearing around it. More than one keg had ended up with us and a decidedly festive atmosphere was heating up—laughter, horseplay, good-natured challenges. Looked a lot like the bush parties we had in high school, except none of us back then had pumpkin-colored eyes.

Dierk walked me around the edge of the clearing, making the rounds. He led me by the hand and I looked down once, catching a glimpse of faint scars in the dancing light. We were tethered by the hands Stohl had bitten that night at the club. The Bite Heard 'Round My World.

I squeezed his hand to catch his attention and he winked at me. He knew what he was doing.

He greeted each Were by name and surname and they replied, greeting him by title with a fist-to-heart salute. The first ones to do it startled me with the handsomeness of it—the interplay appealed to that old-soul part of me. But when they turned to me as we prepared to move on to the next group, they addressed me. As if I mattered.

And they wished me luck.

For a moment, I swallowed my tongue. Quickly, I dragged up that part of me that pretended like I knew what to do. I sincerely thanked them, even reaching out to the closest man to touch his arm.

I didn't think about it. I just did. The moment my flesh met his I felt Dierk stiffen beside me. The man just grinned and performed the same fist-to-heart salute he had done to Dierk.

The others did the same.

Dierk waved and steered me toward the next group. I

leaned into Dierk and whispered. "What just happened?"

"Something just short of a miracle." His half smile looked painted on, as always, but I saw a triumph in his eyes. "You have won them over."

"Because I didn't run screaming?" If that was the case, I should have won them over weeks ago.

"Because you made yourself familiar with them."

We were too close to other people to continue our private discussion. I breathed a little easier and tried acting like they were just people. I think it was the first time I let myself admit they actually were people.

Dierk approached Cacilia's group last. I don't know if it was intentional or coincidence or what but it was still too soon for me. She responded in sullen tones and when the others finished with their pleasantries to me, she just smirked.

"Have fun in the woods tonight, Sophia." Of course, it was said in a tone that implied if she could catch me and eat me, it would be her having all the fun.

I took the high road. "Thank you."

Fuck it. High roads were boring. I tilted my head and gazed up at Dierk, running my free hand up his arm. "I'm having so much fun already."

"Ladies." Dierk bowed his head and excused us, pulling me through the mingling Weres toward a pair of camp chairs. Wow. Thrones. These people really went all out for their royalty.

"Really, dear." He steered me toward one of the chairs and motioned toward the group at the nearest keg. "The first night of the moon isn't the best time to antagonize a Were."

"Relax, Dierk. I've been antagonizing her every day for three weeks. She's used to it."

"I hope. Ah, *danke*." He took two plastic cups from

someone and handed me one. Red Solo cup full of beer. Fancy living, here I come.

I sipped it, relieved that it wasn't cheap light beer. Ooh, did I detect a trace of orange? I'd have to find out what kind it was. I'd finally found my beer niche. Settling back into the chair, I craned my head toward a faint sound. Dierk looked at me over the rim of his cup.

"Is that water?" It sounded like a brook nearby, the gentle rush of water over stone.

He nodded and pointed. "The lake is down there. It's a beautiful thing when the moon is high."

"You sound like you have been here before."

He nodded. "Once. We usually find similar locations wherever we travel with first timers. Water births are easier."

Uck. Sounded—Wereish. And slippery. Once more the image of Toby's violent change flashed in my mind and I shuddered. I didn't want to think about the yuck factor right now.

I kept my phone in my palm all evening, stealing glances at the countdown app and wondering when it would begin. The only thing I felt was the slow building of anxiety. It started as a clothes-too-tight feeling but at an hour until full, it was full-blown turtleneck pressure. And that was despite my copious ingestion of beer. Considering beer usually resulted in a clothes-too-loose feeling, I realized I could have been feeling a lot worse.

"Are you waiting for a call?"

I quick covered the phone, belatedly realizing he'd finally noticed. Well, it wasn't like he was going anywhere. I offered him the phone.

He took it and grinned. "Look at that. From the *Witchkinder*, I assume?"

Dierk scrutinized the screen a moment before closing his

eyes. After a moment, he nodded and handed me the phone. "*Ja*, that's about right on the nose."

People began drifting off from the fire circle in ones and twos, disappearing into the darkened trees. Cacilia lingered with her group, trying to catch Dierk's eye. He never looked at her. The disappointment and anguish was plain on her face. All she wanted was attention. I feared to look at her, to set her off by intruding on something so personal—

Then I realized I wore that same expression for a year and a half, when I spent every waking moment hoping just for a look from Marek. I loved him, even at his worst, and knew if he could have seen how I felt, the pain our separation caused me, he would have stopped avoiding me.

I glanced at Dierk. A look from Cacilia would not change his heart tonight. He needed to put her pain to rest and to remind her he loved her in that own special way. I tapped his leg and pointed surreptitiously to Cacilia. "You need to speak to her. She's hurting."

He hid behind his near-empty cup, finishing the drought. "Why do you care?"

"I don't," I lied. "But I have to pee and I don't want her jumping me behind a bush. Keep her busy."

He nodded. Raising his hand, he beckoned to Cacilia. She eyed me up as she approached us.

"Excuse me, please," I said to them both, did an awkward little curtsey thing and turned to leave.

Cacilia grasped my sleeve. "Good luck, Sophia. Don't be scared."

"Should I be?" I eyed her and slowly tugged my arm from her grasp.

"No." She spread her hands. "This close to the moon, you should never be afraid. This is the one time when you finally have someone else taking care of you."

Her voice, stripped free of the mean tone she usually used with me, sounded raw and vulnerable. I trusted she meant what she said.

I smiled as much as I could, and worried it looked less than sincere. However, since standing up, I realized how bad I had to go and I was holding onto my bladder by my teeth. I waved before ducking under the branches to find a spot. I went far enough away to give them space but not so far that the firelight couldn't make shadows dance through the leaves around me.

I buried the used Kleenex—it mulches, right?—and headed back to camp. Cacilia and her group were making their noisy way through the bushes. Dierk stood and stared at the fire. We were the last left at the clearing.

"We will go down to the water now. We will be alone. No one will watch us there." He stood up and brushed off his jeans. "You can disrobe to whatever degree you find comfortable. Better to leave your belongings here, instead of scattered through the forest. Your first time, I mean. Some consider the scavenger hunt in the morning to be equal fun."

No way. I was prepared. Kicking off my sneakers, I pulled my hoodie off and slid down my sweatpants, dropping them on my chair before stepping into flip flops. All I had on was an old cami-and-shorts sleep set I'd gotten at a Pink sale a few years ago. If he thought I'd go skipping through the woods stark naked, he was wrong.

Still, it was the barest I'd ever been in front of him since the Bite. He'd stripped down as I did, but he was now barefooted in boxer briefs. The firelight danced across his skin, showing every contour of muscle, the ridges of his abdomen, the nice little bump of shoulder muscle that made any guy look like he had the ability to turn into the Hulk. And I couldn't help but notice those sweet little abdominal cuts that dove from his hips into his briefs.

This was forty? Oh, hell yes. It was damn good to be the king.

I pried my gaze off the rest of his body and managed to find his face. He delighted in the way I looked at him. He was a very happy man.

I peeked a little lower, wondering just how happy he was. He must have known what I was thinking because he closed the distance between us and drew me against him, chuckling.

His skin was warm, as if he'd been standing in the sun. I nestled against his warmth because he'd been right—it was chilly up there in the mountains. Dierk ran one hand up my back under my hair, fingers at my neck, while the other hand explored the curve of my waist, my back.

He grinned, licked his lips, looked around us. His hair had tumbled around his face, giving a hint of shadowed maturity beneath the boyish charm. "I am so very pleased it is you who stands here with me."

My heart pounded, part anxiety, part skin rush. "Will you sing to me?"

"My dear, I will sing to you every day, every night for the rest of my life."

The tenderness in his tone made my heart ache. Right now, at this moment, that's what I wanted. Just—not the Were stuff.

I didn't know what to say. Thankfully, he leaned down for a kiss, one of those wonderful warm kisses of his, and I abandoned my doubt. If I could be kissed like this, loved like this, held like this, for the rest of my life—didn't joy always come with a price?

Being Were would be the counterbalance. It was an equal weight, a fair price.

He broke the kiss. "Let's go down to the water. We

should be ready for the moon. If we stay here…well, you should never place the bedding before the wedding."

I laughed. "Are you trying to tell me you're a virgin?"

He squeezed my hand and led me away from the fire circle. "Tonight, we are. This is the first day of an amazing run. I cherish you, Sophie. You will see. It will be magic."

We followed a thin winding path through the brush, Dierk leading me carefully, holding branches and limbs aside. He led the way through the dark as if the path had been lit. The sounds of water became louder and louder, and it wasn't long before I spied the lake through the thinning trees.

And I saw the moon.

It hung in the sky, big and bright, untarnished. Stars blazed in the heavens, undimmed by the thickness of city lights. Here, the sky was naked and pure, inviting us to admire its beauty.

Moonlight rippled across the water, illuminating everything it touched. I could see clearly in the dark, thanks to the moonshine. Along the shoreline, moonlight skipped across wet stones, the curls of water lapping the rocky shore.

I saw the touch of moonlight everywhere, and the pearlescent glow stole my breath away.

Dierk, still holding my hand, gave me a squeeze. "You see it, don't you?"

"What?" I whispered.

"The lay of the light. We are still nearly ten minutes from full, but you can see it, can't you?"

"The moon is so bright. It's like the middle of the day out here."

"Not just the brightness—the life of the light. The pulse of life, like breathing silver. The sound—" He let go of my hand and walked into the water, slow careful steps, arms spread wide. "Can you hear Her?"

All I could hear was the thump-thump of my pulse in my ears, my ragged breathing. "Ten minutes. Oh. Oh."

"Come to me, my dearest. Just come out, stand in the water with me."

I rubbed my arms, trying to smooth the goose bumps. "It's got to be freezing."

"You won't mind it. Come, take my hand." He reached back for me, one hand entreating.

I stepped carefully into the water, gasping when a small wave lapped higher than I expected. The bite of cold was momentary. Slipping my hand into his, I walked out to where he stood. Together we waded deeper, stopping when the water licked at my chest.

"I can control my *Wolf*," Dierk said. "I will wait until you Change so that you are not afraid. All you have to do is breathe, and watch my face. I will be right here."

He kissed me again, cupping my jaw in his warm hands. I reached up and placed my hands over his, trying to breathe. I felt like I was running out of air.

"Will it hurt?" I clutched his hands, waiting for the pain. The water was cool, chilling me. I barely felt the rocky bottom of the lake. It felt like I was floating, drifting. I had no anchor.

"Shh…" He whispered against my mouth, resting his forehead on mine. "The *Leni* is kind. Your Turning will be easy, graceful. My mother told me about hers. It was…gentle. One day, we will talk about it with our own son."

Suddenly, my skin began to twitch, like a million little fingers plucked at me. It didn't hurt, but it did very little to ease my anxiety. I gasped.

Dierk nodded and stepped backwards, away from me. "Just breathe. I will be right here."

I looked down at my arms, rubbing them wildly. I couldn't stand that twitching. The sensation intensified. I felt like I had the DTs and I wanted to crawl out of my skin.

Over the noise of my splashing, I heard the call of a woman's voice, a language I didn't recognize. It was inside my head and outside my head at the same time. I didn't know the words but I knew what it was saying, and it was going to drive me insane.

"Sophie." Dierk's voice sounded tight-rope balanced, in control but knowing a misstep would be disastrous. "Look at me. Just look at my face, Sophie."

I couldn't focus on him. Not when someone else was so intent on grabbing my attention.

The plucking. The voice. It was her again.

A wolf howl laced through the night air, followed by another. Then another.

And I recognized their voices. God help me, I knew it was Janssen who howled first. I heard Olberich and Cacilia follow. I shouldn't know that—I didn't want to know that—wild eyed, I scoured the darkness for Dierk. *Please, make sense of this—*

Dierk reached toward me, reaching but not touching. "Don't fight, Sophie! Breathe it out, it will pass. Just breathe. I can't hold back much longer!"

I wanted to yell, *I am breathing, dammit!* But what came out of my mouth was something unintelligible and defiant and I howled with it.

It was her. It was that voice. She was in my head and she was the one that plucked at my skin and she would drive me insane with it if she didn't stop—

"Who are you?" That voice, that couldn't be the moon. The moon was just a toy to her. I was enraged. All this time I'd been led to believe one thing and now I saw I'd been wrong—they were all wrong. I let myself swell inside, unclamped the safeties around my barriers and I let all of what made me *me* just take over. "You are not the moon. You are not the Goddess!"

Whatever this entity was, it eclipsed even the moon, the Goddess, the feminine divine that drew the Were to her bosom in nurturing protection. This was an interloper. This was a power that knew me and targeted me and I was through being a target.

Spinning my barriers out like a web, I cast myself upwards and grabbed the moonlight. I pulled the night sky down to me with the power of the emotion that I felt. I seized the moon, that piteous toy, yanking it free from her grasp. I threw it far from me and far from her and I screamed, swirling words of a lunar language—

Dierk howled my name, his voice seeping into the mellow music of a wolf. He fell backwards away from me before disappearing under the water. I forgot all about her.

"Dierk!" My scream echoed back and forth, against the water, the rock, the forest. I screamed his name over and over. He was nowhere. I sloshed toward the spot where he'd been standing, reaching down into the water, dragging the depths for him.

That's when I noticed I still had arms. Hands. Skin.

The sound of splashing sounded off to the side, near the shore. A huge wolf, shining obsidian in the moonlight, made its way out of the water before turning back to look at me. Golden eyes shone in the dark.

Dierk's eyes.

I ran to him, with all the grace of a cow on meth, splashing and nearly tumbling over once I got to the shallows.

He simply watched and waited, all the while whining. Wincing, my mom used to call it, that whistle-sound a puppy made when in distress.

I sank to my knees, oblivious of the rocks and scattered river debris, and knelt before him in the mud. Nose to nose. I reached up to touch him, the thickness of wet fur, the ropes of muscle beneath his skin.

Dierk. Wolf. One.

Reaching around him, I hugged him closer. He rested his head on my shoulder. He trembled. Was it the cold? I hadn't thought to pack a towel—

He winced again before withdrawing from my embrace, nosing me to my feet, pushing me toward the path. He wanted me to leave. I didn't think I'd find my way in the darkness without him.

I turned my back on Dierk and the moon-filled lake and put one foot in front of the other, feeling my way through the trees, one branch at a time.

The peace of the night was suddenly shattered by the force of Dierk's howl. I knew it was his. I knew his voice. His howl was the sound of a heart breaking, a soul tearing into tatters, a promise being broken. I felt those same pains and I wanted to howl back.

I knew I never would.

Morning found me stiff in places I'd forgotten were mine. No matter how comfortable people claim bucket seats to be I'm sure they didn't mean for them to be slept in. I'd have a mark from the seatbelt thing for at least a week and I hated—absolutely hated—sleeping on my back.

Didn't help that I'd been in a motor vehicle accident less than forty-eight hours ago. Those aches and pains had worked their way to the surface, too. I'd fumbled through the glove box but couldn't find any ibuprofen. Werewolves obviously didn't know what glove boxes were for.

I lamented the state of my hair in the vanity mirror (aptly named by the way, since who the hell worries about what their hair looks like after sleeping in the car?) when a flash of color caught my eye.

Dierk was coming up from the woods.

Talk about mixed feelings.

On one hand, I was glad to see him. The woods weren't exactly my favorite place to be alone, locked doors are not.

More so, I missed him.

On the other hand, last night he changed into wolf more or less right freaking in front of me. It wasn't a total surprise or anything, but still. Thankfully it wasn't anything like when Toby exploded into an ooey gooey ball of Were. Apparently, it was good to be the king.

This morning he looked like he always did—head up, eyes alert, gait relaxed. His clothes were a little rumpled, his hair was wet and slicked back as if he'd had a dip earlier. He carried his shoes.

When he saw me watching, he waved. I turned the key a half click and rolled down the window.

As he got closer, I saw what could only be sorrow in his eyes. We spent a long moment looking at each other, in silence. There were no words, yet oh, so much passed between us.

He looked around, lifting his chin, and I knew he was tasting the air. "Room in there for me?"

"I hope so. I don't want to flip for the trunk."

I got out so he could climb in and he adjusted the seat to a comfortable reclining position. Once he was settled, I got back in and sat on his lap, leaving the door open so my legs hung outside. Now, this was comfortable, I thought I could have spent the night like this. No problem.

And that's when I realized what it was that I wanted and what it was that I couldn't have and I ached at knowing that they were the same thing.

"Have a good night?" I asked.

"It could have been better." His voice was soft and craggy, like his morning beard.

"I am sorry," I whispered.

He shook his head a little as he rested back against the seat, rolling it side to side.

"Don't be. You've done nothing wrong. Destiny

chooses, not us." Dierk sighed. "If it were my choice, I would have you. Already I feel as if I'd betrayed destiny just by holding you now."

"So that's that?" I blinked against the sting in my eyes. "One night makes all the difference?"

"You did not change with the moon."

"That doesn't mean I haven't changed." I felt like I was being strangled but I couldn't say the words. I didn't think it mattered now, anyway.

He wrapped both arms around me and hugged me against him.

"My Sophie," he said softly. "To think that I'm always going to be in love with you...It makes it all the harder, because I can never have you. I can never be allowed."

He let out a deep shuddering sigh, and even though he made no sound, I knew he cried.

The sound of footsteps crunching on gravel made me sit up.

Dierk remained motionless, eyes closed. "It is Stohl."

"He's not happy," I said. For the first time I caught a thin stream of emotion coming from the werewolf. Uh-oh. Can't be good. "He's really not happy."

I unfolded myself and got out, and Dierk followed.

Stohl stalked toward us, a play of emotions fleeting across his face as if he couldn't decide which one to wear. When his gaze settled upon me, however, his eyes flashed with anger.

Great. Stohl was having an issues-with-Sophie day again. I hid behind Dierk, keeping a wary eye on the other man.

"Stohl." Dierk tensed, but kept his voice level. He must know something was wrong. There had to be, if the Were was so angry I could sense it. "Good run last night?"

"No." The word was clipped, even more curt than

Stohl's usual.

"Why not? Good weather, good moon."

"Was it? I didn't notice."

"Stohl." Dierk sounded apprehensive. "What is wrong with you?"

Stohl flexed his hands, making and breaking fists, and took a menacing step toward me. "Ask her."

"Me?" Oh, geez. Here we go again. "What did I do?"

"You poisoned me." His venomous eyes glared, his lips curling to reveal clenched teeth.

"I am waiting for explanation," Dierk said.

"She poisoned me. She did not change, and my bite is the strongest. I've never failed to turn a human. She did not change, and last night, neither did I." Anger turned to hate as it simmered on his emotions, and I knew I was in immediate danger.

I could feel Stohl because he wasn't Were anymore.

Dierk didn't even turn around to look at me; he remained a barrier between us as he sheltered me behind him. "You claim this woman's blood prevented you from your change last night."

"No, it was no mere prevention. She has killed the moon. She has destroyed everything within me that feels the moon, and I will kill her for it."

"If—" Dierk spread his arms out, increasing the barrier. "If she has done this, your vengeance is the least important of issues."

"How can you say that? I am no longer whole!"

"You are no longer cursed."

In a swift smooth movement, Dierk deposited me behind the shelter of the open car door before standing in front of Stohl, nose to nose. It wasn't confrontation; Dierk was only scenting him. Examining him. "No longer...cursed. You smell human."

"I am not human." Stohl spoke through clenched teeth. The anger was dissolving, replaced again by kaleidoscopic emotions. Confusion. Astonishment. Fear. "I am Were."

"No," Dierk said, his voice reasonable. "You aren't. And if you threaten my woman again, you will not be able to defend yourself against me."

"You choose her over me." Stohl's mouth hung open in disbelief. "I have been your brother for decades."

"Yes, and still you fight against my choosing a woman."

"Only that woman."

I rolled my eyes at him. "Settle down, wolf boy."

Stohl bunched his fists and leaned into his stance. "Don't call me *boy*."

"Don't call him *Wolf*." Dierk reached into the car and dug out his cell phone. Stohl tried to growl at me, but instead of menace, I heard only a man's impotent frustration. "Stohl, get in the back seat. It's an order."

Stohl gave him a measuring look and I thought he'd fight him. Instead, he swallowed hard as if fate had given him too big a bite. He went around to the driver's side and got into the back, slamming the door hard enough to rock the car.

He didn't say a single word all the way back to the city. He didn't make a peep as he listened to Dierk's conversation with Tancred. He didn't utter a single threat against me. Stohl just looked out his closed window and watched nothing.

Dierk took him back to the Windwood, where Tancred came out to the car for a brief consultation. After making an assessment, they escorted Stohl inside, before Dierk emerged alone twenty minutes later. I waited in the car with the remainder of a cup of Starbucks chai latte; the coffee joint was the only drive-thru food we passed on the way back into Balaton. I knew the two of them had to be starving for more than coffee and biscotti. Strangely, though, none of us had an appetite.

As he got back into the car, I saw the crease between his brows. Even his usual vague smile seemed to be slipping.

I waited for him to say something, but he'd clicked on his seatbelt and pulled out of the spot without speaking. Guessed it was up to me to ask. What else was new? "What will happen to Stohl?"

"Why do you ask?"

I shrugged. "Well, I mean, if it was my fault that he didn't change—"

"You keep saying things like *sorry* and *fault.* You don't control any of this."

"Dierk, Stohl bit me. He said I was the only one who never turned. It sounds like I did something."

He pursed his lips and snorted. "Did you wake up the morning of the day we met and say, 'I think I'm going to unTurn a werewolf?'"

"No." I made a sour face at the ridiculous question.

He nodded once, a hard dip of *exactly so.* "Did you wake up yesterday and say, 'I think I will resist changing with the moon when Dierk takes me to the mountains'?"

"No." My sour expression relented

"Did you say," his voice choked a bit and he cleared his throat. "'I think I will turn destiny's course and sunder Dierk's hopes that he has finally found his lifemate'?"

I said nothing.

He rapped his knuckles against the window as he waited for a car to pass. "You can't apologize for something you did not intend to happen."

And yet, I'd gotten so good at it. "What will happen to Stohl?"

"Why do you ask?"

"I... don't like him. I won't even pretend to, not even out of sympathy, but I can relate to what he might be going through. Kind of. I know he's mad at me and that he's scared."

Especially since Tancred told him his options. The options weren't attractive by any means. Tancred was treating him like a failed bite case. It was either bite repetition or an amnesia treatment.

Stohl took the prognosis with a stony expression. His emotional storm gnawed at me. Probably only because I felt so damn guilty about it.

"He wanted to kill you on the spot, you know." Dierk grimaced. "Had he been Were, I would have had to fight him. Considering his determination, I might have had to kill him. Stohl was always hard to control on full moon days."

"If he was Were, he wouldn't have been so hot to kill me."

"Perhaps," he said, but his voice was a little too mild.

I snorted. He didn't need to tell me the obvious.

"Do you still care?" He gave me a leveling look.

It wasn't enough to cow me. "Maybe. Are you going to tell me, or not?"

"Stohl will be fine. He always lands on his feet."

"Like a cat?"

Dierk chortled. "Don't let him hear you say that."

"Then don't tell him. So what will you tell the pack when I don't come back with you?"

His mouth wore a half-frown. "I don't know."

"Will you lose face?"

"It's not face I'm worried about. It's you."

"Why? I thought Stohl was out of commission for now."

"Yes, but...if it's true...if your blood removed Stohl's curse...you will be hunted."

I closed my eyes and pressed my head against the window. Just great. First DV, now werewolves. Once, just once, I'd like to be hunted by someone I'd want actually catching me.

I looked at Dierk and refused to finish the thought. "I don't suppose I'll have you around to protect me."

"I will when I can." Mild words. Too mild. "When I'm here."

"And that will be?"

His voice took on the broad sound of his public persona, The Showman. "The next time we tour, of course."

"Swell," I said. "I'm back to being a freaking groupie again."

"Yes," he said with a laugh. "But you are my groupie."

It was better than nothing, I supposed, and despite all outward appearances, I usually ended up with nothing.

I spent the rest of Sunday in bed, watching Netflix. I armed myself with a thermos of Darjeeling, a tub of chocolate peanut butter ice cream, and my cat. We watched Ghost Hunters International until I couldn't keep my eyes open anymore.

Euphrates wouldn't let me out of his sight. Every time I went to the bathroom or to the tea pot out on the bar, he was two steps behind me, complaining and warning me not to stray too far.

I didn't venture out to the rest of the house. I knew it was empty. No Shiloh, no Rodrian. No Toby or Dahlia. No calls. No texts.

A little piece of me was disappointed. But that was all—a little piece.

Monday morning, now, that was something I dreaded. I had to go to work and see Barb. I went in early, finding the office still at half-lights, but Barb's office glowed. She was a start early, quit late kind of person. And she was salaried, too. That sort of rubbish gave me the creeps.

I tapped on her door.

She waved me in. "You're here ridiculously early."

"Eh." I shrugged. "Traffic was light."

"How was your weekend?"

Where should I start? Hopefully, she wouldn't remark on the trousers and long sleeve shirt I wore to conceal the bruises. I busied myself at the coffee station, selecting an Earl Grey cup and popping it in the brewer. "You know. Same old, same old."

She pulled her glasses off and sat back in her chair. "Jasmine won't be in anymore. She was involved in a car accident."

"Oh, no." I stiffened. Better play it safe and not say anything to incriminate myself.

Barb looked away. Her eyes were red and weary, and I knew she'd taken the news really hard. "Apparently she was with a guy. They were driving too fast. The car was demolished. They died at the scene."

I set my cup on the desk and reached for her hand.

"I just don't understand it." She shook her head, still having trouble processing the tragedy. "Jim and I did everything we could to get her on the right path. She was trouble in high school, she was dropping classes in college. When she began to practice Wicca with her—church group, I'm not sure what it's called—she leveled out. You know? She seemed happy. She changed her focus at the JC, taking more science and history. I thought, that's what she needed. Religion. A community. I don't know a damn thing about that religion but I know it made her a better person. And just when I thought she would be okay—"

"Barb, I'm so sorry."

"No. I'm the one who is sorry." She pulled herself together and reached down to open one of the desk drawers. "They recovered some things from the car. I think you'll recognize this."

She set my cat lady coffee mug on the desk.

My breath just about turned to gum in my throat and I choked. I'd forgotten I put that in my purse Friday. It had rolled out when my purse dumped in the car.

Did she know I was in the car? Did she think—

I just stared at the mug. I didn't know what else to do.

"Yeah, well." Barb shook her head. "They thought it was hers. They gave it to me when we went to ident—I took one look at it and I knew. I knew."

Her voice trembled. Not with sadness. Her words had too sharp an edge.

"You think you know someone. You think that you have a relationship, that you have a good influence and then, this. You really find out the truth. All those tiny unspoken things you see in a person's eyes."

Barb lifted her gaze and looked at me. "I'm so sorry, Sophie. I didn't know she was stealing from you. I don't know if she took anything else but I won't make excuses for her. I should have known."

She fisted her mouth tight, forcing back something. The light in her eyes made me suspect it was a scream.

Barb recovered from the flash of raw pain, smoothing her expression into more reserved lines. "But—did you ever know somebody that, no matter how screwed up they are, no matter how bad, did you ever feel like you could…save them? Redeem them? Get them to wake up and look at you and realize that you are completely ready to love and accept them? That if they'd only open their eyes, open their hearts to you, your love would be enough?"

I turned my head, unable to stop the tears from swelling. Barb didn't know she was laying out my life, one soulmate at a time. One failure at a time.

"Why do we try to save these hopeless cases?" Barb's voice was so plaintive, so bare. I could tell she needed me to tell her something wonderful and wise.

I had no advice for her.

I just didn't know.

On Tuesday, the pack assembled at the Masons Lodge, courtesy of the local werewolves. It wasn't just Dierk's pack; it was the masters of each of the local packs, too. Dierk figured that if Stohl was going to be at a safe house for the next month, the pack leaders had to be in on it as well.

I hadn't seen or heard from Dierk since he had driven me home on Sunday. He must have had a lot of internal stuff to sort out, between me and Stohl, so I didn't call. He needed the space and I didn't want to intrude. He sent a text overnight Monday, telling me he would send a car for me at lunch and I should be dressed.

A little impersonal, but I wouldn't fault him for it. The king had a lot to deal with.

Janssen picked me up and joked about shallow things. Every now and then I'd catch his eyes in the rearview mirror. He wasn't as light-hearted as his jokes would have me think. He looked nervous.

I made him nervous.

He led me into the lodge and escorted me to the front of the room where Dierk and Tancred sat, facing the assembly. A seat had been left open for me. As I walked to the front of the room, a murmur ran through the crowd.

I recognized several of them from the weekend I spent in Dierk's court.

Tancred wasted no time. "I am calling for protection for Dierk's woman. Will I have full swearing?"

"For Dierk's mate? Of course," said the one of the pack leaders. "Whenever she is in our city, she can call on our pack for protection. She will be pack to us. You have our oath."

"We agree with pack master Calhoun. Pack is pack," said another.

"Yes," Dierk said. "But Sophie is not pack."

Calhoun looked confused. "But you performed the *Leni.*"

"We did. Sophie did not change."

"My condolences to you. And to you, as well," he said, and dipped a sympathetic nod toward me. "Our oath still stands, pack or not. The Moon has seen something in her worthy of Wolf. Sophie will be treated like one of our own."

I breathed a tiny sigh of relief and said a prayer of thanks.

"Thank you," said Dierk. "My entourage and I will be leaving very shortly, with the obvious exception of Stohl, who will be staying with you for an indefinite time."

"About that," said one of the Were. "The reason for his stay is not so obvious. Is he injured?"

"Yes." Tancred nodded.

"Was it attack that injured him?"

"No." Tancred was sticking to monosyllabic answers.

The Were persisted. "Who did it?"

"Sophie did," Dierk said.

Calhoun choked. I smiled sweetly at him; if I could have dimpled, I would have. Dierk only raised his eyebrows at him and politely waited for him to regain his composure.

"I underestimated you, Miss Sophie," the Were said.

I shrugged. "No biggie."

"We all underestimated her," said Dierk. "Apparently Sophie has unTurned Stohl."

He said it the way someone would have said: apparently, Sophie has bought a new pair of Colin Stuarts. The only difference was that there were no admiring glances at my feet.

A rumble went through the group. It sounded like muffled thunder.

"That has never happened." Calhoun's eyes flashed pumpkin-bright.

Tancred spread his hands. "It has now."

"In legends, maybe."

"And in truth," Dierk said. "How else do legends come to be?"

"So, what is she?" Calhoun stole a furtive look at me, looking worried I might spring. "A witch? A god?"

"We are not sure." Dierk still hadn't done more than glance at me. He'd squared his shoulders and addressed the assembly as if I wasn't present. Up until now, I figured, you know, king and all, has to do the courtly thing.

But I've done the courtly thing with him. Now, I wasn't *with* him. The disconnect was acutely painful.

"I had hoped that elder pack members may have some insight," Dierk said.

Tancred briefly described what we knew, but it didn't take long to relay. Stohl bit Sophie and never changed again. End of story.

Calhoun seemed to have taken the lead position for the assembly and left his seat in the group, walking up the aisle toward me. "And ever in your life, have you noticed anything strange about yourself?"

"Sure," I said. "I can walk on my tiptoes and I read faster than anyone I've ever met. Oh, and I'm Sophia to the Demivampire."

Can people bristle? I knew that they wouldn't like hearing the word Demivampire, but I hadn't expected bristling. Even some of Dierk's pack shifted uncomfortably in their seats.

Tancred stood, drawing the prickly attention away from me. "The Sophia may or may not be the source of Stohl's affliction... I mean, predicament."

"Your woman is DV?" Calhoun gave Dierk a look of disbelief, his mouth hanging open. "And still you performed the *Leni*?"

I couldn't believe I was saying it but well, I was. "Do I smell DV to you?"

I meant it in a nice, smart assed way, but apparently the pack leader interpreted at it as an invitation. He calmly approached me, leaning close and inhaling me. I tried not to squirm.

"No," he admitted. "You smell human."

"There you go." I craned my head back and away from him. *Personal space here, hello?* "Besides, if I had been, Stohl would have flown the coop by now."

Calhoun still stood in front of me and he looked terribly confused. "He'd what?"

"Flown away, you know?" Still the blank stare. Sigh. Very slowly, and as politely as I could, I enunciated. "Turned into a falcon."

"You mean the *Wolfram*?" said Tancred. He leaned forward in his seat to look around Dierk at me. "That's just a legend."

"Right," I said. Didn't Dierk tell him? "And so is the Sophia, and yet here I sit. I have seen it happen."

"I can vouch for her," said Dierk. He sat like a stone statue, his voice as personable. "I have spoken with her DV and I have seen the *Wolfram*. It is no usual bird. I have also questioned the young werewolf whose blood was taken by the DV who is now *Wolfram*. It is legendary, yes, but it is also fact."

Calhoun had resumed his seat, shaking his head.

"This is a lot to take in. When you called us here today, I honestly thought it was to introduce us to your mate. The *Leni* ritual is legendary enough for us, but I thought that would be the extent of it. This—" He made a wide gesture, taking in Tancred, Dierk, and me. "This is too much."

"Do you reconsider your oath of protection?" Dierk asked quietly. The words hung in the air and he reached for my hand, making an obvious show that I was somehow still his.

The gesture felt little more than ceremonial.

"I do not take back the oath." A man stood near the rear of the room, and I saw it was Thorpe, the brute from the bowling alley. "She is an uncommonly good person. She has a sense of honor and mercy that many of us would do well to imitate. Those qualities deserve protection."

Calhoun marked him before turning back to us. He looked at Dierk's hand upon mine and measured me carefully with his eyes. I knew he was considering my ties to the DV. But in the end, it was Dierk he honored.

"No," he said at last. "You have our oath. I'm not sure what she is, but she is valued by you. Even if the *Leni* failed, she is still valued by you. I have testimony from my wolf. I would not deny a woman protection.

"But—" He held up a hand and I saw determination in

his eyes. "But we must examine Stohl, and this woman's role in his change. She is a threat to all Were and must be controlled."

"A threat?" I snorted. "Yeah, I guess so, if I went around making you guys bite me all the time."

"A threat nonetheless." Dierk released my hand. "I call for a second oath. An oath of secrecy. No one outside this room can know. I call upon all pack to make this vow. It is not an option."

Another Were, a woman I didn't recognize, called out from the side of the assembly. "How can we be sure the DV will not use her against us? Her blood may be a weapon."

"Hey, now." I held my hands up. "The DV don't use me. I give. They do not take."

"Do they not?" This curiosity-laden question sounded from a corner of the room.

"No, they don't," I insisted as I craned my neck, trying to find the speaker.

"But you have scars on your skin." Curiosity twisted into something malicious and I knew—I just knew—who it was without seeing her.

"No crap, Cacilia." I held out my hand. "Stohl wasn't trying to be neat."

"Not that scar. The other. Or, perhaps…your throat?"

My blood ran cold.

"Just what is your point?" Beside me, Dierk leaned forward, ready to protest, but I silenced him with one hand upon his. "Make it now or shut up."

"My point is that you are marked by DV in several ways. How do we know you have not been sent to destroy us? A bomb that detonates once you are thoroughly surrounded by us?"

I was tired of this broad. She was worse than Stohl.

Every frickin' time we were in the same room, she caused trouble. I stood up and marched to where she lounged in her chair, arm hooked over the back, long legs stretched out.

Dierk hissed my name, but I ignored him.

"Do you think I asked Stohl to do this?" I held my hand up to her face for inspection, but I could not disguise my anger and it looked like a threat. "Have I invited anyone else to do the same? Have I tried to entice anyone else to do the same?"

"You have done nothing but entice since the cursed day you came to us," she snarled. Cacilia stood, her heels giving her the advantage of height. "You use your filthy Sophia powers to cloud my master's mind and trick him into asking for the *Leni* ritual. You eliminate his strongest fighter. You seek to destroy us all."

"Cacilia." Dierk stood and used the Royal Voice. "You go too far."

"I have not gone far enough," she growled. Before I had a chance to react, she seized my arm and twisted it behind me, holding suddenly clawed fingers to my throat. "I won't bite her and be poisoned, but I can remove this threat to our people quickly."

Dierk stood and slowly approached, one careful footstep at a time. He was only looking at Cacilia. "You made an oath to protect her."

I didn't dare breathe. The painful twist she gave my arm made it easy to hold a hitched breath.

"I made no such oath! I only made oath to protect you. To love you. And still, you chose her." Ragged words revealed the pain and resentment she must have felt since the moment I came into the picture.

"*Ich bin der König,*" Dierk said softly. "And the king's mate is always chosen by the *Leni*."

"And why do you not choose with your heart?" Cacilia's anguish twisted me inside, and despite the immediate danger of having my throat ripped out, I felt guilt for being the one to cause those feelings. "It's your heart you must live with all your life. You chase destiny, as evasive as tomorrow on the horizon. But your heart beats, day in, day out, the only sound when all else is silent. Why do you not listen to your heart?"

"I do, Cacilia," he said softly. "I do listen to my heart, and I tell you, in all honesty, never has it called your name. You love me blindly and you've chosen not to see that I have never loved you in return."

Cacilia was shaking now, a tremor that rocked us both. She slipped into emotional shock and she yanked up on my arm. I bit my lips together to keep from crying out. I didn't want her to remember me.

The sharp points of her claws pressed into my skin, wicked needles of pain. I closed my eyes.

Dierk's voice was tender. "Let go, Cacilia. You have to let go. You can't do this anymore."

"You don't love me." Her voice was a strangled whisper. "All I have done, and nothing in return."

Her hand clenched and the claws broke the skin. Needles became searing screams. Please, please, please, don't rip down.

"No, not true," Dierk said. "You are *meine Wolfin*. You are my pack."

"No, I am not. I denounce you. You are my pack no longer." She threw me at his feet and I hit the ground, hard. Cacilia ran from the room.

There was a scramble of sound as several followed after her. Dierk helped me up, lifting my chin to examine the wounds. I dug a tissue out of my purse and pressed it to my neck.

He issued me back to my seat, the lines of his face drawn in a deep sorrow. Her denouncement had wounded him. More than anything else, he fought for unity amongst his kind. Cacilia was close to his heart, and her betrayal would hurt him as would no other.

Dierk only allowed himself that briefest moment to mourn before forcing his attention to the matter at hand. The luxury of personal grief was not his to enjoy, not while he had to be king. He drew a deep breath and turned to face the room, standing in front of me. "Anyone else in this room care to make retractions?"

The room was silent.

"I speak for the Priestess of the *Witchkinder.*" A thin melodic voice piped up from the side and people turned in their seats to see who'd spoken. I recognized the plume of black feathery hair at once. "Sophia Galen will be fostered by the covens of the East."

Dierk leaned toward Tancred. "Did you know about this?"

Tancred shook his head.

"Why are you surprised?" I leaned and looked at the men. "Nakia was really sweet when she came to the office."

"Yes, she was." Dierk trained his gaze back upon Alise. "So, *Witchkinder.* Your priestess is laying a claim of her own?"

Alise lifted her chin. "No, sire. Not a claim. Simply an offer of protection. The moon has a great interest in Ms. Galen, and we are to foster her within our ranks."

"And do you have any more within your ranks who are like-minded to Jasmine? I will permit no trespass upon this woman."

Alise didn't cower. "Understood, sire."

Dierk nodded and sat back, seeming to keep an eye on Alise. "Agreed, with the understanding that frequent report will be made through Tancred. Is that clear?"

"Yes, sire."

Dierk gestured to Tancred. "Finish here, please. Report to me in two hours."

He stood to leave, bowing slightly and sweeping is hand to indicate I should rise before leading me from the room. He walked separately, two steps in front. Janssen followed behind. No hand holding. I swallowed hard and locked my head upright, chin proud, expression dignified.

Trying not to feel like a political nobody.

Dierk wanted to see Stohl before driving back to Balaton. Janssen carried two duffle bags into the Bayridge safe house, a simple three-story single detached home on a street crowded with similar homes. Small yards, street parking, children playing. Bayridge was Were suburbia.

Stohl met us on the front porch, careful to avoid looking at me. I chose the porch chair closest to the steps in case I had to make a run for it. Didn't know how good a plan running was when dealing with creatures that liked to chase things, but Dierk wouldn't let me stay in the car. He said Stohl needed to face reality, and I was part of what he had to face.

"They are going to convert me," Stohl said. "It begins tomorrow."

Dierk's expression was one of patient persuasion. He shook his head and reached out to clasp Stohl's shoulder. "I don't think you should do it. You never wanted this life."

"It is my life."

"And you hate it. You cannot lie to me, Stohl. I am your king and I am your friend. You never wanted this."

"But my bite was the strongest—"

"Because your bite was the angriest. It held the most passion. You, above all others, felt cursed. You were always angry. When you gave your bite you gave it with anger. Anger because you believed someone took your life and gave you another in its place. You felt betrayed. You felt denied, and whenever you gave your bite, you wished for another to suffer as you have."

"Wishing doesn't make something so."

"Sometimes it does. Relative to the world in which we live, Stohl, we are magic. We are Were because of something magical that lives inside us. Blessing or curse, it is all magic."

"Then why don't all wishes come true? I thought you wanted her." He gestured at me with a sharp darting swipe. "What about your wish?"

Dierk stood and walked to the steps, herding me in front of him. "If all our wishes came true, they'd lose their meaning. Denial of one thing gives us appreciation for the others."

He slipped in a CD as he drove me back to the Stocks and the sounds of speeding guitars and crashing drums swallowed the silence. I jumped in my seat when I heard a much younger Dierk's voice shouting out of the speakers.

"Holy cow," I said. "What year was this?"

"Eighty-nine." He grinned, looking every one of those twenty-odd years younger. "A little on the thrash side, you think?" He shook his head playfully like a head banger, earning some puzzled looks from people on the sidewalk alongside us. I smiled politely and gave them the horns up salute as the light turned green.

I laughed as he sang along. Well, I guess it wasn't really singing; he was more or less shouting quietly.

"Don't you remember this?"

"A little. I was more into Bon Jovi at the time."

"Oh yeah," he replied. "Pretty boys and their pop music.

I thought you liked real rock."

"I do. It's just that your later albums are a lot more polished."

"A producer and a real studio tend to have that effect on your sound. But this, this is where it all began. This is where we realized we were not going to play in basements and woods and bars forever. This album was a dream come true. Just listen to the words."

"Those are words? It sounds like *gahdahgahdahdahda*."

"Must I put you out on the curb?" He scolded me with a wag of his index finger. "Now. Listen to the words."

We listened. It was easier to interpret. The sound, though, man—the music had an unfamiliar groove, a heartbeat beneath the surface of the song.

"That was Rudy," he said. "My first bassist. He wrote that song just after he'd been bitten and you can hear how he felt. The anger. The fear. In anyone else they would be blind emotion. But when there is music behind the words, emotions gain purpose. What a brilliant lyricist he was."

"What happened to him? You make him sound all past tense."

"Because he is passed. Rudy was killed in a succession challenge the year after this came out."

The song ended, and in between the tracks silence dragged a little. He clicked off the radio. "Rudy wrote most of the songs on this. After he was gone I took inspiration from his memory and used the lyrics as a chronicle. Who we are and what we are. What we live and die for. I started to write the literary reference songs to keep the mainstream interest, but it's the Were tales that mean most to me. They are what make me feel like a real bard. I sing our history, and most of the world is unaware."

"Like me," I said. "I listened for years and never suspected they were any less imaginary than your fantasy music."

"Exactly, but now you know. Can you listen to us the same way again?" I don't think he meant the question to be rhetorical, but I didn't answer him. "So, you don't listen to the early recording." He ejected the CD and handed it to me. "Listen to it again, just for me, sometime. Go beyond the non-Bon Jovi and really hear us. Even then, we were an all-Were group. Try to hear us as we were—young, full of rage and wonder, full of life and promise, ready to take on the world."

He drove up the long driveway, a little more slowly than he usually did, and parked in front of the porch. He peered up at the house through the windshield as he turned the key in the ignition.

I didn't move. I just sat and stared out the window, feeling very different than the day he'd first driven me home.

"You will be okay without me." He sounded confident. "The oath, I mean. The Were won't give you any grief. Someone will always be looking out for you."

"Oh," I said. "That. You, um… when is your flight?"

"Early tomorrow. Short layover in London, then home. I have been away much longer than anyone anticipated."

Tomorrow. Just like that he'd be gone.

"If you are ever in Mannheim—" He flipped down the visor and slid out a manila envelope, handing it to me. "You have this, at least."

I peeked inside. My passport. I folded the envelope shut and stuck it in my bag. I pinched my lips, hiding the grimace. "I… don't travel much."

"I know," he said quietly.

"Do you think we will stay in touch?"

"Of course." He smiled and smoothly hid the lie in his eyes. "Of course, we will."

Always the rock star. Make this star-struck girl feel like she's really a special one. All the world is a stage and each life is just another scene to get through. Just leave on a high note, Soph. I reached for the handle.

"Oh, I almost forgot." He fumbled in his coat pocket and pulled out a small box. "This, I got for you. It would never be for anyone else. If nothing else, remember me."

"Always," I whispered. I held the box so tightly my fingers hurt. "Remember me, too."

"Destiny may have another future for me, Sophie." He searched my eyes, treating me to one last glimpse of coffee and champagne, the king and the commoner. It would be a flavor I wouldn't soon forget. "But your name will always be carved upon my heart."

I watched his car pull away, his farewell kiss still tingling on my lips. I didn't have to open the box to know it held a ring. It was probably beautiful. Maybe one day I'd open it and find out.

No matter how I criticized Dierk for listening to destiny, I knew I was being hypocritical. After all, I'd been content to allow destiny to push me around for a long time now. At least he was man enough to admit it out loud.

Maybe the happy puppet is the one who loves his strings rather than the one who would hang herself fighting them.

I don't know what I expected would happen now that the *Leni* was over and Dierk was gone. An oppression had been lifted, a heaviness to the air that I had only noticed once it was gone. I learned how to breathe deeply again. Although my future with the Were and the *Witchkinder* was still murky at best, the almost-overwhelming anxiety over turning Were was over, for good.

Dierk had once told me he thought lycanthropy was the ultimate vaccine. I guess he never figured he'd be faced with a mate who had an immunity of a different kind altogether.

I tried to look on the brightest side of things. At least I'd never have to worry about Turning. Didn't think I'd be tempting fate by encouraging bites any time soon. I was still a bleeder. And bleeding still sucked.

And, although I enjoyed that particular sense of relief, I wasn't at peace. Relief from one stress only made it possible for me to concentrate on another.

Rodrian.

I hadn't seen him since Saturday morning. I'd called, but hung up when it went to voicemail because I couldn't find the words. I wanted to say *Come home* but wasn't sure what he called home anymore since Aurelia got her teeth into him. It wasn't like the Stocks was his actual home, anyway. But it was my home, and he was my family, even if he didn't want to be family anymore.

I called it his home. In my heart, that was all that mattered.

I texted him a few times from work on Wednesday, but heard nothing back. Nothing on the answering machine when I got home, either. I'd resigned myself to another evening of microwave fried chicken and reruns of *Supernatural* when the doorbell rang and I felt a pulse of DV power.

I was so relieved I didn't even question why he didn't just come in. He knew the alarm code as well as I did.

But I did know that sometimes Rodrian fell back on antiquated manners and stiff protocol when he wasn't sure familiarity was appropriate. He'd always been a gentleman, albeit a scandalous one.

I punched in the code and yanked the door open, expecting a huge hug, manners or no. The power was a strange shade of Rodrian, as if he were so excited he couldn't think straight. That made two of us.

Safe to say I was perfectly stunned by the blast of power that sent me staggering backwards as if I'd been hit by a cannon ball. I tripped over my feet and landed hard on my backside, head dazed and vision swimming, squinting and trying to see what had hit me.

When I heard the click of hard heels on the tile, I pushed into the steely wall of DV power. Not Rodrian. That had been a ruse. Someone pretending to be him. Someone who knew him well enough to fake him.

Only one someone could have done all this. Only one person would have.

"Aurelia." I sucked in another breath, sharp pain between my lungs. "Get out of my house. Now."

She stalked toward me, one *snik* at a time, dropping the power ruse. "You just cannot take a hint, can you?"

I gathered myself and tried to push to my feet but she was next to me in a flash, her hand on my head, nails poking into my scalp. She gave me a rude shove downward that sent sparks of pain down my neck, and I hit the ground with my shoulder. I bunched up my barriers, intending to contain her.

She just laughed and bounced my shields back at me. The collision of our powers set up a reverb that made my ears and the front of my brain throb.

"I don't know why you even came back here. You are no longer a necessary resident. I have come back for my mate and my children. They don't need their Were-whoring nanny any longer."

I pulled up my knees, trying to curl up to protect myself. Some lame instinct to protect my vital organs. Never mind, I was being pummeled from the inside by a vicious female DV. I couldn't even begin to imagine what she'd be like if she Fell.

She kicked me onto my back and placed one foot onto my chest. If she stepped down, that heel would skewer me. The look of sadistic delight on her face was a perversion. How anyone so beautiful could be so ugly—

Aurelia flattened her power against me, squashing my barriers. I couldn't fight back, I couldn't breathe past the pain in my chest. She leaned down over her bent knee, smiling. "In fact, I don't think anyone needs you."

She shifted more of her weight onto my chest, the heel

digging in like a dagger and I just mentally screamed, unable to think through the panic.

Suddenly, the pressure lifted and she was off me, away from me. I rolled, curled and defenseless, wondering where she went but too afraid to unhunch my shoulders. I couldn't see her feet anywhere.

"What are you doing?" Her voice was a furious screech. "Put me down!"

"I'm not doing..." I couldn't get the air in to speak over a breathy gasp, let alone a full sentence. Screw it. I got onto my hands and knees and looked for her. She squalled like a cat getting her temperature taken, and I followed her voice.

To just below the chandelier. She was dangling in mid-air, kicking and clawing and swinging like a helpless puppet, suspended by an invisible hand.

"Give me one reason why I should."

The voice that answered her was familiar yet foreign, naked anger darkening the tone. I'd know that voice anywhere but never, ever heard it speak with such blackness.

I had to look. Had to see her because I never though her capable of such force. I turned my Sophia sight toward the maelstrom and—blinked. Seeing wasn't necessarily believing.

Shiloh stood in the doorway, still dressed in her training fatigues. Her eyes blazed, hazel and hate-filled, as she stared up at her mother. "Tell me why I shouldn't pull you apart and throw you away?"

"My daughter—" Aurelia started, but her words choked off.

"No. 'Daughter' isn't a word you deserve to own. A daughter is loved, and cherished, and nurtured. Not abandoned. Not manipulated." She spread her arms, her hands in pale fists. "I am not your daughter."

Aurelia dropped like the invisible hand dropped her and she hit the ground in a crouch, staring up at Shiloh. "You have forgotten your place."

"No. I learned it, thanks to you. I am Demivampire. I am Thurzo. And I do not know you."

"Your family is your place." Aurelia stood, pulling her skirt back into place. She wiped her nose, rubbing a thin red stain between her fingers. "Your father and your mother, your siblings—"

"My family is my place. And Sophie is my family. If you ever so much as curl your nasty lips at her ever again, I will not hesitate to destroy you. Get out."

Aurelia took a step toward her. "Shiloh—"

"Get out!" Shiloh roared, voice of a siren and power of a storm.

Aurelia tossed her head, flipping her hair back. A tiny trickle of blood had leaked from her ear. She didn't waste a glance at me as she stalked to the door. She didn't disguise her power, though. She wanted me dead, and was extremely pissed that she'd been thwarted.

I got a disturbing sense of *again*. She'd been thwarted again. Things began clicking into place and I didn't want them to. I'd have given anything if they didn't.

When Aurelia passed Shiloh, the girl snapped out a hand and snatched Aurelia by the neck, stopping her in her tracks and making her teeter on her toes.

"Don't come back here again, Aurelia." Shiloh swiveled her head, her eyes cold, and a grim pleasure on her face. "Unless you'd like to spar."

Aurelia pinched her mouth shut and wrenched herself free, an unreadable look in her eyes. She left without speaking a word.

Aurelia's power disappeared as soon as she left the house. Vanished. Gone. Like a storm suddenly blew over.

Thanks to Shiloh.

Her brow lightened when Aurelia's presence left and she ran to me, helping me to my feet and walking me slowly into the den.

Walking hurt. Sitting down hurt more. I'd really landed hard. Great. On top of everything else this month, I probably had a broken ass. How spectacular.

Shiloh didn't say much. I still had a tough time accepting what had happened. That I wasn't safe in my house, unless I had Shiloh to protect me.

"Thanks, kiddo." I gingerly tried to adjust a pillow behind me. "I don't know what I would have done if you didn't—"

"Shh." She smiled, a sweet Shiloh smile. "I'm going to run upstairs and bring down dinner. Whatever you made smells incredible."

The microwave chicken. Huh. Forgot all about it.

"Sophie." She stopped at the door. My neck was stiffening up and I couldn't turn all the way around to see her. "I just want you to know…I wanted to kill her for hurting you."

"Shy, you can't—" I huffed out, knowing what it was like to really hate someone enough to want them gone. "Don't take that onto yourself. That's what hurts your soul. That kind of hate. Don't ever give into that kind of darkness."

"But I got you, sunshine. You can just fix me up when I get too far gone." Her voice held more buoyancy than it should have. "Be back in a hot minute."

And while I sat on the couch, waiting for her to return, the pain of my injuries and the stress of the last month all melted away into a new worry that formed and solidified in my chest. If Shiloh actually thought she could take any risk because the Sophia was just down the hall, she'd really take them. The recklessness of a teenager who had the power of a Thurzo, whose cusp had been supercharged by the Sophia's blood—

What had I created?

What kind of trouble would she get into?

And what if I couldn't always undo the damage?

When I got home from work the next day, Rodrian's car was parked in front. There was no mistaking the touch of his power. I chided myself for allowing Aurelia to fool me, and for allowing my emotions to cloud my judgment. Awake. Aware. I could never let my guard down again.

My doubts lifted once I walked inside. The first thing that struck me was the sense of openness in the house, as if a great oppression had been lifted. I hurried upstairs, finding Rodrian in the office, the balcony doors wide open, fresh air pouring in.

He sat in the center floor, staring at nothing, weathering a storm on the inside. When I knelt down beside him, I touched his shoulder. He only lifted a folded sheet of paper and showed me what was written upon it.

See you next year, darling.

There was only one reason she'd write that note, those words, that timing. Only one reason she'd risk running into Shiloh. I knew what that meant. Aurelia was in a family way again.

That's why she said *siblings* to Shiloh. Shiloh had only ever known her sister. And now, there was a baby on the way.

I couldn't look at Rodrian for a few days after reading that. Sure, I knew they were together, and she was his mate, after all. But the thought of them together like that—it made my stomach hurt. I had no right to the anger, the disappointment, not when I'd been spending every evening with Dierk, chasing my own temporary destiny.

It was almost a welcome distraction, in a way, because it enabled me to avoid asking what had happened the night he had shifted forward on his evolutionary clock. His power felt murky, unsettled. She'd damaged him in more ways than one, with promises of more conflicts to come. Rodrian had led a sheltered life, more or less, while Marek was around. He'd never borne this kind of agony.

He needed time. He had a bit of true soul-searching to do, and I couldn't interfere with it. In a way, he needed to feel bad about what he'd done so that he wouldn't repeat the mistake. I never struggled with anything the way I struggled to give him the space he needed. I knew it was for the best but my heart screamed at me for allowing him to continue in his despair.

I didn't want to do it. I had to. If I didn't let it sink in, he might be fooled into doing it all again.

I put all my energy into researching the Horus equation. I still had a purpose. There was still Marek. I didn't need to let him down the way I kept letting everyone else down. However, as the days wore on, I knew I couldn't avoid Rodrian forever.

Rodrian became more and more withdrawn. He had a perpetual sense of wanting to spill his guts but he wouldn't do it. On the occasions he did speak, it was trite and trivial.

He never talked about the things he'd done with her. His shame was a glow that he couldn't dampen on his own, and I knew from his lengthy silences and burdened sighs that he tried everything he could to rationalize his behavior.

Finally, I couldn't take it anymore. One evening, I cornered him in the den, and told him enough as enough already.

I pushed him down onto the couch and straddled him, pinning his shoulders to the tops of the cushions. Copper heat burned within his eyes, his surprise and involuntary physical lust playing in his parted lips, the lines around his eyes, the weight of his hands on my hips.

I set him straight real fast. This was not sex.

I washed him clean with the coolness of the Sophia, trapping him in my arms and my barriers and my power. He would not deny me. I washed him, flooded him with all that I knew of him—his strengths, his charm, his kindness, his love, or whatever it was, for me. I held him down, quelling his struggles.

He wanted to suffer. He wanted to be punished. And I wouldn't let him punish himself over her anymore.

When I rolled up my sleeve and pressed my forearm to his mouth, silently begging him for the communion, the connection, tears rolled down his cheeks. He didn't feel he deserved it. He was not redeemable. He was past saving.

And I denied him his hell.

When he succumbed to me, when he could resist me no longer, he took my arm in both hands and broke the skin. He didn't use sex appeal to hide the pain.

I smiled, a hard determined smile that matched the iron I knew was in my eyes. I had wanted it to hurt, too, and I enjoyed it every bit as much as if he'd brought me to a throbbing conclusion.

That pain was sacred to me. When we finally released

each other, I knew he'd be okay—his guilt had dimmed, his need for punishment forgotten. I gave him that blood because I wanted to undo the damage she'd done to him that night she pushed him onto blood rush. I had a life to repay because that kill was my sin, my doing, for not seeing what she was sooner. I should have been there—

And no, the irony was not lost upon me. I was the one who wanted the pain, the punishment. It wasn't a sacrifice I'd make for anyone else. Rodrian was mine to guard, just as Marek was. I had a duty to save them. The entire time I was off with Dierk, no matter how much the situation was out of my control, I still had a duty to the DV. To my DV.

I pulled my arm from his mouth before he could tidy the wound. I wanted that mark as a reminder.

Over the days that followed, things slowly returned to normal. Shiloh stayed home more often, and Dahlia and Toby came to watch TV. Nobody said anything about kings or destinies, and nobody mentioned the tell-tale mark on my arm, or the even more obvious change in Rodrian. He was acting more like his bossy jerk of a self and the battles with Shiloh and curfews were quickly becoming legendary. The Stocks were starting to feel like home again.

And the *Wolfram* still flew in my skies.

Early one morning, I stood on the balcony, listening to its greeting when it spied me on my own perch, reminding me it still lived, still needed me. I traced my finger over the mark of Rodrian's bite, over and over, imagining the scar and its position over the line of vein on my forearm gave the impression of the shape of an *ankh*, the symbol of life. The shape of a miracle. It reminded me what I had to do.

I was in the business of salvation, and it was time to get back to work.

The office was getting back to normal, too. There was no

more talk about interns.

One day, after lunch, I got a visitor. When Stohl stuck his head into my office and asked for a minute, I just nodded, speechless.

I wasn't sure if he was Were again. Truthfully, I just tried to forget about him and hoped he would do the same to me. Guessed not.

"Hello, Sophie." He sounded stiff, like blue jeans dried on a line.

"Hello. Can I do something for you?"

"I wanted to stop in." He looked over his shoulder as if concerned somebody might overhear and lowered his voice. "To apologize."

"For what?" I waved him in and he closed the door behind him. Was there a twelve-step program for Weres I didn't know about? I thought of Toby's past crusade to Boy Scout me and cringed. Not again.

"For being difficult, mostly. But more because I gave you a hard time when you were with Dierk. If I had just left you alone, he could have been happy for a time, at least."

"Oh." All my smart-assedness and my indignation poofed away and I sobered. "How is he?"

He shrugged, his hands in his pockets. "I don't know. We don't really talk."

"Are you…"

"Were?" Again, a look over his shoulder. It seemed automatic, as if he spent a lot of time checking to see who followed. Now I recognized the look in his eyes. Hunted.

I didn't fear him anymore. I feared *for* him. My concern for Stohl, of all men, unsettled me because it made the line between friend and enemy too blurry to feel safe.

"No," he said, oblivious to my deductions. "I decided to wait before I went for therapy. I need time to make sure it's what I really want."

"But I thought they'd give you an amnesia treatment if you didn't, ah, convert."

"Dierk intervened. He gave me a choice. I chose to keep my memory, because it's my life. I need all of it, good and bad. I made mistakes, and I don't want to make them again unknowingly."

"I understand." I met his gaze for the first time, and connected with him briefly. He nodded, acknowledging it, before stiffening once more and looking over my head. "Are you going to stay here in town?"

"For now. The pack has requested that I remain. I think they want to keep track of me. I cannot say I blame them. I'm human again, and I know too much. And considering the kind of person I am, I don't blame them for not trusting me." He hunched his shoulders as if apologetic, but I suspected otherwise. His species may have changed overnight, but I doubted the same happened to his personality. "I don't miss it, you know. Full moon was last week."

"I know." I'd never gotten around to deleting the app Nakia had given me the month before. Thankfully, the moon and its crazy lady didn't try talking to me again. Then again, I didn't give it much of a chance.

"I only know it because I watch the sky out of habit. She does not talk to me anymore. I do not hear her voice. Ironic, isn't it? You were the target. You were supposed to be the victim, and you are the only one who came through all this unchanged."

I crossed my arms and looked at him. He didn't look angry or frustrated, only looked confused. Maybe that was what made him look so human now. When I first met Stohl, he had a sense of boiling under the surface, like the magma chamber under Yellowstone. Always angry, always ready to explode into action, making him easy to define in two simple words: dangerous potential.

He didn't look human now just because he was no longer Were. Come to think of it, I'd never really seen him as wolf. Now, Stohl looked human because he finally acted human.

I thought about what he said: I was the only one who came through all this unchanged. Sometimes men could be so stupid. Instead of arguing, though, I just shrugged. "There was no way of knowing what would happen. You don't always get what you want. It's the not getting that makes us appreciate what we have."

He nodded as if I'd said something wise. I supposed he took my words and extrapolated them to fit the confines of his new reality.

Fine by me. I supposed that's why so many people read my column. No matter what I said, my words could mean just about anything to anybody. They were as accurate and as intensely personal as a newspaper horoscope.

I guessed he didn't have anything else to say, because he gave me a nod and left. I didn't expect a toodle-loo or a hug or anything so his departure made me feel relieved more than anything else. Go, before you decided you needed me, or, worse yet, decided I was the one to blame, after all.

I peered after him, watching him walk away. I supposed I wanted to be sure he left. Were or not Were, I didn't trust him. He never stopped looking around as if he expected someone to pop out at him. Paranoia has a way of making even the toughest guy look vulnerable. Oh, how the mighty have fallen.

Honestly, I didn't feel bad at all. Stohl had been a menace and the world was better off now that he could no longer infect people with his hate.

Maybe I didn't have the right to pass judgment. It wasn't

like I changed him on purpose. I simply wasn't interested in feeling guilty about it. I had enough stuff bringing me down. I'd gotten better at picking my battles, and this one definitely wasn't mine to fight.

I closed the last report cover and rubbed my eyes, disappointed but not surprised. Placing it upon the stack, I leaned back and sighed.

My allegiance with the *Wolfenkinder* had opened new avenues of cooperation. One benefit was that I'd been able to gain access to hybrid research no DV had ever seen before. The Were laboratories in Delaware were just as advanced and as extensive as the DV labs in Bluebell, and apparently they've done work on their own wasn't part of the DV/werewolf co-op.

Unfortunately, none of it was helpful. The Were labs hadn't come any closer to duplicating—or undoing—a hybrid any more than the DV had.

My last hope had run out. I guessed Marek really was gone for good.

I pushed back from the desk and stood to look out the windows. It was so hard to admit defeat. I had really thought I'd find something in all that research, but I had nothing to show for it.

Maybe if I'd tried to stay objective it wouldn't have been so bad, but I'd read Marek's journals. I had finally heard his thoughts his feelings since he'd stopped seeing me. Knowing how he'd felt about not wanting to leave me, knowing now that there could have been hope for us after all—and watching it float away like dust motes when I closed that final research report.

I wanted to scream, but I didn't. I did the only mature thing that I could.

Crossing the office to the stereo system, I rooted around until I found the CD Dierk had given me. I read his curving European handwriting and smiled a little, missing him already but glad that things had worked out the way they did.

I'd learned to love the man, but never, ever did I want to become Were. My monthly troubles were trouble enough on their own without adding howling at the moon to them.

The music was loud, and I turned it up even louder. The sound was heavy and tribal, classic rock and thrash. Not pretty boys' music. It was unpolished, primal, and I remembered why I favored their more recent work. I sank down in the chair, closed my eyes, and just listened.

Dierk had told me so much about his journey through life and through music. These songs were the beginning. They deserved to be heard.

The boldness and the beat chipped away my frustration. He had told me his bass player wrote these songs to conquer hopelessness. Life went on. Everything managed its own way somehow. There is yet hope. I just don't know where.

Yet, I amended.

The last few years of my life had completely rearranged my perception of life, of love, and of hope. I supposed near-death experiences and attacks by vampires and werewolves played a big part in those changes, but that wasn't all.

It was being needed by so many; it was being loved by such remarkable people; it was the experience of grief so profound that the world could fall away and I'd never notice; it was belonging and being valued in an otherwise impersonal and stranger-filled world.

And while I had developed some of these things at one point or another in my life, they took on new meaning and new depth the day I visited a museum and crashed into a stranger named Marek.

The song faded at the end, and in the lapse I heard the scream of a bird far across the field. Going to the window once more, I scanned the sky, wondering if I could see it. Wondering if it was the *Wolfram*. Wondering if it was mine.

The CD played on, and the notes of an acoustic piece tripped like a medieval fountain. It was one of the bardic songs that Dierk had mentioned. I listened and distractedly watched for the bird, pushing open the door. I leaned out as the music streamed out around me.

The bird flew high on a warm spring thermal over the patch of woods standing to the north. It circled lazily; was it hunting or relaxing? It edged closer, but never close enough for me to see it well.

I gave up and wandered over to the stereo to restart the track. I closed my eyes again and listened. *Ocean's Daughter* it was called, written like a bard's tale and set to a minstrel tune. I recognized this song, although I didn't know it well; maybe I'd heard it long ago, or maybe the melodies were recycled in later songs.

Now, for the first time I listened to it carefully, word for word. Halfway through it, I sat bolt upright, eyes wide, wondering if I'd heard him right.

Before the music ended, I flew out the door and down the steps, calling for Rodrian as loudly as I could.

Shortly, he joined me in the office listening to the same song. His hands were folded and he rested his chin upon them, eyebrows bunched in concentration

He signaled to me and I paused the CD. "What does he say right there?"

"*The wolf is gone, that lived in me, a bitter empty shell,*" I said.

"Are you sure?"

I nodded.

He rubbed the tip of his nose. "I don't know how you can even tell what he's saying."

"I read the lyrics online." Which was part of the truth, anyways. Fact was, I knew his voice now.

Resuming the track, we listened to it all the way out. I shuffled through the papers on my desk to find the song sheet I had printed.

"Well?" I asked.

"Well, what?"

"Ocean's Daughter. She turned a Were into a regular person."

"It's just a song, Sophie." Rodrian pinched his brow, looking weary.

No, it was more than a song. Rudy may have written it, but we just lived through it. I felt the gut-connection, a tight one that wouldn't let go. "A song that was written by werewolves."

"That doesn't mean it's real."

"It may," I said. "I haven't told you about Stohl."

"Great." Rodrian looked away, hands on his hips. "Another Were boy-toy?"

"Hardly. He hated my guts."

He snorted, looking somewhat mollified that I hadn't

had every mutt in the pack lapping at my heels. Rodrian was such a petty jerk sometimes. And it was so nice to have him back. "What about him?"

"He was the one who bit me."

Rodrian's temper ignited faster than a superhero yelling *flame on!* His eyes were angry and bright. Glinting with vengeance. "Was he, now?"

"Relax," I said. "He can't hurt me anymore. Well, I guess he could. Anybody could. I'm not bulletproof, and I don't always watch crossing the street—"

"Soph," he interrupted.

"Right. Stohl bit me, and when the full moon came I didn't change and neither did he."

He actually looked surprised. "He didn't?"

"No, he didn't." I shook my head and flopped into my chair. "None of them would discuss much in front of me. Not in English, anyways. But he's human. Dierk knew as soon as he smelled him, and I felt him. I mean, you know, felt him."

Rodrian rubbed the back of his neck. "I never thought it was possible. Why you?"

I restarted the track and fast-forwarded it to the line *lady white, with brightest blue of eyes.* "Think it was a Sophia?"

For she was Ocean's Daughter—and she has killed the moon.

Gunshot-memories echoed in my head.

Stohl's voice: she killed the moon.

The priestess: Ocean and his children.

"Any possibility that word can get out?" Rodrian's voice may have sounded smooth, but I felt his anxiety trip up the waves of his power, like ripples on a pond. "This is dangerous news. There are a lot of people who would try to use you."

"What else is new?" I sighed. "I don't know about DV or vamp, but I shouldn't have any Were or *Witchkinder* trouble."

His skeptical expression urged me to tell him of the protection agreements Dierk had forged before he left. Rodrian nodded thoughtfully as I told him what the Weres and the witch had said.

"That was good of him to do," he said. "An oath to the Were King won't easily be broken."

"Yeah, well. He was kind of sweet on me."

He looked sour but refrained from commenting. "So. Let's say you are Ocean's Daughter. What's it mean to us?"

I looked him straight in the eyes. "Everything."

"Everything, how?"

"Rode, if I am Ocean's Daughter or whatever—if Stohl wasn't some fluke—then maybe—" A shrill scream of falcon made us both look up. "Maybe I can bring Marek back."

Aerogenetek Laboratories. The building felt empty, but I'd called ahead to make sure my connection would be around.

The last time I'd been here, I'd met with the head technician. Kevin Corby had seemed nice enough but looked really doubtful when he handed me the flash drive Rodrian requested. He didn't think I'd get any closer to solving the Horus Equation, as he called it, than anyone on his team.

He didn't know I'd end up with a team of my own. Shoot, I didn't know, myself.

Funny thing, destiny.

Funny, too, that decades of research on the DV side and an equal amount by the Were labs did nothing on their own. Then there was me, stuck in the middle, pulling it all together. Always in the middle. Always trying to desperately make sense where there wasn't any.

I looked up at the rear view mirror. In the back of the SUV was the *Wolfram*. He was stuck in the middle, too.

And we were both ready to pick a side.

I clicked my tongue and it swiveled its head toward me, whistling softly through its beak. The hood had kept it calm for the ride out. I refused to think it looked like an executioner's mask. This had to work. I would not accept anything less than perfect success.

I cracked the windows and locked the car, stowing my keys and digging out the key card that would allow me to get in. Kevin's office was on the lower level, near a staircase leading up to labs and an aviary at the back end.

I knocked twice and stuck my head in. He was typing but waved me in when he saw me.

"Can you help me with something?"

Kevin looked surprised. "What do you have?"

"A specimen. By the way," I added. "Bring a gauntlet."

He followed me out to the car, and I lifted the hatch to show him what was in the back. The huge gyrfalcon, hooded and quiet and very big swiveled its head toward us.

"I'll say. Where did you get him?"

A thousand glib responses flashed through my head, but the bird cocked its head at me and I decided to be straight. "It's Marek."

"Marek... Thurzo? You're kidding me, right?"

I shook my head. "Afraid not."

He puffed out a breath and I could sense his doubts. "Marek is this bird?"

"Yeah. I was there when he shifted. He had a Were confrontation, and when things got...bloody, this is what happened."

Kevin was floored. "Marek had increased the funding for hybrid research a few years ago and now he's a hybrid?"

"*Wolfram*," I corrected. "Hybrid sounds like a car or flower. The German Weres call him a *Wolfram*. It means wolf-raven."

"Weres? Well, did they mention any developments? Because we haven't gotten any farther than we already were."

I bit my lips a moment. "I've gone through some independent lab files—"

"Independent meaning Were?"

I nodded. "Nothing new."

"Okay." He eyed up the patient bird. "So what do we do?"

"This is a true *Wolfram*. Take samples, but don't hurt him. When you're done, I want to run something by you."

"Fair enough." He waved the gauntlet at me. "You want to do the honors?"

I strapped on the heavy leather armguard, trying to ignore the smell. It was well-used, and by well I meant tremendously soiled. Hooray. "He doesn't seem to go to anyone else, so I guess I will."

An hour later, we sat upstairs in one of the labs. Kevin had prepped slides of blood samples. I sat quietly next to a perch he'd brought up from the aviary, trying not to watch the *Wolfram* pick apart a strip of rabbit meat.

Kevin worked quickly and quietly. "I would never believe it if I didn't pull the samples myself. No wonder we never got anywhere with the hybrids. I don't think we ever had a real one. This is... unbelievable."

He went over to another set of computers. "There is more than one type of DNA being mapped. The bird is chimeric. Oh, wow," he said, raking his hair back. "Do you know what this means? I don't even know where to start. There is so much to do!"

"Later," I said, looking at the falcon. "A test of my own, first. If it fails, then I will release him to limited study. Post mortem."

"What?"

"Marek wouldn't want to live this way. He does not want this. You can anesthetize him for certain tests, but then..." I looked him directly in the eyes and added the authority of the Sophia behind it so that there would be no doubts. "Euthanize him. Release him."

Kevin looked down at the lab station for several long moments. I could tell from his power that he didn't like what I had to say. He had spent a long, long time studying this phenomenon and waiting for the right bird to come along. He could not reconcile finding one and losing it again so quickly.

The *Wolfram* keened softly to me and I held my fingers to its beak. It nibbled them, not hard enough to break the skin, but with enough force to pinch. Love pecks, right.

"What is your test?"

I stroked my fingers down along the feathered breast. "We need to feed him my blood."

Kevin seemed taken aback. "Well, never thought of that. Why?"

"Swear you will keep all of what I say confidential."

"Sure."

"No, Kevin. Not sure." I thinned my shields and reached for his power, snagging the corner of his essence and snapping him into full attention. The edges of my vision lightened, took on a bluish tint. The light blazed from his eyes, a rose-gold gleam. "I want you to swear yourself to me. Swear your secrecy, even on pain of death."

I wasn't sure if I had the right to command such a thing, and I was even less sure of its ethical consequences. Didn't matter. Right now, ethics would only get in the way.

Kevin looked as if he'd fall to his knees if I didn't release him. I did so and tucked the Sophia back down deep, deep inside. The light lingered in his eyes for several heavy breaths.

"I swear. I would have sworn before you touched me like that but..." He mopped his forehead. "I am yours and will never betray you."

Satisfied, I nodded. *I am yours.* Another one. Pretty soon I'd have to start a roster to keep track. "My blood has an adverse effect on werewolves. My European connection gave me a copy of an old legend that may have been Sophia-inspired. It was accidentally tested earlier this month."

I briefly explained the basics of what happened to Stohl.

"No flipping way." He shook his head. "Great gods. What a day this is turning out to be. Can I call in at least one or two of my staff? I can't be the only one to catch this bombshell."

"I'm sorry, Kevin. You can't do that. Too much of this information puts me at serious risk. You must keep this absolutely confidential." I called the Sophia just enough to light my eyes, to make him remember his vow.

It worked. His power took on the soft color of acquiescence. "So, what do we do? Let the bird bite you?"

"Uh, how about no? Ick. That's too much Alfred Hitchcock for me. Can we do a—I don't know, a line in?"

"Wouldn't it be easier to inject it?"

It was gut-sense that tugged me toward it. "Marek turned after he attacked a Were, and then Stohl bit me. The blood has to be consumed."

"Maybe a GI tube, then?"

I nodded and rolled up my sleeves as he began gathering supplies. "Does he have to be awake for this?"

"No, it would be easier to get the tube in if he's not awake. Even if it's Marek, I doubt he'd cooperate."

The *Wolfram* keened again, and I blew gently on its feathers, admiring the play of black feathers on white. It twisted its head and clicked its beak at the stream of my breath. "Just don't hurt him."

Kevin approached from behind. "Do you think you could hold him while I give him the injection?"

I nodded and took a deep breath. "Are you ready for this?"

The *Wolfram chuuup*ed softly and shook his feathers out, spreading his wings reflexively, almost like a knuckle-cracking.

"Okay." I stroked my fingers down its head, over its back, then gripped him gently with both hands.

Kevin administered the dose and backed away as if he expected to be bitten, but the *Wolfram* only turned its head. Dignified. The slight lift of beak reminded me of the way Marek used to look down his nose when he was being snooty. I banished the memory before it could change my mind.

"Huh," the technician said. "King of falcons, that's for damned sure."

The dose administered, I felt Marek relax slightly in my grip. "I think he'll let you carry him now," I said.

Kevin put on the gauntlet and the *Wolfram* stepped carefully onto his arm. The drug acted quickly. The bird was unconscious by the time Kevin lay him down on the table.

I hopped up onto a second gurney. If this didn't work—

No, couldn't think like that. It had to work. But if it didn't—he'd never wake up again.

I realized I'd never had my last words.

Maybe this was better. What could I say to a bird?

Kevin peeled the wrapper from a needle. "How much blood do you think this will take?"

"Not much, I don't think. The last two incidences were just bites." I shuddered. "How much blood in a bite?"

"It varies. Were they attack bites or feeding ones?"

I grimaced and tried to avoid retching. "Hello, human here."

"No need to remind me. I've been breathing you in all morning." His tone was clinical and held none of the seducing playfulness of Rodrian's voice. It was about as sexy as a Pap smear. But still. Words like that had a personal effect on a girl, Sophia or not.

"Attack bites."

"I think an ounce would be the limit. We have to consider the size of the bird." He fitted the open and of the catheter to a valve that was already connected to the G-tube. "I'll adjust the flow rate to deliver it in a two-minute time frame. That's slow enough to monitor him and stop it if there's a problem."

He flipped the switch on a monitor, and it beeped as it came online. After entering a few settings on the keypad, he began stripping off plastic sheaves to reveal wires. "These are just leads. I'll monitor his temperature and heart rate during the transfusion."

He pulled off several pieces of surgical tape to secure the leads to the falcon, which was starting to look like a pile of lab recyclables, its body hidden beneath tape and wire.

The only thing left to do was to insert the feeding tube. Thankfully, Kevin stood between me and the bird as he did it. I didn't want to watch.

Finally, Kevin had the bird prepped. Marek and I were connected by tubes, distantly and clinically. Coldly. The telemetry unit beat with the rhythm of a mechanical heartbeat. I stared at the instrument over the falcon's prone body and prayed.

"Okay," he said. "Everything's hooked up." He tied a tourniquet around my arm and gently tapped the vein. I closed my eyes when he pushed in the needle; not because I was squeamish, but because I didn't want to see his expression. Clinical or not, I could sense his eagerness to see my blood, as if he were witnessing a holy relic. It unsettled me.

He withdrew the needle, leaving the thin catheter in place. A scarlet thread unfurled through it and he adjusted the clamp, watching my blood drip into the timing reservoir. "All set," he said.

"Do it," I whispered.

He rolled the stopcock on the *Wolfram*'s line and the red thread slid toward the falcon. I stretched out my awareness, hoping that maybe the stream of blood would act as a bridge, a connection, but it didn't. It was still just a falcon, and an unconscious one, at that.

I stared at the clock. The minute hand swept like a scythe, cutting down the seconds. Time itself could not stand against Death.

My mind drifted back over the last several weeks. Each morning I had gone out into the back yard to where Marek's memorial stood. I'd stare up at the big perch on top and scan the sky for the *Wolfram*. His shrill whistles would slice right through me, his wing beats making me wince. Even while he circled overhead, each moment seemed to take him farther from me.

I'd ventured down into the woods in search of a sturdy branch, rigging a makeshift perch in the back of the estate's SUV. He'd watched me, every step of the way. And when I had sat in the open hatch this morning, and called his name, his right and true name, the *Wolfram* swooped out of the sky. First, to land on the memorial perch. Then, into the hatch. He leaned and picked at the hood I'd bought, letting it dangle from his beak, before hopping up onto the perch like it was something he did every day. I closed the hatchback like I'd closed a book.

And then there was Dierk.

Dierk was home in Mannheim. I'd received a few e-mails from him, just superficial check-ins. You can't put the right words in an email; you can't plumb the depths of an unspeakable emotion. There was only one way for him to know how I felt, and that could only happen if he held me and I thinned my shields and I sought the wind with the moon on our backs. He'd taste it, run through it, glean it from me if I'd still been the half of his whole.

But I wasn't.

I never told Dierk what I planned to do today. I only thanked him for the CD and told him how interesting it really was, told him I could picture his high top sneakers and jean jacket while he sang. I made no mention of "Ocean's Daughter" or my plans for the *Wolfram*.

I never told him how much he'd come to mean to me, either. So many little things. So many big things. I never told Dierk any of them.

Maybe I wouldn't, either. It's not like we really had a future together, destiny or not. I never could have been able to live as Were, Dierk or not. The letter I wrote to Rodrian before the full moon was still in my office. My contingency plan. Maybe I didn't turn. Maybe I couldn't, after all. But just in case... Rodrian needed to know what to do, just like I knew what I had to do with Marek.

"One minute," Kevin said. The telemetry unit beat, then staccato tones. "His temp is rising. Heart rate jumped."

"Good sign?"

He peered at a strip of thermal paper that spewed a stream of data from the telemetry unit. "Don't know yet. Could just be a reaction to the infusion."

I drummed my fingers. Come on, come on, come on, Marek. You'd have to still be in there somewhere.

"Thirty seconds."

Please, you couldn't have run out of second chances.

Suddenly, the telemetry went nuts, the beeps coming so close and so fast that it sounded like a shriek.

"I have to pull the line," he said, voice taut. With a snap of his wrist, he rolled the valve shut.

"What's going on?" Panic rose in me like mercury in a hot thermometer. He was in my way and I couldn't see the falcon.

"I don't know." He braced the bird and pulled the line free as I clamped off my catheter.

The shrieking continued. I felt like I'd soon start. "What can you do?"

"Nothing. It was time. We had to stop anyway. Grab some cold packs from over there in the drawer. We gotta get his temperature down."

I ran to the drawer, pulling out the packs, cracking them and feeling the chemical chill spread. Feeling the dread spread through me.

Suddenly, the beeping melted into a long, unbroken wail. It was the sound I didn't want to hear.

"Shit," I whimpered. The machine displayed flat lines and zeros. "His heart—it stopped."

We killed him. I stared in horror at the *Wolfram*. I killed him, I killed—

Kevin snapped off the sound control. "I can try and resuscitate."

I shook my head and scratched it with both hands. "No. I really didn't have any hope it would work. It's just that…it made sense, for one moment…"

My lungs squeezed, my breaths reduced to gulps. I wouldn't bring him back just to be a falcon for the rest of his life.

"Are you all right?" Kevin peered at me, and I could feel the pity on his power. Why did I always end up piteous?

I shrugged, wiping tears. "Yeah. I just thought—"

"Yeah. For a second, so did I."

"Right." I hiccupped. "I didn't think that it would kill him. I just—"

"Look," he said. "How about you go down to the lounge on the first floor. I'll just clean things up a little and then bring him down to the car for you."

"Okay." I nodded emphatically "That's nice. Okay. I'll just... bathroom?"

"Down the hall on the right."

I ran out.

I shouldered the restroom door open, pushing it with all the rage and the desperation and the unrequited hope I'd carried around with me for the last two years. I slammed it hard against the wall, wanting to feel the force of impact under my hands, wanting to shatter this ridiculous veneer I wore, the one that told everyone that everything would be okay. I kicked open a stall door, slammed it shut, and fumbled at the lock, trying to put up another layer between me and my damnable decision.

And when I realized I'd never be able to hide from it—from any of the things that caused me pain—I howled. I released a jagged scream that echoed off every shiny surface and I screamed, dredging up every ounce of agony that had made itself a home in me. I screamed it up and out in a terrible flood.

And when I was empty, the tears rose. I just sat down on the edge of the toilet seat and cried. What an appropriate place to lose the last drop of hope I had in me.

I couldn't hide in there forever. Somehow, I had to walk out, drive home, go on. Cold-water rinses did little to restore my complexion. I did the best I could and went back outside. I noticed the door didn't have a single mark on it, despite the sound and fury with which I'd battered it.

Nothing I did ever mattered.

I heard Kevin's voice as I came out. He was in his office at the far end of the hall and stuck his head out the doorway. He held a phone to his ear but covered the receiver with his hand. "I'll meet you downstairs, Sophie."

Weary, I headed for the staircase. I had to pass the lab where we had been and I paused. Should I look in one last time? Would he still be lying there, a lump under a plastic sheet?

A gentle DV vibe reached me and I sighed. I guessed one of the staff had wandered upstairs. Hopefully Kevin would keep everything confidential. I ignored the vibe, not wanting to deal with anyone else right now.

Not when I had to arrange a burial for hope.

I meant to continue on and head downstairs, but at the last minute something made me change my mind. The vibe was stronger, almost familiar, and I was curious to know who it was. I needed someone familiar right then. I thought about the drive home with the fallen *Wolfram* in the back of the SUV, and I didn't want to drive home alone. Maybe it was someone I could talk into going with me because I didn't want to feel like I was driving a hearse, because he was dead. Dead.

I had difficulty forming the words in my mind, because disbelief wouldn't allow them. Marek was dead.

"Hello?" I called. "Did someone come up here?"

There was a clatter in the lab as if something had been knocked over and I stopped at the door. Someone was in there with the *Wolfram*.

Something red and liquid filled me. What if they did something to him? What if they were carving him up and dissecting him?

Oh, hell no. No one would touch him as long as I lived. I rushed into the room at a charge. "Stop! Who said you could be in here?"

He turned around shirtless, pulling the plastic sheet hastily around his waist. His hair hung wet and heavy, dark and damp, bangs long, back short, yet almost familiar--

A flash of emerald through the thick strands. Deep voice that sounded confused, a rasp as if he were afraid to speak out loud, as if he'd forgotten how. "Sophie?"

That voice.

I did the only sensible thing and promptly fainted.

"Sophie?"

Was I dreaming?

How long since I'd heard that voice, the deep rumble of bass I felt as well as heard. Lately, I had only heard it in dreams. So, dreaming. I must be.

I squeezed my eyes shut, feeling the oblivion of unconsciousness slip away as alertness crept in. I covered my eyes with my hands, trying desperately to hold on to that sweet dream that allowed him to whisper my name. Once more. Just once more before I woke and had to go back to living without him.

"Is she okay?" The Philly twang was unmistakable.

Kevin? Why the hell would I dream about him? Unless…

I suddenly couldn't feel my hands and feet. Afraid to open my eyes now. Absolutely terrified.

I felt the muscle, the strong arms cradling me and I unraveled my barriers, just the tiniest bit.

Marek. Whole and pure, strong and restored, bright and concerned. His power caressed to me like a spring wind, warm and wonderful. Tears brewed and slid out of my still-pinched shut eyes. My breath hitched.

Oh, my God. Him.

He shifted to a more comfortable position and rocked

me to his chest. His heart, strong as a lion, beat against my skin. The tremor echoed through me.

"Open your eyes." Marek's voice held a playful tone. Concern faded rapidly into simple joy.

"I can't," I whispered.

"Why not?" His scent, sandalwood and leather, surrounded me in a glow of warmth and remembrance and promise.

"Because." I whimpered and my throat fisted again. "If you're a dream, you'll just disappear."

Close to my ear, soft puffs of breath warm against my cheek. "I promise. Not a dream."

I drew a shaky breath and pouted, trying to hold it until it steadied. I didn't want to cry. I wanted to be happy. I was afraid I would only be disappointed.

"Sophie, my dearest. . ." Fingers trailed along the side of my face and he gently smoothed my hair back, tugging my hands away from my eyes. "I am real."

I cracked my eyes and looked up into his face, still so handsome, even without the fierce stubbornness. So much younger, looking so rejuvenated, and his power, his soul—

"I am whole." He laughed in happy disbelief. "I'm whole again. You did it, Sophia. You saved me."

His eyes were bright with his power and his joy. I slid my arms around his neck and he lifted me in an easy movement, holding me against him a moment. He lifted and spun me in a happy circle before letting me to my feet, embracing me once more, his face buried in my hair. "You saved me."

Within the hour, nearly every Demivamp I knew had gathered in Marek's office. It was an anti-funeral party, and I had trouble keeping my barriers up. The joy and the happiness were like a tsunami.

I wanted to roll with those feelings. I was afraid, though. Afraid to feel too much happy. Happy had been so alien for far too long.

Kevin had been on the phone with Rodrian when I went into the bathroom. He figured I needed a ride home. Rodrian was already on his way when I discovered Marek.

Rodrian arrived somber and grave since Kevin had warned him that I'd shown up with a falcon and it hadn't survived. He must have sensed that strange, familiar power because he sprinted up the stairs.

He was confused. I felt that a mile away. He knew his brother's power.

Rodrian burst into Marek's office, eyes wild. "Sophie? What's going on?"

Then he saw him.

Marek practically launched to his feet to embrace his brother, a wrap of arms. Rodrian pulled away to search his brother's face, mouth agape.

Marek laughed, enjoying his brother's befuddlement.

Rodrian looked at me once, awe and joy in his face. But there was still a brief flash of something I decided to let slip. I couldn't bear to think of it right then.

Joy and pain.

It faded as quickly as it had appeared, and he reached out to me, pulling me into the middle of their embrace. One big happy family. At last.

"Hey, you." The sweet bass notes of his throaty murmur sent shivers down my neck.

I turned away from the kitchenette counter, seeking him. I needed to see him. I wanted to touch him. It was the only way to be sure he was real.

Every moment seemed so fragile, as if I were trapped in a crystal ball of a dream. After being apart for so long, after the torture of watching him in a form I couldn't reach—this miracle seemed so fragile. Anything could shatter it.

"Hi." I dipped my head and hid beneath my bangs, suddenly shy. It was new all over again. The discovery. The infatuation. Not just because we'd been apart but because, somehow, his soul had been renewed.

Wiped clean. Completely indulgenced, like a special blessing from the Pope. His ordeal had been a miracle in the truest sense of the word, because when he found his form again, there wasn't a trace of evolution to be found.

It was like he'd been cured, cancer free. Full hit points.

The grimness, the desolation, the desperation was gone as well. He was completely brand new.

New—and, different. I hadn't thought about the subtle change too hard. I was still getting used to him simply *being*.

I sort of missed the grumpy. He obliged by acting stern and forbidding but the amused glint in his green eyes always gave it away. If I didn't know better, I'd swear he was stoned.

"You're up early." He leaned in the doorway, arms crossed over his broad chest.

"Habit. Very bad habit. I forgot how to stay in bed."

His smile grew smoky, secretive, making my belly flip-flop. "It would be a pleasure to remind you."

I smiled behind my bangs again, feeling my cheeks warm. Blushing bride syndrome. "Want some? I made a fresh pot."

At his nod I poured a second cup, watching the stream of dark amber. Such a pretty color. The taste was bright and earthy, like sunlight in a forest, a sweet fruity hint of possibility that surprised you after you swallowed, disappearing quickly. It made you drink again. I found Nirvana in a ceramic mug, after so long a Purgatory of generic tea bags. I'd never miss coffee again.

"What's this?" Marek, who always had been a tea drinker, made an appreciative face at his own cup. "It's wonderful."

I sat across from him at the snack bar. Sure, I had a little guilt and conflict but they mingled well within my Paradise regained. The shadows made me whole. It was who I had become and I was, for once, happy to be me.

"Darjeeling." I decided to tell him the truth, even if it was as vague as a tea leaf fortune. "I learned to love this stuff."

Epilogue

The afternoon sky was ceilingless, an open bowl of blue cobalt that grew deeper as my gaze turned upward. White clusters of clouds, their billows soft enough to lie upon, scattered across the heavens, capturing the golden glow of the sunshine.

Although it seemed like my work was never done at *The Mag*, I decided that skipping out on a half-day wouldn't make much of a difference to the column. I worked through lunch to send out the market subs so I could face the weekend with a clear conscience.

Traffic was light as I drove to University Heights, and I slid the Cavalier into a parking spot that seemed to be waiting just for me, directly across the street from the University Museum. Hoisting my purse, I grabbed an envelope from the dash and strolled into the stately brick courtyard. Sunshine glittered from the dancing water of the fountain, radiated from the basking cobblestones of the walkway. Summer had come early.

After a springtime of temperate indecision and weather that couldn't make up its mind, the afternoon spoke of auspicious optimism. The season was a goodness that sank all the way to the bone, renewing my spirit and reminding me how good it was to be alive.

Truly alive.

And, despite being the type of day that demanded every window be opened and every person run outside to play, it wasn't enough to keep me from hurrying across the stones toward the door, envelope in hand. It had been an invitation.

I flipped over the envelope and tugged out the folded card, tilting it over my open hand. Out slid a plastic badge, burgundy and white, emblazoned with the Museum logo and the words LIFE MEMBER. I received the gift today, tucked into a vase of roses that had been placed on my desk, waiting for my arrival at work. The card had not been signed, but it did not need to be.

There was only one person who would have sent it.

I flashed the card as the admissions clerk, who waved a brochure at me. I glanced at it as I walked through the atrium, climbing the staircase that lead to Old Egypt. NEW EXHIBIT OPENS. The date was a few days off. I wondered if I'd get a sneak peek at the work in progress. Blood hummed in my ears, my heart fluttering at the thought of what secrets I'd discover in that old kingdom.

The great hall that housed the temple exhibit hadn't been altered much since the last time I had visited. Breathing deep the dry air and its dusty fragrance, I scanned the room, noting each great column and each shadow that danced around them.

Stepping deeper into the room, I passed the *stelae* and the sculptures in their glass cases, approaching the centermost of the carved columns. Ceiling lights dropped down rays of yellow illumination, reminding me of the sunlight outside. I smiled, feeling like sunlight followed me wherever I went. Even when I travelled to dimly lit temples, seeking the deepest shadows.

My unspoken thoughts gave animation to the shadowy stillness, and a beautiful darkness stepped out from behind the column. Surprise gripped my breath and held it.

His hair, pulled back into a blunt tail, was black as night, his skin white as the constant moon. Long sideburns trimmed his sculpted face, drew my eye along his strong jaw, to the cleft chin, upward to those perfect lips. But when the dark lashes lifted, eyes seeking me, those eyes shimmered with an emerald glow that made me forget all else, save him.

Marek stowed his leather journal inside his breast pocket and leaned against the column. His posture was relaxed, one hand in his pocket, the other at his side. His lips parted, a hungry anticipation playing upon his mouth. He'd been waiting.

My captive breath released, I walked across the tiled floor, the click of my heels the only sound. A few steps from the tall shadow, I paused. I'd been waiting, too.

His free hand lifted, holding a single rose. Marek raised it to his mouth, rolling the flower against his lips. The deep scarlet petals caught the light, a sanguine glow, and he extended the rose toward me. I heard the swift intake of breath the split second before I heard his voice. "Happy birthday, love."

That voice, still so deep and smooth as the day we'd first truly met, here in this room, on this very spot. I didn't celebrate birthdays back then, not back when I merely existed. Back then, a birthday was a line of data, a simple fact of having been born.

Now I lived. We both did.

I closed the distance between us, gathering the blossom up to my cheek. His hands slid around me, palming my arms before splaying fingers across my back. His embrace was all-encompassing, the heat of his body as penetrating as the sunshine itself. He was heat and light, and as I reached upwards to catch his spill of kisses, I basked in the glow of his power.

"Marek," I whispered. "You remembered."

"I remember everything," he said, the bass notes more rumble than words. He pushed my hair from my shoulder, revealing my throat, and brushed his fingertips against my nape. "There is nothing I wish to forget."

Shivers tumbled down my neck, tingles that dripped a steady stream across my skin. His touch, his voice, his power. My paradise, thusly defined.

He released me, reluctance playing in his lingering touch. Only his gaze held me, a breathy pressure of green gem light. His eyes rarely went out these days, I noticed, his Demivampire light impossible to dim for the sake of public appearance. He'd taken to wearing black polarized lenses to obscure the light, to hide it from human passersby. I was one of the privileged few.

He noticed the rapture with which I beheld him and he smiled, a deep spread of pleasure. I was one of the privileged few who got to see that smile, who was permitted to see a side of him that been hidden away for so long.

"Come," he said. With a tilt of his shoulders, he bowed and gestured to the side room, a bright white light beckoning to us through a boxy arch. "The new exhibit awaits. I wanted you to be the first to see."

I linked my arm with his and we strolled into the next room. New exhibit? The thought was a bit disappointing, since traditionally the next room had housed the Isis

Collection. The goddess had always occupied a special place in my old soul, and I'd be sorry to see it go.

However, Marek's power trilled along the edges of my shields, rippling and eager. It was hard to remain disappointed when he felt like that.

"Are you a curator now?" I teased, giving his arm a squeeze. Mmm. Muscle. I grinned. Well, it was my birthday, after all. I squeezed again, spoiling myself.

"I exert an amount of...influence." He paused at the door before we could turn the corner. "Close your eyes."

He stepped behind me and covered my eyes with one of his hands, steering me forward with the other. The ceremony of it made me laugh.

When he removed his hand, however, the laughter died in my throat, replaced with a staggering sense of astonishment.

The Isis Collection hadn't been removed. It had been embellished.

A cartouche-inspired sign hung from the center of the display. *ISIS AND HORUS.* A smaller sign beneath read *Wisdom of the Mother, Strength of the Son.* Now, the great painting of Isis, previously the center of the exhibit, was mirrored by an equally ornate image of Horus. Throughout the room, statues and carvings depicted the falcon-headed deity in all aspects of his reign.

"And Rodrian?" I ran my eyes over every little detail, feeling I could lose myself in this room and never be lost again. "Did he have something to do with this?"

I felt the sudden turbulence in Marek's power, like a stone dropped into a stream. A disruption of his lightness. It was more than a cloud upon the face of the sun. It was a total eclipse.

This was the toughest part of being a Sophia. Knowing that something troubled Marek, darkened his very heart, and having to be strong enough to wait for him to confide in me. Some things couldn't be oracled away. They had to be entrusted.

His brow flinched and he swallowed with visible effort. "No, love. He's still away on business."

Marek could fake a nothing-is-wrong tone all he liked. I knew better. Rodrian's sudden departure wasn't something Marek was ready to talk about. All he'd say was *they had words*. Words that made islands out of men.

And I was pretty sure my name had been one of those words.

I didn't push the issue, even though he wasn't the only one who felt the pang of Rode's absence. Perhaps he wasn't my mate, but Rodrian had become as near to me as my shadow and his absence was unnatural. Unnerving. And I was unwilling to pretend I wasn't as hurt as his brother.

I stifled a sigh and put on my strong face. When Marek was ready, I'd be ready. Right now, I could do only one thing. I should be content with living in the moment, and this was pretty wonderful as far as my moments usually went.

I drifted to the wall where a local artist's work paid homage to the god. *The Eyes of Horus*, read the brass placard on the wall near the frame. One eye was the sun, the other, the moon. I reached backward for Marek, who laced his fingers with mine and leaned down, his mouth at my ear.

"Look closely."

I turned my head and stepped closer, stopping a foot away from the frame. It wasn't until the light reflected across the surface that I saw what he'd meant me to see: the brushstrokes weren't simply the result of spreading paint on canvas. They created a pattern that could only be seen from up close.

The brushstrokes spelled out my name. My title. My

destiny.

SOPHIA.

I turned back to him, hiding my mouth behind my fingers. I couldn't get the words to come. My speechlessness earned a deep chuckle.

"Sophia. The Greek word for wisdom." He walked backward a few paces, opening his arms wide. "All this is for you. What you've done, what I know you will do. What we will do. Together."

I laughed and ran to him, allowing him to sweep me up in his arms. He spun me gently, and for a moment, all the universe revolved around us.

Together. I couldn't imagine a more perfect destiny, or a better way to surrender to it. After years of losing and wanting and struggling and surviving, I knew one thing.

It was time for us to live.

Together.

THE END

ABOUT THE AUTHOR

Ash Krafton is a speculative fiction author from the Pennsylvania coal region. If she's not writing, it's probably because she's distracted by all the cool junk on her desk or by the stacks of books that have grown up around it.

She writes novels, short fiction, and poetry for mostly adult audiences. (She's *mostly* an adult.). Some of those novel titles include:

The Books of the Demimonde: urban fantasy trilogy

Enter the world of the Demimonde.

Look outside your window. Same old town, same streets, same people, same stories you've lived all your life. Or... are they?

Sophie Galen is an advice columnist from the suburbs of Philly. Like many sensitive women, she's done her best to create a shelter for herself in order to live in a safe, predictable world, protecting her vulnerable self: her mind, her heart, her soul.

Then he came into her life and blew the walls in.

When Marek Thurzo arrived, he brought with him all the secrets she never wanted to know: the world outside was not what she thought. There were people and creatures and powers she'd never dared to believe exist and at the very center of this humongous supernatural web was one single person.

Her. The Sophia. The one hope for redemption for the Demivampire race.

Some days, she still can't wrap her head around the whole thing. Other days...

...she's ready to do whatever it takes to protect her Demivamps, no matter the obstacle, no matter the enemy, no matter the personal cost.

While meeting her deadlines, of course. Who says a girl can't multitask while saving the world?

Bleeding Hearts (Demimonde #1)

Blood Rush (Demimonde #2)

Wolf's Bane (Demimonde #3)

WORDS THAT BIND: *paranormal romance*

Social worker Tam Kerish can't keep her cool professionalism when steamy client Mr. Burns kindles a desire for more than a client-therapist relationship—so she drops him. However, they discover she's the talisman to which Burns, an immortal djinn, has been bound since the days of King Solomon…and that makes it difficult to stay away from him.

Ethical guidelines are unequivocal when it comes to personal relationships with clients. However, the djinn has a thawing effect on the usually non-emotive Tam, who begins to feel true emotion whenever he is near. Tam has to make a difficult choice: to stay on the outside, forever looking in…or to turn her back on her entire world, just for the chance to finally experience what it means to fall in love.

Words That Bind

She also writes New Adult spec fic as **AJ Krafton**. Her debut, THE HEARTBEAT THIEF (Victorian fantasy) is a little bit Jane Austen, a little bit Edgar Allan Poe, and a whole lot of stealing heartbeats in order to stay young and beautiful forever...

How far will Senza Fyne go to avoid Death?

The Heartbeat Thief

"There was something smart, ominous, and romantic about this strange story..."
Rated 4.5 stars on Amazon reviews!

Join the Fictitious Initiative...

If you'd like an email whenever Ash (or AJ) has a new release, great giveaway, or special offer, you can sign up on her website or online at http://eepurl.com/wAm2T. Your email will never be shared and you can unsubscribe at any time.

Thanks for reading!

Word-of-mouth is crucial for any author to succeed. If you've enjoyed reading this book, please consider leaving a brief review—just a line or two is fine, and it may help another reader decide to give this book a try.

And if you *really* enjoyed reading it, tell a friend. Friends share :)